Two Bodies Are Better Than One

OTHER TITLES BY ERICA RUTH NEUBAUER

Jane Wunderly Mysteries

Murder at the Mena House

Murder at Wedgefield Manor

Danger on the Atlantic

Intrigue in Istanbul

Murder Under the Mistletoe

Secrets of a Scottish Isle

Homicide in the Indian Hills

Two Bodies Are Better Than One

ERICA RUTH NEUBAUER

Published by Thomas & Mercer, Seattle

www.apub.com

EU product safety contact:
Amazon Media EU S. à r.l.
38, avenue John F. Kennedy, L-1855 Luxembourg
amazonpublishing-gpsr@amazon.com

ISBN-13: 9781662535949 (paperback)
ISBN-13: 9781662535932 (digital)

Cover design by Faceout Studio, Molly von Borstel
Cover image: © CSA-Images, © Ben Stevens, © Francesco Marzovillo / Getty; © kosmofish, © New Africa, © Lana Sham, © Dana Zurkiyeh, © wallerichmercie / Shutterstock

Printed in the United States of America

For Jessie and Shannon, who never stopped believing in me.
And for Megan, who never stopped believing in Lorraine.

Chapter 1

Tuesday, June 13, 1989

The immaculate expanse of lawn that Lorraine took so much pride in was interrupted by a body. A dead body, to be precise. One that had not been there the night before.

Lorraine stood with hands on hips, the Minnetonka moccasins she'd slipped on squishing slightly in the damp grass. When she'd seen the lump marring her lawn, she quickly turned off the sprinklers, and now she watched in bemusement as water ran from the dead man's shiny bald head and *drip drip dripped* off the slightly misshapen nose. It had a nice rhythm, that drip, and she let herself enjoy it for a moment before heaving a sigh and, with a glance around to make sure she wasn't being watched, toed the man's meaty calf with the tip of her moccasin. Just a little poke to make sure he was really dead. Satisfied that he was, she sauntered back into her two-story bungalow, the yellow siding cheerful in the growing light. The color was bold for the neighborhood, annoying several of her neighbors, which gave Lorraine a zing of pleasure. As she climbed the front stairs, her eyes drifted across her prizewinning rosebushes, in full bloom and softly scenting the air. A cool morning breeze off Lake Michigan caressed her arms, raising a smattering of goose bumps. She briskly rubbed a hand over her exposed flesh and considered her options.

1. Drag this idiot around back, dig a hole in the garden, and use him as compost. It would save a few bucks—Lorraine wouldn't have to buy quite so many bags of fertilizer from Menards.
2. Drag this idiot into the basement and dump him in the freezer, let him cool off until she took a trip, somewhere nice and wooded, like Minnesota. Or even one of the Dakotas—less wooded, but there was a lot of empty space for dumping a body.
3. Let the police deal with this mess.

It didn't take long for her to form the conclusion that there was, unfortunately, really only one viable option. There were enough secrets buried in the flower garden, and it wasn't worth the effort of digging a grave in order to clean up someone else's mess. Fifteen, twenty years ago she might have considered it just to avoid the inconvenience of calling the cops, but she didn't want to disturb the flower beds.

She sighed. The police would have to be called. And since the man's hands were tied behind his back with nylon rope—indicating something other than natural causes—it wasn't going to be a quick pickup. Lorraine looked at her watch. This was going to make her miss her appointment with Cynthia, her aerobics instructor, wasn't it?

Well, shit.

Lorraine went inside, heading straight to the olive green rotary phone sitting on her gold-flecked Formica counter, and stuck her finger in the clear plastic dial, spinning nine-one-one and waiting for dispatch to pick up.

"911, what's your emergency?"

"Sheryl, I got some trouble over here."

"Mrs. Highsmith? Dat you?" Sheryl's gum cracked on the other end of the line, and Lorraine grimaced at both the sound of the gum and the poor grammar. The woman likely reeked of Juicy Fruit. "What kinda trouble you got over dere?" Sheryl asked.

"There's a body on my lawn," Lorraine said with a great deal of patience and enunciation. More than this woman deserved, certainly.

"Oh jeez Louise! I'll get the chief over by you real quick. You need an ambulance too?"

"No," Lorraine said. "We're past that."

"Yeah, no, for sure, but golly! Well, okay then," Sheryl said, then hung up to call in the cavalry, or so Lorraine assumed. While she waited, she sat at her kitchen table and sliced open a few of the envelopes she received every week for her advice column. Most people who wrote letters to Dear Lorraine were absolute fools, but now and then she got one that could genuinely benefit from her advice. Not that anyone took her column seriously, although people really should. She'd started the column as a lark, applying for the job at the *Sheboygan Bay Chronicle* when they'd advertised it. She'd been offered it immediately—she'd always been a strong writer—but it had taken some convincing and a few years to talk them into letting her do it her way. It started with a sly comment slipped in here or there, until finally she'd been given clearance to write exactly what she wanted, and the paper called it "satire."

It had more than doubled the popularity of the column. The paper was happy, and she got to speak her piece. The added bonus was that, as a popular columnist, she had an easy in for finding out anything newsworthy that happened, well before the general public. Like whether any issues with the Chicago mafia were creeping north. Lorraine kept a close eye on anything the Outfit—the uppity name the mob liked to use for their operation—was up to, for her own sake.

Lorraine tugged the dustcover from her typewriter, a sheet of paper still wrapped around the roller from her last typing session, and scanned what she'd written. She was nearly finished with her latest column, due at the end of the week. She picked up where she'd left off, punching out the last few lines. She considered starting on the next bit of advice, telling the local yokel who'd written in about her twelve-year-old stealing the Miller High Life to drink even shittier beer if she didn't want her kid to chug it like Yoo-hoo, but the singing tone of the doorbell interrupted the clacking of her keys.

Lorraine strolled to the door and found the police chief standing there, which sent her eyebrows reaching for the sky in surprise. Just behind Chief Schneider was the only female on the force, Michaela Zenoni. Hadn't she read something about this woman being promoted to detective recently? Squinting, she thought back. Yes, she had read that, in her own paper. From the article, she'd sensed that the reporter was skeptical about the choice, even as they touted the fact that Detective Zenoni was a "local made good," but that didn't matter in the long run, not really. The fact that the detective possessed a vagina made it impossible for her to do a man's job, didn't she know that? Didn't everyone?

"Body's over there." Lorraine gestured vaguely toward the side yard.

The chief's small eyes bulged slightly, his salt-and-pepper mustache twitching, but he didn't say anything, instead rubbing his fingers against his chief's badge, pinned to the left breast pocket of his white uniform shirt; the gold had been polished to a near mirror finish. The chief certainly looked the part of city official, perfectly pressed and serious, but words seemed to have escaped him. Behind Schneider, Zenoni closed her eyes briefly, then crossed the lawn, camera in hand, ready to start photographing the crime scene.

"You okay, Hans?" Lorraine liked to use the chief's first name and only his first name. It riled the man up, and that was fun.

Chief Schneider huffed. "I was going to ask you the same thing." When she didn't respond, he huffed again and fired another question. "When did you find the body?"

Lorraine sighed and grabbed a navy windbreaker from the hall closet and stepped outside. She supposed there wasn't much to be done for it—she'd need to hang around and supervise. Her time would be better spent doing other things, like finishing her column or bouncing around in aerobics class, but this was what happened when someone dumped a body on your lawn.

Could this be a message from her past? She'd changed her name and moved numerous times, ending up here, in the place where her late husband had grown up, with a new look and zero intention of navel-gazing about what she'd left behind. But she'd lived in Sheboygan Bay for a decade now, and while she'd never admit it, it was possible that she'd gotten a little too complacent.

Had someone discovered who she really was?

Chapter 2

LORRAINE

Tuesday

"You don't recognize him?" Chief Schneider asked. "I guess why would you, you haven't been here that long."

These little darts did get under her skin, even if she never let on. How was a decade in this shithole not that long?

Reading the chief's body language, Lorraine suspected he didn't know what to do about this corpse since they so rarely had murders in this sleepy little lakefront town. His shoulders were practically hugging his ears, and his fingers were caressing that badge like it was a genie lamp. And a dead stranger on an old lady's lawn? Unfamiliar territory for sure.

Not that she thought of herself as an old lady, not by any stretch. But she knew what other people saw when they looked at her, and she'd learned it was best to play to their perceptions.

"I don't recognize him. You should see if he has a wallet on him," Lorraine suggested, maintaining her suitably distressed look but nodding toward the corpse.

Schneider snapped on latex gloves, then paused next to the body, obviously not wanting to touch the dead man but believing he had to since there was an audience. He gingerly patted a back pocket of the man's dark trousers, even darker since they were soaked through. Clearly finding nothing, Schneider patted the other pocket, and with two fingers, delicately reached in. Lorraine was amused to see that the chief's eyes were squeezed shut while he did this.

The wallet retrieved, Schneider jerked up and took a large step back from the body, then looked at the water-saturated wallet. A few solitary drops of water trickled from the wallet and down the chief's forearm, causing him to shudder violently. Whoever this dead guy was, his clothes were sopping wet, and now Schneider's arm was sprinkled with dead-guy water.

Lorraine watched as the chief gave another full-body shudder and hid a grin. This was turning out to be worth the price of admission.

Schneider cracked open the black pleather wallet, worn down to nothing but fibers in a handful of places. He pulled out the license tucked behind the little plastic window and squinted at it. "It says here he's Douglas Rupp." Schneider paused. "Shit, I think that's Marjorie's brother. He moved away years ago, became a cop in Milwaukee, but he grew up here."

It was easy to read the subtext there—*he's still one of us.*

"I wonder if she's spoken to him recently." Schneider sighed, shaking his head sadly. "She lost her chance, if she hasn't." He continued riffling through the battered wallet and removed another card, this one laminated in plastic. "Whoa. Looks like Rupp was a licensed private detective." He waved the card at Lorraine, who took it from his hand, touching the edges only, and frowned at it before passing it back and wiping her fingers on her blue polyester track pants.

"I wonder what brought him back home?" Schneider mused.

Lorraine had a few guesses, more like worries, really, about why a private detective might have been watching her, but she kept them to herself.

Chapter 3

DETECTIVE MIKE ZENONI

Tuesday

Chief Schneider and Lorraine Highsmith were watching Douglas Rupp's body being zipped into a black body bag and loaded into the ambulance. At least the EMTs had taken care with the body—Mike had once seen an elderly man's body roughly pulled from a wheelchair, and the sound the head had made bouncing from the chair to the ground had stayed with her. Haunted her, really. She'd been too green at the time to object, a brand-new officer on patrol, but she carefully supervised Rupp's treatment today.

Mike had already finished inspecting the lawn—there wasn't much to see, since the sprinklers had run for a while before the body was found—and she joined her boss and Mrs. Highsmith, shooting the lookie-loos in the street an occasional dark look. She'd warned them once already to keep their distance, and they'd reluctantly retreated across the street for a time, but they were drifting back, jockeying for a better view.

Her boss looked her over. "Good job not getting sick at the sight of a dead body, Detective."

Mrs. Highsmith locked eyes with her, a moment of sisterhood, gone in the flash of a lightning bug when Mike turned to smile at her boss. "Thank you, Chief." She patted the trim waist of her pleated gray dress slacks. "Always did have a strong stomach." She thought about her boss's own squeamishness at touching Rupp and smiled just a touch wider.

Schneider grunted. "Shouldn't Rupp have checked in with us? I thought that it was protocol for private investigators to let us know they're working in the area."

Mike was pretty sure that this was something Schneider had seen on reruns of *The Rockford Files*. "I'm not sure, sir. We could ask Carla, see if Rupp checked in at the station."

The chief bobbed his head emphatically, clearly excited about something he could control. "I'll do that. I'll have a chat with Carla about keeping me up to date on what's happening in our community. As my secretary, that's part of her job. We wouldn't want people thinking that I don't know what's going on in my own town."

Mike nearly sighed but swallowed it back, which morphed it into a little burp that she just managed to cover with her hand.

Mrs. Highsmith ignored Schneider, watching the ambulance pull away from the curb. "I think maybe I should come with you to tell Marjorie about her brother. I didn't know him, but the news will be tough for her to hear. Might be easier coming from me." The woman's dark eyes were trained on Chief Schneider, who avoided making eye contact in return.

Mike had noticed it several times, that people avoided looking Mrs. Highsmith in the eye, although it was hard to put her finger on why. There was nothing terribly remarkable about Mrs. H.; she was about the same age as her mother or a little older. Maybe because she wasn't warm and fuzzy, smelling of freshly baked cookies and giving out hugs? But Mike's mother hadn't been that, either, even before she walked out on her family. If anything, this brand of older woman should feel familiar. But there was something . . . not *right* about Mrs. Highsmith that she couldn't quite figure out.

Huh. What exactly did they know about Mrs. Highsmith? She narrowed her eyes slightly at the older woman while she thought. She worked for the paper, wrote some kind of column and maybe did the occasional article, but Mike couldn't come up with anything else off the top of her head.

You know, it was pretty weird that Rupp's body was dumped here on Mrs. Highsmith's lawn. It probably wasn't related, but Mike wouldn't leave that stone unturned. She would do some digging on Mrs. Highsmith, see what crawled out.

Ew. *That* was a gross analogy. Even though she was the one that thought it up, it made her skin feel tight, her stomach squidgy.

Quickly turning her attention to her boss, she opened her mouth to object to a civilian tagging along on a death notification, when her boss nodded, decision made. "It's not protocol, of course," the chief said. "But you're right, this will be difficult for Marjorie to hear, so I think having you there to give her the bad news is a good idea."

A few minutes later, Mike watched as her boss and Mrs. Highsmith got into the chief's unmarked car and pulled away. She shook her head. It was hard to believe Schneider was taking Mrs. Highsmith along with him. Actually, scratch that. She *could* believe it. Her boss hated making death notifications nearly as much as she hated making them. In fact, it was downright shocking that the chief hadn't made *her* do it. And while she was relieved not to be on her way to Marjorie Rupp's, they really should be taking Mrs. Highsmith's statement right now. Not to mention how *stupid* it was to take someone who worked for the newspaper along on police business. Sure, Mrs. Highsmith was an advice columnist, but she worked for a newspaper. And with a front-row seat to this story, why *wouldn't* she write this up?

Schneider probably hadn't thought of any of this. She wondered whether it was worth mentioning later, or if she'd be accused of being hysterical again. She was really fucking tired of hearing *that*.

Mike's gaze fell on the little shed in the back of Mrs. Highsmith's yard. There was a huge lock on the door, and when she'd given it a shake, it had held tight. There was no reason to search the thing, not without a warrant, but she was curious about what an old lady would keep in there. Probably just old gardening supplies and not a stack of bodies. No, that was just her colorful imagination, right? Or too many zombie movies, like the ones she'd watched with her pops.

Mike chuckled at the thought of a bunch of bodies, stacked like cordwood in an old lady's shed, but made a note in her notebook to learn what she could about Mrs. Highsmith just the same.

Chapter 4

LORRAINE

Tuesday

Marjorie Rupp lived on the south side of town, where the property taxes were a lot lower, as were the incomes. On the way there, the chief's squad car thumped over a pothole that seemed to have its own pothole, banging the bottom of the car so hard that Schneider gave the dash a pat and muttered an apology before pulling into Marjorie's cracked driveway.

Lorraine looked at the house as she leveraged herself out of the passenger seat. Marjorie's stoop was a concrete slab that had been poured sometime in the last century, given up hope, and was crumbling into dust at the edges. The shack itself was an ugly two-story box with siding that was likely made of asbestos. That, at least, was hanging on to the bitter end.

Schneider knocked on the screen door, the thing juddering precariously in its frame. "Just a minute," a scratchy voice griped from somewhere within. A woman wearing a faded housecoat with a tropical theme answered the door, lit cigarette in hand. The pattern placement made it look like a toucan was perched on her left breast, and Schneider was immediately transfixed by it. Marjorie opened her mouth, then closed it again, apparently deciding to ignore his reaction. She gazed at her visitors without blinking for a long moment, sucking in nicotine, before giving a nod. "Well, you better come in." She left the door open and disappeared into the dim interior, leaving them to follow her.

Schneider gave a small shrug and went first, leaving Lorraine to close the battered front door and bring up the rear. They settled themselves in Marjorie's faux-oak wood-paneled living room, which was stuffed to the hilt with a jumble of furniture. Nothing matched—it looked as though Marjorie had spent the last decade scouring every garage sale in the county and hauling things in, lack of space be damned. The overstuffed brown-and-gold floral chair that Lorraine was perched on was entirely uncomfortable, and the burnt orange easy chair that Schneider had chosen didn't look much better.

"Marjorie," Lorraine said, breaking the awkward silence, "this chair is stabbing me in the ass. I think it might be a loose spring. Why do you keep this thing?" She shifted in an attempt to find a better position.

Schneider stiffened at this opening salvo, but both women ignored him.

"I like looking at it." Marjorie put out the cigarette she'd been holding, but not before she lit another Virginia Slim off the butt of the first and regarded her. "And I don't get much company."

"I can see why," Lorraine said. She glanced at Schneider, wondering if he was going to tell Marjorie the reason they'd stopped by. When he said nothing, rubbing his gold badge and staring at the floor instead, she sighed. "Marjorie, your brother is dead. I found him on my lawn this morning."

Chief Schneider gasped. On the way over, he'd rambled on about how good it was that Lorraine was along so she could soften the blow. It was obvious the man assumed she would have some words of wisdom for Marjorie or would at least break the news gently.

Fuck all that. She never had any intention of playing along. It was one of the perks of aging—you didn't have to play by the rules anymore.

And as long as she looked the part, she could get away with saying whatever she liked.

Marjorie blew out some smoke, not bothering to direct it toward the ceiling for her guests' comfort, and in fact might have been blowing it in their direction deliberately. "I figured that something happened to him and that's why you all came by. Well, the chief at least." She spared him a single look before turning back to her. "Why'd he bring *you* along?"

"I think the better question is what was your brother doing in town?" Lorraine asked, face placid despite her irritation at the question. "I thought he left years ago."

Marjorie shrugged. "He did, and then he came back."

Lorraine looked at her expectantly.

"We weren't close," Marjorie said with a wet cough. "But he needed a place to crash while he was doing one of his 'investigations.'" Marjorie used air quotes around the word, the ash on her cigarette balancing precariously as she did so. Schneider breathed an audible sigh of relief when she finally tapped it into the brown glass ashtray on the side table nearest her elbow. It looked like it had been swiped from McDonald's, and it likely had been. "Couldn't turn down family, no matter how much I disliked the man."

"You didn't get along with your brother?" Schneider piped up.

"No duh. You know he was a cop, right? Down in Milwaukee, went through the academy for the city." Schneider shook his head, and Marjorie sighed. "Doug was a real piece of work. A knuckle-dragging caveman—couldn't get along with women and sure didn't think they should be doing a 'man's job.'" Marjorie obviously loved doing air quotes. "He was stuck in the past as far as that shit went." She rolled her eyes. "He got fired from the department a few years ago for harassing some poor young woman on his shift. He went private after that."

"We found his license," Schneider said.

"Good for you," Marjorie replied. From the look on Marjorie's face, Lorraine could tell that they shared the same opinion of the chief—mainly that Schneider couldn't find his ass with both hands and a map.

"Can I see where he was staying?" Chief Schneider asked.

One of Marjorie's eyebrows crept up, ever so slightly. "Sure. It's up the stairs. First room on the left." Marjorie gestured with her head but stayed seated. Her chair was obviously more comfortable than the others in the room.

Schneider stood and headed that way. Lorraine only waited a beat before following behind. As soon as they started up the stairs, both she and Schneider understood why Marjorie had stayed where she was. The staircase was narrow, and the ceilings were low, the sloping of the roof bringing the outside walls in at a steep angle. Schneider stepped into the room where Rupp was staying, while Lorraine watched from the doorway. The bed was along one of the lowered eaves, pushed up against the wood paneling, and she wondered how many times the man had hit his shiny bald head climbing out of bed. The image made her smile, just a little.

There was a beat-up dresser and a nightstand in the room, but no other furniture and no closet. A blue duffel bag had been tossed next to the dresser, pressing down the shaggy gold carpet. Lorraine's lip curled at the thought of what might be crawling in the funk.

Schneider grabbed the duffel bag and set it down on the bed before zipping open the top and rifling through. She opened her mouth to suggest he wear gloves but then shut it again with a snap.

Not her circus, not her monkeys, not her fingerprints.

The chief removed everything from the bag, piling the clothes in a heap. A pair of bleached jean shorts, a couple of collar-stained polo shirts, and a gaudy Hawaiian shirt, as well as some Fruit of the Loom tighty-whities with fraying elastic, went onto the bed. A file folder was the only real item of interest, unless you counted the half-used tube of Sensodyne toothpaste. No toothbrush, so either he'd taken that with him, or he just ate the stuff.

Schneider set the duffel bag aside while Lorraine eyed the pile of things it had contained. "Shouldn't there be a weapon of some sort?" she asked. "If he was a private eye?"

Schneider gave a start, suddenly realizing she was there. He paused with the folder in his lap. "Oh, yah. Yah, probably. He didn't have one on him, did he?" Lorraine shook her head. "I wonder where that could be."

"Marjorie!" She turned her head and shouted in the general direction of the stairs.

"What?" came the equally loud reply from the sitting room.

"Did Doug have a car with him?" Lorraine bellowed.

"Yeah, he drove up here. A piece-of-shit Corolla."

She lowered her pitch back to a normal speaking voice. "There's your answer."

The chief had flinched with each shout, his hands jerking toward his ears but not coming close enough to actually cover them. "Erm, thanks. I'll have Detective Zenoni put out an APB for it."

Schneider looked down at the file folder in his lap and started reading the papers inside, his lips moving as he read.

"What does it say?" she asked when Schneider flipped to the second page.

"Looks like Doug was investigating Julian Baker." Schneider looked up, puzzled. "I don't know him, do you?"

She didn't know Baker personally, but he'd certainly been on her radar. And Lorraine's radar was *not* where a person wanted to be if they were interested in staying above ground.

Chapter 5

LORRAINE

Tuesday

"I should go talk to Julian Baker," Schneider said. He hadn't moved from his position on the bed and appeared to be talking to himself rather than her.

Lorraine studied him. On the one hand, she definitely wanted in on this investigation, otherwise she'd just be replicating the police's efforts. She had no intention of ignoring a dead body on her front lawn; she needed to figure out whether someone from her past had resurfaced or whether someone in town had finally learned who Lorraine really was. And of course, once she'd figured out who had the absolute *balls* to dump a corpse in her yard, she'd take care of the matter.

She'd have to be careful, though. She worked for a newspaper, and the cops were likely to put up a fight about her nosing in on their murder. Well, regular cops would. It wouldn't be hard to manipulate the chief into letting her tag along with him on an interview.

"Didn't you assign Detective Zenoni to the case?"

Schneider looked affronted. "Yeah, no, yeah, I sure did. But you think I can't interview someone? I'm real good at it, I'll have you know.

And besides, I'm just talking to him, having a little chat—the detective will do a formal interview later."

Lorraine held up a hand. "Oh, no, Hans." She drew out the *o*'s, imitating a native Wisconsinite, ingratiating herself while smoothing his feathers. "I have no doubt you're a skilled interviewer." This was a lie. "And it's a good idea. Let's go talk to him."

Schneider gave a firm nod, and her mouth tipped up in a little smirk as she followed him back downstairs. Shit, he was easy to manipulate. Too easy, really. It almost took the sport out of things.

Although she had a sneaking suspicion his detective wouldn't be nearly so easy to get around.

Julian Baker lived a quarter mile from Lorraine, the houses here not just facing the lake but actually on the water, tucked just far enough back that they were on solid soil, but close enough that Lorraine thought folks should be nervous about the cliff collapsing into the lake. As they pulled up, it became immediately apparent that Baker had recently built the place. It was an ugly two-story cubic design of glass and dark-stained wood. A two-car garage extended into the driveway with a lot of house on top of it, maximizing the water view on the other side. It was a hideous house-beast, hulking and clearly blocking the view of the houses across the street.

Chief Schneider gave a little whistle. "Nice place."

Her only reply was a twist of her lips.

They walked to the front door, and the chief pushed the bell, a cheerful little tune playing inside. A pretty blond came down the short flight of stairs and leaned to glance out the frosted glass beside the door. She paused, then opened the door, her hair already blown out to maximum volume, bangs curled like a claw scratching up from her forehead. The woman's makeup was also thickly applied, although she was wearing spandex pants, leg warmers, and a shoulder-baring top that made it seem like she was about to do some home Jazzercise and jump around with Jane Fonda.

Regardless, she looked a little surprised to find the police chief standing on her front stoop, but gave Lorraine only a cursory glance. "Can I help you?" she asked. Her eyelashes fluttered slightly at the chief, and Lorraine rolled her eyes. No one noticed.

"Is your husband at home?" Schneider asked.

"Of course, Chief Schneider. Please, come in." The blond led them up the beige carpeted stairs and into an open-concept room decorated in chrome and leather. Despite the modern decor, a ceramic sculpture of three dolphins leaping out of the water perched next to the fireplace, and Lorraine was tempted to kick it out of principle. They lived on Lake Michigan, not the ocean. The closest thing to a dolphin they'd see from their oversize living room window was a giant carp flopping in the waves.

The woman—Sharity, it turned out her name was—went to fetch her husband, and the chief took a seat while Lorraine examined the framed photos on the mantel. Sharity was clearly fifteen or twenty years younger than her husband, a trophy wife in spandex. From the photos, or lack thereof, it looked like they didn't have any children, the lucky bastards, although it was unusual for a nice Midwestern couple to go childless. Maybe Baker was shooting blanks.

Julian Baker entered the room, greeting the chief with a hearty hello and a very awkward handshake. This was because he was sporting an enormous white bandage on his right hand, so he was using his left to shake, forcing the chief to use his nondominant hand also. Baker turned to Lorraine and paused. "Mrs. Highsmith?"

Lorraine didn't offer a hand, but she did offer a greeting. "That's my name, don't wear it out."

Julian made a weird face, unsure what to do with that, then turned his attention fully to the police chief. "What can I do for you, Chief Schneider?"

"Have you seen Doug Rupp around lately?" Schneider asked. She was amazed that his first question didn't involve the cartoonishly large bandage on Baker's hand. It was difficult to focus on anything else.

Julian tilted his big, half-bald head as though considering the answer to this question, his hands behind his back as he shifted his weight back and forth on his feet. Lorraine watched this pageantry and knew that whatever came out of the man's mouth was going to be a lie. Or a half truth, at best.

"Boy, I haven't seen Doug in years," Julian said, eyes flicking to the window. He wore skimpy pleated white shorts topped by a pink polo shirt, and a thick gold chain, much like Schneider. The chief's glistening chain peeked from his uniform shirt where his tie should have been, but where an extra button was undone instead. Schneider claimed that this made him look "approachable." Lorraine wondered if a good yank on the chain would pull chest hair out. Something to keep in mind for the future—for both of them.

"It looks like Doug was investigating you," Schneider said. "You have any idea why that would be?"

Julian blinked hard, the most ingenuous reaction she had seen so far. The man was honestly surprised.

He blinked again. "I'm shocked to hear that. I can't imagine why he would be investigating me." Julian cleared his throat and reached his good hand up to tug his earlobe. "Do you think he's been . . . watching me?"

"Well, we can't say for sure," Schneider said.

Lorraine interrupted. "But I'd say it's a good bet that he was."

Both men swiveled their heads toward her position near the fireplace, looking like they'd forgotten she was there.

Lorraine took advantage of the moment to address the bandage in the room. "What happened to your hand? You applying for a role on Looney Tunes? Let me guess, it was an anvil."

The chief's mouth dropped open, and red spots appeared high on Julian's cheeks. "No, it was an accident in the kitchen," Baker said, his tone abrupt.

"Just stitches? Gotta be something more serious, a bandage like that."

Baker visibly stiffened. "I lost a finger."

Lorraine nodded. That at least might be true, but the rest of it? All lies. Because no way was this guy spending time in the kitchen. And he lost a finger, how exactly? Slicing vegetables? Not a chance.

Julian cocked his head at Lorraine. "You know, you look like that statue inside Mary Ann's Frozen Custard. The fiberglass one."

That statue was hideous, malformed, and a crime against art—a melting woman with twin braids and an orange ball cap. It was rumored to represent the owner's mother, but God help him if it did. Not to mention, she looked nothing like that statue, and they all knew it—the man was being offensive simply to be offensive. Well, two could play at that game.

"How exactly did you make your money, Julian? This is an awfully nice place. Good view of the surfers in their tight little wetsuits. You like looking at men in wet suits?" She nodded toward the windows that took up the entire wall with an encompassing view of the lake. The wind had picked up, and the waves were frolicking now, with some fool on a surfboard braving the icy water out past the stone breakers. It never ceased to amaze her that these idiots surfed Lake Michigan, which was frigid even during the warmest summer months. In fact, Sheboygan Bay was known for its surfing, which was even more ridiculous.

Baker and Schneider both looked uncomfortable at her question, but she didn't break eye contact with Baker, fully expecting an answer. What did he think would happen when he started talking shit?

He cleared his throat. "Uh, investments. I like to invest in our community."

It appeared that was all Baker was going to say on the matter. She was about to ask another pointed question when Schneider spoke again.

"Well, thank you for your time, Julian. If you think of anything, please call the station."

Lorraine's eyebrows disappeared into her hairline. That was really all they were going to ask this dipstick?

"Should I call you directly, Chief?" Julian asked.

Lorraine watched as Schneider shifted on his feet. "Well, ya know, I think Detective Zenoni will be heading up this investigation, assisted by Sergeant Hannigan and the day shift. I'll be supervising, of course. New detective and all."

"Of course," Baker murmured.

Lorraine pursed her lips as Schneider herded her to the door and back to his unmarked squad car. Schneider dropped into the driver's seat with barely a glance around, but she surveyed the street before getting in, catching sight of a shitty white Corolla down the block, an older model with rust spots near the wheel wells. She'd bet money that car belonged to Rupp, but the question was, should she mention it to the chief?

"Lorraine?" Schneider'd gotten into the car and leaned over the middle console, peering at Lorraine where she stood.

She sighed. It probably wasn't worth keeping it to herself since the cops would find it eventually, Zenoni most likely—the detective appeared smarter than the average small-town cop. But if she threw Schneider a bone now, maybe she could leverage that to her benefit down the road.

Lorraine bent down a little to speak through the cracked passenger window. "See that car there?" She pointed down the street. "It's an old Corolla. Might be Rupp's—it's the right color."

Schneider twisted around in his seat then sprang from the car like a jack-in-the-box. "By God, Lorraine, you might be right."

They left the squad car and walked down the street to where the Corolla was parked. The asphalt road was starting to cook in the summer sun, and the faint smell of rubber and oil kicked up with every step.

The chief shaded his eyes to peer into the driver's side window while Lorraine tried the passenger-side handle. No joy.

"Is your side open?"

The chief gave a little start, then tried the handle and pulled the door open. Schneider stood there, peering inside, then shut it again before Lorraine could make it around to his side.

"We need to call a tow truck and have this processed at the station," Schneider said decisively.

It was bullshit timing for the chief to suddenly follow protocol—she should never have told him about the car in the first place. The smart choice would have been to keep it to herself and come back later to go through it.

With gloves, of course. She was no amateur.

But lesson learned. She would keep everything to herself from here on out until she was *sure* she was finished wringing every last drop of usefulness from whatever it was she gathered.

While they waited for the tow truck, Lorraine walked around the Corolla, peering in through the windows. There was nothing much of interest—crumpled McDonald's bags and Styrofoam sandwich containers tossed behind the seats, a half-empty box of Kools on the passenger seat, but not much else. If there was anything worthwhile to be found, it was in the trunk. Lorraine stood at the back of the car and sniffed but didn't smell anything out of the ordinary, and in this heat? There would definitely be a smell if someone was squeezed in there. No blood dripping onto the pavement, either, so it was a safe bet that the trunk was clear of bodies.

A pity, that. Sometimes two bodies were better than one.

Chapter 6

MIKE

Tuesday

Once her boss and Mrs. Highsmith left, Mike quickly finished up at the scene and headed to the hospital down south in Sheboygan proper. She was worried it would take a lot of time out of her day, but the trip to visit the medical examiner was blessedly brief. Dr. Schneider didn't have a solid cause of death yet—she'd been just about to crack Rupp open when Mike scurried out of there, but she'd estimated his death at between two and five in the morning. That was useful. And hopefully Dr. Schneider would get back to her soon with just how the guy had died.

It was still wild to Mike that Dr. Schneider—a stunning redhead with a medical degree—was married to her boss. She shook her head every time she thought about it and promised herself not to slum it when it came to dating. At least, not *that* far down.

Mike was now an hour into typing up the report on Rupp's death, with too many pages left to go. She sighed and flexed her fingers. A cup of coffee would be the bee's knees right about now. But first, she had to call Steph and let her know she wouldn't be at the rink tonight.

Once a week, Mike drove down to Sheboygan to teach girls how to roller skate at the big indoor skating rink. Her friend Stephanie Gayle took over when Mike couldn't make it, but it was always a big fat bummer when work got in the way of a little fun. Not to mention how good it felt to give those girls some confidence, even if it was just on skates. It was something she sure coulda used as a kid.

Steph said she could cover for her, so Mike hung up, then left her cramped office and passed through the open room where a handful of scattered metal desks were shared by the patrol officers. If anyone was around, they tended to go quiet when she came through, but it was empty, so there was no awkward silence for her to endure, no feeling that she was conducting a one-person parade while projecting confidence she didn't really feel.

Near the door to the hallway hung a motivational poster that read **Teamwork**, with a picture of some Canadian geese on it. She hated Canadian geese—all she could think about every time she passed the poster was how much poop those flying assholes left all over the city sidewalks. Every summer, there was an infestation of the creatures, hissing and shitting everywhere.

But yeah, sure, teamwork. That's what geese were about.

Besides, what did teamwork have to do with the police? Mike had never really felt like teamwork was what cops were about, not for her, anyway. Maybe the guys felt like they were part of some kind of "brotherhood," but she wasn't privy to that, no matter how many beers she drank with them, or how many jokes she cracked at her own expense. She'd even opted to go by her childhood nickname "Mike" instead of the full Michaela, but that hadn't helped her either. It actually seemed to make people uncomfortable, much like her height, so she'd decided to just lean into it. Let them be uncomfortable.

Anyway, the point being, in the end, they were never going to let her in. Especially not now that she'd made detective instead of one of the good ole boys who'd applied.

Walking down the brightly lit hallway toward the break room, she could hear the chief talking with his secretary—probably grilling her about whether Rupp had ever checked in with them. It would be easier to grab a cup of coffee and return to her desk, but Mike wanted to hear what Schneider had to say, so she walked the rest of the wood-paneled hallway and popped her head through the doorway. A large metal desk occupied by the chief's secretary sat behind a chest-height counter. That counter was all that separated the police from the tiny lobby where the general public could wander in, which they often did—usually to narc on barking dogs and speeding neighbors.

The chief's office was located directly behind Carla's desk. The man could have had a cushy office in the back of the building with lots of windows and a view of the city administrator's building, but Schneider preferred to be out front, where everyone in town could see him as soon as they walked into the station. Mike thought it would feel super exposed, but Schneider loved being seen—the face of the department, he liked to say. She was surprised they didn't have a department crest with his literal face on it. Or maybe just his mustache.

The chief was standing in front of Carla's desk, and the secretary was eyeing him with absolute disinterest, her chair swishing side to side like a cat's tail.

"Nope. Never heard from him," Carla was saying.

"Are you sure?" Schneider coaxed. "Maybe you wrote it down and lost it."

Carla just shook her head before spinning back around to her typewriter. Mike was never exactly sure what she was typing, since there was no chance the chief had that much dictation for her, but if Carla wasn't filing her nails, she was either typing or reading a romance novel, with the kinds of covers that made Mike blush. Not that she was a prude, but to have that kind of thing at work felt *brazen*.

Maybe Carla was writing a romance of her own. Mike stifled a giggle at the thought, not because it was unlikely, but because it would be kinda hilarious to write something so . . . *sexy* at a police station.

Anyway, Carla had clearly dismissed her boss, who watched her for a moment before mumbling something and stalking back to his office. "Mike! Get in here!" the chief's voice came seconds later.

Mike passed Carla. "Afternoon, Carla. How are ya?"

"Above ground," she said, her fingers not pausing.

"You betcha." That exchange was pretty representative of their usual conversations, other than asking Carla for office supplies or messages. The secretary wasn't one for chitchat.

Mike stepped into her boss's office and took a seat in one of the chrome-and-brown Naugahyde chairs. "How'd the notification go, boss?"

Chief Schneider's lips pressed together as he played with a pen on his desk. "Not good. Well, I suppose Marjorie took it well enough. And we learned that Rupp was investigating Julian Baker. I even found Rupp's car—it was parked on the street in front of Baker's place."

A jolt, and then excitement fizzed in her veins. This sounded like a solid lead. "How'd you learn all that?"

Schneider leaned down and rummaged through the duffel bag at his feet, then pulled out a folder and passed it to her. "Here ya go. You'll want to read this."

Mike gave it a cursory glance before lobbing her next question. She would read it super thoroughly later, plus go through Rupp's duffel bag for herself once her boss had gone home for the day. "You talked to Baker? Did he have anything to say?"

Schneider shook his head. "He said he didn't know Rupp well and had no idea he was back in town."

Mike already knew in her gut that the first part was untrue. Baker and Rupp had been tight in high school—they'd been a couple of years ahead of her, but she remembered them palling around together. There had been another two guys in their little group of misfits, the kids with long hair who smoked pot in the woods before and after class, sometimes during. She was having a hard time remembering exactly who the others had been, but Baker *definitely* knew Rupp. Now, whether or not Baker knew his old buddy Rupp had been investigating him was another story entirely.

She would follow up with Baker ASAP to get those other names. "And the car?"

The chief checked his watch. "I have to leave soon, but it should be in the lot out back. I had it towed here." He frowned. "Did you see the medical examiner?"

Mike hid a smile at the chief referring to his wife so formally. "I did." She relayed everything she'd learned and ended with, "Dr. Schneider said to pick up shrimp. She wants you to make scampi for dinner."

Chief Schneider beamed. "It's her favorite."

The boss left early—presumably to buy shrimp—and as soon as he did, Mike snagged the blue bag from the evidence room, where her boss had finally logged it. She dropped the bag on her desk, then checked the halls one more time to ensure Schneider hadn't come back before holing up in her office. She was pleased that no one else seemed to be around, either—she knew any one of the patrol guys would dime her out to the boss just for shits and giggles if they caught her doing anything Schneider wouldn't like. Schneider hated when his mistakes were pointed out, which meant he sure wouldn't like her checking his work by going through this bag, especially if she found something he'd missed, which was likely. It wouldn't be the first time, or the last, and the boss did not like being corrected.

Did the snitching and surveillance mean she was always looking over her shoulder? Sure, but it made her a better cop, ensuring she did everything by the book.

That's what she told herself, anyway.

Feeling assured that she was alone, she snapped on latex gloves, then carefully removed every item from the bag, stacking it all neatly on her desk. As each item surfaced, she searched it thoroughly, every pocket and hem, even checking to see if the bag had a false bottom, but it was as dry as a popcorn fart. She blew out a sigh and a curse. There wasn't much here—the folder the chief had given her was the most interesting thing by far. She replaced everything, then carried the duffel back to the evidence room and grabbed the plastic evidence bag that held Rupp's keys.

Mike caught herself jangling the set of keys on her way to the back door, and stopped abruptly, holding them carefully by the ring instead. It couldn't hurt anything, but it felt wrong somehow. Too cheerful. It wasn't as though she could shake evidence off them, but it felt disrespectful all the same. A man was dead, after all.

The driver's side door opened without the key—the chief had obviously left it unlocked, and she closed her eyes before shaking her head. Good thing she'd come out when she did, before some civilian got the bright idea to poke around in here and contaminate evidence. It wasn't like the police department had a secure parking lot; they were right on the street, a couple of diagonal painted lines for anyone to pull into. She looked at her hands—still gloved—and got to work.

The glove box held nothing but a half-empty carton of Kools and some paperwork for the car. Under the seats and in the back footwells, there was nothing but fast-food wrappers, and the ashtray was overflowing with cigarette butts—Dr. Schneider had been right, this guy did *not* take care of himself. Mike went through every dirty wrapper and used napkin, even poking a finger through the filthy ashtray, hoping to find something of interest.

Zilch. Nada. Bupkus.

Frustration was starting to build, but she took the keys and went to the trunk.

Now things were cookin'. She took it all in with a quick glance, immediately dismissing the ice scraper and the bag of sand. A pint-size car like this, it was no surprise that Rupp had sand in the back, both for weight and to throw down for traction if the car got stuck in the snow. Ice scrapers were common as cows too.

What *was* interesting, though, was a rusty shovel, crusted with dirt and resting on a relatively new tarp. She picked up a corner of the tarp with two fingers, gingerly pulling it up a bit, looking for stains but finding none. She turned to the lightweight climbing ropes coiled in the corner next to a beat-up pair of tennies, a good brand, Nike, but beat to hell. She poked at them and wrinkled her nose at the smell coming from the shoes, not super noticeable unless you brought your face close in. It smelled like . . . well, like pig shit. Which was a distinctive smell. Wherever Rupp had been wearing these, it was likely close to a pig farm, or at least a place that kept a few. Mike leaned down toward the shovel and gave that a sniff as well, but the crusted dirt didn't smell like anything.

Interesting.

Other than those few items, the trunk was empty. It was a real suspicious collection of things for anyone to be carrying around—all of which would need to be bagged and tagged and logged into evidence, of course. But the stuff in this trunk raised an awful lot of questions, starting with: Why did Rupp have all this shit? Was there another victim that hadn't been reported missing yet?

And had Rupp been the one to make them disappear?

Chapter 7

MIKE

Tuesday

Mike ended up staying late at the station to finish typing her report, so she was glad she'd made the call to Steph—she never woulda made it to the rink in time. Her legs were itching for a quick roll, but she knew it was better to get the reports done on the same day, when her memory was fresh, rather than let them go until the next. It was the right thing to do. But of course, this was yet another thing her boyfriends never seemed to understand—that sometimes she needed to stay late to get things done rather than let them go.

Men really seemed to be nothing more than a hassle. Fun to look at, exhausting to maintain.

Speaking of, even with her office door closed, the activity at the officers' desks in the room just outside was distracting, and she was finding it hard to concentrate. It sounded like Patoka had arrested someone for drunk driving, and the young man was loudly complaining that his cuffs were too tight and *goddamn it, officer*, he hadn't been drinking. The door muffled the voices, but she could still hear the kid slurring his words. She rolled her eyes and tried to mentally shut out the noise, even more difficult now that Officer Swartz had joined the fray, filling the room with his own clacking typewriter. Christ, if only this station was bigger—then maybe she could have an office away from all this.

Of course, she *should* have the big office at the back of the building, the one Chief Schneider could be using, but the two sergeants shared it, and when she got promoted, she was given this one and told she should be grateful for having one at all. After all, she wouldn't want to inconvenience the men, would she? Make them move and share a much smaller space? She'd bitten back all her objections, smiled with too many teeth, and agreed that this office was fine for her. Perfect, even, for a working detective.

Ah, who was she kidding, she knew how she'd gotten promoted to detective. She dearly wanted to believe it was because of her hard work and diligence—all that doing the right thing—but in a dark corner of her heart, she knew it was because Chief Schneider thought it would be good optics to have a female detective so he could keep bragging about his "modern department." There'd been a photo shoot that still made her cringe when she thought about it—the chief had made her crouch down so she didn't appear taller than him, even though she was, by a good amount. She'd avoided looking at the paper the day it ran.

After finally finishing up and pulling the last sheet from her typewriter, Mike clipped all the pages together, then leaned back in her seat. She didn't know what to make of the stuff she'd found in Rupp's trunk, although her imagination had some wild ideas about what that equipment could be used for, like digging a grave. How many bodies were buried in the Kettle Moraine, with no one the wiser? There weren't a lot of big predators in the area to dig up shallowly buried remains, and honestly, if someone went deep enough into the forest, it would be easy to dispose of a body without it ever being found. Or if hikers *did* eventually find one, it would be nothing but bones.

She shook her head at herself. There had to be a more reasonable explanation—she just needed to figure out what it was. She'd looked through the daily logs, and there was no one else missing right now, so it was unlikely that Rupp had offed someone.

The pig shit in Rupp's trunk, though. That smell was unmistakable. And pigs were known to eat *everything*, bones and hair and all.

Mike heard her pops's voice. *Child, you don't have any facts, just a wild imagination and zero evidence. This isn't* Murder, She Wrote, *and you are not Jessica Fletcher.*

"I'd rather be Cagney. Or even Lacey," she muttered, then groaned when a hot wave of guilt rushed through her—she really should go visit, even though it was depressing. Most times he didn't even know who she was anymore. But she still needed to stop by, take him some McDonald's since that was the only thing he seemed to enjoy. It had been about a week since she was there last, or was it two?

She grimaced and tried to ignore the sour guilt curdling her stomach.

After taking a swig of lukewarm water from the bottle on her desk, she pulled out her notebook and made some notes on Mrs. Highsmith. She needed to get a formal statement from Mrs. H., but she also wanted to do a background check, see what turned up. Of course, that meant she needed to find out where the Highsmiths had lived before moving to Sheboygan Bay. Once she had that, she could call the local department and see if they had any files on Bob and Lorraine. She was awfully curious about them—Mrs. Highsmith kept to herself a lot, especially since her husband had passed, and didn't seem to have friends in town.

And why *her* lawn?

Mike grabbed the report and opened her office door, then passed by Patoka's drunk driver, a young man in tight acid-washed jeans and a sleeveless flannel shirt, hanging his head between his knees and looking half passed out. She tossed a good night to both officers, which was met with silence, then headed to Carla's desk to drop her finished report in the basket.

"You still here, Sergeant?" Frankie Sanders had wandered in, late for his shift as usual.

She didn't bother mentioning it, or correcting Frankie on her new title—Mike wasn't Sanders's direct superior anymore, thank *God*. If it were up to her, they'd have fired Frankie years ago for gross incompetence, but Frankie was related to someone on the town board, so it was nepotism, pure and simple, and they had to keep him.

Lord save them all from small-town politics.

She dropped her report in the basket. "Frankie, what are you doing up front?" There was no good reason for the man to be lurking around Carla's desk.

Sanders looked everywhere but at her, adjusting his utility belt before reaching up to stroke his bushy mustache, stretching over the top of his mouth and down to his chin on both sides like a wooly waterfall. Whatever the man was up to, it wasn't good, so she herded him out to the hallway. "You looking through the chief's files again?"

"What? No, I don't even know how to get in there," Sanders protested, but he let himself be shooed out of the area.

"Just keep out of there, will ya?" Incredible that the one thing Sanders was good at was breaking and entering. "And if the medical examiner calls tonight—"

"Dr. Schneider? The chief is a lucky man, that's a sweet piece of ass. I should ask her if she wants to see my new hot tub." Frankie looked Mike up and down, thick eyebrows waggling. "Unless you want to. I bet you got a hot little two-piece. I wouldn't mind a look, even if you do chicks."

Mike paused before replying. "Do you mean chickens? I have a dog, but I don't keep chickens," she said slowly, maintaining a lot of eye contact. It usually shut men up.

But Frankie didn't catch her drift. "No, chicks like women. Like, you're into women."

She didn't bother stifling her sigh. But she decided to address only part of the nonsense and ignore the rest—it really didn't pay to say anything. She knew from experience that he would claim he was kidding, and can't she take a joke?

"Here's some free advice, Frankie. Don't let the chief catch you talking about his wife like that."

"Nah, he wouldn't mind," Sanders said. "Now what about the doc?"

"Never mind." Mike would just call Dr. Schneider the next day and see what she'd learned from the autopsy. Frank wouldn't be able to take a coherent message anyway. "Have a good night. Try to write some tickets, maybe."

"You too, Sarge."

Mike walked to the back of the station and stuck her head into the sergeant's office. Rich Johnson was sitting behind his desk, pawing through a stack of reports. "Hey, Sarge, just a heads-up that Frankie was skulking around Carla's desk again."

Johnson stopped what he was doing and sat back in his chair. "Breaking in, you think?"

She nodded, then paused and leaned against the doorway. Johnson had always been pretty decent to her, hadn't made any of the usual cracks about her "butch" haircut, or at least not to her face. And that counted for *something*. "Do you know anything about the Highsmiths?"

Johnson took off his square black glasses and blew on the lenses, then used a desktop napkin that looked reasonably clean to wipe them. "Bob and Lorraine, right? Live over on the lakefront?" She nodded again, and Johnson kept going. "I thought he dropped dead not too long ago. Weird, 'cause he was a runner too. Out running along the lake every morning."

"A good reminder that running is bad for your health." It was a joke, but Johnson just looked at her, then went back to wiping his lens smudges around, moving them from place to place. "Do you know anything about her? Lorraine?" Mike asked.

Johnson put his glasses back on his beak-like nose and shook his head. "Nah, but the chief might. He and Bob went to high school together and were fishing buddies when Bob moved back. They used to do catch and release over on Elkhart Lake, pretty regular I think."

That was interesting, and something she hadn't known. It made sense why the chief had insisted on showing up at Mrs. Highsmith's house that morning, then.

She had one last question. "Do you know where they lived before?"

Johnson was already turning back to his stack of reports, red pen poised. He shook his head, attention already on what he was doing next. "Around Chicago maybe?"

Mike thanked him and went out the back door. It hadn't been the *most* useful, but it was better than nothing.

Chapter 8

LORRAINE

Tuesday

While she waited for it to get dark, Lorraine worked on her column, shuffling through letters and deciding who would benefit most from her advice. There was a lot of trouble with mothers-in-law, kids of all ages, and cheating husbands. No big surprises with those. The one from a young woman with a roommate keeping a snake as a pet was intriguing, though. Without advising harm to animals—readers hated that—she could suggest some other ingenious ways to horrify him. Some Godfather-type action.

Or was that inviting trouble from her past?

Lorraine moved on to a different letter, one where the writer was being asked to sneak ashes of her dead father out of an urn to give them to her mother. This was safer territory and entertaining to boot.

Unfortunately, it was also fast work, and once she finished, she checked her watch and sighed. Still too early to head out. She pulled the paper from her typewriter and decided to turn her attention to a news article about Rupp. This type of writing was more challenging—ensuring the juiciest bits of news were up front, and everything was tight and concise. Readers rarely made it to the bottom of these articles, unlike her column. She did several drafts of the first few paragraphs until she hit upon the perfect flow, then pulled the paper from the machine and highlighted the paragraphs at the bottom. Tomorrow she'd type the article from scratch, starting with what she had here. After that, she would inform her editor, Jim Higgins, that the paper would be paying her for a new article that they could expect shortly.

Checking her watch again, she was pleased to see it was finally late enough to get moving, and she covered her typewriter before heading to the garage. She gave her bicycle a quick pat as she passed but opened the door of her wagon and dropped into the driver's seat.

Lorraine tended to ride her bike for short trips around town because even though she drove a sensible wood-paneled station wagon, she'd bought the largest model, and it took just a little too long to find good parking spots, especially downtown, where the angled street parking was tight. But the Behemoth—as she affectionately called it—had a hell of a lot of room in the back, and you couldn't beat the gas mileage for the size, both excellent selling points.

You never knew what you might need to transport over state lines.

She made sure she had Bob's binoculars, the ones that he'd bought to watch birds—honestly, what a boring pastime, but it had made him happy, and sometimes he'd brought her a dead one to stuff—and slid the station wagon out of the garage and onto the street. It was finally dark, which was useful. Of course, even more useful were the dark clouds blanketing the sky, blotting out the moon, manufacturing a more complete darkness. The summer air was thick with moisture, telegraphing an impending storm. She hoped it would hold off for a few hours—rain would make covert spying difficult. She navigated to Baker's place and parked a block away, with a full view of his driveway, avoiding the wide yellow spotlights cast by the streetlights flickering on.

Lorraine was a little amused to realize that she was parked in nearly the same place that Rupp had been. But she had no intention of meeting the same fate as that jackass.

A red sports car—was it a Corvette? Either way, it was a classic and clichéd midlife crisis on wheels, and it was parked in the driveway. It *had* to belong to Julian, and she hoped that he wasn't already in for the evening. While she waited for something to happen, she played a game she'd invented for herself long ago: observe and deduce. It was exactly what it sounded like—she observed what she could, and like Sherlock Holmes, tried to deduce what she could about the person or people based on what she saw. It helped keep her mind sharp. For instance, the house directly next to where she was parked had a large wooden swing set that clearly hadn't been used in some time. So the kids had aged out of it, but were still at home, based on the brand-new minivan in the driveway. Middle schoolers, then, or early high school, but not yet old enough to want wheels of their own.

Other than the monstrosity that Baker had built, the houses here were oversize but tasteful, built around the turn of the century or just a little later. This was the wealthiest neighborhood in the city, with the houses and the vehicles to match—like that minivan. Top of the line, and probably had all the amenities, like automatic windows and maybe even those newfangled CD players.

Lorraine wondered how many of these folks had made their money in toilets—Kohler was within commuting distance, and a sizable portion of the working-class population traveled from Sheboygan Bay to work at the toilet factory there, especially since most of the local factories had shuttered. Of course, the folks on this street weren't screwing on flushers, they were probably engineering the damn things or some such nonsense. Or even more probable, simply sitting at a desk, twiddling their thumbs and collecting fat paychecks.

Upper management. What a joke.

A few fat drops on her windshield turned into a deluge within seconds, the clouds letting loose their bottled-up rage. She had to crank up her window, which meant the windows were now fogging up from nothing more than her breathing, making it even more difficult to see. Maybe it was time to pack it in for the night. Lorraine turned the car on, but instead of putting it into drive, she hit the button for the front-window defrost. Although, should she turn the air on, or blast a little bit of heat? She never could figure out the best way to defog a window, summer or winter. There was an alchemy to it that seemed beyond the reach of mortals.

About the same time her windshield started to clear, the rain began to ease up, so she idled for a few minutes instead of taking off. Her eyes swept the neighborhood again, looking for changes in the landscape, when she saw the light above Baker's front door flip on. Finally! She sat up straight in her seat, ready to throw the Behemoth into drive. But the minutes stretched out again, and just when she was starting to think it was a false alarm, Julian stepped outside. While the man climbed into his overly sporty car, dwarfing it with his bulk, she put her hand back on the gearshift and idly wondered what bullshit excuse he gave his wife when he went out at night. If he even bothered to give one.

Baker pulled onto the street and zipped off, Lorraine struggling to keep up with him, even on the city streets. The man was a terrible driver, even worse than her, dodging around the few scattered cars out on the road, as though the two seconds he saved in doing so were going to be his very salvation. She was so busy cursing his driving that she nearly missed him pulling to a stop in front of Mary Ann's Frozen Custard. It would be convenient to blame this near oversight on his bad driving, or even the rain, but that had nearly let up. It was aggravating to admit that the real reason she'd almost missed Baker was that it was now a struggle to see at night, especially when the streets were wet and shiny. It was hard to make out where the lines were—they seemed to absorb into the asphalt entirely, leaving a blank black canvas, only reappearing with the sun.

Lorraine cruised past Mary Ann's, then pulled an illegal U-turn at the next intersection and parked several spaces down from Baker. Was he doing an after-dinner ice cream run? With the gut he was hauling around, she really wouldn't recommend it.

She left her car running with the lights off, waiting to see what happened next. She couldn't quite see inside the front window and was considering getting out and casually strolling past when Julian came out empty-handed and got back into his Corvette. He pulled out and took off at far too fast a clip, tires chirping, but this time Lorraine had a good idea where he was going, so she didn't bust her ass to keep up.

Christ, why didn't they make these station wagons with more pickup?

Lorraine cruised through downtown, then through the run-down area of town where Marjorie lived, before hitting an industrial area to the south. Just on the other side of the paint factory and a few other ugly commercial buildings was the seedier bit of Sheboygan Bay, not too far from Interstate 43. Here was a Chi-Chi's, a strip club, and a truck stop, as well as a handful of roadside motels.

Sure enough, a few minutes later she found Baker's car parked at one of the nastier motels—the Sea Breeze, an especially absurd name since they didn't live near the sea. Lorraine pulled into the parking lot and set up on the far side, away from the front desk, both car and lights turned off this time. There was no one parked near Julian's Corvette, nothing to be seen but crabgrass hunkered down in the concrete's many cracks, so she was feeling confident his mistress hadn't arrived yet.

But when time slipped away and no one else arrived, she grew impatient. She stepped out of her car and stretched, arms overhead, side to side, then reached for her toes. Sitting for so long made her muscles tighten up—she had to be mindful of that. It was work to stay limber, which was why she took her weightlifting, circuit training, and aerobics so seriously. She even lifted some weights in her garage when she couldn't carve out time to hit the gym. Her body might be pleasantly padded these days, but it covered a strong core of muscle. Would she rather sit and stuff her dead birds? You bet your ass, but she set an egg timer whenever she sat down—she couldn't afford to sit for too long, couldn't let her muscles atrophy.

Of course, there was less to taxidermy now that Bob was dead.

No, she hadn't stuffed him. Although what an exciting challenge that would have been.

With nothing more than a quick glance around the deserted lot, Lorraine headed for the motel room directly in front of Baker's car. She didn't even have to put her ear to the door to hear the distinctive noises of sex. Loud sex, and by the sound of it, whoever he was with was a real performer, since there was no chance she was enjoying herself *that* much. But at least she was in the spirit of things.

She could bang on the door and roust them, but she hadn't come this far to reveal herself and the fact that she'd been following Baker around town. She played with the zipper on her windbreaker, considering, then headed for the front desk. If Julian and his mistress were regulars, maybe the clerk knew who the woman was.

And then who knew where the evening would take them?

Chapter 9

LORRAINE

Tuesday

The girl at the front desk had been entirely unhelpful, but she'd also failed to look up from her blaring television, meaning she was unlikely to know what Lorraine looked like. This was an upside to the apathy of today's youth—if Detective Zenoni came to talk to this kid, she wouldn't be able to describe her.

If Lorraine was really lucky, the girl would forget she'd been here at all.

Sitting in her car, she eyed the door to room number five in the rearview, waiting for Baker to emerge, sweaty and gross. In her mind, anyway, although how could he not be? She'd heard enough to know he'd be lucky to get out of the room alive—a heart attack was surely coming for him. A man of his age and girth shouldn't be exerting himself so much.

That poor woman. Or man, Lorraine supposed it could be one of those, too, although it had definitely sounded like a woman.

Lorraine shuddered, pushing away further images of a naked Baker from her ripe imagination, concentrating instead on what she would say to the man when he finally emerged from the motel room. His earlier dig about her resemblance to that hideous statue was still roiling in her blood. The last time someone had made the mistake of commenting negatively on her looks, he'd become fish food floating in the Mississippi, a single gunshot wound through the back of the head. Clean. Precise.

Her lips slowly slipped into a grin as she recalled the pleasure she'd gotten from dispatching *that* guy. He'd been a low-level guido with a big mouth, and the higher-ups with the Outfit hadn't even blinked at the loss. Besides, that's what she was known for—dispatching mob fuckups and cleaning up messes. Sure, she'd started out running numbers for a neighborhood wannabe, but over time she'd worked her way into a job for guys who were actually with the Outfit, despite the fact that she was a woman. She'd been one of the only women that Joey Epstein trusted, as a matter of fact, because she was smart, efficient, and deadly. And most importantly, she kept her mouth shut, unlike Virginia Hill. That was a woman who didn't know when to shut her trap, and she'd paid the price with her life.

Even now, years later with a new name, Lorraine knew to keep her fucking mouth shut.

She was interrupted from further reminiscences by the door to room number five cracking open, and her focus became razor sharp on her current prey. Julian was halfway out the door, tucking his shirt back into his pleated pants, when the young woman behind him said something. He turned and snarled, although at this distance, she couldn't tell what was said. He continued out the door, followed closely by his mistress, who was wearing only a T-shirt and nothing else—a decent Donald Duck impression, really.

Who was that? She looked familiar. What was her name? That was definitely the girl from the gas station, and Lorraine dredged up the fact that the girl had her entire name spelled out on her name tag, which was a weird choice. Carrie Ann Williams, that was it.

Well, whatever Carrie Ann said next caused Baker to turn quickly and take a solid swing in her direction, putting his substantial weight behind his meaty fist. Carrie Ann ducked like she knew it was coming, like she expected as much from this man. Or maybe any man.

That wouldn't do at all.

The blow neatly avoided, Carrie Ann hustled back into the hotel room and quickly slammed—and presumably locked—the door. Baker was stomping back to his car, about to use his key to unlock the driver's side door, when Lorraine left her own seat and sauntered around to the trunk, popped it open, and hoisted up the back hatch before hopping up to take a seat, legs swinging against the back bumper. Before Baker could compress himself enough to squeeze into his matchbox car, she put two fingers in her mouth and blew hard, the short, sharp whistle giving Baker a start. His head swiveled left, then right, searching for the source, and she watched his eyebrows crease into a frown when he spotted her.

He stood for a long moment, clearly considering whether to bother approaching, but curiosity must have won in the end, because he slowly closed his car door and crossed the lot, coming to a stop a few feet away from her.

"Whaddaya want?" Baker was clearly still in a temper.

"You're awfully grouchy tonight. Couldn't get it up?" Before the man could respond, she patted the car's wide-open trunk next to her. "Have a seat."

"Why would I do that?" Baker sneered.

"So I don't rat you out to the police for domestic abuse and cheating on your wife."

"You can't prove any of that, and besides, so what? Fooling around isn't a crime."

Lorraine shrugged. "Well, *you* can't prove that I don't have a whole raft of Polaroids of you and that young woman doing the dirty tango. I'm happy to post them all over town, you know. I could even get them featured in the newspaper, make sure this whole town knows you're an abusive prick. You'd be great front-page news."

Baker studied her for a long moment before crouching to get his big head beneath the raised hatch, turning, and settling his considerable bulk next to her. The poor Behemoth's back end dipped hard with a creak, and she hoped she wouldn't need to have the struts replaced. Or the axle? Whatever part of her car this idiot was currently damaging.

Of course, even if he did break something, it would be worth it—Baker had taken the bait. She fought a smile, saving it for later.

Her purse had dipped forward as the car had, bumping into her back, and she took the opportunity to turn slightly and pretend to putz with it as she pulled a hypodermic needle from the outside pocket where it had been stashed and tucked it beneath the purse. All this happened in a matter of seconds, quick enough that Baker didn't bother to look at what she was doing.

"What is it you're actually involved in, Julian? Guns? Drugs? Prostitutes?"

Baker's eyebrows went up, emphasizing how far back his hairline had receded. "You have an overactive imagination, Mrs. Highsmith."

She gave a casual shrug, eyes boring into him. "That may be so, but the fact remains that you're into something, something that doesn't include vague 'investments.'"

"Are we done here?" Baker looked as though he was about to launch himself from the trunk, so she put a hand on his arm to stop him.

"How many women have you taken a swing at, Julian? They can't stick around for long after." She moved her right hand to the hypodermic behind her.

"What I do with my lady friends is none of your business," Julian blustered, looking as though Lorraine might be the target of his next swing.

All this was enough of an answer for Lorraine. As he started to push himself up, she stabbed him in the love handle with the syringe, depressing the stopper and hiding it again before he had a chance to process what had bitten him. It was a technique she'd learned from her mother at the psychiatric hospital—a nurse for many years, Lorraine's mother had been quick as a hiccup with a syringe when one of the violent prisoners got out of hand. In and out, *boop*, there's your sedative, enjoy your linoleum-floor nap.

Of course, this wasn't a sedative.

"What the fuck was that?" Julian shrieked, sitting back down and slapping at his side, lifting his shirt and looking for the culprit.

"A bee maybe?" She stood and gave a little stretch. "Wasps have been real bad this year. That's probably what stung you."

The digitalis was already working its magic. It was not a small dose, and this would all be over quickly.

"Oh, my heart, it's too fast. What's happening?" Julian was listing to the side now, one hand to his chest. She gave him a little push backward so he was more fully in the trunk. Then, with some considerable effort, she got his legs into the back as well. There. Baker was all tucked into the trunk, still moaning.

With a quick glance around to ensure no one was watching, she shut the hatch and dusted off her hands, then pulled the car keys from her pants' pocket. Baker had landed on her purse, but she could retrieve it later.

Once he was dead.

Chapter 10

MIKE

Wednesday

The next morning Mike stood in front of her closet, hands on hips, and tried to decide what to wear. Cheesus crisp, she missed wearing the uniform. It took all the guesswork out of mornings, trying to put together a getup professional enough for a detective but not so fussy that she would get ridiculed by the guys. They didn't need any more ammunition. Although she didn't miss the Sam Brown utility belt pulling her pants straight down when she snapped the belt release. Those belts were *heavy*, all that gear strapped to your waist.

In the end she grabbed a gray plaid jacket and matching trousers, with a white silk blouse. Classy, right? Before she put on the jacket, she slid the shoulder pads out. They were en vogue, but her shoulders were already broad—she didn't need neon signs screaming *Lookee here!* She checked herself out in the mirror and gave a nod. Not bad. In fact, she looked a little like Melanie Griffith in *Working Girl*, and that was definitely a win. She let her enormous gray-and-white Great Dane Zeus out into the yard—no time for a walk this morning—then made herself coffee and poured it into a large thermos.

She waited impatiently while Zeus finished his business, turning what little grass she had a grody shade of brown. The dog was so tall his head came nearly to the top of the chain-link fence, so it was more for show than anything—if he wanted to, Zeus could leap over it, although she wasn't sure the dog realized this. All in all, Zeus was just a big baby and not too adventurous, and he was real good about coming when called. She patted him on the head when he loped back. "I'll take you for a nice long walk tonight, boy. I promise."

He slobbered on her pants in reply. She sighed and mopped herself up with a kitchen towel, then headed for work well before she actually needed to be there. It was drilled into her to be early—her pops always said, *If you're five minutes early, you're late.* Besides, she had a murderer to catch, and you couldn't do that by sitting on your ass at home. In all the detective novels she read—Ed McBain was her favorite—the cops barely slept until they tracked down the killer. That wasn't reasonable, of course—she needed at least seven hours of sleep to function. And if she couldn't function, she definitely wasn't going to solve this.

Was there time to stop at the bakery for a blueberry muffin? She looked at her watch and decided not to waste even the extra fifteen minutes—probably more than that 'cause there was always a line. She could grab a packaged Little Debbie from the box of snacks in the break room—she had seventy-five cents in spare change at her desk. And even though the little cardboard payment box was on the honor system, she always paid, even though she suspected Frankie just pocketed all the money at night.

Mike parked in the lot at the back of the station and came in the rear employee entrance, but instead of going to her desk, she headed for the front and leaned against the doorway to talk to Carla. "Any messages for me?" When citizens called after hours, they left messages on the department answering machine, which Carla listened to every morning.

Carla didn't look up from whatever she was typing. "Nope," she said.

Mike paused. It really would be nice to be friendlier with Carla, have an ally here, someone who knew what it was like working with all this baton-swinging testosterone every day. Honestly, they'd worked together for more than five years—it was weird that they'd never really had a conversation.

"Did you have a good night?"

At this, Carla froze mid-keystroke and turned slowly toward her. Her brown eyes, magnified behind the square brown plastic glasses she wore, studied her. Mike's skin felt tight under the intense observation.

"It was fine. How was yours?" Carla said slowly, every word careful and clear.

Mike nodded, regretting her urge to start this conversation. "Good, it was real good. Low key, you know?"

Carla blinked at her a few times, then nodded, slowly turning back to her typewriter, the chair screeching its complaint. Carla took a long drink of her coffee before her fingers were back at it on the keys. *Clackity, clack, clack.*

Mike could feel her face flush, although there was no good reason why. It had been a totally normal thing to ask a coworker, right? Luckily, she was interrupted from having to obsess about it further by the chief barging through the door behind them.

"Detective! Why are you just standing here?" Schneider asked.

She was tempted to ask her boss why he was actually at work at a decent hour, but bit her tongue instead. Truth was, she had to bite her tongue so often around her boss it was shocking she hadn't developed a lisp. "Just talking to Miss Robinson, here." She really should end that with a *sir*, but she couldn't bring herself to do it.

"Mmm." Schneider tried the door handle to his office. "Why is this unlocked?" he muttered to himself. Mike nearly told him that Sanders had been back at it, searching through files, but her boss was already settling behind his desk and moving on. "I spoke to the medical examiner last night," Schneider said.

After following the chief into his office, she took a seat in the chair closest to the wall this time, hoping it might be more comfortable. Nope, still stiff as a billy club. "Did she have anything interesting to say?"

The chief was interrupted from answering by a little bell, signaling that the front door had opened and a member of the tax-paying public had arrived in the front lobby, an area no bigger than three wooden caskets laid side by side. Four orange molded-plastic chairs lined the back wall, FBI wanted posters hanging precariously above them, dangling from strips of yellowed Scotch tape. The detective twisted in her seat to peer through the glass window behind her, the chief leaning over in his own chair to do the same.

Mike couldn't help a sigh as she turned back around. She had a list of questions to ask her boss about Mrs. Highsmith, but she couldn't exactly do that while the woman was here.

"I brought kringle," Mrs. Highsmith announced. She held a bakery box aloft and made prolonged eye contact with Carla. Mike heard a swooshing noise and stifled another sigh—Carla had motioned the busybody through the little swinging door separating the public from the police. There was a pause as Mrs. Highsmith offered a section of almond kringle to Carla—who politely declined—and then there she was in the doorway, box in hand.

Mike recognized that box—it was from the bakery where the eye candy named Jamie worked.

"Lorraine, what are you doing here?" the chief asked.

"I've learned a few things, and I assume you have, too, being the hardworking public servants that you are." She smiled, the movement creating creases where none had existed before. "So, I brought kringle for you to eat while we discuss developments."

Mike waited for her boss to object to this, but he was busy craning his neck to see over the side of the bakery box. Mrs. Highsmith opened it and smoothly served kringle on a napkin to each of them.

"Mrs. Highsmith, you know we aren't going to discuss the case with members of the public." Mike set her piece of kringle on the edge of the desk. It *did* look good, certainly better than the mushy, plastic-wrapped Little Debbies in back, but she wasn't sure she could morally eat what felt like a bribe.

"You'll be delighted to learn that I come to you as a member of the fourth estate, then."

Mike frowned and glanced at her boss, whose face was sugar glazed, mouth open, mustache delicately dusted with powdered sugar. If only the public could see him now.

"I'm covering the murder for the paper," Mrs. Highsmith clarified.

This wasn't good news, as far as Mike was concerned. Quite the opposite, really. She opened her mouth, but Mrs. Highsmith interrupted her, cutting her off before so much as a syllable could pass her lips.

"First, I'd like to know what you've learned from your wife, Hans," Mrs. Highsmith said.

Schneider took a bite of his almond kringle, powdered sugar drifting from his mustache and settling onto his loudly patterned tie. "This certainly changes things, you working for the paper on this one."

Mike watched her boss's mind work, such as it was, and had a sneaking suspicion she wasn't going to like what came next.

Chapter 11

LORRAINE

Wednesday

Lorraine and the detective watched Schneider's mind struggle through possibilities. A little torturous, but Lorraine was still feeling confident that she would get what she wanted out of this exercise.

"We're not ready with a statement for the press, boss," Zenoni said.

Lorraine narrowed her eyes at the other woman, then smoothed her face back out. Mike Zenoni was going to be trouble—she'd known it from the first moment she'd laid eyes on her.

The cogs finally ground to a halt in Schneider's head. "I'm afraid the detective is right, Lorraine. We don't have a statement yet." He hurried to add, "But we'll call you as soon as we do. I'm glad you're the one who will be writing this up."

This wasn't going to plan, which was frankly surprising given what she was working with, as far as the chief went, anyway. After what she'd learned the previous night, Lorraine had decided she could use information in trade. After all, the cops were bound to learn things that she couldn't—like what the doctor had found during the autopsy—and she could trade the few scraps of information she'd picked up. It was a fair exchange, and it was annoying that the chief wasn't playing along.

Lorraine shook her head. "Hans, even after I found Doug Rupp's car for you?"

Zenoni squinted her right eye. "Chief, I thought you said you found the car." Schneider was finishing his chunk of kringle, looking longingly at the box resting on the edge of his desk and ignoring both women. Perhaps if she tossed them another tidbit of information, in addition to the baked goods, she could wear Schneider down. Then the detective would have to fall in line. Zenoni was smart, too smart, but her position was tentative—she wasn't likely to go against her boss. Not this early in her career.

Lorraine baited her hook again. "Very well, I learned something about Julian Baker last night, and wouldn't you like to know what that is?"

Both the chief and the detective tilted forward in their seats, fully focused on her now. "What did you learn?" Zenoni finally asked.

Lorraine decided to go for playful here. "I'll tell you if you tell me what Dr. Schneider found in the autopsy."

"Not a chance," Zenoni said without missing a beat, leaning back in her chair.

"I'm afraid I agree with the detective, Lorraine," Chief Schneider said, his voice regretful. "We can't leak police information to a civilian."

"Even if I'm working for *The Chronicle*? And even if he was found on *my* lawn?"

"Not even then," Zenoni said, after a quick glance at her boss. "But we can let you know when we have a formal statement for you."

Well, it had been worth a shot. Nothing ventured, nothing gained, as her mother had parroted with a shrug after every failed relationship. But the chief looked as though he either had something to say or a touch of indigestion. If she was lucky, it was the former, and tossing out her last scrap of information would get her a goody in return.

"Did you know that Baker has a mistress?" Lorraine asked.

Detective Zenoni blinked hard, once. "How did you learn that?"

Lorraine chuckled. "A woman has her ways. You should know that, Detective."

"That son of a gun," Chief Schneider said. "I never would have guessed it of him, especially given . . . well, given his wife and what she looks like. Do you know who the woman is?"

"I do," Lorraine said. "It's Carrie Ann Williams."

Schneider and Zenoni both frowned, clearly not familiar with the name. Lorraine shook her head at them, feeling a little zing of triumph at knowing someone they didn't. Wasn't she the *outsider*, after all? "She works at the gas station—the Amoco."

"Over by the liquor store? The one on Main Street?" the chief asked.

Lorraine didn't bother to point out that there were only a handful of gas stations in town and exactly one of them was an Amoco, so it was pretty obvious which one she was referring to. "That's the one."

Schneider nodded, sitting a little straighter in his chair. "Detective, I want you to talk to this Williams. See what she knows."

Zenoni nodded, the normally unlined skin around her eyes pulled tight. Unsurprising, but interesting—Schneider annoyed his new detective. Could Lorraine use that information to her advantage? Maybe.

She tucked it away for later.

Lorraine shot over to the Amoco, then ambled into the building. With a glance, she took in the best place to stand so she could hear everything, deciding on the row of bagged chips immediately to the right. Feigning great interest in the selection of Doritos, she waited. After a minute or so, the door dinged again and she heard footsteps enter, move toward the counter, pause, then come up directly behind her.

"You can't be here," Zenoni said.

Lorraine turned with a smile and shrugged. "It's a public space, isn't it? I need to buy a snack." She held a bag of Cool Ranch Doritos aloft.

The detective's face brewed like the previous night's storm, and she was quiet for a long moment, studying her. "I get that you've got a job to do, but so do I. I don't want to see any part of my investigation in print, or you won't get a statement from us at all."

This felt like an idle threat, and they both knew it since Schneider would rather die than miss seeing his name in print, but she tipped her head in acknowledgment, then moved down the aisle toward the coolers, where she stood, eyeing the cold drinks. Coke, Mello Yello, Tab. She snagged a can of Dr Pepper and meandered toward the register, pausing here and there to peruse other items for sale. The Amoco really was a decent little convenience store, with its rows of candy and crunchy snacks and even a whole section of tacky local gifts. A small rolling cooler offered bags of cheese curds and shrink-wrapped beef sticks—Lorraine was always suspicious of how long that shit sat around. It seemed like a fast track to being confined to the toilet. But a small glass-topped cooler stood next to the counter, and she browsed the frozen ice cream treats inside. These were tempting—she always did enjoy a Drumstick.

Red Garlock, the station owner, stood behind the register sucking on a cigarillo, blowing foul smoke into the air, watching Lorraine slide her items onto the counter. Detective Zenoni glanced between Lorraine and the owner, then simply addressed Red, ignoring Lorraine. "Is Miss Williams here today?"

"That bimbo didn't show for work today, which is why I'm behind the register." Puff, puff, blow. "I should know better than to hire good-lookin' women."

Lorraine waved an exaggerated hand in front of her face, making her thoughts on the clouds of foul smoke quite plain. He saw it, but ignored her, taking a moment to look Zenoni up and down before appearing to dismiss her as not attractive enough to waste breath on.

This needled Lorraine. The detective was no Miss Dairyland, but she was fine, cute even, although that haircut wasn't doing her any favors. Too close to a curly mullet. But who the hell was this guy, to be passing judgement on the women around him? This horse's ass, with his sagging jowls and bulbous red nose. Not that she thought Zenoni was sorry to miss out on his disgusting brand of sexual harassment—she undoubtably got plenty of that at work.

This exchange was putting Garlock on her list of men to annoy. High on the list, really. His particular brand of misogyny reminded her of the stepfathers Lorraine had endured as a girl. Big men, like this one, quick with a fist, dumb and ugly to boot. Men like this needed a little misery injected into their lives to balance the karma in the world.

For a brief moment, the world around her stopped moving, and she slipped back in time, back to the asylum where her mother worked the night shift as a nurse. Muted screams echoed down the hall, mixing with the jangle of an orderly's keys and rhythmic pounding on a metal door, the smell of unwashed bodies and unflushed toilets so pungent you could reach out and grasp it.

She'd sure learned a lot of ways to mete out karmic justice there, learned to weigh whether someone—well, men—were redeemable or irredeemable. But that was a whole scale unto itself, and meting out that kind of justice took planning and care. She'd learned from a master.

"When's the last time you saw her?" Zenoni asked. The detective was doing a fine job so far, so she saw no need to interrupt.

Garlock scratched behind his ear. "Day before yesterday."

Zenoni had the gas station owner look at his employment records in the back and give her Carrie's address while she continued to pretend that Lorraine wasn't there. That was fine. Lorraine just sipped her soda—a little treat, since she normally tried to avoid sugar—and observed her, which was clearly making the detective uncomfortable. Zenoni was avoiding eye contact, but her cheeks were getting red, either in irritation or anger. Or embarrassment? It was hard to say.

The address that Garlock came back with was an apartment on Carriage Drive, and as soon as she heard it, she hustled out the door and back into her car, determined to beat Zenoni there.

Of course, the detective had the advantage of lights and sirens, so she was able to get there before Lorraine this time, but not by much. Lorraine broke every rule between the Amoco and that side of town, shrugging off the possibility that she might get a ticket, and pulled into the parking lot just as Zenoni was opening the front door of the shabby redbrick building.

This part of town was close to where Marjorie lived—lots of brick apartment buildings that had been built decades earlier, the area hovering between okay and unsafe. Lorraine hustled into the building right behind the detective, wrinkling her nose at the pungent cooking smells lingering in the hallway, something thick with onions and an unidentifiable spice, gone sour now. Zenoni was knocking on the door of Carrie's apartment, and it opened just as Lorraine joined her.

Zenoni was clearly displeased at Lorraine's presence, but she put on a neutral face when the door swung open, ever a professional. When Carrie saw who was in her hallway, she cocked her head to the side, blond hair pulled into a ponytail and secured at the front by a blue terry sweatband. "Oh, I'm sorry, I don't go to church."

"No, I'm the police," Zenoni said, pulling her badge off her belt and then holding it aloft. "Detective Zenoni, but you can call me Mike."

"Oh," Carrie said, looking even more confused. "I didn't know that was possible."

"A female detective? It's a real thing," Zenoni said with a lot of patience. "Can I come in?"

Carrie looked between Zenoni and Lorraine, touching the neck of her oversize sweatshirt that had slipped off one shoulder but covered her spandex pants and pink unitard. "I was just in the middle of a workout."

"This won't take long," Detective Zenoni said, "since I'm the only one coming in." The look she gave was stern.

Lorraine shrugged. She'd let the detective have this. "I'll wait out here, and when the detective is done, I'd like to speak with you for *The Chronicle*."

Carrie Ann's face lit up. "Will my name be in the paper? That would be wicked. I've always wanted to have my name in the paper."

Zenoni had already stepped inside, and Lorraine saw the detective briefly close her eyes, but Zenoni still insisted that Williams shut the door behind her, leaving Lorraine in the hall. No matter, she would wait this out. There was little doubt Williams would talk to her, especially if she promised to drop her name in the article. In fact, she'd probably get *more* information than Zenoni.

It was only ten minutes or so before Zenoni reappeared, giving Lorraine a dark look as she brushed past her and left the building. Lorraine was sorry she couldn't follow the detective to her next interview, but she'd figure it out. In the meantime, Carrie Ann was holding the door wide open for her.

The inside of the apartment was no less grim than the hallway, dingy, bare white walls and stained gray carpet the dominant features. At least the woman had gone to the trouble of hanging some curtains in a green-and-pink floral pattern. A stiff-looking brown corduroy couch and two wicker chairs were what Carrie Ann Williams called furnishings, and Lorraine frowned at the discolored couch cushions before opting for a chair. There was less chance of sitting in something questionable, although she also knew that if she moved wrong, the woven seat would either give way or a piece would come loose and stab her.

"When was the last time you spoke to Julian Baker?"

"Uh, who?" Carrie Ann asked, pulling at the hem of her sweatshirt.

"Now, Carrie Ann. I saw you with Julian at the motel last night. There's no need to lie to me. I promise I won't put this part in the paper." That was a lie, of course. This was exactly how Carrie Ann would get her name mentioned in the paper.

Carrie Ann looked surprised, then worried, but Lorraine kept her dark eyes fixed on her. It only took a second before the young woman broke down and admitted everything.

"It's true. I've been seeing Julian behind his wife's back." Carrie Ann wailed. "But he swears he's going to leave her."

Lorraine studied the young woman, concluding that Williams couldn't be much younger than Julian's wife, a fact that was confirmed moments later.

"That bitch shouldn't have been so mean to me in high school." Carrie Ann paused. "Oh, you wouldn't know that, you're not from here. We went to high school together, and his wife was awful, just awful to me." Carrie Ann's lips, pink with a sticky-looking gloss, did a pouting thing that Lorraine found off-putting. Did that kind of thing appeal to men? And why would you exercise wearing that shit? She'd bet her hair stuck to it.

"Ya know, I might not be from here, but I had my fair share of mean girls *and* boys growing up," Lorraine said. "It's tough going to school in a small town, isn't it?"

"Jeez, I didn't think they even had schools when you went," Carrie Ann said, wide eyed.

Lorraine clenched her jaw but moved on. "They sure did. Now, about Julian."

Carrie Ann frowned. "He was supposed to call me this morning but didn't. He's usually pretty good about things like that, so I waited here, but I still haven't heard anything. Mr. Garlock won't let us use the inside phone for personal calls, he's so *lame*. And I can't hear the pay phone outside, so I like, just didn't go in." She was tugging on her sweatshirt again. "Do you think Julian is okay?"

"I'm sure he's fine. Do you know anything about his work?"

Carrie Ann shook her head. "I just know he's in investments. And that he can afford pretty much whatever he wants."

Lorraine didn't figure cheap blonds and plastic cars were that expensive, but then, what did she know?

Other than why Julian Baker wasn't making that phone call, of course.

Chapter 12

MIKE

Wednesday

It was becoming really hard to ignore Mrs. Highsmith, but at least she'd listened and stayed in the hallway while Mike conducted her interview. She really didn't want to arrest Mrs. H. for interfering with the investigation—she could only imagine how much shit the county guys would give her for that, bringing a little old lady into lockup. So she was relieved that Mrs. Highsmith had followed directions. With any luck, Mrs. H. would get what she needed for her article and butt out, leaving her to do her job in peace.

A little voice in the back of her head piped up. What would Mrs. Highsmith ask once she was gone? It was kinda tempting to stay behind and listen to her interview Carrie Ann. Would she get something different out of the young woman? She'd had good intel about the mistress, but that was all Mrs. H. had, right?

Mike had one foot outside already, but looked back at Carrie Ann's door, which had just clicked shut with Mrs. Highsmith inside. It wouldn't hurt to put her ear to the door, see if she could hear anything.

She crept down the hall and pressed her ear close to the scratched wood. It was almost like she was in the room. Christ, this place was built like papier-mâché. Mrs. Highsmith asked some simple questions, the same ones that Mike had started out with. Then Mrs. H. confronted Carrie Ann, announcing that she'd seen Carrie Ann and Julian together the night before.

Mike's mouth dropped open. This was *definitely* worth staying behind to listen to. What had Mrs. Highsmith been doing at that motel? She would for sure be asking questions about *that*.

"Miss Williams, I think you should call your job and explain why you didn't show up today. So that you still have a job to go to," Mrs. Highsmith said. You know what? This was actually good advice.

"And tell him that I can't work because I'm having an affair with a married man? That won't look good." There was a mumble she couldn't make out; then Carrie's voice got stronger. "No, I'll just go to work tomorrow after I've heard from Julian and tell Red that I had laryngitis."

A pause. "Does Mr. Baker talk to you about his business? Anything you can tell me?" Mrs. Highsmith asked. "Is there a reason he goes to the ice cream shop but doesn't buy ice cream?"

That was a weird question. Had Mrs. H. seen something interesting at the ice cream shop? Man, that old busybody had been busier than a raccoon at a trash buffet.

It looked like Mrs. H. *had* seen something, since Miss Williams had plenty to say on this matter. "For sure. Yah, he does go there a lot, but he doesn't like sweets. I asked him about it once, 'cause he's always stopping there but not for very long. All he would tell me was that he had business there." She sounded annoyed by this. "And like, he wouldn't say anything else, like he didn't trust me or something. Lame sauce."

Mrs. Highsmith barely paused long enough to take in the other woman's answer before firing off the next question. Probably a technique to keep Williams off balance, which Mike filed away as useful. "Why were you bumping uglies in a motel if you have this apartment?" Mrs. H. asked.

In the hall, Mike's eyes went wide as saucers, but Carrie Ann seemed to take the question right in stride. "I have a roommate. Ricky goes to bed pretty early, and Julian is not . . . quiet." Carrie Ann was quiet, then apparently felt the need to clarify further. Maybe because Mrs. H. gave her a look? "In the sack. Julian is not quiet in bed. And he's not here right now, so I can say that." Carrie Ann sounded defiant now.

"Thank you, Miss Williams. I'll let you know if I have any other questions."

"When will the article be in the paper?" Carrie Ann sounded eager for the answer, and Mike felt a wash of sympathy for her. Whatever Mrs. Highsmith wrote, it wouldn't be complimentary, but the girl was clearly too dim to realize it.

This was also Mike's cue to leave. She had every right to be where she was, but she'd still be embarrassed if Mrs. H. caught her standing at the door, a little kid eavesdropping on her parents. No, it was much better to confront her outside.

Mike went outside to wait, leaning against the door of Mrs. Highsmith's station wagon. The thing was a beast, which wasn't a surprise. Old folks seemed to have a real thing for driving enormous cars. Slowly, too, and in the fast lane, which never failed to spike her blood pressure.

Mrs. H. emerged from the building moments later, not even breaking stride when she saw the detective leaning against her car.

"Thanks for buffing the old girl. She could use it."

"No kidding, you ever bother to wash this thing?"

Lorraine shrugged. "That's a waste of money."

"It also seems like a waste of money to spend this much on a car and let it go to shit."

"Your definition of shit and mine appear to be very different, Detective. You should get out of the city more."

Mike shook her head and got down to what she really wanted to know. "Why were you following Julian Baker last night?" It was the only explanation for what Lorraine had asked Carrie Ann.

Mrs. Highsmith didn't even pause to think about the question. "Because I wanted to see what he did and where he was going. That's what a journalist does. Investigates. So they can write a story."

Mike narrowed her eyes slightly. Mrs. Highsmith wasn't wrong, but it sure felt like there was more to it than that. Her gut said so, at least. *Follow the facts, not your gut* is what she heard, but for once she ignored her pops's voice, pushed it away. She was onto something here, she was sure of it.

"And that's all you saw? Mr. Baker stopped at Mary Ann's and then met Miss Williams at the motel?"

"So formal, Detective. They have given names."

"And you're avoiding the question," she shot back.

Mrs. Highsmith smirked—there was no other word for it. "That's all I saw, Detective, before I went home and tucked myself into bed."

"You didn't see him leave?"

Lorraine's mouth twisted. "I didn't want to wait around that long. The noises coming from that room were . . . unseemly."

Mike grimaced, then waited a beat to see if Mrs. H. would admit to anything further, but it was clear she was simply waiting for whatever came next. "Where did you and Mr. Highsmith live before you moved here?"

This time Mrs. Highsmith's eyebrows popped up, just a little. "Rockford, Illinois. Going to do a little digging, Detective? You won't find much, I'm sorry to say. Just a couple of boring old fogies, living uneventful lives."

But they hadn't always been old, had they? And was it her imagination or had Mrs. Highsmith's face tightened, just a little?

Or maybe that was amusement. Because Mrs. H. seemed super amused now.

"No one says fogies anymore," Mike said without thinking.

"Hmm. Thank you for the pop-culture lesson, Detective." Lorraine moved past her and reached for the door handle. "May I leave now?"

Mike nodded, and pushed away from the huge vehicle, brushing off the seat of her pants as she strolled over to her own car. She was still going to do some digging. Because something wasn't copacetic here, regardless of how fast Mrs. H. spit out excuses.

Minutes later Mike pulled up in front of Mary Ann's Frozen Custard. Everyone referred to it as an ice cream shop, which they sold, sure, but the soft serve that was so popular was actually custard—right there in the name. Mike wasn't sure why that bothered her, but it did.

On the short drive she'd considered getting on the radio and calling in a request for a background on Mrs. Highsmith, but she didn't want to alert her boss that she was doing it. Not that Schneider had a right to object, but she was pretty sure he would. He'd call it a waste of her valuable time, even though her gut said it wasn't. So she'd just wait until she got back to the station, then call down to the Rockford PD and have them pull any files they had.

Was it worth calling in a request to Chicago right away? That would be a pain in the ass, such a huge city with a lot of red tape, so maybe she'd just start with Rockford, see what turned up, and go from there.

Mike was acutely aware of Mrs. Highsmith's car, which had pulled out just in front of her and was clearly heading for the custard shop as well. Was the news article the only reason Mrs. H. was so interested in snooping around? She tried to put herself in the other woman's shoes—an old lady, her husband dead, no real friends in town, and then a fresh corpse turned up on her lawn. And her reaction had been really weird—Mrs. Highsmith had hardly seemed bothered, and wouldn't most people be horrified? Shaken? Unable to look at the dead guy? Mrs. H. had been none of those things. Of course, it hadn't been a bloody scene, not at all. So maybe that was why Mrs. H. had seemed to take it right in stride.

Plus, she was writing it up for the paper, which wasn't ideal for the police, but it did explain why she was poking around. But was that it? The only reason?

Or was it also because Mrs. H. was bored and a little lonely?

Mike pulled onto Main Street and saw Mrs. Highsmith springing out of her car and trucking up the front walk, through the glass door of the custard shop before the detective could even pull into a spot. She took the time to lock her car before crossing over and following her inside. Mrs. H. was quick on her feet; she'd give her that.

The old bat was waiting just inside the door.

Mike cocked her head, motioning for Mrs. Highsmith to go ahead of her. "Age before beauty, Mrs. H."

Lorraine snickered at that but let it pass. "You're not going to stop me?"

"No, by all means, go ahead." Mike was gonna wait until Mrs. H. was done asking her questions before asking her own, without an audience, of course. She'd learned a few things from listening to Mrs. Highsmith's last conversation, so maybe Mrs. H. would let something else slip, some other juicy bit of information she was holding back from the police. And since Mrs. H. was with *The Chronicle*, people might actually talk to her, hoping to get a mention in the paper, like Carrie Ann.

Mrs. Highsmith narrowed her eyes at her, then shrugged and sauntered the last few steps to the ice cream counter. The place was empty, except for an acne-ridden high school kid lounging behind the glass display, reading a beat-up paperback. Mary Ann's uniform consisted of an orange shirt and matching ball cap—they weren't doing this kid any favors.

"That's a terrible uniform. Orange isn't your color, sport," Mrs. Highsmith said. Mike felt herself nodding but stopped abruptly. It was super rude, even if she did agree.

The kid looked offended, then shrugged it off. "Pays better than most places in town."

"It would have to," Mrs. Highsmith said. "Is your boss here?"

The teenager shook his head. "Still too early for Craig."

"How about Julian Baker? Have you seen him in here? More than a usual customer might come by?"

"Like, I don't know who that is." The kid picked up his paperback again, trying to either hide behind it or make them disappear. It was a Stephen King novel, *The Stand.*

"He's a middle-aged gentleman, wears a lot of polo shirts. The ones with the little alligators," Mrs. Highsmith said.

The teenager looked balefully at her over the thick fan of pages. "That could be any hoser in town."

"He's balding and getting real fat around the middle." Mrs. Highsmith held her hands out, indicating Baker's belly. "Lots of chest hair and a gold chain that you shouldn't be able to see, but he makes sure you can." She shook her head, looking to Mike. "I've never understood about men and gold chains. Makes 'em look like assholes." Here again Mike was inclined to concur, but this time managed to keep her head from bobbing in agreement. Mrs. H. paused, clearly annoyed with the kid. "Has a big bandage on his hand right now. Looks like a cartoon."

A light bulb went on, and the kid nodded. "Oh, for sure, that guy. He never gets ice cream, he's always just here to talk to the boss."

"Thanks, kid," Mrs. Highsmith said with a nod.

Mike took a few steps to the door and swung it open for Mrs. Highsmith. Mrs. H. didn't say anything as she swept past the detective, which was fine. Then Mike shut the door and braced herself against it, holding the long metal handle to make sure Mrs. H. stayed on the other side.

"There's nothing else you can tell me about Mr. Baker?"

The kid was good and annoyed now, heaving an exaggerated sigh as he dropped the book as far as his waist. "Who are you?"

"I'm Detective Mike Zenoni. I'm investigating a suspicious death, so anything you can tell me about Mr. Baker would be useful." She pointed at the badge clipped to her waist as proof.

"That murder, you mean."

Word spread fast in a small town. Even the kids were talking.

"And?" she prompted.

A shrug of disinterest. "I never talked to the guy."

"And you didn't hear what he was talking to Mr. Youngblood about?"

The kid—Brian, according to his name tag—rolled his eyes. "I got other shi . . . stuff to do."

Mike nodded, then came forward and slipped her card across the counter. Brian picked it up and ran his eyes over it before tucking it between the back pages of the paperback. With any luck, he'd use it as a bookmark, keeping it handy. "Call me if you think of anything."

This time Brian ignored her, making a deliberate show of going back to his book. She gave her head a little shake as she headed out the door. At least the little shit was reading. In her experience, readers tended to stay out of trouble with the cops, or at least they had when she was in school.

But why was Baker here so often if it wasn't for the custard?

Chapter 13

LORRAINE

Wednesday

It was obvious the kid behind the counter didn't know what was going on in the place—his head was buried in his book when they came in, and it went right back to his book as soon as Detective Zenoni walked out. But it was nice to get confirmation that Baker spent a lot of time in there, and not for the ice cream. Or custard. Whatever.

Lorraine had been right about Zenoni, too—the detective was crafty. It was clear from her questions that Zenoni had listened in on her conversation with Carrie Williams. On the drive over, she reviewed that conversation a few times to make sure she hadn't given anything important away. And then at Mary Ann's, Zenoni had obviously decided to take a back seat and let Lorraine go ahead so the detective could see what else she might learn.

She needed to be very careful indeed.

There were a couple of raggedy-ass picnic tables in front of Mary Ann's, painted brown once upon a time but with weathered bare wood showing through split paint, giving them a zebra effect. Lorraine was perched on top of one of them now, her feet flat on the bench, watching Zenoni exit the shop. The detective seemed taken aback at how she was sitting, maybe surprised that she could still hop up there, and seemed poised to make a comment when her attention snagged on a figure about to cross the street toward them. Both women watched as the man checked both ways for traffic as though they lived in some kind of booming metropolis instead of a quiet town with just over six thousand people. She narrowed her eyes. It had been some time since she'd bet on the ponies, but she'd wager this was the owner of this joint. Something about him exuded proprietor—maybe it was the confident way he walked, or how he frowned briefly at the roof of the building.

If the roof was in as bad a shape as the tables, he had reason for concern.

They both waited until he was close enough before either of them spoke. "Craig Youngblood?" Zenoni asked.

"Sure am!" Youngblood said, his voice brimming with obviously false cheer. He was yet another middle-aged man with a close-cut dark mustache starting to show gray. At least he still had a full head of hair.

As far as Lorraine could tell, anyway. She'd have to give his hair a tug to make sure it wasn't a rug, but she was pretty sure it was his own. And she was also pretty sure that Youngblood would object if she reached out and tested her theory. Zenoni, too, probably.

"You're not wearing the ugly orange shirt," Lorraine said. The black Nike polo he was sporting was far more attractive than the uniform he made his employees wear. Far more expensive too.

Youngblood's expression closed down, less friendly now, and she enjoyed this display of irritation. "Yeah, well, it's different for the boss, you know. I'm not behind the counter very often. Even when I am back there, people know who I am."

Lorraine stared at him, unblinking, causing him to shift on his feet. "I have some questions about Julian Baker."

"What about Jules? Has something happened?"

Interesting that this was his first question. Kinda like he *expected* something to happen to his buddy.

Zenoni held her tongue, even now, clearly waiting to see what Lorraine asked. She decided to oblige the detective and reassure her at the same time. "Nothing has happened to Julian Baker. But he seems to be a regular at your store, and he's not here for the custard. What can you tell me about that?"

Lorraine was watching Youngblood carefully, and it was easy to see how hard he was working to keep his face still and blank. He'd be terrible at poker.

"Well, he and I went to school together, and we're still friendly. A fishing trip here and there, ya know." Youngblood was standing perfectly still now, arms held stiffly at his sides.

"That's all there is to it, huh?" Zenoni finally piped up.

Youngblood gave a smile that only moved the bottom half of his face and then nodded. "Of course, Detective."

Zenoni's mouth, a cute little cupid bow, crooked up at one side, and she reached up and scratched the permed curls above her ear. "Seems like an awful lot of 'stopping by' for the occasional fishing trip."

Youngblood's small brown eyes did some calculations, flicking between the sky and the sidewalk. Lorraine had a feeling she knew what was coming next. "Well, he was having trouble at home. Needed someone to talk to about things."

"Trouble like an affair?"

Youngblood cocked his head, then gave a little nod. "I guess I can tell you that, yah, his wife was stepping out on him."

Both Lorraine's and Zenoni's eyebrows went up at this announcement, and Youngblood looked from one to the other but didn't say anything further.

"Do you know who she was cheating with?"

Youngblood shook his head, then checked his watch. "I don't. And I'm sorry, but I really do have work to do." He suddenly seemed to realize that he'd been speaking to both a police officer and a reporter, because he stammered, "And none of this is on the record, Mrs. Highsmith. I wouldn't want to see any of this in the paper. Any of what I said."

Not too bright, this one. "Oh, of course." This was a lie.

Youngblood squinted at her. It looked like Zenoni was trying to cover a smile, which was a little surprising. Maybe the detective had a sense of humor? She'd have to, wouldn't she, working in this dump.

"I'll be by later this afternoon to have a formal chat with you," Zenoni said. She sounded casual, but there was an edge to the look she gave Youngblood, a clear warning that they *would* be talking more later. The ice cream man didn't say anything, just scurried inside, probably to call Julian.

Lorraine nearly snickered—he'd have a hell of a time getting in touch with his buddy Baker. She looked at the detective. "You think that hair is real?"

Zenoni's mouth quirked up farther. "On his head or his chest?"

This time Lorraine snorted, and the detective walked off without a goodbye. Lorraine called over to her, "See you at Rupp's in Milwaukee, Detective!" She'd already found Rupp in the phone book and jotted down his address; she was just testing the waters.

The detective stopped, then turned to look at her, hands on hips. Zenoni sighed and retraced her footsteps.

"Mrs. Highsmith, this has been . . . interesting." Zenoni's mouth tipped up in a half smile again. "But if you show up at Rupp's apartment, I will have to arrest you for interfering with a police investigation." The detective shook her head. "I don't want to do it, but I will. So please be reasonable. Go home and write your article. You've got plenty to work with."

"A good investigative journalist wouldn't sit at home, Detective," she countered.

"One that wants to stay out of jail would."

Lorraine didn't respond, just gazed placidly at the detective, and Zenoni finally shook her head one more time before strolling back to her unmarked squad and getting in.

Would she actually do it? Lorraine wasn't so sure. If it was anyone else, she'd have pushed that envelope a little—okay, *a lot*—further, certain that they wouldn't follow through on the threat. But Detective Zenoni was turning out to be a bit of a wild card—she was a young woman in a man's world, and she couldn't have gotten there with *no* backbone.

Lorraine was still heading to Rupp's place; that wasn't even a question. She was just going to be extra careful to stay out of sight.

Lorraine pulled out first, deciding to gas up her car and give the detective a healthy head start. She trundled over to the gas station and pumped her gas before heading in to pay and pee—a good idea before the hour-plus drive. She fired up the Behemoth again, then drove down Main Street past the cream brick buildings that housed second-story walk-up apartments perched over mom-and-pop businesses below, through some residential areas, and then over to Highway 23. She'd be on this for fifteen minutes or so until she hit the interstate running south.

Midwesterners loved to describe distance in terms of time instead of miles, and she'd adopted the habit, if only just to communicate with the locals. It was one of the few idiosyncrasies she'd picked up after moving so far north. That one she could handle—it was the accent she was thrilled to have avoided. Hers was still neutral, unidentifiable. There was nothing to point to her childhood in upstate New York, or any of the places she'd lived in between then and now.

The obnoxious billboards picked up as Lorraine climbed the ramp onto I-43, looming over the corn fields. She especially hated the religious billboards—like this one, a simple black background that read **Where are you going?** in huge white letters. *None of your business* was what she usually muttered out loud. Although, she *was* amused by the juxtaposition of these religious billboards immediately followed by ones advertising sex shops—**Hell is Real** followed by **Private Pleasures XXX**. Just in case you needed to hop off the interstate to buy a dildo. She would do it, too, if she thought it would get back to the religious whack jobs and make 'em mad.

In the end, all that nonsense did was distract from the subtle beauty of the state, the rolling green farmland that picked up as soon as the city ended. She even found the views relaxing on occasion—it was precisely what you would expect of Wisconsin, just rolling farmland dotted with big red barns and fields of black-and-white cows. Like a toddler's toy set, come to life.

But today she wasn't relaxing into the drive. Today as she drove, she barely saw the landscape as she reviewed what she had just learned, imagining that Zenoni was doing the same ahead of her. Baker's wife was cheating on Baker—what was good for the goose was good for the gander, as they said. It was an interesting bit of information, although it was clear Youngblood knew more. A lot more. Of course, regardless of how Lorraine had to extract the rest of the story from him, the fact remained that it didn't make much sense for either of the Bakers to hire Rupp if they were both having an affair. Even if they wanted a divorce, proof of infidelity wouldn't help them in Wisconsin, since it had just become a community property state. Which meant that the *why* of the divorce didn't matter—you had to split your assets right down the middle. There was a chance that the Bakers weren't up on the new law, but anyone looking for a divorce would have quickly learned that bit of news. It was one of the first things you did when you wanted to get unhitched—find out what the damage was going to be.

Which meant there was another reason Rupp had been watching the Baker house. Lorraine would bet money it had to do with Baker's "investments," whatever the hell that meant. When someone was as vague about their investments as Baker was, she assumed that they were involved in something illegal. That had been her experience anyway, when she'd worked for the Chicago Outfit.

But digging into Baker's financials wasn't something she was interested in doing, even if she could get her hands on those kinds of records. Tracing money and looking at numbers—that was a fine job for the detective to handle. Lorraine would let Zenoni do all the dirty, boring work to see where Baker's money was coming from. And once the detective had done that, she would weasel the information out of Schneider. Freeing her from having to do any of the grunt work.

Chapter 14

MIKE

Wednesday

Doug Rupp's apartment was on the north side of Milwaukee, just off Appleton Avenue. Many of the businesses had gone out, **For lease** signs in the windows, and everything that was left had iron bars over the windows and doors. Numerous buildings had plywood tacked up where there'd once been glass, and Mike had to avoid a pool of sparkling shards on the street when she pulled up in front of Rupp's building. His address was a two-story brick number that had probably seen its heyday back in the 1930s, a downhill slide ever since.

A glance along the block told her that Mrs. Highsmith wasn't here. Not yet, anyway. Mike had no doubts that Mrs. H. would show up at some point, and this time she would actually arrest the old biddy for interfering. It would be humiliating, dragging her into county lockup, but she would do it. Especially if Mrs. H. showed up before Mike was finished searching Rupp's apartment. She looked at her scrawled notes from the drive—pretty legible this time. She mentally high-fived herself, then got out of the squad, scoping out the street from the sidewalk, not missing the twitching window coverings, proof that the residents were clocking her right back. Assorted trash gathered in patches, like the grass that should be growing but had clearly died out long ago.

Bleak. This part of town was friggin' *bleak*.

Mike pushed through the inner door, which was unlocked—another mental high five, 'cause, man, things were going *right*—before checking out the dingy patterned carpeting, stained far beyond whatever color it had started out as. The walls had probably started out white, too, but the marks and gouges and yellow hue shrieked of decades of neglect. The cigarette smoke tainting the air was the only thing that was recent, besides the small pile of McDonald's wrappers just inside the vestibule.

It was, in a word, a shithole.

A wall of dented and scratched metal mailboxes took up the space between the inner and outer doors. Almost none of the boxes had name tags, and the ones that did had faded to nothing. Mike found the box that matched Rupp's apartment number and flipped through keys on Rupp's fat key ring until she came across one that was significantly smaller than the others. She grinned when the key slipped easily into the hole and popped the lock. Rupp had been gone for over a week, so there should be a bunch of mail. She put her hand up like a catcher's mitt as she swung the little door open but was surprised when nothing came out. Huh. There wasn't a single piece of mail to be seen.

Mike slowly closed the metal door, then relocked it. Okay. So either Rupp had a PO box, or he'd had the post office hold his mail, knowing that he was going to be gone for a while. Interesting. Most people wouldn't do that if they were going to be out of town for only a week—so how long had Rupp planned to be back in Sheboygan Bay?

The detective started on the inner door leading into the building, systematically trying keys. After going through a quarter of the ring, she found a key that worked and made her way upstairs to the second floor, where Rupp's apartment was located at the far end of another yellowed hall. There weren't many signs of life in the building beyond an apartment or two with televisions roaring through flimsy wood doors. She doubted Rupp had been killed anywhere near this place, so they probably wouldn't need to do a door-to-door, but if they did, she would send a patrol guy to handle it. Someone capable and good with people, like Patoka.

The key ring, one more time. She jangled the set, then started at the beginning and one by one tried the keys in the door. It took longer this time, and she gave a victory cry when a key finally turned in the knob. She pushed the door open, a wave of ammonia hitting her in the face as a matted ball of gray fur raced through the open door past her legs, before careening around the corner.

"Shit!" she said, watching the fur-beast disappear. This day was taking a turn. Should she try and catch that thing? She wasn't into cats, but it felt real shitty to let the thing disappear into the bowels of this dump. It would likely get let outside and then get hit by a car, which was a gruesome way to go.

Mike grimaced, then pulled Rupp's door shut and hurried after the cat.

She made it to the basement—as gross as the rest of the building—and caught a glimpse of gray fur zipping into the laundry room. She peered behind the row of banged-up washing machines and saw the reflection of one eye. Jeez a flip, was this a one-eyed cat? She sighed. One eye or two, this was gonna be a pain in the *ass*. At least no one had opened the outside door and let it out into the street already.

Mike was still crouched down and staring behind the row of dented machines when a tenant sauntered in carrying a plastic laundry basket brimming with dirty clothes. She jumped to her feet and ran a smoothing hand down the front of her trousers, trying to recapture some sense of authority. She was a detective, dammit, not animal control.

The tenant was somewhere in his fifties or sixties, with a lined face and a full head of hair. He slid the blue basket onto a washing machine and lifted an eyebrow in her direction. "Lose something, miss?"

"Yeah, a cat. At least I think that's what it was," she added in a mutter.

"Mmm," he said. "And who are you, exactly?"

"I'm Detective Mike Zenoni with the Sheboygan Bay Police Department," she said, pulling her badge from her belt and holding it up.

"Well, that's a new one," he said. "I didn't know there were any of those."

She didn't have to ask what "those" he was referring to. "Can you help me catch this cat?"

The tenant was filling a washing machine at the end of the row. "Hell no." The man gave her a skeptical look. "But I guess you can use this basket. If you can get that thing out from behind there."

Better than nothing, she supposed, crouching down again to eye the little beast, who hissed and backed up a little farther.

Fucking great.

Chapter 15

LORRAINE

Wednesday

As soon as Zenoni's feet hit the stairs descending to the ground floor, Lorraine trotted up the stairs and slipped into the apartment. Good thing the detective hadn't relocked it—Lorraine didn't think she had enough time to pick it. In fact, she was quite aware that her time here was limited—she needed to work fast and get out before Zenoni returned.

Holy shit, the smell was overwhelming, her eyes watering immediately from the stench of cat piss. But she pulled her shirt over her nose and pressed through, anxious to see what she could see before the detective came back. A quick glance around the living room showed a big chalkboard with shit taped up all over it—photos clearly taken with a long lens, newspaper clippings, and a few notecards with scrawl, arrows chalked between things. She whipped her trusty little Kodak out of her purse and snapped a picture, advanced the film and snapped another one—*click*, advance, *click*, advance—before heading toward the bedroom in the back. It was as filthy as the rest of the place, dirty laundry and crusty plates on every available surface. She took a picture to inspect later, although at a glance there wasn't anything here. Except, of course, the prescription bottle on the dresser, half full of white pills.

She quickly swiped *that* into the side pocket of her purse. If she was lucky, those pills were something useful—she'd figure it out later.

Nothing else was of immediate interest, so she did a quick perusal of the bathroom, grabbing the bottles of prescription meds from the medicine cabinet, then stashing them in the same pocket. A quick look at the kitchen—nothing juicy, although plenty of things that were rotten—and Lorraine was ready to leave. She hitched her purse higher on her shoulder when she heard voices in the hall, just outside Rupp's door.

Fuck.

Lorraine glanced around wildly, realizing there was no good place to hide. Retreating to the bathroom or bedroom wasn't a great idea—the detective would be thorough, that was for certain. Hiding in the closet or behind the moldy shower curtain wouldn't give her cover for very long.

Lorraine did the best she could, standing against the wall where the door would open and swing against her. She braced herself for a long moment, barely breathing, sucking in her stomach and hoping the door's angle would look natural. It took the detective several long minutes, but the door finally swung open, bouncing gently against Lorraine's midsection. Her heart was beating fast, her breath almost nonexistent. She'd be lightheaded soon.

Zenoni gave instructions to someone, then picked something up and moved into the apartment.

Lorraine's breath stopped completely. Would Zenoni be able to get through the smaller opening of the door? Or would the detective turn around and see her tucked back here?

The detective's mind was clearly elsewhere as she walked past carrying a laundry basket that rocked in her outstretched arms. As soon as Zenoni disappeared into Rupp's bedroom, Lorraine slipped from her hiding spot and hit the hallway.

Where she found the man Zenoni had been talking to.

He raised an eyebrow. "I'm guessing you ain't supposed to be here."

She quickly reached into her purse and pulled out a twenty. "You never saw me," she said quietly as she passed it over. She didn't wait for his reaction before she was moving down the hall.

She hit the front door, pushed it open, and was back on the sidewalk before the detective was any the wiser. Or so Lorraine hoped. Even if the twenty wasn't enough and the nosy neighbor dimed her out, Zenoni hadn't seen Lorraine and wouldn't be able to *prove* it had been her.

Lorraine glanced up at the building, clocking the dirty windows, and continued hurrying until she reached the opposite side of the building from where Rupp lived. She slowed her pace then, feeling secure that she'd made a clean escape, and let herself enjoy the rush from the close call as she sauntered to the building's parking lot, where she'd left her wagon, partially hidden between a rusted-out conversion van and a pickup truck with three flat tires. The pills were burning something of a hole in her purse, but she knew she couldn't take the time to inspect them here.

First thing she *would* do, though, was find a one-hour photo place, preferably here in the city, where no one knew her and wouldn't ask what this roll of film was all about. They weren't supposed to look, but of course, they did. There was a touch of voyeur in everyone.

Still riding the high from her escape, she made her way to North Avenue in the Washington Heights neighborhood and found a Fotomat tucked between a corner bar and a pawn shop. Lorraine went into the photo shop and slipped an extra ten to the greaseball behind the counter. Was he going to look at the photos? Without a doubt. But since there were no naked ladies, she didn't think this guy would pay her strange pictures much mind.

Twenty minutes later, Lorraine had her little paper packet of photos and got back in her car. She glanced up and down the block, but the street was conspicuously empty this time of day, people either at work or still sleeping one off. She flipped the top of the envelope open and thumbed through the still slightly tacky prints. There weren't many—only the ones she'd taken in Rupp's apartment. Another reason it hadn't taken long to develop—she hadn't used the whole roll.

From her quick perusal she could tell the ones of the chalkboard were the most interesting and would need closer scrutiny with a magnifying glass, which she'd left at home. She'd pore over the rest as well, just to make sure she hadn't missed anything, but she had a gut feeling—or maybe it was just hope—that whatever had gotten Rupp killed was somewhere here on this board.

Chapter 16

MIKE

Wednesday

Mike was carrying a plastic laundry basket with a towel pulled tight over the top, barely containing the hell beast inside it. She was holding the basket away from her body, and her arms were starting to shake a little with fatigue. But it was totally necessary—one of the swipes from an angry paw, claws extended, had popped out the side of the basket and snagged her blouse already. She'd gotten lucky—it hadn't torn, just left a little hole. She was keeping her fingers crossed that a run through the wash would shrink it back up.

The helpful tenant—George, it turned out his name was—was following at a respectful distance.

"Imma need to wash both that towel and that basket," he grumbled.

Mike didn't bother responding with anything but a sigh. At Rupp's door she set the basket on the floor, stepped on one side of the towel, and kept a firm hold on the other. The basket rocked a few times, and staying in a crouch, she reached up with her free hand to twist the knob and pop the door open. "Could you hold this towel so I can find a box or something?"

"Uh-uh. I ain't touching that," George said, arms folded over his crisp white wifebeater. It looked new out of the bag. In fact, everything about George's appearance was tidy and crisp— it was no surprise he didn't want to get involved with this box of claws, although it *was* a surprise that he lived in this place.

She sighed again. "Could you go look for a cat carrier then?"

"You gotta be out your mind, lady. Whatever you're here for, I ain't getting involved. I just want my basket back."

This time she closed her eyes. "Okay, just wait here then. I'll find something." Mike picked the basket back up and scurried over the threshold, fighting the rocking as the cat yowled and hurled itself at the sides. She was tempted to just let it go, but she'd sustained enough injuries that she wasn't about to give up now. No, now she was pissed. She would rescue this goddamn cat if it was the last thing she did.

The smell in the apartment was *thick*, and Mike did her best to breathe through her mouth, which honestly didn't improve anything. It felt like the very air was burning a path right through her—was this how a fish tossed onto the ice felt? Fucking *torture*. Using the tips of her fingers, she twisted the doorknob of the hall closet, while gripping the basket, and jerked the door open. A quick glance told her there was nothing useful here—it was just old sports equipment, ratty towels, and a few rolls of toilet paper. At least those looked new.

She got the basket into the bedroom and sent up a silent thanks to whatever resided in the clouds above that the closet here was wide open, the shuttered sliding doors pulled off to each side, leaving a gaping hole in the wall, speared by a rusty metal rod. Fuck, yes! There was an old cat carrier on the top shelf.

But how to get it down without releasing the kraken?

It took nearly fifteen minutes, but she managed to get the rusty carrier down and the irate cat stuffed in it. She was bleeding in a couple of new places, but she would clean up and slather herself with antibiotic cream as soon as she got out of here.

Leaving the cat on the floor of the bedroom, she went back out to the hallway and returned the basket and towel to George.

"You gonna need to get those looked at," he said, pointing his chin at her assortment of scratches.

"I will." She pulled her slim little billfold out of her back pocket, fished for a ten spot, and passed it over to George. "Thanks for your help."

George looked at it for a long moment, then shrugged. "I didn't do nothing. I will keep this, though." The bill had already disappeared into George's shorts.

She cocked her head at him. Did he know something he wasn't telling her? "Do you live on this floor? Do you know anything about the guy who lived in this apartment?"

"I keep myself to myself," George said, already backing down the hall. "I don't even talk to the folks on my own floor. Or no one else, for that matter. Have you *seen* this place?"

She gave a resigned nod and watched him go, then turned back to the apartment. She really wished she had a bandanna or something to tie over her nose, although the smell was so thick it probably wouldn't help. Even the Vicks-under-the-nose trick wouldn't mask the smell—it would only add to the burn. Best to get this over with, and fast.

The kitchen held nothing good, although someone needed to clean it out before all kinds of vermin decided to move in. The living room was next, and her interest immediately snagged on the chalkboard. She needed to inspect the rest of the place first, *then* let her attention be totally absorbed by the chaos on the board, but she was excited by the possibilities here. She'd take photos of this before she moved it to the car—there was no chance she was leaving it behind.

You know what? A quick look at this wouldn't hurt anything but her sinus cavities.

In the center of the board there was what was clearly a surveillance photo of Julian Baker. There was another of Craig Youngblood and a third man she vaguely recognized but couldn't quite put her finger on his name. Sheboygan Bay was a small town, but there were still people she either didn't know or couldn't immediately place. And boy, age wasn't helping this guy's case.

She'd figure out who he was, first thing.

Several articles from the *Sheboygan Bay Chronicle* were taped up, a few featuring Julian Baker in his role as the local Rotary club president, including an award he'd received for civic excellence. Mike rolled her eyes at that, but then her attention snagged on something else. The corner of a Post-it note stuck out from behind Baker's picture, making her fingers tingle with the temptation to grab it, but she didn't want to move anything before she took pictures.

With some effort, she pulled her attention from the board and went back to searching the rest of the place, although sifting through the junk in the living room didn't reveal anything interesting, and neither did the bathroom. Mike breathed through her shirt for a second while she thought. It was strange that there weren't any medications around, right? Dr. Schneider'd mentioned how Rupp didn't take good care of himself, and someone like that usually ended up on meds for blood pressure or cholesterol or something like that, didn't they? Of course, Rupp was probably the kind of guy who only went to a doctor if his arm was falling off.

And at the end of the day, it probably didn't matter since Rupp had been murdered. Before leaving town, Mike had radioed the station on the private channel to learn the cause of death, and Schneider had reported that the man drowned. People didn't drown on dry land, meds or no meds.

The bedroom was both filthy *and* disgusting, and she was more than a little glad for her latex gloves. Crusty tissues were piled on the floor next to the unmade bed, and a quick glance beneath revealed some raunchy porno magazines. Nothing that could get you arrested, but they were real cringe worthy—it looked like a lot of whips and chains. Where would you even buy something like this? Waldenbooks sure as hell didn't carry this kind of shit—it was probably mail-order only.

With a shudder, she picked through the rest of the bedroom, but there was nothing else worth writing home about, and feeling slightly deflated, she headed back into the living room. That Post-it was singing a siren song, so she went down to her car, propping the vestibule door open, and grabbed the Polaroid camera from the trunk. A quick glance up and down the street revealed nothing of interest, including Mrs. Highsmith's tank masquerading as a station wagon.

Good.

Back in Rupp's apartment, Mike snapped photos of the board and set them on the counter to develop. Once that was done, she pulled the yellow Post-it out from its hiding place. It had a short message and a date. *Drop LMP, 6-18-89. 11p.m.* Huh. She didn't know what *LMP* was, but the date was this Sunday night.

Chewing that over, she gingerly grabbed the board—it was just large enough to be awkward, even if it wasn't heavy, and she hauled it down to the car, struggling all the way. It wouldn't fit in the trunk, so she slid it into the back seat footwells, keeping her fingers crossed nothing would fall off. After double-checking that the board was secure and she hadn't lost anything on the sidewalk, she locked the car and headed upstairs one last time.

She took a final look around before she picked up the cat carrier, which immediately began rocking as the cat yowled and fought. This was going to be even tougher to get downstairs than the chalkboard, and she couldn't help her sigh. Why did everything have to be such a fight?

Her mind tumbled over the cryptic Post-it for the entire drive north, while she did her best to ignore the ruckus from the back seat. The chalkboard was a barrier between her and the beast, but it didn't do much to muffle the noise. And what on earth was she going to do with this cat? There was no way she was taking it home with her. Maybe Rupp's sister would like to have it? Since it had belonged to her brother and all?

Yah know, Rupp sure didn't seem like a cat guy. Was he keeping it for someone else? Of course, he really didn't seem like *that* kind of guy either. There were no signs of anyone else in the place, and there wasn't a photo of someone with a bull's-eye drawn around them either—nothing screaming that Rupp had disappeared someone. Other than the murder kit in his trunk, of course. She would search the stuff on the board real thoroughly at the station, though, make sure there was nothing pointing to another missing person.

She hated to admit it, because it had seemed like such a juicy idea, but maybe, just maybe, this little theory of hers had been a bridge too far. Maybe Rupp really had just been investigating his old high school buddy and hadn't tossed a different victim to the pigs.

Mike was relieved as she pulled up in front of Marjorie's house. She pulled the still-yowling cat from the back seat and carried it to the front stoop, setting it far away from her so the thing couldn't swipe her legs—it had a real surprising reach. She knocked and waited a long while for Marjorie to come to the door, the cat rocking and screeching. How the hell did the thing have the energy to keep up a full-scale assault?

"Shhhh. She won't keep you if you don't knock it off," Mike told the beast.

Marjorie finally came to the door, but simply looked at her through the screen, taking a long draw on the cigarette in her hand. "Help you, Detective?"

Mike's face creased in sympathy. "I'm so sorry for your loss, Miss Rupp."

Marjorie didn't say anything, just made a sort of grunting noise, then gestured with her cigarette for the detective to get on with it.

She cleared her throat and pointed to the cat carrier sitting as far from her feet as possible while still on the stoop. "I have your brother's cat. I thought you might like to give it a home."

Marjorie took another drag off her cigarette, eyes narrowed. "You're kidding, right?" She tipped her head at the carrier. "Sounds like a

Tasmanian devil, I'm not letting that into my house. I got good furniture in here. Nice try, Detective."

Mike stared at her, mouth slightly open. "You really won't take the cat?"

"You hearing okay?" Marjorie bit back.

The detective blinked at her a few times, honestly surprised at the rudeness. But then, grief showed up in lots of ways, so maybe this was how Marjorie handled loss. "I'll be back tomorrow to talk to you about your brother, if that works for you."

"As long as you don't have that nasty-ass cat with you." Marjorie gave a little salute with her cigarette, then closed the inner door.

With a sigh, Mike picked up the carrier and gingerly took it back to the car, making sure it didn't come within swiping distance of her body parts. That did not go as planned. What was she going to do with this thing now?

Mike decided to stop by Baker's house and talk to his wife while she figured out what to do with the cat. The Bakers had been cheating on each other, and she wanted to know who Sharity was seeing on the side. Did she know the guy? Did Julian know him? It might have nothing to do with anything, but it was important to get a full picture. And it would be great if the wife would clue her in on what Baker actually did for a living.

She pulled into the Bakers' driveway, hoisted the cat carrier out of the back seat, then set it gently on the asphalt next to the car. "You get some fresh air while I talk to Mrs. Baker," she told the cat, who simply yowled in return. Maybe it would figure out how to escape, and the issue would take care of itself. It was a mean-spirited thought, and she immediately felt bad for having it, but really, the cat was possessed by Satan. She'd rescued it out of obligation and then spite, and now she was stuck with it. And there was no way she was taking it home to terrorize

Zeus. Her dog was the size of a small pony, but he was a big baby, and this demon would beat the shit out of him.

She traipsed up the driveway and rang the doorbell. The doorbell played a little song, and she heard a woman's voice inside call, "Just a minute!"

A few beats later and Sharity Baker opened the door. She was wearing a cozy gray robe, holding it closed at the neck, despite the fact that it was pretty late in the afternoon, nearly suppertime.

"What gives, Detective? This isn't a great time, ya know." Sharity didn't look surprised to see Mike, but she did shoot a fast glance behind her.

It gave Mike the distinct feeling that someone else was in the house. "I need to ask you a few questions about your husband. I was hoping this was a good time."

Sharity cocked her head slightly. "I haven't seen or heard from Julian since last night." She shrugged. "He probably just made like a bread truck and rolled out of town."

Mike narrowed her eyes slightly. "Did he take anything with him? Anything that makes you think he just took off?"

Sharity shook her head again. "Yeah, no, he didn't take anything but his keys." She cocked her head. "Honestly, I just assumed that he took off with his girlfriend, but now that you mention it, he didn't have a bag or anything with him. So that's bogus. Especially 'cause he's real particular about his socks—like, he won't put ones back on his feet if they're already worn. So if he's gonna be gone overnight, he always packs up a couple pairs. But I guess he could just go to Shopko to grab new ones."

Mike paused, trying to tread really carefully. "You knew about his girlfriend?"

Sharity shrugged. "Oh, yah. Everyone did."

Sharity's casual attitude toward her husband's mistress was definitely odd, but Mike put that aside as Sharity signed off on the paperwork Mike handed her, after asking whether her credit cards would be tracked as well. Mike assured her that only her husband's would be tracked, so the blond relaxed and signed off on all the dotted lines.

As Mike pulled away, she focused on what she'd just learned. Neither Sharity nor Carrie Ann had seen Julian since the previous evening. Could Baker have gotten spooked and disappeared? What would have sent him running out of town now that Rupp was dead? Unless Baker had been the one to take Rupp out. The chief had seemed convinced that Baker was telling the truth, that Julian had been surprised that Rupp was dead, but when had Chief Schneider been right about anything?

And what about the finger Baker was missing? Had that really been a kitchen accident?

Chapter 17

LORRAINE

Wednesday

It had been a long day, and Lorraine was feeling stiff from so much inaction and time sitting in the car. As soon as she got home from Milwaukee, she went inside and worked out the kinks in her muscles with some stretching.

That wasn't the only reason she was stiff, of course. Despite her well-thought-out setup, it was hard work moving a dead body.

Speaking of, Lorraine went down the wooden stairs into the cellar and popped open the top of her oversize chest freezer. Julian Baker was starting to look nice and frosty, which was good since bodies really did reek after a day or so. When she'd stuffed him in, his cologne had been so pungent she'd nearly expected it to turn into its own layer of ice. It hadn't, which was disappointing, but at least there was no odor at all now.

She sighed, closing the top again. The man shouldn't have taken a swing at his mistress in the parking lot where Lorraine could see him. Carrie had managed to avoid his fist—the young woman ducked like she had plenty of experience—and Lorraine had seen enough. Baker had sealed his own fate, really, and he'd lost a lot more than his finger.

Her only regret was that she hadn't been able to do proper planning. It was rare that her temper got the best of her these days, and she liked to do quite a lot of research on a man before passing judgement. Although, stabbing Baker—even with a needle—had felt good, and she was grateful she'd had the foresight to bring the bottle of digitalis and hypodermic along. It had been a long time since she had scratched the itch.

So much for retirement.

But it was helpful when a man like Baker revealed himself, since he was exactly the type that gave her a zing of pleasure when she dispatched them—women hating, fist throwing. The type of man who had no trouble taking what he wanted, even from a young girl. A carbon copy of the men she'd endured throughout her childhood. Her mother had always had terrible taste in men, and Lorraine had been the one to endure the repercussions. It was impossible to decide which was worse—fighting off grown men who found their way into her bed in the middle of the night, or spending nights in the asylum while her mother worked, essentially raised by the criminally insane.

She sometimes wondered which camp her birth father had belonged to.

The flower beds technically still had room, but she was loath to dig up anything, let alone her rosebushes. It was hard fucking work keeping roses alive through a Wisconsin winter, and it had been years since she'd had one die on her. So that left the question about where to get rid of this idiot—it had to be somewhere he wouldn't be found. Dropping a body into the lake was entirely too risky, even on Lake Michigan—you had to go out a long way, and it was hard to push so much dead weight over the edge of a boat without capsizing, not to mention whatever heavy thing you weighed them down with. That was a younger woman's game. Besides, there was never a guarantee that the corpse wouldn't fill with gas and float to the surface, no matter what you strapped them down with.

No, it was best to leave Baker where he was until the case was over and the heat had cooled off. She just hoped she wouldn't have any other additions, since there wasn't room in the freezer for anyone else—Baker was a large man. A perfect example, really, of why she had a pulley system set up, anchored into the floor joists above the freezer so that she could get a body in with minimal effort. Same with the wooden ramp she'd built that covered the stairs running from the backyard to the cellar floor. A plastic sled was most handy—once you got a body onto it, it would zoom down the ramp and right into position to be hoisted up and into the freezer. A car with a big trunk and a sturdy wheelbarrow filled out the system nicely.

Bob had never asked questions about any of it. It had been part of the reason that she'd agreed to get married in the first place—he wasn't curious, enjoyed a certain amount of humiliation, and kept out of her way. It had helped that he also hated unfinished basements and kept clear of the whole thing. Too dank, he'd said. Reminded him of his childhood for some reason or other. Not to mention, her taxidermy equipment creeped him out, and as far as Bob knew, the entire basement was dedicated to it—as long as Lorraine appeared with the occasional mounted bird, he had no reason to question any of it, or so much as poke his head through the door.

Lorraine double-checked that the slanted cellar doors were padlocked from the inside—one could never be too careful—and went back upstairs. She really needed to figure out who had left Rupp's body on her lawn. Lorraine had begun to think it was unlikely that her past with the mob had resurfaced—those people had long memories, but more than thirty years long? Doubtful, right? Not many lasted that long with the Outfit, anyway, so most of the guys who wanted her dead were probably dead themselves. The mob often killed their own, which should have eliminated most of her problems.

Although she'd never stop looking over her shoulder. Just in case.

Which left the possibility that someone in town had learned about her rose-garden graveyard. And if that was the case, that person would have to be eliminated. The only way two people could keep a secret was if one of them was dead.

And it sure wasn't going to be her.

There was a red light blinking on her answering machine, and she hit the play button. "Hey, Lorraine, it's Jim, your editor. Just wanted to call and give you some exciting news—your column was picked up for syndication! You'll be famous! Not to mention the bigger paycheck. Give me a call back, and we can discuss details. Talk to you soon!"

Well. That was interesting news.

Fame was a pass. It sure wasn't appealing to someone who was trying to hide from her past. Even a bigger paycheck wasn't much of an incentive—the paper barely paid enough for her car insurance each month. It was a joke, really. But it kept her busy and, more importantly, provided cover for the investment money coming in that she actually lived on. She'd been smart when she was young, set herself up nicely, laundering plenty for herself. And syndication meant the neighbors might not raise an eyebrow if she spent a little more, treated herself to that Jacuzzi hot tub, because *shit,* those jets would feel good on her sore muscles after a tough workout.

She'd give Jim a call back later to get details, which would be a good time to tell him about the new article she was writing for them too.

She checked her Swatch, noting the date, and sighed. She needed to turn in a new column within a few days, and that meant she needed to respond to at least one more letter to round out what she already had. Then she could work on typing up her article about the murder—she didn't have a deadline for that, obviously, but it was in her best interest to get it started now. She'd already decided to put a little line at the end telling the public to call the newspaper with any tips—it would piss Zenoni off, but it could bring in some interesting leads, and that would be worth it. And it wasn't like *she* was going to be answering the phone, writing down tips.

Lorraine sat at the kitchen table and uncovered her typewriter, popped her reading glasses on, and perused the stack of letters that sat in a wire basket next to it. Her favorite was about a man who wanted his cousin to stop telling the family that the baby growing in her belly was his. Her response was to call that man out as the undercover cousin lover that he was.

Men really were disgusting.

There was one other that jumped out at her as interesting, and she set the rest aside to stash in a large cardboard box in her garage. She didn't want to dispose of anything permanently in case she needed to bang out a last-minute column and had nothing new to work with, so she hung on to old letters. For a while anyway. Once the garage box was filled, she emptied it and started over.

An hour later, and she had a decent draft of her column, and she slipped it into an envelope, addressed it to Jim Higgins, and popped a stamp on it. It looked like the mail had already come today, so instead of sticking it in her mailbox with the flag up, she'd run it over to the post office.

That onerous task done, she took a break and poured an iced tea from the fridge before taking a seat in her comfortable leather recliner while considering her next move. She'd write the article for *The Chronicle* next; that would be quick and easy. But once that was done, she needed to go back to figuring out who was behind this body dump. She didn't give a shit about *why* Doug Rupp had been killed; she just needed to know who had done it and why Rupp had wound up on *her* lawn.

It would be most inconvenient for someone to have learned who she really was and leave Rupp as a warning. She didn't have room in her freezer at the moment.

Chapter 18

MIKE

Wednesday

In the end, Mike dropped Rupp's hellcat off at the local humane-society shelter. She quite literally cringed to think about what would happen to it, but Jenny had been working intake, and that woman had a real soft spot for tough cases, so maybe she would take the cat. Or at least try to rehabilitate the thing until it could be adopted.

It was unlikely, but possible, right? If pineapple could go on pizza, anything was possible.

Next stop was the police department, where she hauled Rupp's chalkboard into evidence after studying it and taking a bunch of notes. There was plenty there that was intriguing, but the most pressing thing was that Post-it, with its date roaring up quick. Mike's last task was to call the Rockford PD and ask them to pull any files they had on Robert and Lorraine Highsmith. The desk sergeant on the other end of the line took down her request and said someone would call her in a couple, three days. Hopefully they would find some dirt, give her some sort of insight into Mrs. Highsmith.

Mike went home and let Zeus out, then rolled her own chalkboard into the living room. It was super nerdy, but she liked to organize her thoughts about a case, and honestly, this was the best way to do it. And doing a little extra work in her off time was perfectly fine, especially now that she was single. Which was great, honestly. A murder required undivided attention, and a boyfriend could be worse than a dog, begging for attention.

She scribbled the date from the note she'd found next to *LMP* and circled both several times. Whatever was about to happen was going down soon, and she needed to figure out what it was. There was only the smallest chance that it wasn't something big. But how to figure out the what and where?

She sighed. It was times like these when she wished her dad was still with it enough to run things by him. He hadn't been a detective, but he'd been real street smart, able to put himself in the shoes of criminals—she'd always thought he should have been a local cop instead of a statie, although she'd never said *that* out loud. But on her earliest cases, when she'd still been on patrol and even after she'd made sergeant, it had been a total lifesaver to talk things through with him over a beer. He'd always helped her see a different side of things—it had made her a better cop.

Tears filled her eyes, and she blinked them away. He was still here, sort of, and she should be grateful for that much, right?

Guilt pooled in her gut again, twisting up through her veins. She *really* needed to go see him.

Yah know what? After she knocked a couple of things off her list, she would, she really would. Of course, it was quite a list. She needed to pore over Baker's bank statements, which Sharity Baker had signed off for her to get from the bank. Only the ones Sharity was listed on, of course, and Mike suspected that wouldn't be the case for all of them. Julian Baker seemed like the kind of guy that would have a couple of accounts hidden from his wife, so Mike would need the judge to sign a search warrant for those too. But maybe something from the accounts would point her toward what *LMP* was.

It was . . . well, *troubling* that Baker appeared to have gone missing. Okay, missing or disappeared, but either way it was not good, especially since it happened right after he learned Rupp was dead. She needed to talk to the motel clerk where Baker "met" with Carrie Ann Williams the night before and see if he'd noticed anything unusual too. She glanced at her watch, then at Zeus, who had curled up on his giant floor cushion as though the dog hadn't spent the entire day on the couch, which he wasn't allowed on. Not while she was home, anyway. The dog hair ratted him out every time, but it was hard to get upset with him.

Yah know, a trip to the motel shouldn't take long, and maybe she'd get lucky and the same clerk would be working tonight. She could just go by there really quickly and still be home in time for *Dallas*. She'd be *mortified* if anyone at work found out that she loved soap operas—what a cliché, right? A woman watching soaps. But they were totally escapist. She could enjoy some onscreen drama without having to think about anything—she did enough thinking during the day.

She paused at the door, casting a longing gaze at her colorful skates, sitting neglected. Fingers crossed she'd have this wrapped up by next week so she could get back to those kids at the rink. Okay, fine, she loved skating as much as they did, maybe more. And teaching the girls gave her an excuse to get her own exercise after class.

Mike pulled up to the Sea Breeze in her unmarked squad a few minutes later, glad she hadn't bothered to change out of her work clothes yet. It was usually one of the first things she did when she got home, pants and bra *off*, but tonight she hadn't. Maybe because she knew in her gut that she wasn't done for the night.

It took nothing more than a quick glance around the parking lot to spot a car that looked a lot like Julian Baker's, a red Corvette. There weren't many cars here—no mystery why—and she pulled into an empty spot near it. She got out and checked the license plate against her list. Sure enough—this was Baker's.

Mike headed to the front desk, smiling at the dour young woman who was watching a small television behind the counter. She couldn't have been more than twenty, wearing high-waisted acid-washed jeans and an ironic T-shirt that said, **FINE, THANKS**. At least Mike assumed it was ironic.

"You want a room?" The clerk didn't even look up to ask the question.

"No, I just have a few questions." She had her badge at the ready to prove she was a detective, but the kid hadn't bothered to so much as glance her way yet. "Do you know the owner of the flashy sports car out there?" she asked.

"Nope."

"Were you here last night?"

"Yup." The clerk was doing her level best to ignore her. It was almost impressive really. Or would have been if it weren't enough to make eye twitching a hobby.

A sigh escaped her lips, and she moved toward the end of the counter where the TV was perched. All it took was a little reach, and she was able to grab the electrical plug and yank it from the wall. Height *did* have benefits, and long arms were one of 'em.

"Are you trippin'?" The clerk stood up, completely affronted.

"I'll give this back once you finish answering my questions." She waved the end of the plug.

"You can't do that!"

"It looks like I just did."

"This is bogus." She glared for a few seconds. "What's your damage, anyway?"

"I'm Detective Zenoni." Not really an answer, but close enough.

"No way."

"Way." Mike was fast losing patience with this girl.

The clerk squinted at the badge she was holding up, then crossed her arms over her chest. "Fine. What do you want to know?"

Thank the heavens and three backup singers *that* was over. "Did you see Julian Baker check in last night?" She described the man, and the clerk tipped her head to the side.

"Sure, he's a regular. Usually here with some betty or another."

By the power of Grayskull, Mike hoped Julian didn't have more than one mistress. "Great, and he was here last night?" At the clerk's annoyed nod, Mike continued. "Did you see anything unusual?"

She rolled her eyes. "I mean, what's unusual in a wastoid place like this?"

Mike nodded. It was actually a fair question. "Anyone out of the ordinary, then? More weird than usual."

The clerk, her name tag reading **Noneya**, thought about the question. "Yeah, there was a Q-tip here. We don't get a lot of those."

Mike cocked her head. "A Q-tip?" No way a place like this gave out freebies.

Another eye roll. "An old woman. Gray hair."

That could be only one person. Mrs. Highsmith had known an awful lot about Baker's extramarital affair, so this just confirmed how she'd come by the information.

"And did you see Mr. Baker leave last night?"

The clerk shook her head. "Nah, I just know about the old bag because she came in and asked some questions. I don't pay attention to what happens in the parking lot. I figure that's their own business."

"Are there video cameras in the parking lot? Or on the building?"

Noneya laughed out loud. "Are you crazy? This place? The owner isn't gonna invest in some high-tech shit like that."

Fair enough. Sex workers and drug dealers and guys like Baker were the only clients at a sleazebag motel like this one. None of them would use a place with cameras—it wasn't good for business. "Thank you for your help, Noneya." She paused. "Is that short for something?"

Noneya looked her dead in the eye. "Yup. Short for Noneya Business."

Everyone was a comedian.

Chapter 19

LORRAINE

Wednesday

It had not escaped Lorraine's notice that she needed to do something with Baker's car. She'd left it in the motel parking lot overnight, figuring it would take the cops a few days to realize that Baker was missing. But she was quickly realizing that while underestimating the police chief was fine, she needed to keep a close eye on Mike. It was a real pain in her ass that the female detective was competent, clever even.

Of course, it was still nothing like going head to head with a tough Chicago copper, like she had back in the old days. Those guys, you had to either bribe 'em or fight 'em. She liked a good fight, but a lot of those palms were also pretty easily greased.

Zenoni was young and naive, but she didn't seem corruptible. A real shame, that.

Once it was dark, Lorraine pulled her bicycle out of the garage. She double-checked that Baker's keys were in her purse, which she tucked into the front basket. She'd learned early on that it was helpful to go through her victims' pockets before popping them in the freezer—they became entirely too difficult to search once frozen through, and things snapped real easily. Fingers, toes, wrists. It was a mistake you had to make only once to remember the lesson.

Lorraine stuck to the sidewalks instead of riding on the streets. She needed to take care of this little task under the cover of night, which required dark clothing, precisely what a bicyclist should *not* be wearing on the roads after sundown. No matter, the sidewalks were nearly deserted this time of night anyway, and the few pedestrians she did come across—well, Lorraine rode straight for them, forcing them to jump out of her way.

It was the little things that brought her joy.

It took her over thirty minutes to pedal to the motel on the outskirts of town. She was grateful that the humidity had dropped after the storm, and the breeze coming from the east off the lake was chilly now, cooling her sweat. With a shiver, she approached the motel, sticking to the sidewalk on the other side of the road while she cautiously scoped out the parking lot.

Shit. Detective Zenoni was here.

Lorraine tucked herself into the shadow of an abandoned Hardee's and watched. Zenoni was on high alert, judging by the look on her face as she left the motel's office. She made her way over to Baker's fancy sports car and walked around it, trying the doors. But Lorraine's luck was holding tonight because Baker had locked his car up before coming over to hers. She didn't remember that, but he clearly had.

After circling the car several times and peering in through the windows, Zenoni stood, hands on hips, scanning the parking lot, before walking slowly back to her car. Lorraine stayed stone still as Zenoni's eyes brushed over her but didn't stop. Even if she'd spotted her, Lorraine wasn't worried—she was an expert at coming up with excuses. And this article she was writing was an excellent one.

Zenoni finally pulled out of the parking lot, turning toward town. Lorraine waited several long minutes before walking her bike across the street, making sure the detective wasn't doubling back. She doubted she would, not tonight anyway, and when Zenoni returned tomorrow, this car would be long gone. She hoped the detective would assume that because the car disappeared overnight Baker was still alive. Who else could come and take a locked car?

Lorraine surveyed the car in annoyance. This expensive piece of shit was going to be too small for her bicycle, especially the trunk, which meant she would have to leave her bike here and come back for it. What a pain in her hemorrhoid.

She tapped her lip, thinking about where to stash the car for now—a long-term solution was another thing entirely. There were other hotels that were definitely a step up from this shithole, but they might have cameras in the parking lot. The quality of the recordings was never good, but even still, not worth the risk. So that wouldn't work, although it would be fun to send Detective Zenoni on a wild-goose chase, talking to clerks, looking at camera footage that would go nowhere.

You know, that *was* a delightful idea. She just had to be careful not to be seen.

Chapter 20

MIKE

Thursday

Mike drank her first cup of Maxwell House in the living room while staring absently at her chalkboard and thinking. Zeus was at her side, sitting and patiently waiting for some head scratches, occasionally nudging her hand with his nose. He did not need to stretch to do this.

She obliged her big baby, scratching his head and giving ear rubs as he leaned into her leg. "I hope Rockford gets back to me with some dirt on Mrs. H. soon. I guess she could just be nosy because of the article she's writing?"

And loneliness. She'd bet money that Mrs. Highsmith was lonely.

Speaking of, Mike needed to go see her dad. She speared her watch with a glance and grimaced—she'd put it off too long. Today after work, after she crossed a bunch of things off her list. She really needed to stop and see him, even if her dad wouldn't know the difference, because *she* knew that she'd been avoiding it. She gave a firm nod. Yes, she would grab some McDonald's and go over there tonight once she'd finished as much as she could for the case.

First, though, she'd take a quick swing past Baker's house, just out of curiosity, to see if she could catch a glimpse of Julian Baker. Turning onto the street, she nearly hit a parked car in surprise. Holy cripes almighty, there was Baker's red Corvette, parked on the same block as his house. In the street, though, which was super weird, what with all that empty driveway.

Mike pulled up behind the car, got out and circled it, although she saw nothing different from the night before. She pulled on the handle and found it locked. Again.

Her mind was racing. Did this mean that Baker had come home? But why hadn't he parked in his driveway or pulled into the garage? Who else could have moved the car? His wife? His girlfriend? She needed to talk to Carrie Ann again. For now, though, she parked and rang the Bakers' doorbell. She heard some noises inside and rang the bell again. This time she could see someone behind the frosted sidelight, shuffling down the stairs.

"Detective Zenoni, it's awfully early," Sharity Baker said through a wide crack in the door. Her hair was a mess, and she was once again wearing the fluffy robe pulled closed at the waist. Mike was pretty sure there wasn't anything beneath that robe—hopefully that belt would continue to do its job. Contrary to the rumors around the department, she did *not* enjoy naked women.

"Oh, please, call me Mike," the detective said. This didn't elicit a response, so she barreled ahead. "Mrs. Baker, have you seen your husband?"

Sharity looked more than a little annoyed. "I told you yesterday, I haven't seen him."

"He hasn't come home?"

Sharity just shook her head, starting to pull the door closed.

"Then why is his car parked out front?"

The door stopped abruptly, then swung wide open. Sharity pushed open the screen door and stepped onto the front stoop in her bare feet.

"What the fuck?" Sharity said. Then her head cocked. "Why is it parked on the street? Julian never parked on the street."

"I was wondering the same thing. Unless he didn't want to wake you or your . . . friend . . . by opening the garage door?"

Sharity ignored the inference that she had an overnight guest in the house. "The garage door does make a gnarly noise. He's been meaning to call someone out to have that fixed." Then she shook her head. "But like, nothing in the house has been touched."

"Are you sure? He didn't come in for some clothes or a change of socks? He has a weird thing about his socks, right?"

Sharity stared at her for a few beats before responding. "I'm sure."

Mike considered that and then nodded. "Well, thank you for your time, Mrs. Baker. Please let me know if you hear from your husband."

Sharity didn't answer; she simply stepped back into her home and shut the door firmly behind her.

Mike had only one question on her mind as she drove away. If Julian Baker hadn't driven his car home, who had?

Or maybe Baker returned to town? But then where would he be hiding? He clearly wasn't at home.

Chapter 21

LORRAINE

Thursday

Lorraine was up before the sun to get her workout in, but she hated it. She hated mornings and wasn't too fond of working out, either, but she forced herself to do both because it was necessary. Her aerobics instructor Cynthia was a morning person, but at least not an overly cheerful one, and it really *was* the best time to use the gym before all the macho men started showing up. There was too much grunting and posturing—after listening to a few minutes of it, she wanted to take a hand weight to someone's head. A couple of good whacks would stop the animal noises, but it really wouldn't do, what with all the people around.

It was a good workout that morning, and Lorraine stuck around for a little bit afterward to use the weight machines. She liked to ensure she did plenty of weight training in addition to the cardio. Lorraine was doing a set of curls when the sight of a dark-haired man with very Italian features caused her to freeze, hand weight curled to her chest. It stopped her heart for a second, but she quickly remembered that Tommy Carbone would be in his eighties by now, not a young man like this one, wearing tight shorts that displayed his tiny package.

Even still. She decided to pack it in for the morning and head home.

Lorraine was pleasantly sore as she showered at home, the incident at the gym nearly forgotten. She hated the doing of working out, but the after was a good feeling. As she toweled off, she caught sight of herself in the full-length mirror. She looked good, a side benefit of all the time she spent sweating and pumping iron. She had a touch of padding, but that was natural at her age and frankly looked better than those skinny minnies who looked like a brisk wind would knock 'em over.

Her mind wandered back to Zenoni and her doubtless confusion at finding Baker's car back in front of the Baker house and the fruitless investigating she would do all day long. She smiled, a Cheshire grin. Of course, she'd been very careful both in the car and out of it—Zenoni would find no trace of her, but she knew the detective would look.

It should keep her busy for a while.

In the meantime, Lorraine would head out to talk to John Hooper, the third man in the photo she'd seen in Rupp's apartment. She was hoping that her luck would hold, and Hooper would know what all this was about.

The residential streets of Sheboygan Bay quickly gave way to fields of corn, already knee high, probably from the last few soaking rains. Most of it was likely cattle feed, although she did pass one little stand selling sweet corn, the piles of green husked corn looking lonely with no one keeping an eye on them. She knew from experience that these stands had nothing more than a little metal box to put your payment in—an insane way to run a produce stand, since anyone could walk off with an armload of vegetables and all your money. She passed a field of spotted cows, then another, before turning onto county Highway N. Within a minute, she found herself caught behind a large piece of farm equipment—a combine maybe?—and she swerved well onto the left side of the road to get around the enormous John Deere, its tires stretching past the top of her station wagon.

She didn't get very far before she needed to slow, looking for a little red placard with numbers on it, trying to match the north and west coordinates to the ones she'd found in the phone book under Hooper's name. She finally spotted it, the green metal stake it was attached to sitting crookedly in the ground. It had probably been hit by a snowplow once or twice—folks out here had to replace a lot of mailboxes and markers in the spring.

Lorraine pulled onto a long gravel drive, dust kicking up in her wake, and parked in front of the gray clapboard farmhouse at the end of it. She didn't need to knock on the front door—and she was glad, since the weathered porch didn't look entirely sound—because she could see Hooper in the nearest fenced-off area, chasing a large flightless bird with a floral pillowcase. Laura Ashley maybe?

Bemused, she wandered to the weathered metal gate near a barn that had once been red and hitched one foot up on the bottom rail as she watched Hooper chase the emu in ever-widening circles.

"What the hell are you doing?" Lorraine shouted. The circles were boring. She wanted something else to happen.

Startled, Hooper stopped dead, nearly tripping over his own feet, and the gray bird quickly changed directions, charging at Hooper, hissing loudly and clacking its beak. For a few minutes the emu chased Hooper, occasionally kicking at him with its talons, which delighted her to no end, and she gave herself over to a fit of rusty laughter. Within moments, however, and much to her dismay, Hooper used the turnabout to his advantage and whirled on his heel with the pillowcase wide open, causing the bird to run headfirst into the linen. With its head suddenly covered, the bird came to an abrupt halt and collapsed to the ground, legs folded neatly beneath it. Panting heavily, Hooper gently secured the pillowcase before bracing his hands on his knees to catch his breath.

Now that the show was over, she was impatient to get on with it. "I've got some questions to ask you, John."

The bird turned its covered head in her direction at the same time Hooper did. "Let me just get Hector into the barn." Hooper replied. Lorraine rolled her eyes and waited while he got the now-docile bird back on its feet and led it into the peeling red building. Minutes later the large wooden door hanging from a surprisingly well-oiled metal track on the side of the building slid open, and Hooper emerged from the dark interior, wiping his hands on his already filthy jeans as he came toward her.

"What can I do for you Mrs. Highsmith?" Hooper asked. Sheboygan Bay was pushing six thousand people, but it was still a small town, so she wasn't surprised that John knew who she was even though the two had never had a formal conversation before. Especially after Bob's turn on the city council in a fit of civic mindedness—everyone seemed to know the Highsmiths after that.

The farmer didn't bother holding his hand out for a shake, though he did absent-mindedly smooth his reddish-brown beard with it, causing her to grimace. A smear of dirt on his bald head told her that he had recently run that hand over his scalp as well. Disgusting—it was probably bird shit, and he was smearing it all over himself.

"I need to ask you about some old friends of yours." Lorraine got right to the point. "Doug Rupp and Julian Baker."

"Ah." Hooper said. He pulled a startlingly clean handkerchief from his back pocket and rubbed it over his head and face before turning his attention to his hands. He concentrated on this task and kept his eyes on what he was doing, neatly avoiding eye contact. "I haven't talked to either of those dudes in several years."

This was a bald-faced lie. As someone who told a lot of them, she was pretty adept at recognizing them. Glancing around the property, taking in the falling-down outbuildings and the rickety-looking fences, she gathered that emu farming was not terribly profitable. The large barn Hooper had come from looked reasonably well maintained but was in desperate need of a paint job and probably more. Although the same could be said for most of the aging barns in the state, Hooper's property seemed especially hard luck.

In the distance a flock of emus could be seen, thirty or so birds bobbing, pecking, and scratching at the field, and a handful more lying on the ground, looking like feathered beanbag chairs with beaks. Lorraine wondered why he'd been fighting with Hector in particular but decided she didn't care enough to ask. She was more curious as to why John Hooper would bother to lie to her.

"Several years, huh? Then you would be surprised to hear that Doug Rupp was just found dead on my lawn."

Lorraine was watching Hooper closely, and when his head came up with wide eyes, it appeared genuine. Which meant John Hooper was not the one who'd killed Rupp and left him on her front lawn.

"Shit" was all Hooper could say.

"Shit, indeed."

John seemed to suddenly remember his manners. "I'd invite you inside, but my wife was just trying to get the baby down for a nap."

Lorraine had no desire to get involved with any part of that, babies or wives or going inside the house, although it made her wonder if she should have brought along a hot dish. She kept a couple frozen in the freezer for occasions like this, when she wanted something from someone. Folks around here cracked wide open when you brought 'em a hot dish. "Oh, that's fine, I prefer the fresh air anyway." She really should have put *fresh* in quotes, since the occasional breeze carried a whiff of something quite unpleasant—bird shit was a revolting smell and turned her stomach—but she didn't plan on staying much longer. She'd already learned much of what she needed to.

"When was the last time you spoke to Julian?"

Hooper cleared his throat, still absently wiping his hands on the rag. "Gotta be going on five years now. Right before he got married, maybe . . . I think I saw him at the Mucky Duck." The local watering hole was known for its surly bartenders and stuffed ducks—many of which had been mounted by Lorraine herself. Even still, Lorraine had never been since she preferred to do her drinking at home. But it was useful to know where both Julian and Hooper frequented, even if she didn't believe for a second that Hooper was telling her the entire truth.

"And Rupp?"

"Oh, ya know . . . probably about the same." Hooper tried to make eye contact with her and failed, turning to squint at his flock of emus instead, as though they were doing anything remotely interesting. They were not. Large flightless birds did not provide a lot in the way of entertainment outside of the initial chase she'd had the pleasure to witness.

"I see." Lorraine cocked her head and considered the ways she might get John Hooper to tell her the truth, but standing in his yard was not going to be where it happened. "Well, if you think of anything helpful, please give me a call. If I'm not home, leave a message." She handed him a little business card with her phone number on it. Her late husband had had them made up for her, and while she thought they were silly, they did come in handy at a time like this.

"Oh, I will Mrs. Highsmith. You have a good day now, yah?"

"Mmm." She grunted, already walking to her car. Hooper gave a stiff wave and scurried back into the barn, presumably to deal with Hector the emu.

John Hooper was hiding something. There was no doubt about that, and he was the best lead she had right now. And while she didn't have any truth serum, sometimes alcohol had the same effect. Or perhaps something even stronger was called for.

It was time to look at those pills she'd liberated from Rupp's filthy apartment.

Chapter 22

MIKE

Thursday

Well, Baker's car had thrown a big ole wrench into her morning. First thing, she got on the radio and requested a day shift officer. Once they showed up, she'd have them do a door-to-door and see if anyone saw the car being dropped off. Once that was in the works, Mike could get on with today's tasks. She flipped through her notebook to her list.

See if Rockford got back to me about Mrs. Highsmith
Talk to John Hooper about his high school buddies
Find out where Baker might be hiding
Figure out what "LMP" is before Sunday night
Go see dad

That last checklist item cramped her stomach. Shit, how awful that she even had to write that down on a list of things to do. What did that say about her?

She did her best to push it from her mind, although the *ick* feeling in her stomach stuck around. Mike covered the last line with a pinky finger and scanned the brief list again. Item number four should really be at the top—Mike was *very* aware that there was a ticking clock with that one. Something was going down on Sunday night, and she needed an idea of what that was so she could get prepared. She was holding out hope that one of the guys in Rupp's circle would give her a clue.

Mike sat up straighter in her seat, trying to relieve the strain in her back. The pressure of a homicide investigation felt heavy, like a thick bulletproof vest squeezing her chest and shoulders toward each other. She'd been involved in homicide investigations before, of course, but they'd been drug related, which gave you a real limited pool of suspects—it was almost always someone in the "business." And drugs were big business here—Lake Michigan was an easy way to move product up and down the state. This murder was different, though, and the pool was much wider. She was feeling the pressure to dig up answers, fast. It wasn't just that the chief was breathing down her neck—and he was, leaving messages on her machine and notes on her desk—but she could feel the looks from the other officers, wondering why she hadn't solved this yet.

This was what she'd wanted, though, right? A chance to prove herself as a detective. And to prove herself as a woman in this dick-saturated field, although she'd never say that part out loud.

"Detective! You're needed at the high school," Chief Schneider called from his office as soon as she stepped through the door. When would she learn to only use the employee entrance instead of taking a shortcut through the front? Mike rubbed the bridge of her nose and glanced at Carla, who gave her a sympathetic look before she trudged into Schneider's office.

"I really gotta keep working this homicide," she started to argue, nearly adding "like you keep reminding me," but Schneider interrupted her.

"Yah, yah, but there's been an arrest at the high school, and then you can get back to that," Schneider said, then added, "I don't know why it's taking you so damn long, anyway."

She ignored the dig. "What about the school resource officer? Or can't you take care of this one?" The words were out before she could debate the wisdom of their release.

Her boss stiffened noticeably before leaning over slightly to peek out his office door, making sure there were no citizens present to overhear what he was about to say.

"You know that the high school prefers that I stay off the grounds," Schneider said in a quiet but intense voice, then paused. "Besides, the SRO said it might be related to a case you've been working."

Mike sighed. She'd nearly forgotten that the chief was pretty much banned from setting foot on school grounds. He was only allowed on the premises in extreme circumstances since an *incident* a few years earlier that Schneider worked hard to keep under wraps. He'd been pretty successful too—only a handful of folks knew about it.

Every summer the department put on gloves and scoured the countryside around their small town, pulling up ditch weed—low-grade and frankly shitty marijuana that grew wild alongside the county roads. The officers then took it to a secret location, where it was destroyed. Except for one particular year when the chief filled the back of his pickup truck with the plants and then drove to the high school to assist with football practice, leaving his truck—and the marijuana—completely unattended in the parking lot. No one but the chief was surprised when it "mysteriously" disappeared from the bed of his truck. The principal, Tom Carter, went through the roof, but agreed to keep it quiet as long as the chief stayed off school grounds after that.

Mike closed her eyes before mentally scrapping her plans for the day. Or at least for the morning. "Do you know which case?"

Schneider shook his head. "All I know is a burnout who barely graduated a few years ago was found on school property selling drugs to students. He's being held in the main office for you."

Mike nodded and left Schneider's office. It should be a fairly straightforward arrest, and then she could get back to what she was doing—investigating a goddamn homicide. Before scooting out to her car, though, she walked through the back offices to see if the day shift supervisor, Sergeant Hannigan, was in.

He was. "Sergeant, I'm happy to see you. How would you feel about sending someone over to do an arrest at the high school?" Mike asked.

"Nope," Hannigan said, without even turning around. "The chief assigned it to you—I already offered to send Patoka, and he shot it down." Hannigan spun around in his chair and eyed her. "What else?"

"How do you know there's something else?" she asked, genuinely curious.

Hannigan just looked at her.

Mike shrugged. "Fine. There *is* something else. Could you send someone over to interview Baker's neighbors and see if they saw anything last night?" She explained about the unexpected return of Baker's Corvette to the street in front of his home. "I can write down the questions they should ask." She took a step toward his desk, looking for a pad of paper.

Hannigan held up a hand. "I think my guys can handle it," he said. "They don't need a script. A car was found this morning, and you need to know if anyone saw it get there, yah?"

She nodded. She'd really rather write the questions down, but now that Hannigan said it out loud, maybe it *was* overkill. But then her mouth kept going, like it had its own motor, independent of her brain, which *was* telling her to shut up. "Are . . . are you going to write it down?" But that was a reasonable ask, right? People needed to write stuff down to remember it.

Hannigan maintained direct eye contact while he took a pen from his uniform pocket, reached behind him for a pad of Post-it notes, and wrote down *car found*. He held it up and showed it to her, his movements slow and deliberate.

Mike knew that Hannigan was making fun of her, but instead of calling him on it, she thanked him profusely for his help and took her leave.

Kill them with kindness. So far it hadn't changed anything, but it might, right? Especially if she could get her brain and her mouth to work together.

Josh Stanley was sulking in the principal's office when Mike arrived at the high school a few minutes later. A sprawling one-story brick building on the outskirts of town with small square windows squinting at the sun, it looked like any other school that had been built half a decade earlier and not updated since. No amount of wax could hide the last fifty years of scuffing on the flecked linoleum floors, and the banks of gray metal lockers lining the hallways were battered and beaten, clinging to one another to survive the storm of students for another year.

The school resource officer, Marcus Stroh, hitched up his pants a bit as she came into the office. "Caught him red handed." He nodded toward the principal's desk, where a bunch of baggies were spread out. At a glance, it looked like mostly marijuana and a little crack. "I'd a brought him into the station myself, but I'm not supposed to leave the grounds."

"You said this might have something to do with the Rupp case?"

Stroh frowned. "Dat murder? Yeah, no, I didn't say nothing like that. I thought you'd done some drug arrests last month." He nodded toward the baggies. "This could be related."

Mike stifled a sigh. That meant literally anyone could have finished up this arrest, but she was already here, so she might as well get on with it.

"You want to explain why you were selling drugs to schoolkids?" she asked Stanley, trying to ignore the patchy porno mustache clinging to the young man's upper lip.

Stanley turned his face away, arms crossed over his chest. She shook her head and gathered all the drugs into an evidence bag before cuffing Stanley and walking him out to the car.

Stanley's lips were pressed shut on the way to the station, and he refused to utter a single word right up until she had him in the tiny interrogation room in the back. There wasn't room for more than two people in there—three if absolutely necessary, but that was a sardine-can squeeze.

She got Stanley settled into one of the chairs and then took a seat in the folding chair across the table. "Well," she said, popping a fresh cassette into the tape recorder that dominated the small tabletop, then clicked the record button. She made sure the tape was rolling, then gave the date and time and her own name before stating that she was interviewing Josh Stanley, then read the kid his Miranda rights.

Stanley was finally looking nervous, but he still didn't say anything, including asking for a lawyer, his cuffed hands twisting in his lap, the metal quietly clinking.

"What do you think we'll find when we search your place?" Mike's voice was casual, and she tipped back in her chair. She wasn't worried about getting Stanley to talk—this idiot had been caught red handed by the SRO, who even now was writing out a statement to be delivered to the station later. She'd thought about taking Josh Stanley directly to the county jail and filling out the arrest paperwork there, but wasting thirty minutes interrogating Josh at the station wasn't going to hurt anything. The detective was already behind for the day—she'd be working late no matter how long this interview took, and the little interrogation room *did* make people uncomfortable. Close quarters and no air flow were a great combo platter for that.

Josh shifted in his seat, and little beads of sweat popped out on his forehead. The kid wasn't too far out of high school himself, thus the patchy porn-stache. His greasy brown hair was short and spiky on top, with a long rattail in the back, scraped into a ponytail and held with a red rubber band. There was a sizable gap between his two front teeth, and a smattering of dandruff on his black AC/DC T-shirt. She could tell that the kid was considering his options, which weren't great, honestly.

This was light years from a first offense, so she led with that. "You'll definitely do some time for this one. Selling drugs to kids."

"I don't sell to anyone under sixteen," Josh said defensively, raising his cuffed hands up and bending his head down to awkwardly wipe sweat from his forehead.

"A real model citizen," Mike said, her voice as dry as the Sahara. "Tell me, Josh. What will I find when I get my search warrant?"

Josh scratched his ear, raising both hands to do it. "I mean, it's hard to tell whose stuff is whose in the house, you know?"

"Whose stuff is whose?"

"Yeah, like, which are my drugs or my dad's drugs."

It was a struggle not to palm her own face, but she managed it. "I see. Your dad's dealing too?"

"I mean, who do you think taught me how?" Josh looked genuinely confused at the question. "He's not gonna be in trouble, too, is he? He'll be so pissed at me." His dull blue eyes squeezed shut.

She left that little gem alone. "You both working for the same person?"

Josh took a second to think, and she cocked her head. Was he trying to come up with a lie or deciding whether to answer at all? Hard to say.

"Look, I don't know who we work for. My dad doesn't neither." At her skeptical look, Josh became insistent. "For real! We get our instructions on my dad's beeper." Before she could ask where these mysterious messages came from, Josh shook his head, dandruff flying. "The number we gotta call back changes a lot. I think the dude goes to different pay phones." Josh looked proud of himself for coming to this conclusion, even though it was an obvious one.

Mike knew a thing or two about how drug gangs worked, since she'd done a stint as the department's narcotics officer before getting promoted to detective. It was honestly shocking how many drugs were here in Sheboygan Bay, which was nothing but a small town when it came down to it. But they had the lake, which was likely where the stuff was coming in—Sheboygan Bay had a small port, mostly unregulated, and it was way too easy to move drugs in and out on private boats. Much like the crack cocaine in some of those baggies she'd packed up, real nasty shit, and getting more popular by the day. From what the news said, anyway.

The point being, Josh and his dad were low-level dealers. There was likely a middle manager above them, and then at least one more person in charge of the larger operation above *that* person.

"You think the DA would give me a break if I give you some information?" Josh suddenly asked.

She raised an eyebrow. "I thought you didn't know who you worked for?"

"I don't, but I *do* know something about Julian Baker."

Mike leaned back in her seat again, crossing her legs, making sure her expression was *super* bored. But holy macanoli, things were finally getting interesting.

Chapter 23

LORRAINE

Thursday

Lorraine had been so focused on getting home and inspecting the photographs, she hadn't had time to deal with the prescription bottles that she'd swiped from Rupp's apartment. Once she was safe in her kitchen, she rifled through her purse until she found them, then lined them up neatly on her counter. One by one she opened them, tipping the pills out to see if they were what they claimed to be. There was nothing interesting here—blood pressure medication, speed, and some expired bennies that might come in handy someday, but it wasn't until the second-to-last bottle that she became intrigued. The label said that it should contain extra-strength acetaminophen, but there were unmarked white pills inside instead. She tipped a few into her hand, double-checking for the stamp indicating what they were. Nothing. She then cautiously sniffed the pills—again, nothing. If it were Tylenol, there would be a slightly bitter smell.

Hmm. What an interesting quandary. She sat and pondered how best to figure out what these pills were. Should she taste a bit of the residue? No, too risky. She was 95 percent certain that what she had here was not Tylenol.

Rupp was a dirtbag through and through—that much was obvious. This left her with a theory about what the drug was, and it wasn't something that was prescribed by any doctor here in the states. Not a legitimate one, anyway. But who could she test the drug on so she didn't need to take any herself?

An hour later and Lorraine was wearing a black dress accentuating the fact that she worked hard at staying in shape, even though she was dancing the tango in her early seventies. She applied some makeup, accentuating her dark eyes, and surveyed herself in the mirror. She looked great, if she did say so herself. After grabbing her purse—making sure the mystery bottle was safely tucked inside—she pulled on black flats. Heels were a thing of the past. She hadn't worn heels since, well, she couldn't remember, and she wouldn't ever again, even if they had made her calves look especially good.

She grabbed a bottle of water and pointed the Behemoth south toward Milwaukee. There was no way she was going to pull this off in a city as small as Sheboygan Bay, not this little experiment. She had a general idea about where the nicer hotels were in Milwaukee, downtown and close to the water, and traced a route on her fold-out map before she left. She kept the map open on the passenger seat just in case she needed to double-check her route, but she'd always had a keen sense of direction and wasn't terribly worried.

Once downtown, she avoided the valet attendants in front of the Pfister and parked in a surface lot several blocks away. She double-checked her makeup in the rearview mirror, then sauntered along the sidewalk toward her target destination. From a distance, the hotel was nothing but a large square with a tall toilet roll slapped onto the side of it, but it was the nicest hotel in the city once you walked through the doors. Vaulted ceilings boasted gilded carvings, with an enormous chandelier gracing the center space. Lorraine carried herself as though she belonged there, welcomed by the doorman and garnering several friendly nods from staff and visitors as she made her way up the richly carpeted marble stairs to the hotel bar, where she settled onto a plush stool at the far end. It was a prime vantage point for observing other customers.

The bartender stopped by to take Lorraine's drink order, and since she was out of town and could drop the bullshit for an evening, she ordered her favorite: a Manhattan neat. She couldn't stand the sickly-sweet things that people were drinking these days, Long Island iced teas or cosmopolitans. Fruity shit with umbrellas was not for her.

While he mixed her drink, she surveyed the other patrons at the dimly lit bar. So far, there were only two possible targets—men who were clearly there on their own. The first one was a definite no. He was within ten years of her, but it looked as though he was made of dough, especially around the middle. If he lifted his shirt and nothing but loaves of bread fell out, she wouldn't have batted an eye. She would simply nod, her suspicions confirmed.

The bartender delivered her drink, and she took a sip, approving. It was higher shelf—that rail shit would give her a headache just short of a migraine, so the additional cost was worth it. Besides, she wasn't planning on paying for any more of these. Lorraine turned her attention to the second man as a potential target. He was probably a few years older than she was, but kept himself in decent shape, and had a vague resemblance to James Brolin, with thick eyebrows and an equally thick mane of hair, although his was now silver. The distinct lack of a wedding ring was also helpful. Yes, he would do rather nicely. And if the drug wasn't what she suspected it was, she wouldn't even mind sleeping with him.

She may be getting on in years, but she wasn't dead.

Lorraine took another sip, and the Brolin look-alike glanced her way. She gave a coy look over her glass, and he smiled slightly. Lorraine could turn on the charm when she wanted to; it was just that she didn't often want to.

The man picked up his drink and came to her side of the bar. "Is this seat taken?"

She smiled and cocked her head at him. "It is now."

As the man slid into his seat, he introduced himself. "James."

"Hi, James. I'm Louise."

"What are you drinking?" James asked.

This conversation was already dull, but this was how the game was played. "A Manhattan. And yourself?"

"More of a vodka man, really," James said. "You in town on business?"

"I am. And yourself?"

James nodded and proceeded to explain whatever it was that he was involved in. Some sort of technology involving IBM and DOS operating systems, green screens and blinking prompts. She tuned out immediately, nodding at the appropriate times and smiling. When the bartender swung around and asked if they wanted another round, the obvious answer was yes, and James put them on his tab. Lorraine smiled coyly and thanked him. But then conversation droned on forever—men never stopped talking about themselves or bothered to ask any questions, and it was entirely too easy to lob the occasional generic question to keep him going while she tuned out. They were sipping their second drink together when James excused himself to use the restroom.

Here was the one great thing about men of a certain age—those old prostates required a lot of bathroom breaks. It was the perfect opportunity, and she took it, discreetly scooping a little pill out of the bottle and dropping it into his drink, disguising the move as though she were taking a little sniff, swirling the liquor around, the little white pill quickly dissolving into nothing.

She was confident no one had seen her.

James returned, and Lorraine asked him some other inane question, which set him off again. She sipped slowly on her Manhattan, watching him slurp down whatever it was she'd just slipped him. It didn't take long for him to start slurring his words slightly. A few more minutes and he seemed confused.

Perfect.

"James, why don't you show me your room?" she suggested, putting her hand on his thigh, suggestively inching it up his leg.

James nodded and stood unsteadily. She wrapped her arm around him, pretending to nestle up to him, and caught the bartender's eye on their way out. "Charge it to his room?"

The man nodded and gave her a wink.

In the elevator, James was having trouble standing, which made her a little nervous. She needed him to get to his room under his own steam, or this little experiment would be over, and she'd have to hit another hotel. Or come up with another plan altogether.

"Are we going to have sex?" James asked.

"We sure are. We just have to get to your room first," Lorraine said.

The elevator came to a stop, and she managed to get James into the hall, the couple waiting for them to exit giving them a strange look, but Lorraine whispered, "A little too much to drink." The woman nodded knowingly, giving her own partner the side-eye. Lorraine smiled slyly, before directing James down the hall with a little push. He stumbled over his feet, and she braced herself against the wall to keep him upright, then got him moving forward again.

"This is a lot of work," she muttered.

"Wha's tha now?" James asked.

She didn't respond but did make a mental note that he was with it enough to respond to her—that would be helpful when dealing with Hooper. The real question would be how much he remembered the next morning.

Because Lorraine was now sure she'd been correct about the powder she'd found in Rupp's apartment. It was a date rape drug.

Chapter 24

MIKE

Thursday

Mike dropped Josh Stanley at the county jail after getting his full confession and promising to talk to the district attorney on the kid's behalf. She would actually do it because she was a woman of her word, not because she thought Stanley would get any kind of deal, not when he was selling drugs to schoolkids.

But at least the guy had given her some interesting information to work with. Because according to Stanley, Julian Baker was heavily involved in the drug sales going on around town. Stanley said he'd seen Baker's fancy-pants Corvette leaving the drop site more than once.

But even *more* interesting was the rumor that Baker had stolen a shit ton of money, and no one knew where it was or what he'd done with it. This was somehow common knowledge around town even though she hadn't heard squat about it. Of course, people didn't like to gossip with her around, being a detective and all. Even when she'd been a patrol cop, folks shut down when she walked into a room. It stung a little. She was a local, after all. But she'd grown a thicker skin in the years since; it just meant she had to be sneaky to get information.

Mike swung by her house on the way back from county lockup to let Zeus out. While she waited for him to finish his business, she stood in her living room, eyeing her chalkboard. She added *drugs* in the center and circled it a couple of times, then put *stolen money* next to it. Could that be what all this was about? Drugs and a cache of stolen cash? She repeated the phrase out loud a few times, the rhyme fun to repeat.

Okay, from what Josh Stanley had spilled, it was easy to figure that the drop on Sunday was drugs. The only question now was *where* that was going to happen. At *LMP*, most likely. But what did that stand for?

And who'd hired Rupp to investigate Baker? Was it the person Baker had stolen the money from? It was real easy to believe Rupp had taken on a drug dealer as a client. It seemed like a perfect skeezeball match, actually. But it still left the question of who'd killed Rupp and dumped him on Mrs. Highsmith's lawn. The big boss?

Mike had treated herself to a Nintendo gaming system last Christmas, writing her dad's name in the "from," before sliding it under the tree. He couldn't buy her gifts anymore, but she could pretend it was from him. Anyway, in *Super Mario Bros.*—her favorite—there was a big boss at the end that you had to defeat to rescue the princess. This was exactly what that felt like. But the princess in this case was a butt-load of money.

Of course, now that she knew about the missing money, the fact that Julian was missing a finger was even more interesting. Could his missing digit have been a warning from the money's owner? The big boss? She'd ask Sharity Baker, but a guy like Julian wasn't gonna admit something like that to his wife. Maybe he'd talked to Craig Youngblood? She made notes on the board to talk to both again.

So maybe the big boss—whoever he was—had hired Rupp to find the money because taking Baker's finger hadn't been enough for Baker to cough it up. That made sense. But why would the big boss kill Rupp? Especially while he was still staking out Baker? Wouldn't that defeat the purpose of hiring him if you didn't let him finish the job?

Her thoughts flitted to her dad. What would he tell her? *Everyone you talk to is lying, about something or other.* That was good advice. The chief thought Baker's surprise about Rupp surveilling him had been genuine, but that didn't mean it was true. Maybe Baker *did* off his buddy. Although, what would Baker's motive be?

It was so frustrating that Baker wasn't around to interview. Shit, if it had been up to her, she woulda dragged that guy into interrogation and grilled him harder than a Fourth of July weenie.

Her dad woulda argued that she was still missing something with Baker, though, so she put a question mark next to Baker's name. Her dad had loved to argue with her, and she'd never been able to tell if it was serious or just to make her think. Truth be told, he hadn't been interested in discussing—or arguing about—anything other than sports or police work, just one more thing that had pushed her into the field. Otherwise, what would they have had to talk about?

Mike flinched—it stung that she didn't have either of those things to discuss with him anymore. Or anything, for that matter, like if she should start going by her full name. Her pops was where she'd gotten the nickname Mike from, after all. He'd called her Little Mike from the first moments she could remember, which made sense, since the name Michaela was really just her pops's first name with an *a* slapped on the end. If she'd been a boy, she woulda been a junior, for sure.

She'd always wondered if Pops would have been happier with a boy, since he'd raised her like one.

Ugh, this train of thought wasn't useful. It took some effort, but she pushed thoughts of her pops aside.

Now. All this guessing meant that Rupp's murder was still a big question mark. So were Julian Baker's whereabouts. The thing with Baker's car was strange, though, its moving from the seedy motel to the street in front of his house. Who woulda done that? It seemed unlikely Baker would have left it on the street, not an expensive car like that. And it was super unlikely that he could have gotten in and out of his house without his wife knowing. That woman seemed to be at home—and in bed—quite a lot. She woulda heard something. It would be interesting to know who Sharity was seeing, though, since they'd probably been hooking up before Baker took off. This secret boyfriend might know something too.

All in all, it was likely that Baker *had* skipped town, probably with the stolen money. Josh Stanley couldn't tell her exactly how much it was, but it would have to be a lot for the big boss to take a finger, right?

Zeus came back inside, and she shut and locked the back door, still thinking. She patted her dog on the head, then walked to her car. It was time to get back to the office and start writing up a warrant to track Baker's bank activity. If the man had a stack of cash, it would be pretty easy to change his name and set himself up with a new life and a new bank somewhere far away. But hopefully Baker hadn't been able to take all the money with him, and he'd slip up and make a withdrawal from a TYME machine somewhere or use a credit card. Then she could narrow down where he'd escaped to and bring him back for that grilling.

Mike imagined Baker with black grill marks on him and grinned.

Then she shook her head. Drugs. The drugs would explain why Baker was always so vague about his line of work and where his money came from. She shook her head. She never woulda figured, but as her pops used to say, *It takes all kinds*. Now she just had to figure out where Sunday's drug drop was happening. Then they could stake it out and bust whoever was in charge.

Back at the station, she checked her messages. Yes! Mike did a fist pump because there was one from Rockford with a note to call them back. She excitedly punched the numbers into her phone, practically dancing in her seat while it rang. It was pretty late in the day; hopefully they hadn't gone home yet.

"Rockford Police Department, this is Sergeant Wilkerson. Can I help you?"

"This is Detective Zenoni; I'm returning your call. I requested information on the Highsmiths who used to live in your community." Mike did her best to drop her voice low and sound professional.

"Oh, yeah." There was some shuffling of papers in the background. "We looked at our records and had a clerk do some digging at the courthouse as well. Only thing we came up with was a marriage license for Robert Highsmith and Lorraine Conrad, dated, ah, 9-20-71."

"Huh. That's all there is? Nothing on Lorraine Conrad?" *Whoops.* Her voice had crept up. Why did it do that, get kinda high, when she talked on the phone?

"Yeah, nothing on her, just the marriage certificate. Sorry there wasn't more. But we have no other records of either one."

She thanked Wilkerson for his help and slowly hung up her phone. Something didn't feel right there. Shouldn't there be tax records if they'd owned a house in Rockford? It was also hard to believe that there was nothing on either of them if they'd lived there for even a couple of years. People got at least one speeding ticket, right? Filed a complaint against their neighbor's dog or something stupid like that. It was weird that there was none of that. No one could stay *that* far under the radar, could they?

At least she had Mrs. Highsmith's maiden name—Conrad. She'd try to do some digging with that next.

Chapter 25

LORRAINE

Friday

The smell of coffee woke Lorraine up the next morning. She had planned to leave once she'd finished interrogating James—about nothing in particular, but it was fun to get some practice in—but she needed to figure out how much he remembered in the morning. So, she'd waited for James to pass out, then she carefully hung up her dress and crawled into bed beside him, sleeping like the dead, conscience unbothered.

Lorraine opened her eyes to find James standing there in a robe, holding two cups of coffee, one of which he offered to her, smiling sheepishly. She took it but immediately set it on the bedside table without taking a sip.

"Good morning," James said. She could tell he was feeling uncertain, especially when he cleared his voice a few times and took a drink of coffee before speaking again. "I had room service bring up some coffee."

Lorraine gave him a winning smile that didn't reach her eyes, but few people ever noticed that. "Thank you. Did you sleep okay?"

James nodded vigorously. "I did." He paused. "Did you?"

She smiled, coy this time. "I did. I had a great time last night." She watched his reaction closely.

The man nodded, although his brow was furrowed a bit, obviously trying to remember. "I did too. It was . . . fun."

"Especially that last part."

James nodded again. "Yes, especially that part."

She was delighted, the smile reaching her eyes for real this time. The man didn't remember a bit of what had happened. He thought they'd had sex the night before and simply didn't remember.

Perfect. This drug was perfect for her purposes.

Lorraine unselfconsciously bounced from the bed, found her bra on the floor, hoisted her tits in, and fastened it before strolling to the closet to retrieve her dress, then slipped it over her head.

"Oh, you're . . . leaving already?" James was uncertain again, although he'd clearly been enjoying the show.

"Mmm." She made a little noise. "I have to get back."

"Oh, okay."

She cocked her head, considering. Should she stay for a quickie with this man? He was fit enough to be worth her while. She glanced at her watch, then shook her head. Nah. She had to get back to her place. She needed to write her article and figure out how to slip this drug to John Hooper, tonight if possible. She didn't want to waste any more time fooling around with this lame-o. He probably couldn't get it up anyway.

She smiled at James and gave him a little finger wave on her way out the door. If only he knew just how lucky he'd gotten the night before. To still be above ground, and all.

Lorraine hadn't had any of the coffee James had sent up to the room, so she stopped at a vending machine on her way to the lobby and grabbed a Coke. The caffeine should be enough to stave off any kind of headache she would get from not having her morning coffee. Normally she wouldn't drink something with so much sugar, but she thought she deserved another treat. A mini celebration, if you would.

Back on the highway heading north, her stomach growled. Loudly. She would need to eat something soon, or she would end up with that headache anyway. Did she have anything at home? Mentally reviewing the contents of her refrigerator, she decided to treat herself further by stopping in downtown Sheboygan Bay and getting a pastry or two from the bakery. It was early enough in the day that she would be able to burn everything off.

The Lakeside Bakery was busy with people grabbing goodies on their way to work. Lorraine considered aborting her mission—this was a ridiculously long line, but after a moment decided to suffer through it. Her blood sugar was getting far too low for anyone's good.

The local Lutheran minister was ahead of her in line and gave her a friendly hello. He was one of the few in town that was overtly friendly to Lorraine. She figured it was because he hadn't given up on getting her to set foot in his church and toss cash into his coffers.

It would never happen.

But she *could* use this to her advantage. Lorraine returned his greeting, then put a hand to her head.

"Are you all right Mrs. Highsmith?" he asked, concern evident.

"I'm just feeling a little faint. I haven't had enough to eat this morning, that's all. I should be fine." She wobbled a bit on her feet.

"Oh, we can't have that," Pastor Zarling said. He tapped the shoulder ahead of him in line, and soon she found herself being shuffled to the front. There was some grumbling, but no one wanted to tell Zarling to fuck off. He was a man of God. They did give her dark looks, though, which she thoroughly enjoyed, although she managed to stifle her delight and maintain a suitably pathetic appearance.

None of this applied to Jamie Sprout, however. Lorraine suspected—but wasn't sure—that the man was just stone stupid. Jamie was certainly attractive—tall and muscle bound, biceps flexing every time he picked something up, and when he bent over? She would bet you could bounce quarters off that ass. All in all, he presented a pretty picture, but she had long suspected there was no one home upstairs. When she got up to the counter, she ordered a lemon-blueberry muffin and a bran muffin.

"Good morning, Mrs. Highsmith! It's a pleasure to see you! It's been a while," Jamie greeted her, punching buttons on the register in front of him. "Why are you so dressed up? Did you have a date?" Jamie gave a saucy little wink.

She didn't have a fast answer for that, which she blamed on the low blood sugar. It was *not* that she was getting older and her brain wasn't churning out snappy replies as quickly as it used to. Jamie grabbed her muffins and put them in a bag, then passed it across the counter with another wink. "I get grumpy before breakfast too." He gave Lorraine a friendly wave, then continued smiling until the next person took Lorraine's place in front of him.

She shook her head and went to one of the empty tables that had just been vacated. She was well into enjoying her muffin when Detective Zenoni pushed through the door. Lorraine would love to know if the woman had made progress and learned something useful, but she wasn't about to ask her. She simply picked at her muffin, chewing thoughtfully, watching.

Interesting. Detective Zenoni hadn't taken her eyes off Jamie Sprout since she'd walked through the door, not even to peruse the baked goods on display, which were honestly worth a gander. She also seemed a little tongue tied when Jamie greeted her with his usual sunny disposition. Could the detective be enamored of the clerk? He was blond and cute, tall and had a vague resemblance to a current popular actor—Lorraine couldn't remember the kid's name exactly, Feldman or something—but Jamie pulled it off. It was impossible to tell how Jamie might feel about Zenoni in return, since he treated everyone precisely the same way, but that wasn't important. What was important was that this crush was something that she could use against Detective Zenoni. Something that would distract Zenoni from whatever she was up to.

It was always good to have some ammunition in your pocket.

Chapter 26

MIKE

Friday

Normally Mike would have avoided the bakery during an investigation—she didn't need to ogle the eye candy, not when she had plenty of things to think about, or waste time standing in what was always a long line. But she'd burned her last pieces of bread in the toaster. It was probably time for a new one anyways—it was real unpredictable, and if you took your attention off it for just a second too long . . . well, burnt toast. But there was no way she could start her day without at least *something* to eat, so a trip to the bakery had been her only choice, really.

Dang, Jamie *was* handsome; his white Chiclet smile really lit up a room. When he turned it on full force, she fumbled her words a bit, but that probably had more to do with the lack of breakfast, which was why she was here in the first place.

"Good morning, Sergeant Zenoni," Jamie greeted her sunnily, then frowned. "Oh, no, it's Detective Zenoni now!"

"I wish you would call me Mike." She smiled, but it was an unfortunate facial expression, caught somewhere between good morning and *I smelled something terrible.* Just as well that she wasn't actually interested in him. She'd work on the weird expressions, though, in case she ever decided to go on a date again. In a couple of months, maybe, after this case was wrapped up. Which it would be, tighter than a burrito.

Jamie cocked his head slightly. "Of course. It's just hard to remember since you're a girl." His smile was wide and easy. "What can I get for you?"

Mike ran a self-conscious hand down her gray tweed suit coat. At least she looked like a girl, right? Giving her head a little shake, she placed her order—two muffins to go—and let her mind wander, running down her list, while Jamie bustled about behind the counter.

She would *not* ask him if she looked like a girl. She would not.

Jamie brought the bag with her muffins to the register. "Do you need anything else? We have dog biscuits." He indicated a glass jar on the display case filled with cookies. Cookies that were distinctly penis shaped. "They're the North Point Lighthouse," he said proudly. Had he baked them himself? Wowza. They were certainly . . . something.

Mike nodded uncertainly and accepted her bag with the muffins. "Thank you." She lifted the bag in an awkward salute. Did this guy somehow know she had a dog? Or was he just making polite conversation? It would be real creepy if he knew about Zeus, eye candy or not.

"You're so welcome!" Jamie replied.

She turned, still wondering about Jamie's dog biscuits, and for the first time noticed Mrs. Highsmith sitting at a table near the door. How had she missed her? Mrs. H. was pretty dolled up for this time of day, too, which was weird. Her getup wasn't what Mike wanted to discuss with her, though.

She took a seat across from Mrs. Highsmith, making brief contact with those dark, unreadable eyes. Mike pushed away a slightly ick feeling in her stomach, then reached into her bag to pull out her own muffin. "I thought I'd join you, Lorraine *Conrad*."

Mrs. Highsmith took a bite of her bran muffin, brushing crumbs from her lap casually, not reacting to the use of her maiden name, not in the slightest. Mike was sure this was careful, though. "Did you, now?"

Mrs. Highsmith said. "I hope you gave my best to the Rockford Police Department."

Their eyes met and held. "You didn't own a place there?" Mike popped some muffin into her mouth.

Mrs. H. turned her attention back to her own treat. "Rented."

"Mmm," Mike said around her mouthful of muffin. "And where did you live before you met your husband?"

This time Mrs. Highsmith gave an alligator smile. "Oh, you'll have to work much harder than that, Detective."

"Not even a hint?"

Mrs. Highsmith shook her head, clearly enjoying herself. "Where's the fun in that?"

"I'll find it. Whatever it is."

"It's good to believe in yourself," Mrs. H. said. The condescension was clear, but it only strengthened her resolve. She *would* learn what this woman was hiding. Because there was obviously *something*, a big something if Mike's instincts were correct.

"Now, if you'll excuse me, Detective, I have things to do." Mrs. Highsmith stood and grabbed her little paper bag of bakery goods and sauntered out the door, leaving a mess of crumbs and a wrapper on the table.

Mike watched, eyes narrowed, chewing thoughtfully. She finished her muffin, then cleaned up the table, casting one last glance at Jamie—she'd never seen him around her neighborhood, so how could he know about Zeus? She didn't like the idea that someone—anyone, really—might be tracking where she lived.

Unless it was all perfectly innocent, which she supposed it *could* be. She'd let it go for now, but only because she needed to get to work solving a murder.

Mike didn't bother stopping at the police station, instead heading straight out to John Hooper's farm. If her boss didn't see her, maybe she wouldn't get roped into doing something that wasn't connected to this case. She only had three days to figure out where that drop was going to happen, after all, and every hour wasted did nothing but tick the clock down further, a clock she was all too aware of.

She found Hooper's driveway, and as she pulled close to the house, dust from the gravel driveway coating her car, she noticed that Hooper had wild asparagus growing in the ditches along his driveway. A lot of it had gone to seed already, but down in the long grass, there were still some good stalks that could be picked. She hoped Hooper wasn't mowing them down.

There was a car in the drive that seemed vaguely familiar, but it didn't belong to Hooper. Mike racked her brain, trying to remember how she knew that car, but couldn't come up with an answer, so she got on the radio.

"Dispatch, meet me on channel two, please." Rather than talk to Carla on the channel that everyone in the county used, she would make this request on their private channel, the one assigned to their department.

"Go ahead," Carla said moments later.

"Can you run a plate for me?"

There was a long pause—she could practically hear the sigh over the radio—before Carla told her to go ahead with it. Mike read off the plate number, and then there was a long, several-minute wait while Carla looked the car up in the department computer. At least she hoped she was. While she waited, Mike opened her door to let a breeze in—it was hot as Hades without the AC going, but she didn't want to risk running the battery down.

"It belongs to Grace Baker," Carla finally reported.

"Thank you!" There was no response on the other end, and after a beat she flipped back to the main channel.

Grace Baker. Julian Baker's sister. Well, *that* was interesting. Grace had been on her list of people to talk to, so she could kill two birds with one stone here.

Mike got out of the oven formerly known as her car and shut the door, relieved to be outside, although the breeze out here wasn't exactly fresh. She gave her pits a quick sniff—nope, not her—then eyed Grace's car. Mike didn't believe in coincidence, so there was a reason that Grace was here, a reason probably related to her brother.

What *was* that smell, though? Her first thought was a body rotting under the porch, but then she looked out over the fields and saw the flock of emus. Bird shit was almost as bad as pig, so that had to be it. Not another body, poorly hidden.

Okay, maybe her pops *had* been right about her imagination running wild sometimes.

Mike gingerly mounted the sagging gray boards playacting as stairs and crossed the porch to the front door. She was watching her feet, afraid the wood beneath her might buckle at any moment. A quick knock on the screen door kicked off some intense wailing from a small child inside. Seconds later footsteps sounded behind the surprisingly sturdy wooden door. It cracked open a beat later to reveal John Hooper, bloodshot eyes squinting through the screen.

"I'm sorry to disturb you, John—and the baby—but I've got a couple questions for ya."

Hooper sighed. "It's fine. It's not like the kid was going to sleep anyhow. But let's talk on the porch." Hooper let himself outside and walked to the wooden railing, leaned against it, and crossed his arms.

This was a bold move, since it looked like the sturdy man was gonna break through the wood and go flying at any moment. Mike stayed where she was, on planks that she'd already tested with a gentle bounce, and even still, she made sure those boards weren't too close together and her feet were squarely planted. Just in case. "Is Miss Baker here? I'd like to chat with her too."

Hooper's eyes shifted ever so slightly to the left. "Oh, she's just, ah, talking with Nancy. She came over to help with the baby."

"Great. Maybe when you and I are done then." Mike paused. "How long have Grace and Nancy been friends?" She didn't think the two women actually *were* friends—if she remembered correctly, they'd hated each other in high school. Although, they were all older now, so maybe things had changed.

But even still. Her gut told her that Grace was really here to talk with John Hooper, not his wife and their screaming baby.

"Oh, since high school," John said, wiping a palm on his jean-clad leg and avoiding her eyes.

A lie, then. Not a great start.

"I see. And when was the last time you talked to Julian Baker, Mr. Hooper?"

Hooper gave a little chuckle. "Mr. Hooper is my pops. I'm just John."

Mike said, "Ha ha" rather than give a real laugh, then waited for an answer to her question.

Hooper cleared his throat, clearly uncomfortable. Good. "I guess it must be almost a year now." This was delivered while Hooper inspected his boots, arms crossed over his chest, leaning against that precarious porch rail. It could be that he was thinking, or it could be that he was avoiding the truth. Then Hooper looked up and shrugged, cocking his head slightly. "It's funny. Mrs. Highsmith was just asking me the exact same thing."

This was obviously intended to put Mike off her game, but she wasn't about to fall for *that*. "Oh, yah, the article she's writing." She smiled at John. "Hoping to get your name in the paper?"

Hooper shook his head, and she imagined the farmer looked a little defeated. "Yeah, no, I don't want my name in the paper."

She shrugged. "Might be good for business. All these . . . birds." Maybe Hooper would think that she had suspicions about the farm. Then she quickly changed course, à la Mrs. H. "You and Julian were friends, weren't you? And not just in high school, I've seen you together since then. Why has it been so long since you've spoken? A year, you said?"

Hooper shrugged, but his face tightened. "Things sure change once you've had a kid, Detective. I can tell ya that, free of charge."

She didn't know about that firsthand, but it was probably true. "Don't get out much anymore, huh?"

"I get one night a week to myself—the wife and I switch off. Just to get a break."

Mike nodded. "What about the cash Julian Baker is supposed to have stolen? What do you know about that?"

Hooper went still, even seemed to stop breathing. The only movement she could see was a fast blink—John Hooper was not a very good liar. This was good news for her, though. Because he knew something about the money.

"I don't know what you're talking about, Detective."

"Listen, John. We both know you're lying, so we can talk about this here, or we can talk down at the station."

A series of emotions ran across Hooper's face, and she wasn't sure what would win. Then Hooper sighed. "Fine. Yeah, I've heard that rumor. Although Jules was really tight lipped about it." Hooper was defiant now.

"But you think it was true?"

Hooper nodded. "Yeah, no, yeah. I think it was."

"When was this?"

"I think it happened around the last time I talked to him, so a little over a year ago. He was real nervous but said he had everything handled."

Josh Stanley hadn't been sure, but he'd thought it was a few months ago. So not too far off. "Do you think he paid it back?"

Hooper shook his head. "That I don't know, but he's still alive, ain't he? If he didn't, I can't imagine he'd a stayed alive this long." He paused, considering. "Of course, I heard about his missing finger. I've never seen him cook a day in his life, so I can't see him losing it that way."

And here was confirmation of what she already suspected. An angry boss making a point about stolen money was *way* more likely than a "kitchen accident."

If only Baker was around to comment on it.

"I'd like to talk to Grace. Could you send her out?"

Hooper looked relieved and hurried into the house. Mike waited patiently, although she couldn't hear anything inside. Maybe she shoulda followed him in.

It felt like an eternity later, but Hooper reappeared, looking distinctly uncomfortable. "Uh, my wife says Grace can't talk right now."

Mike raised one eyebrow. "She give a reason why?"

His cheeks stained pink. "Grace is in the bathroom, and uh, she's gonna be in there a while."

Now both her eyebrows were up. "I hope you've got more than one bathroom. For your own sake."

Hooper looked even more uncomfortable, if that was possible. She kinda enjoyed it, making him uneasy. "Well, let her know that I'll catch her at home, then. I hope she's feeling better."

He nodded and scuttled back into the house, then gently closed the door behind himself.

There was zero chance Grace Baker was actually holed up in the Hoopers' bathroom. If you were having that kind of trouble, you'd go to the privacy of your own home. Using a toilet that wasn't your own, even a friend's, was a biscuit away from a public restroom, and the embarrassment would be epic.

No, Grace Baker was avoiding her, which moved her way up the list of people to talk to.

Chapter 27

LORRAINE

Friday

Unsettled was an excellent way to describe how Lorraine was feeling as she walked out of Lakeside Bakery.

"Fuck," she muttered under her breath. What Zenoni had learned from Rockford wasn't a surprise—it was more that Zenoni wasn't willing to let this go. The woman had a suspicious mind. Lorraine might have been impressed if the detective was aiming it at anyone but herself.

She cursed again under her breath. Would Zenoni try to get a warrant for her house? No, Judge Warner would never sign off on that.

Or maybe he would. When he'd run for judge his elections posters had read **CHARLIE WARNER FOR JUGE**, spelled exactly like that. It was inconceivable that he'd won.

Point being, she needed to distract the detective, because if Zenoni saw inside Lorraine's basement, it would be nothing short of a disaster. Her stomach gave an uncharacteristic bubble, and she put an uncertain hand to it before making up her mind. Time to put her earlier deduction to use. Lorraine waited in the shadows until the detective left the bakery and drove away, then marched herself back inside. The line was shorter now, and she didn't have to wait very long to get to the front. "You know, I was thinking about getting a kringle to go. Got any left, Jamie?"

"Oh, you betcha, Mrs. Highsmith!" Jamie studied the bakery case. "I think we still got a cherry or an almond."

"I'll take the almond." She paused. "You know, I've been meaning to ask you, Jamie, are you seeing anyone right now?" This was asked while Jamie slid the large kringle into a thin paper bag made specially for the pastry.

"Oh, I don't date older ladies, Mrs. Highsmith."

She briefly closed her eyes. "Not for me, Jamie. I didn't mean me."

"Oh!" Jamie cocked his head. "Well, not right now, no. After Megan Mueller dumped me, I thought I would take a break and work on myself."

This sounded like some new age bullshit that kids said, but she let that be. "Or maybe you should strike while the iron is hot." Jamie looked confused, so Lorraine barreled on. "What about Detective Zenoni?" She smiled, pushing warmth into her eyes. She'd studied how it was done long enough that it was easy for her now. "She's a nice young lady."

Jamie was thinking so hard Lorraine thought his eyes would cross with the effort. "She is, isn't she? She comes in every once in a while, just like you." Jamie started pushing buttons on the register. "I think she likes our muffins."

"I'm certain that's not all she's interested in," Lorraine said, her voice heavy with meaning.

Jamie looked at her with a quizzical expression. "Our donuts? I thought that was just a stereotype, you know, cops and donuts. Do you think it might be true? She seems to be pretty fit, though . . ."

Lorraine cut Jamie off—this was painful. The boy really was dim. "No, Jamie. I think she likes *you*. Not the donuts. Have you ever thought about going out with her?"

His brow furrowed. "I've never thought about her like that."

"She's awfully pretty, and smart, and I think she might be interested in you." Sometimes all it took was knowing someone was attracted to you to change your idea of them. She lucked out here.

"You really think so?" he asked, his eyes suddenly a little extra sparkly. "Do you think I should ask her out?"

"I do. But how about you give me your phone number, and I'll pass it on to her." That way she'd have proof that she'd done the matchmaking, proof to hand over to the detective. Besides, she had no idea what Zenoni's home phone number was—it was unlisted.

Jamie smiled and nodded happily, then wrote his number on a napkin and passed it over the counter. Lorraine was pleased at how little effort this had required, and now she would look like the hero to Detective Zenoni. It might not get her to completely stop looking into her background, but it should certainly soften her up, right? Not to mention it would give her a marker she could call in later.

Lorraine stopped at home before swinging by the police station. She needed to shower off the night before and change her clothes. It was interesting that no one but Jamie had asked why she was so dressed up for a bakery run on a random Friday, but again, one of the benefits of being an invisible older woman. It worked in her favor, so she didn't spit nails when it happened. Although she did enjoy spitting nails whenever it was warranted.

She washed off her makeup, making certain that any remnants were gone before she applied a fresh coat. Then she dressed in a long denim skirt with an elastic waistband and a striped polyester blouse with a bow that tied at the neck.

On the way out the door, she double-checked that she had Jamie Sprout's phone number in her pocket and headed off to the police station.

She perused the lot behind the station and found that Zenoni's squad car was parked there. Excellent. Lorraine parked in front, then sauntered inside. Carla glanced up from her typewriter, gave a nod, then went back to what she was doing. She could hear the muffled sound of Detective Zenoni speaking with Chief Schneider inside Schneider's office, and she dearly wanted to hear what Zenoni was reporting, but of course, she'd been betrayed by the little bell over the door.

Zenoni and her boss leaned over in their chairs to see who had come in, and when she saw who it was, Zenoni practically leaped from her chair to come out of Schneider's office, brow furrowed. "Mrs. Highsmith. What can we do for you?"

She wasn't put off by Zenoni's clear displeasure at her appearance. "I think the real question is, What can I do for you?" She reached into her pocket and slid the napkin with Jamie Sprout's name and phone number across the counter. Zenoni's face looked confused, which wasn't exactly the reaction Lorraine was hoping for.

"He gave this to you?"

"He did."

Mike was holding the napkin gingerly, like it might disintegrate at any moment. Lord, this girl had it bad. "And he said you should give it to me?"

"He did, and I am sure. He's waiting for you to call."

"Uh, thank you." Zenoni's voice was gruff, but Lorraine wasn't fooled. The detective was delighted at her delivery. Exactly as she knew she would be.

"What are you two talking about?" Chief Schneider called from his office. "Come in here so I can hear."

Lorraine looked at Zenoni, who was suddenly so stiff it looked like she'd been jolted with a cattle prod. But then, with a sigh, Zenoni reached down and opened the little swinging door, then held it open for her as she passed by. The detective followed her into Schneider's office, resignation coming off the woman in waves.

"Hans," Lorraine said, feeling a prick of pleasure as Schneider frowned at her informal greeting. "I was just seeing if Detective Zenoni—"

Zenoni cut her off. "Had left anything at the bakery this morning. I didn't."

She was deeply amused but agreed with the cover story. "What were you two discussing in here?"

"Well, Detective Zenoni was just telling me about her interview with John Hooper. Interesting stuff." The chief frowned, then shrugged. "Now, what were you telling me? Start over."

Lorraine could tell this was the last thing Zenoni wanted to do. "Yeah no, I was done, boss. Nothing else to report."

"Nothing but a stack of stolen money? I'm not sure I believe it, Detective. I mean, otherwise I'd a heard about it. And how would Hooper have known about it? I guess I could believe that Baker was involved in drugs, but to lose his finger because of some stolen cash? It seems like a real stretch."

Zenoni's shoulders were drawn up, and her spine had stiffened. It was clear that the detective really wanted to argue with her boss or maybe tell him to shut his big fat mouth but was restraining herself. Admirable, really, since Schneider had basically just called her investigating abilities into question.

"I think it's likely there's some truth to it, sir. It's a good motive for him to skip town," Zenoni finally said. Lorraine waited for her to continue, but she caught the look Zenoni shot her from the corner of her eye and knew that Zenoni wasn't going to cave.

The chief continued talking, but Lorraine tuned out. It looked like she no longer had a reason to drug John Hooper into telling her anything. She was a little disappointed—she'd gone to an awful lot of work to test those pills. But no matter, she would find another use for them.

Even more exciting, though, was she now had a lead on a stack of stolen money. And it was clear the police thought Baker had left town because of it. Things were really coming together for Lorraine Highsmith.

Chapter 28

MIKE

Friday

Mike knew exactly what Mrs. H. had been up to with the napkin trick—trying to distract her from the case by throwing her Jamie Sprout. Back in her office, she tossed the napkin on her desk and chuckled. If only Mrs. H. knew that she wasn't genuinely interested in the guy. Mike had done her best to play along, though, let Mrs. Highsmith think she was grateful for the number. She liked the idea of getting one over on the smug reporter.

Could she use this number to her advantage, though? She leaned back in her chair and thought about it. Jamie appeared to be dumb as a stump—and was possibly stalking her?—but he also had regular contact with nearly everyone in town. Was it possible that he might know something useful about Baker or Youngblood? Or even about the drug trafficking? It was crazy that people weren't more upset about the drugs in town, but maybe Jamie knew why.

Hmm. Something to consider.

The other thing worth considering was whether going on a date or two with the big ox would spread word around town that she dated *men*. It was fucking aggravating, the rumors and whispers that she was a lesbian.

Was it her height? Or her hair? Maybe she *should* grow her hair out. Try to look a little more feminine, although the prospect just made her tired. She supposed the trouble could also be that she went by Mike instead of Michaela, but she was pretty sure that ship had already sailed.

She shook her head and turned her attention back to the case. The clock was ticking, now only two full days until the drop, and she didn't feel like she was making any progress toward figuring out where that would go down. What would her pops tell her? *Everyone is lying, so talk to them again.*

That was true, although why couldn't people just tell the truth the first time? It would make her job so much less frustrating. If only real life was like one of those McBain novels—she wouldn't have these problems. Anyway, the first person on today's list was Grace Baker, since the woman had obviously been avoiding her earlier. Cornering her at work was the best way to make sure that Grace couldn't keep *that* up.

So, Mike headed to the First Citizens Bank where Grace worked as a teller. There was only one other location, in a town fifteen miles away—it wasn't a big bank. But that was part of its small-town charm. The service was personalized, if not downright personal.

Grace was standing behind the window helping Karen Johnson make a deposit when Mike walked in. She stood patiently in line, ignoring the curious stares from the other ladies who worked there. When Mrs. Johnson finally closed her checkbook, tucked it away, and headed for the exit, Mike stepped up to the counter. "Miss Baker, is there somewhere we can talk?"

Grace glanced around, then at the clock on the wall. "I don't have a break until lunch."

Someone in an office behind Grace called out, "You can use the conference room. I'll cover the front." Mike assumed this was Grace's boss, the only man who worked here. What would that be like? Nearly the exact opposite of her own situation, except for Carla, who was super uninterested in anything even approaching friendly. Did Grace have friends to eat lunch with, people to chat with between customers? That must be nice.

Grace heaved a deep sigh and motioned with her head for Mike to follow her. The detective passed through the little gate that allowed her behind the counter and followed Grace to a small room with a big table, next to her boss's office. Grace closed the door, then took a seat in one of the stuffed faux-leather chairs and sat quietly for a few seconds before she began swinging back and forth. Mike took a seat across from her and pulled out her notebook.

"I hope you're feeling better. Musta been something you ate, huh?"

Grace rubbed at something imaginary on the table. "Yeah, I'm feeling better, thanks."

Mike stared her down for a moment, wanting Grace to know that she knew she'd been lying. "I'm sure you can guess why I'm here," Mike said after the silence had become just uncomfortable enough.

Grace paused for a second, then gave a small nod. "My brother. But we aren't close, Sergeant. I haven't spoken to him in months."

"It's detective now," Mike said with a friendly smile.

"Congratulations," Grace said.

"Thank you." The woman hadn't sounded sincere, but Mike moved on. "Anyway, I know the two of you weren't close, but you probably know more than you think you do."

Grace didn't look convinced of this and pursed her lips.

Mike stared again, letting the silence stretch before lobbing another question and watching Grace's chair twitch, back and forth, back and forth. "Do you know where Julian is right now?"

Grace shook her head. "No, should I? Isn't he at home with his *wife*?" There was a sour note on *wife*, and while Mike didn't write it down, she made a mental note that Grace did not approve of Sharity Baker.

"He is not."

"Huh. Well, I have no idea where he would have gone. Like I said, I haven't talked to him in, like, months." Grace's chair was still twitching, a little harder now.

"And when I get a warrant for Julian's phone records, is that still gonna be true?"

Grace bit her lip, and her cheeks got red as the chair finally stopped. "Fine, I called a month or so ago asking for a small loan. I want to get out of my shitty apartment on Carriage Drive and buy a little place here in town." Her eyes flashed at the memory. "But Julian claimed he was broke and couldn't help me out. Not even an apology or nothing. And I don't believe for a second that hoser doesn't have the money."

"And why is that?"

Grace bit her lip again.

"Because of how much money he's making selling drugs?" Mike asked casually. "Or do you mean the money he filched from his boss?"

Grace's eyes widened slightly. "You heard about that?"

Mike leaned back in her chair. "Everyone has heard about that." This was a lie, which made her stomach flip, but she kept her face neutral.

Grace blinked once, then moved on. "He said all his extra money was going toward paying that back, and he was strapped right now."

"Why didn't he just give the money back?"

Grace shrugged. "I didn't hear this from him, but I think he lost it all. He's always liked the casinos a little too much, and he's dumb enough to think he can beat the house." She rolled her eyes. "I work in a bank; I could have told him the house always wins."

Mike wasn't sure there was actually a connection between those two things, but she let it slide. Because this was the first she'd heard of Julian having a gambling problem. Her gut told her Grace was telling the truth, but it was also true that the siblings weren't close—far from it. Which meant it was entirely possible that Baker *hadn't* gambled the money away, even if Grace assumed that was what happened. Time to change directions. "Why were you out at the Hooper place?"

Grace flinched. "I'm friends with Jennifer Hooper. I wanted to see the baby and also see if she needed anything." Her voice was defensive. "Then I . . . got sick. It was unexpected."

Mike looked at her for a few long beats. Grace's cheeks turned a little pink, but she was sticking with her answer, staring back even as her chair went back to twitching like a cat's tail. If there was a different reason Grace'd gone to the Hooper farm, she wasn't going to admit to it. Not today, anyway.

"What do you know about your brother and Doug Rupp?"

"I heard Doug was found dead on someone's lawn. Like someone knocked him off." Now Grace leaned forward. "Is that true?"

It wouldn't hurt to answer since it wasn't exactly a state secret, so Mike nodded. "But he was investigating your brother. Do you know where Julian gets his money?"

"He would never say," Grace said with a shrug. "I assumed he was doing something illegal, honestly."

"Why is that?"

"He dealt a little pot in high school, and it was easy money for him. I think he got used to cash coming in without having to do much work in return. He's always been a slacker."

"So, you think he was dealing drugs in town."

Grace nodded. "It's one of the reasons we didn't speak. My brother was a dirtbag, and I didn't want anything to do with that life." She sniffed a little.

"And you weren't involved?"

Grace sat back, clearly offended, or at least doing a real good imitation of it. "Of course not! How can you even ask that?"

Mike just nodded. "Do you know who Julian was working for? The person he stole money from?" She wasn't super hopeful that Grace would know this answer, but it was worth asking.

"I haven't the faintest idea, but I heard that's who took his finger." Grace paused here, clearly hoping for a reaction, but she didn't get one, and her face twisted in annoyance. "I got the sense over the years that he had moved up in the . . . organization, I guess you would call it? I don't know how these things work. But he had a beater car that he put most of his miles on, since he seemed to be running all over creation."

Baker was probably getting the larger shipments from the big boss, doing the packaging, then making drops to lower-level dealers. Typical middle manager stuff. Mike thought back to the list of vehicles registered in Julian's name. There was an older model Datsun—she would check with Sharity to see if she knew where it was. If it was missing, it might just be the vehicle Baker took off in. She would also double-check to see if Baker had a boat registered in his name—Lake Michigan was the easiest way to move things in and out of the city while staying off the state police's radar. It was also the most likely spot for Sunday's drop, but Lake Michigan had a real long coastline—the drop could go down anywhere. And if Baker had any smarts, he wouldn't do it right in Sheboygan Bay harbor, which meant a stakeout there would probably be a waste of time. She needed to narrow the field.

Part of her felt like it was a waste of time tracking down Baker, but she also knew that Baker was her only lead who knew where the drop was happening. Not to mention Baker was probably the only person who knew the name of the big boss running the whole shebang. And Mike needed that name if she was going to solve Rupp's murder. Two birds, one stone.

Chapter 29

LORRAINE

Friday

Zenoni was never going to let Lorraine tag along with her, but that was fine. She would simply observe and see what the detective did next. Lorraine watched her walk a few blocks, and when the detective was just out of sight, she moved her car, sliding down the street and into the corner gas station parking lot. She parked at the edge of the lot, where she had an unobstructed view of the street. Two blocks down, she could see Zenoni crossing toward the First Citizens Bank, standing alone on the corner, set slightly apart from the other buildings.

Zenoni was going to talk to Grace Baker.

Lorraine supposed this made sense, but she wasn't sure that Grace would have any useful information. It was well known around town that the Baker siblings were barely on speaking terms. What would be more interesting than what Grace told Zenoni was what Grace did *after* Zenoni spoke with her. That was the real dirt. Because let's be honest, everyone lied to the police, either outright or by omission.

This was a decent place to set up camp, so she shut off her station wagon, cranked down her window, then leaned across the brown bench seat to roll down the passenger-side window. It was already stifling, and she needed a breeze if she was going to stay put for anything longer than a few minutes. Then she sat back to wait.

The only person who so much as looked at her was an old man on a riding lawn mower. He wasn't there to get gas. No, he pulled into a parking spot in front of the glass doors, went inside, and came out a few minutes later with a twelve-pack of Milwaukee's Best. As she watched in her rearview, he settled the beer on his lap and threw it in reverse, then pulled back onto the street, presumably heading back home.

Too many DUIs, no doubt.

The lake wasn't offering up much in the way of a cooling breeze that day, so her face was bathed in a sheen of sweat by the time Zenoni left the bank and started the short trek back to the police station. From her vantage point, she could see when the detective reached into her suit coat and pulled out the napkin, then wiped her face with it before tucking it back. Zenoni hadn't even looked at it, which wasn't at all the reaction Lorraine was looking for.

Huh.

About fifteen minutes after Zenoni had disappeared from sight, Grace Baker poked her head out the front door of the bank and looked both ways. Lorraine wasn't worried about being spotted—Grace was clearly looking for any sign of Detective Zenoni. Seeing nothing, Grace scurried to her car, a yellow Ford Pinto whose glory days were many years past, and didn't they become flaming death traps if you hit 'em wrong? Either way, Grace pulled onto the main road and drove off, Lorraine pulling out just after her.

Lorraine drove carefully. Grace Baker was likely already nervous since she'd just been questioned by the police, so she kept well back from the other woman's car. After pulling up to the next intersection, Grace's Pinto made a right, and Lorraine gunned it down the street in time to see Grace's car turn onto Main Street. She waited at the next stop sign, and when Grace was nearly out of sight, she followed. There were now several cars between the two women, which should assuage any paranoia Grace might be feeling, but now Lorraine was concerned she might lose her. Her lips pressed into a tight line as she rode the bumper of the Chrysler in front of her, rolling her eyes at the religious shit stuck to the back hatch. "Honk if you love Jesus," her ass.

But she needn't have worried. Grace pulled into a parking spot across from Mary Ann's Frozen Custard and appeared to shut off her car. Lorraine drove past Grace's spot and found some angle parking in front of the True Value about a block away, so she pulled in and turned off the Behemoth. She half turned in her seat, but Grace appeared to be sitting tight.

Lorraine calculated her next move. From her vantage point, she couldn't see Grace clearly, although she could see the front door of the ice cream place. But she really wanted to be able to see both at once. Should she risk being seen and go patronize one of the shops across the street? She got out of her car, leaving the windows down and the doors unlocked—this was a small town, nothing was gonna happen to it—then perused the shops. Here the buildings were old, built using a cream-colored brick that was now hard to come by, charming if you were into that kind of thing. Luckily, there was a shitty little liquor store, and Grace was parked a few spaces down from it. It was close enough that Lorraine would be able to see her, but far enough away that maybe Grace wouldn't notice her.

Hitching her black purse up her shoulder, she sauntered down the block and into the Bottle Stop, careful not to glance in Grace's direction. The little bell dinged over her head, and she grimaced as her shoes became sticky on the cracked linoleum beneath her feet. The proprietor slurred a greeting from somewhere deep in the store, clearly hard at work sampling his own wares. She couldn't see him, but she could ignore him.

A cardboard cutout of some redneck race car driver stood life size and listing near the front window. She took up a position behind it, the cardboard man's dead eyes uncomfortably close to her own. She peered through the window and watched as Grace continued to sit unmoving in her car. Lorraine had a clear view of Grace's face and could see that the woman was simply looking into her rearview mirror, but she wasn't checking her lipstick—which was a terrible shade for her coloring—or even plucking stray hairs. Grace was just watching the street behind her.

It didn't take a genius to figure out that the woman was keeping an eye on Mary Ann's Frozen Custard. Interesting that Grace's first instinct had been to talk to Youngblood—it looked like they were both onto something there.

It also looked like Grace had no intention of moving anytime soon. She appeared to be settled in for the long haul, and Lorraine was starting to think that sticking around was a waste of time.

The proprietor was now slurring much too close to her ear, a clear violation of personal space. "Can I 'elp you fin' somethin'?" Flecks of spit landed on her cheek, and she resisted the urge to throw a fist toward the source, but only because she didn't want to risk a broken hand.

"Fuck. Off." She clearly enunciated each word. The grizzled man leaned even closer. He was probably only in his fifties, but his florid complexion and puffy features—from the drinking, no doubt—made him look closer to late sixties.

"Wha' di' you say?" he slurred, barely comprehensible.

Lorraine swung a knee hard and fast toward the man's family jewels, landing a pretty solid hit. The man let out a huge "Oof!" before toppling over, nearly taking out a wall of twelve-packs on his way down. It was shitty Miller Lite and would have been satisfying to watch it tumbling on top of this idiot, but it also would have drawn a lot of attention, which she was trying to avoid. She glanced out the window, satisfied that Grace's attention was still glued to the ice cream shop. Good.

Lorraine took another look at the lump on the floor clutching his junk, shook her head, and walked out, snagging a big bottle of Four Roses bourbon on her way out the door. Either he wouldn't notice, or he wouldn't report it. Lorraine felt sure of that.

Men really needed to learn better.

Chapter 30

MIKE

Friday

Back in her office, Mike stared at the wall and wished that she had her chalkboard here, but there was no way she was bringing that into the station. With Sanders's uncanny ability to get through locked doors, he and the other patrol cops would just break into her office, erase her notes, and draw penises all over it. She didn't know this from experience, exactly, but she'd seen the inside of the men's room. She knew what their artistic efforts looked like.

Anyway, Grace Baker. The bank teller had come up with enough interesting information that Mike was still considering whether she'd told the truth about being involved with her brother's operation. On the one hand, it was unlikely that Grace was involved. Grace really had been madder than a cat in a room full of rocking chairs that her brother hadn't given her money when she'd asked for it, and if she *was* involved, she woulda had the extra cash to buy a place.

Could Grace be a user? Mike shook her head immediately—there hadn't been any signs, not of the hard stuff anyway. And hardcore users couldn't hide the marks for long.

What about Youngblood?

Mike decided she could rule him out as a user as well, but she definitely couldn't rule him out for being involved with Julian's enterprise. Especially since Baker stopped there all the time, like the kid behind the counter said. So what was Youngblood's role? Did he know where the drop was happening? Was he selling through the custard shop?

She sighed, then toyed with the napkin Mrs. H. had given her. Would it be useful to call up Jamie Sprout, see if he wanted to meet her for a drink? Could he know what was going on in town? He *had* been sort of dropped in her lap, and it really was silly to look a gift horse in the mouth.

As a bonus, she could ask him how he knew about her dog.

Mike picked up the phone and called the number on the napkin. She was a little surprised when Jamie answered, and even more surprised when he suggested they meet that very night. Didn't he have anything going on? Plus he'd suggested Café Carpe, a hippie joint with live music, mostly folk, which was *really* not her thing. And who knew what kind of drinks they served there? But she supposed it would be worth taking an hour or so out of her evening to find out what the guy knew about the folks in town.

Now that that was settled, she pulled the list of Julian Baker's vehicles from his file, immediately noting there was no boat. Did Youngblood own one? She made a note to run a search on that, copied a list of Baker's other vehicles into her notebook, and slid the paper back into the file. She kept things locked in her desk so nothing happened to them. As far as she knew, Sanders hadn't bothered to break in here, but she was always on alert.

She glanced at her watch. A call to Chicago to start a background on Mrs. Highsmith would probably take a while. She'd be on hold, or bounced around from office to office, before she found someone to help her. Was it worth taking the time right now? Or should she put it off until tomorrow?

Sigh. Mrs. H. could probably wait.

Speaking of putting things off, she really needed to stop by and see her dad. Even just the reminder crumpled her face into a grimace. She could do it tomorrow, though, right? She'd thought maybe she could squeeze in a visit after dinner, but now she had a date. Ugh. That felt dirty, pushing off the visit to her dad, but not as dirty as the thought that came right behind it. *He won't even remember you were there.*

Shaking *that* grody-toad thought off, she decided to get moving, leaving her office and locking it up. She needed to go by Sharity Baker's and ask for a peek inside the garage.

Sharity answered the door with obvious bedhead, slightly pink and out of breath. She looked annoyed to find Mike on her doorstep again. "Help you, Detective?"

"Can I have a look in your garage, Mrs. Baker? I'm trying to figure out what car Julian is driving, since he brought the Corvette back. You haven't heard anything from him, have you?"

Sharity blew out a breath and reached inside, hitting what was clearly a garage door opener, because the door began to slide open with a great deal of noise.

Oh, Sharity hadn't been kidding about the racket this thing made. It made sense why Julian hadn't put his fancy little sports car in the garage that night, although there was still the driveway. Then something else occurred to her.

"Was your . . . friend parked here in the driveway the night after Julian went missing?"

Sharity flushed a little but met her eyes defiantly. "What if they were?"

Mike shrugged. "Just a reason why your husband woulda left his car in the street."

"Oh," Sharity said, her shoulders dropping back down a bit. "That would make sense, actually. And to answer your other question, I haven't heard a peep from Julian." Now she frowned, which was the closest thing to concern Mike had seen from her. "It is surprising, huh? It's been a few days now. I mean, I do hope he's okay." This was clearly an afterthought.

"Of course. Can I take a peek in the garage now?"

Sharity shrugged and followed Mike barefoot down the driveway, where they could see clearly into the garage. She shrugged again. "Everything is accounted for. This one is mine." She pointed to a dark-blue Volkswagen Golf. "And I parked the Corvette in here after you stopped by last time. I dug the spare key out of the junk drawer."

Mike pulled up the list she'd written in her notebook, checking the two cars in front of her against it. The VW checked out as did the cherry red Corvette. What she *didn't* see was a 1977 Datsun B-210. "What about a gold Datsun?"

Sharity squinted at her, then shook her head. "I don't even know what those look like."

"Interesting," Mike said, more to herself, really.

"Sure, I guess," Sharity said. "Can I go back inside now?"

"Just one more thing, did your husband deal drugs?"

Sharity squinted again, her eyebrows pulling together as she thought that over. "Ya know, that would make sense with a lot of things. Huh."

Mike wanted to do a facepalm on the other woman, but restrained herself. "Have you ever seen drugs in the house?"

Sharity didn't even have to think about that one—she immediately shook her head. "Not even. Like, I kid you not, I thought Jules was some kind of teetotaler. Is that the right word? Whatever, he claimed that he didn't touch anything but booze, and he was real adamant about it."

Interesting. Maybe. But Mike was starting to believe that neither Baker, husband nor wife, knew the other very well. And if Sharity's reaction was anything to go by, she wasn't exactly devastated that her husband had taken off. So far, Mike had no reason to believe that Sharity had anything to do with it, not yet anyway. But she wasn't reacting the way Mike thought a wife should if she really cared about her husband, so she would keep an eye on Baker's wife.

Anyway, if Sharity hadn't seen any drugs in the house, where was Julian stashing the stuff he was running all over the state?

Storage locker. That had to be it, the only logical place, right? Mike crossed her fingers that he'd kept his business local so she wouldn't have to comb through every storage facility in the county.

Of course, there was another question about Julian Baker that hadn't really occurred to her before now, and she was kicking herself for not seeing it sooner.

Could Julian Baker have killed Doug Rupp?

Chapter 31

MIKE

Friday

Judge Charles Warner lived on the north side of town, only a few blocks from where Julian Baker had built his monstrous house. It was the nicest neighborhood in the city, manicured lawns and imposing homes cozied up to the Lake Michigan shoreline. The sun was out today, heating up her car, but a cool breeze off the lake brushed her face as soon as she stepped outside. She paused and surveyed the Warner home, a sprawling split-level, with brown siding on the top and red brick on the bottom, and an enclosed porch facing the lake. By all accounts, the house belonged to Warner's wife, even though Warner was an attorney. Charles—or Charlie as he liked to be known—had a twin brother, and rumor had it that his twin took the bar exam for him, because Charlie never could have passed it. Charlie liked to say that he got the looks and his brother got the brains.

They were identical twins.

Charlie Warner didn't get a lot of business as an attorney, which was why he'd run for judge. And even as judge, Charlie didn't work on Fridays or Mondays as a general rule, which was why Mike had to turn up at the man's house to get things signed.

The detective rang the bell and waited as Julia, Charlie's wife, answered the door. She was tall and slender, with thick shoulder-length brown hair, fine features, and a smattering of freckles across her chest. She wore a simple blouse tucked into flowing gray pleated trousers, a thin gold watch on her wrist. It was a mystery to everyone—Charlie included—why she'd married the man. "Are you looking for my husband, Detective?"

"I am, Julia, thank you so much."

"Can I get you anything? Tea or a soda pop?" This was asked over her shoulder as they walked through the foyer into the wood-paneled living room where Charlie was watching a baseball game that he had obviously taped.

"No, I'm fine. Thanks for asking." She returned Julia's warm smile.

"Charles, Detective Zenoni is here to see you," Julia told her husband from the doorway.

"Who is . . ." Charlie looked up. "Oh! It's that girl cop."

Julia rolled her cognac-colored eyes. "Excuse my husband, *Detective*," she said and took her leave.

Her husband did not pick up on this big hint.

"I'm just watching the game!" the judge called from the overstuffed floral couch. "Brewers against the Red Sox. Baseball, you know. Those are baseball teams. Brewers are lookin' real good this year." A wicker chair shaped like an egg sat next to the couch, flanking the glass-topped coffee table where a cold beer dripped condensation. Mike perched herself on the edge of the wicker egg.

She didn't bother telling Judge Warner that she knew perfectly well who both the Brewers and the Red Sox were. "Just have a couple things for you to sign, Judge."

Charlie Warner glanced over. "Sure, sure. What are they?"

"A warrant to keep an eye on Julian Baker's credit cards—his wife signed off, but the company will still want a warrant. And this is a warrant to see if Baker has a storage locker around here."

Judge Warner finally muted the game and gave her his full attention. "Is this about the dead guy?"

She coughed and placed the paperwork on the coffee table in front of the judge and handed him a pen. "It is."

The judge nodded knowingly. "I heard about that. Glad you're looking into it."

She wasn't sure what to say to this, so she just said thank you. Judge Warner nodded again, very serious, and leaned over to sign the paperwork. She made sure to point out exactly where the judge needed to put his signature, which he did, something resembling an *X* and some squiggles.

Good enough. As long as it was legal.

As soon as she politely could, she extricated herself from the Warner house, but it took much longer than she wanted it to. Judge Warner had insisted that she watch some of the game with him, and despite her protests that she had a lot of work to do, she couldn't find a graceful way to get out of there, so she'd stayed put in the wicker egg, perching stiffly on the thin orange cushion while the judge explained baseball to her. It was more than thirty mind-numbing minutes before Julia came and rescued her, breaking her free from this special sort of hell.

As if Mike didn't know who the Brewers were. She'd gone with her pops to every opening day for *years*, not to mention regular games during the season. Her pops had liked sitting in the top bleachers of County Stadium, even when it was blisteringly hot. They both wore baseball mitts in the hopes they would catch a fly ball.

They never did catch one.

Mike heaved a huge sigh of relief once she was back in her car. It was stifling after baking in the sun, the pleather seats like branding irons beneath her legs, but at least she was out of there and had signed warrants in hand. She'd really been hoping to get a lot more done today—like stop by the U Store It and see if Baker had a unit—but she needed to get a trace on Baker's cards first, which would take a hot minute.

Sharity Baker was someone that Mike wanted to ask a couple of questions about too. Sharity wasn't responsible for her husband's disappearance—probably—but she knew more than she was letting on. She had to. Not to mention, Sharity didn't seem to think Julian would be coming home anytime soon, not if she was letting her "friend" shack up there.

Of course, if Mike were Baker and she'd killed her ole buddy Rupp, she wouldn't come home either.

She checked her watch. Son of a biscuit. She didn't have time to get on the phone with Chicago about Mrs. Highsmith—she only had a few hours before she was supposed to meet Jamie for their "date," so that call would have to wait until the morning. Especially since she had other calls to make first, calls about Julian Baker and where he'd scampered off to.

After calling all the credit card companies and faxing over the paperwork, Mike learned that there'd been no activity so far, but they were at least tracing the cards now. That was enough to decide to call it for the day. Before heading out to her car, Mike swung by the front of the station and wished Carla a good night. She started down the hallway leading to the back exit, then paused and retraced her steps. She stuck her head around the doorway.

"Carla, do you think a woman should wear a dress on a date? Or like, a jean skirt and a blouse? Or is that too dressy?"

Carla turned slowly toward her, surprise written across the secretary's face, but then Carla appeared to actually think about it. She pushed her large glasses up a tiny increment. "It depends on the place."

"Café Carpe."

She shook her head. "Just a casual blouse and a jean skirt if you have one." Carla squinted at her. "A T-shirt would even be fine, if it's a cute one. Fluff your hair up, though, so it doesn't look . . . like that. And for God's sake, put on some eyeliner and mascara."

This was all really good advice—she wouldn't even have *thought* about makeup. She grinned. "Thanks, Carla, you're a lifesaver."

Carla had already turned back to her computer, but Mike could see her little half smile. "You're welcome."

At ten to seven that evening, Mike was standing outside Café Carpe wondering if she should go in or wait outside for Jamie. Go in. She should definitely go in, right? She did the two-step for a while, then finally went inside. It wasn't at all what she'd expected—there was no incense or macrame hanging on the wall. No hippie stuff in the slightest. The exposed brick walls had art hanging on them, and after squinting at a little plaque beneath the piece nearest her, she realized that she kinda recognized the name. A local artist, then. The lighting was low, and small candlelit tables were set up across the floor leading to the stage—a little too romantic for her tastes, but fine. Honestly, she was pleasantly surprised by the place. She was about to head to the bar when she felt a tap on her shoulder. Swinging around, she found Jamie smiling down at her.

Yah know, it *was* nice to have a man looking down at her, instead of up, for a change.

"Hi!" Jamie said. He was wearing a white polo shirt and a dark pair of shorts that hugged the contours of his legs quite nicely, probably his butt too. Not that she was looking.

"Hi. Thanks for meeting me tonight." Mike had put on some makeup, aiming for an evening look, with dark-blue frosted eyeshadow around her brown eyes and blue eyeliner, like Carla had suggested. She had even fluffed her hair up. She hoped she looked okay, because honestly, she had no idea.

"I'm glad you suggested it! I was hoping to listen to the set tonight, but I didn't really want to come by myself." Jamie looked her up and down briefly, nothing grody, though. His eyes caught a little gleam off the dim lights. "You look nice."

She blushed and said thank you while she smoothed her denim skirt. Even if this wasn't a real date, it was nice to be complimented.

She couldn't really remember the last time she *had* been complimented. "Um, where would you like to sit?"

Jamie smiled and led the two of them to a small table for two, close to the stage, but not *too* close—hopefully they would still be able to hear each other. A perfectly average-looking man with an average-looking mullet was setting up with a guitar and some equipment—Mike prayed he didn't suck or she'd have a hard time keeping it together. She had a tendency to giggle in serious situations—even funerals sometimes, which was horrifying.

As soon as they took their seats, a waiter was there to take their drink orders. Jamie ordered an amaretto sour, and Mike ordered a Pabst—she'd never been much of a cocktail drinker. *Liquor is dangerous, but with beer you can keep your wits about you,* her pops liked to say. Usually with a beer in his hand.

"So, you must know everyone in town, working at the bakery, huh?"

Jamie started chattering about his job as she listened with one ear, hoping he'd spill something interesting about any of the people connected to the case, but so far no luck. The man really had a lot to say about yeast, though.

When Jamie's steam train of information finally ran out, he asked about her, in a roundabout sort of way.

"I heard that a dead body was found in town." His brown eyes were wide.

She nodded. "It's true."

"Are you working on the case?" Jamie put his chin in his hand, elbow propped on the table.

"I am." Here was her opening, but what was the best way to approach it? "Did you know Doug Rupp?"

"Who is that?" Jamie asked with the exact same wide-eyed expression.

"Um, the dead guy."

"Oh, wow." Jamie appeared to think about the question. "No, I've never heard of him."

"Didn't you go to school here?"

"Oh, no, I moved here after high school," he said. "How about you? Did you move here?"

"Ah, no, I grew up here." She paused, wondering how far to push her questions about people in town. "Do you know Craig Youngblood?"

"Is he dead too?" Jamie asked, eyes even wider, if that were possible.

She sighed inwardly. This was not going to be a good use of her time at *all.*

Chapter 32

LORRAINE

Saturday

Lorraine sipped her coffee, still brooding over the time she'd wasted the night before. Hoping to ambush Craig Youngblood, she'd camped out at the Mucky Duck, a townie bar on Main Street filled with kids—likely underage—smoking like oil refineries and taking turns at the pool table, trying not to hit their heads on the low-hanging Miller Lite lamp above as they lined up their shot. The joint was headed up by a bartender with a mustache befitting a porn star. That fool had had the absolute gall to start off their interaction with insults, which quickly ended once she'd put him in his place. That had been the only redeeming part of the evening, since she hadn't seen Youngblood and had come away smelling like a smokestack. Even the brandy old-fashioned that she'd ordered had been subpar.

How did you fuck up an old-fashioned at a Wisconsin bar?

Lorraine's doorbell rang, and she frowned. Who could that be? If she ignored it, maybe they would go away.

After it rang a second time, she went to the door and opened it, her other hand still holding the coffee mug that read "Tears of My

Enemies." She almost shut it again straight away when she saw who was on the other side, but there was a fat foot in the way now.

"Marjorie," Lorraine said, pulling the door open again and kicking at Marjorie's tennie-clad foot to dislodge it from her threshold.

"You gonna invite me in for a coffee?" Marjorie Rupp asked, ignoring the abuse to her extremity.

"No."

"Aw, come on. I'll bet you've still got some in the pot." Marjorie was already stepping inside, and Lorraine only had moments to decide how far she was willing to let this go.

Shit. She already had a body in the freezer, and she really should refrain from killing someone else while there was an unsolved homicide in town. Not to mention, she'd already committed one impulse murder this week. It really was best to get organized and plan things well ahead of time. You were less likely to get caught—proven by the fact that she was still walking free.

Lorraine grudgingly led Marjorie to her kitchen, then went to the cabinet and pulled out a mug that read "Unwanted Guest," filled it from her Mr. Coffee carafe, and handed it to Marjorie. The woman read the mug, smirked, and proceeded to take a seat at the breakfast nook table that Lorraine had just vacated. Stale cigarette smoke wafted from Marjorie's long brown cardigan pulled over a brown-and-orange floral sack that apparently doubled as a dress.

"Make yourself at home." The dryness of her tone made it very clear that this was not sincere in the slightest.

Marjorie made a show of looking around, her small eyes taking in everything and adding it up. She leaned back in the wood chair. "Nice place you got here. Bob left you pretty well set up."

That rankled. Lorraine had always been self-sufficient. It was one of the very first things she'd learned in life. "What makes you think Bob had anything to do with this?"

Marjorie scoffed. "Newspapers can't pay this good." She nodded at the table. "And this here table set cost at least three, four hundred bucks new, at a place like Marshall Field's."

In her mind, she imagined hitting Marjorie over the head with a cast-iron pan and found that it was satisfying. But alas, one more pleasure she had to deny herself.

For the moment, anyway.

"So, what have you learned about my brother's murder?" Marjorie asked.

"What makes you think I've learned anything?" Lorraine was less hostile now, more curious.

Marjorie drank more of her coffee, then reached into her peeling faux-leather purse and pulled out a pack of Virginia Slims.

"You're not smoking in here." She really *would* kill the woman if she lit up one of those cancer sticks.

"Nah, I just like to have one in my mouth. I won't light it." Marjorie did exactly that, sticking a long cigarette into the side of her mouth, then let it hang there. Lorraine couldn't take her eyes from it—it sort of bobbled when she spoke. Marjorie even managed to drink coffee around it, which seemed its own sort of magic.

"My brother," Marjorie prompted.

"Right. What makes you think I know anything?"

Marjorie rolled her eyes. "Everyone in town has seen you trailing after that detective, asking questions."

"I only ran into her the one time. It was a coincidence." Lorraine refused to acknowledge she had been following the detective around town.

"And coming to my place."

"That was with the chief." Why wasn't this conversation over already?

"How'd he die?" Marjorie asked in the same tone of voice that she had asked everything else, and Lorraine did respect that. Some.

"He drowned."

"On dry land, huh?"

"That's why it's a *murder investigation*, Marjorie."

"Just double-checking that it was." Marjorie drank some more coffee, the cigarette bobbing but still not interfering with her beverage consumption. Why wasn't it soaked?

"So why are you poking into it? Why follow around the detective and watch her ask questions?"

Lorraine shrugged. "I'm writing an article for *The Chronicle*."

Marjorie's eyes narrowed. "That can't be all. There's gotta be an angle. Something in it for you."

"Writing an article isn't enough? Educating the public?"

Marjorie continued to sip and glare.

"Fine. I was thinking that if I did a good enough job on this, showed them that I could be a real investigative journalist, maybe even solve this murder before the cops, then I could give up writing that silly column and be a full-time reporter." Luckily, this lie came off the tongue easily—she could lie like breathing. It was one of the first skills she'd honed as a child, like tying a shoe.

Marjorie studied her, then nodded. "Okay. That makes sense. You have any idea who might have done it?"

Lorraine gave a quick shake of her head. "I know it had something to do with Julian Baker, but he skipped town." She shrugged. "Maybe he did it."

Marjorie slurped up some more coffee. "Julian was dealing. I'm not surprised things caught up with him." She appeared to think about it a bit. "It might make sense that Baker killed Doug. They were friends in high school, but shit changes when you're an adult."

Lorraine wouldn't know, but she nodded agreeably. With any luck, Marjorie would spread word around town that Baker had killed her brother and then split town. If she and the rest of the gossip mill believed it, well, then Lorraine was in the clear.

She didn't want to waste time keeping an eye on Marjorie, but the woman was getting to be a nuisance. She'd best not pop up again, or Lorraine couldn't be held responsible for where the woman ended up.

Chapter 33

MIKE

Saturday

Her "date" with Jamie the night before had been a complete bust, and a waste of a couple of hours. She'd tried to cut it short, but Jamie had insisted on a second drink, and she hadn't had the heart to tell him no. At least she'd learned that Jamie hadn't in fact known about her dog—he'd just been trying to sell his porno dog biscuits. So he wasn't stalking her. Probably. But that second drink meant by the time they'd gotten out of Café Carpe, it was too late to either see her pops or talk to anyone else on the case. And she'd tried, boy had she tried, but she hadn't spotted Sharity Baker or Craig Youngblood either out on the town or at their own places.

She would *love* to know what either of them had been up to last night, but cruising around town hadn't given her any ideas.

It had given her some theories, though, and she'd added them to her chalkboard when she got home, with little asterisks. The first, and her current favorite, was that Baker had offed Rupp, dumped him on Mrs. H.'s lawn, and then taken off. The chief had said that Baker had seemed real surprised that Rupp was investigating him, but that didn't mean it was true. Everything the chief said had to be taken with a grain of salt, *especially* concerning an interview he'd done without supervision.

The only problem with her theory was she couldn't figure out why Baker would leave Rupp on Mrs. Highsmith's lawn. Dropping a body seemed like a message, but why leave Mrs. H. a message? The old lady was a busybody and a pain in the ass, but she wasn't a drug dealer.

Wait, was she? Mike only considered that for a second before having a good chuckle. God, the very *idea* of that.

Anyway, she couldn't see the connection, although she'd run the scenario through her head a couple of different ways just to make sure.

Okay, what if Baker had left Rupp there as a warning to the paper? That could be, right? She took a sip of her morning coffee, thought about it some more, then nodded and added it to the board. She liked that and would ask Mrs. Highsmith about what the paper had on Baker next chance she got.

Mike glanced at her watch—she needed to stop by the office to check for messages and to see if Hannigan's officers had learned anything from Baker's neighbors. She might as well take the time to call down to Chicago, too, see if they had any scuttlebutt about Mrs. Highsmith. It would be nice to be armed with something when she confronted Mrs. H. again.

It was quiet at the station, not a soul around to notice her charging through. There were no messages on her desk, either, so she shrugged and sat down, then picked up the phone. It took some time, but she finally was transferred to the right department, where a very bored secretary took down the information. She gave Mrs. Highsmith's name and DOB, as well as her maiden name. "I'm looking for anything you have on her, please."

"Sure, sure. Is it urgent?"

Was it? Not really, but records didn't need to know that. "Yes, it is."

There was some scribbling on the other end. "Maybe by the end of next week, okay? We'll call ya."

She thanked the woman and hung up. Fingers crossed they'd find something. There had to be *some* kind of record on Mrs. H., although Mike would be sure to talk with her before that report came in.

Next on the list was the one storage facility in town. The owner, Stu Calkins, hadn't upgraded the place since he'd built it back in the sixties—it still looked like a series of small pole barns with roll up garage doors. There'd been talk about a rival facility opening on the north side of town, a nicer place with cheaper rates, but rumor had it that Stu snapped up the property, and then those rumors died with the deal. It was still an empty lot—apparently Stu hadn't felt the need to actually *build* another facility.

Stu was in the office watching the Brewers play the Tigers when Mike entered. "Morning, Stu!"

Stu returned her greeting, although his attention never left the game. "What can I do for ya, Mike?"

"I'd like to check your records and see if Julian Baker has a unit here. And if he does, I have a warrant to search it."

"Lookin' for anything in particular?" Stu tore his attention from the baseball game with obvious reluctance and looked at the ledger sitting on the counter.

"Drugs," she said simply.

Stu nodded, running his finger down the page. "Lotta drugs in the area."

"Yeah, I don't know why people aren't more worked up about it."

Stu shrugged. "All them factories closed, maybe folks are looking for a new hobby?"

Yeesh. That was a depressing thought.

Then Stu looked up at her. "Ya know, Baker has been renting a locker since I opened the place. He started small, but about a year ago he upgraded to a larger unit," His finger tapped the ledger.

"That's interesting. What number?"

"Unit forty-two," Stu said. "You need a bolt cutter?"

"Yeah, no, yeah. That would be helpful."

Stu reached under the desk and pulled one out, pausing before passing it over to Mike. "Uh, you need me to cut that for ya? It can be a little tough."

"Nah, I've got it."

Stu clearly didn't believe her but also didn't want to leave the game. "Holler if ya need help. That number should be out through this door and to the right. Second building." He pointed in the general direction.

"Thanks, Stu." She was mildly offended that he'd offered her help since she was clearly stronger than a man pushing seventy with shaky hands. But it wasn't worth offending Stu's dignity to point it out.

She crunched down the gravel walkway between buildings, checking each number until she found the unit she was looking for. It looked like a medium-size space. She bent down with the bolt cutter, and after a minute of struggling with it—it *was* awfully hard to get a good angle—she managed to cut the heavy lock off, using her body weight to put some *oomph* behind it. She set both the lock and the cutter down, then slid the metal door up. It was dim inside, but there was supposed to be electricity in these things now, so she used her Maglite to search the walls for a switch.

Ah! Right there. She flipped it on and looked around the suddenly bright space. Great Gatsby, was Julian Baker dealing drugs. There were four tables set up with glassine baggies and scales for weighing, a big enough operation that she actually whistled. A box of pagers sat off to the side. Since she'd been the department's narco officer, she could tell one table had some crack, another was covered in a white powder that was probably cocaine, and another had a big ole brick of Mary Jane. She couldn't say for sure what was on the last table, but if she had to guess, she'd say heroin. A real diversified portfolio.

She retrieved her Polaroid and snapped photos of everything, then carefully labeled each on the white strip at the bottom with the date, time, and exact location. After photographing everything in sight—without touching anything—she moved toward the back, where a big white chest freezer hunkered down in the corner. The closer she got to it, the more she was aware of the faint hum the thing was giving off. How was it even plugged in? These places didn't usually have outlets. She followed the freezer's plug to the electrical box in the ceiling and saw that Baker had done some splicing into the wiring. It was a real dicey job and honestly could have burned the whole place down from the looks of it.

What could Julian Baker have stashed here that needed to be kept cold? It clearly wasn't drugs. Venison? Baker didn't seem like a hunter, though. And why keep meat here and not at your house?

There was another Master Lock securing the freezer top, smaller this time, but still annoying. Mike retrieved the bolt cutter from where she'd left it outside and came back, then easily snipped through this one. She flipped the lid open, and her jaw dropped when she realized what she was looking at. It was *definitely* not what she was expecting, that was for sure.

It was a body. A frozen one, curled on its side, still wearing a blue polo shirt and acid-washed denim shorts. And if she wasn't mistaken, based on the big frosty ginger mustache, she was looking at Dean Lagerfield—Jamie's cousin.

Chapter 34

LORRAINE

Saturday

Lorraine was about to change into her workout clothes when her phone rang. She was tempted to let it go to the machine, but at the last second she picked up the receiver.

"Hello?"

"Lorraine, it's Chief Schneider."

"Hans, what can I do ya for?"

The chief sounded a little out of breath. "There's another body. Another murder."

Lorraine was certainly pleased to have this information, although she was irritated that she'd already turned in her article on Rupp's murder. Would she have to do more work and write another? "That's too bad. I already turned in my article."

"You could write another! I was also thinking that you could call your contacts. Your *media* contacts." There was a pause. "They were interested when I called, obviously, but they said it would take them some time to get a news crew together. It being Saturday and all. I was hoping you knew someone that could make it up here faster."

Did Schneider really not realize that she wrote for a small regional newspaper? She didn't have an inside line to any of the news stations. Truly, the only person she even knew at *The Chronicle* was her editor, Jim. She did everything by mail or by fax so that she didn't have to go into the "office." The last thing she wanted was coworkers, even if it meant she'd have a little more human interaction on a regular basis. That was exactly what she *didn't* want.

She wasn't lonely, goddammit.

But this second murder was probably related to the first. She should take a look at it. "I'll meet you there. Where am I going?"

"The storage facility off Highway N," Schneider said. "I'm headed there now."

Lorraine didn't waste any time. She grabbed her purse and headed out the door, then pulled up only a few minutes after the chief. This was possible because she had an educated guess about where all the police in town were, and she pushed the Behemoth as fast as she felt like. If they were all at the storage barn like she assumed, there was no one to pull her over and chastise her for blowing through a school zone or running the stop-and-go lights.

So far there was just an ambulance crew and a couple of police cars, one of which looked like Zenoni's unmarked squad—there was a distinctive scratch along the back bumper. Chief Schneider was standing out front expectantly, nearly dancing from foot to foot. "I'm thinking they'll be here any minute," he said.

Lorraine nodded. "I made some phone calls, and I'm sure they will be."

She had not made any phone calls.

Schneider's mustache twitched upward. "I knew you would come through."

She thought about giving the man a lecture on his assumption that all publicity was good publicity, because it was inherently false.

Especially if he was trying to run for that stupid position with the police chief's association. The news cycle—not to mention his fellow police chiefs—was not going to be impressed that Schneider now had two dead bodies on his hands and zero suspects. It was something he should be trying to keep out of the papers, not make headline news with, but she decided not to waste her breath. He'd called the papers because he smelled an opportunity to get his face on television.

"I'm going inside."

"You're not going to wait here with me?" Schneider asked, still scanning the highway in both directions.

"I'd like to see for myself what you're about to tell the world."

Schneider looked confused, so she clarified. "I'm going to go take a quick look inside, so I can help you with your statement."

His face cleared as he nodded, although he'd already gone back to scanning for news trucks.

Lorraine left the chief there and went inside the storage facility, passing the ambulance on her way in. There were two EMTs sitting in the front, one reading a newspaper and the other catching a little shut-eye. Neither so much as glanced her way as she passed by them. She supposed they were just waiting for the go-ahead to remove the body and transport it to the hospital.

Once outside, it was easy to follow the noise down the gravel corridor to her right, and she stopped just outside the open door of Julian Baker's unit. Stu Calkins was standing on the other side of the opening, arms crossed, watching the activity inside. He gave her a nod but said nothing, which she appreciated.

Inside, Sergeant Hannigan and another officer were dusting for prints at a table liberally covered with tiny plastic bags and a smorgasbord of drugs. Lorraine looked around—there were a lot of fucking drugs in this room, but she didn't think she could get away with pocketing any. Especially since Zenoni had likely taken pictures of it all and would know if something was missing. A real shame. Free drugs were the best drugs.

Zenoni was currently taking pictures of an open chest freezer with the department's Polaroid. There were only the three cops in the room—Lorraine supposed the department didn't really have the resources for anything more than what they were doing right now, and there was no need for crowd control. Not until their chief called as many members of the media to the scene as he possibly could. Then they could radio another couple of patrol cars over to contain the lookie-loos.

"You trying to get this done before your boss calls every reporter in a hundred-mile radius to show up?" Lorraine's voice was loud in the enclosed metal space.

All three officers jumped. Hannigan and the day shift officer both took a brief look at her, then went back to what they were doing, but Zenoni's brows gathered into a storm before she came forward, dodging the drug-laden tables. "What are you doing here, Mrs. Highsmith?"

"Your boss called me."

Zenoni didn't respond, just pursed her lips.

"He's looking for news coverage. I qualify." Lorraine walked into the unit, passing the tables with only a glance, and went straight to the freezer. Zenoni tried to block her, but she was nimble and peering over the edge before the detective could stop her. The dead man was curled on his side, red mustache frosty. If she leaned far enough over the freezer's edge, Lorraine thought she could see a dark hole on the man's chest. She was careful not to touch anything, though. She was always mindful about keeping her fingerprints to herself.

"Oh, he's good and dead. Pretty frozen by the looks of him." Lorraine felt a pang of respect for Julian Baker, which was unexpected. But it looked like he had a similar MO, and it was only right to acknowledge that. "Do you know who he is?"

Zenoni rolled her eyes. "Of course, I know who he is, but you need to get out. You're contaminating a crime scene."

"I'm careful," Lorraine said, but she'd seen enough, so she meandered back toward the entrance. "Why don't you tell me who the stiff is? You know I'll just ask your boss."

"I'm sure you will," Zenoni said, arms crossed, waiting by the doorway to make sure that she actually left.

Shit. Looked like the detective hadn't taken Lorraine's advice and gone on that date yet. She wouldn't be this owly if she had.

But there were still plenty of reasons for her to be happy about this current development. Now that Julian Baker had a body in a freezer, regardless of who it was, Baker's "disappearance" truly looked like he'd gotten scared and split town. It threw suspicion off her and the body in her own freezer. Which was Julian's, of course.

Chapter 35

LORRAINE

Saturday

Lorraine should get a goddamn medal for self-control these days. Of course, Zenoni was still looming like a gargoyle at the locker entrance, watching her, so there wasn't an opportunity to pocket any baggies on her way out the door, and her fingers still itched with the urge.

Back at Stu's office, she found Chief Schneider with his official police hat on, talking to the two news crews that had shown up. Not bad, really—both of them were bigger stations from the city, and there was even an extra man, probably from the newspaper. Apparently one death in a small town wasn't enough to send out a news crew, but when you combined it with a second body in a freezer, then it was worth sending out the troops.

"The victim's name was Dean Lagerfield," Schneider said into the microphones, leaning forward a little. Lorraine was tickled—she hadn't even had to ask for that little nugget.

"Are these murders connected?" a reporter in the back of the little crowd called out.

"Yes, we do believe the two murders are connected, and we are doing everything in our power to find the man or men responsible," Schneider said.

"Do you have any suspects?" a female reporter with shoulder pads like a linebacker asked.

Schneider blinked once. "We have the investigation under control."

"That doesn't answer the question," a man with a notepad said. "Do you have any suspects? I'm going to guess you don't have anyone in custody."

"This is still an active investigation," Schneider said, defensive.

"Obviously," the man said. He turned to his colleagues. "They don't have any suspects."

Schneider bristled. "Of course, we have suspects, what kind of operation do you think we're running? We have suspects."

Shoulder Pads jumped on this. "Then who are they?"

As much as she was enjoying watching the sharks circle the chum who'd called them there, Lorraine needed to get back to her place. Her morning coffee was taking effect, and she wasn't about to ask Stu Calkins if he had a public restroom.

Back home in the comfort of her own bathroom, Lorraine heard the phone ring. She washed her hands and listened while the answering machine whirred and picked up the message from whoever had called. There was some noise, but it was muffled. Curious, she walked into the kitchen, where the machine rested on her Formica countertop, and hit play.

The person on the other end of the line chuckled, a soft laugh, impossible to tell if it was a man or a woman. There was a beat of silence before they hung up.

What the fuck?

She listened to the message one more time, then dialed star sixty-nine, a little-known feature she'd recently learned her telephone company provided. For a cost, of course. A mechanical voice read her the number that had just left her a message. She swung the plastic rotary dial around and waited while it rang.

No answer. No human answer, anyway. There was a click, and then a message played. *You have reached Julian Baker's answering service. Leave a message.*

Lorraine did not leave a message.

A quick call to four-one-one, and Lorraine had all the landline numbers registered to the Baker household. The number she had just dialed was not one of them. So what other phone did Baker have? And who was using it? She did not like to be toyed with, and she didn't like not knowing the full layout of Baker's setup. He didn't have an office; his wife had said that. But did Baker have one that Sharity didn't know about? It was possible—she doubted Sharity knew about the storage unit with the drugs and the corpse either.

Where would Baker have kept an office? And why didn't the operator have it listed?

Lorraine decided this called for a trip to see Baker's side piece, Carrie Ann, since she'd been the last one to see Julian alive. Besides Lorraine, of course.

Red Garlock was behind the counter of the Amoco again, smoking his life away. Lorraine's lips twisted, but she pushed a question past them all the same. "Carrie Ann in today?"

Garlock shook his head. "She was nice to look at, but I fired her ass. Too many times she just didn't show up. Can't afford that kind of scenery."

"You're a pig."

Red's eyes widened. "What did you say to me?"

Lorraine leaned across the counter and enunciated clearly. "You. Are. A. Pig." Red's face turned the color of his moniker.

Pleased with this result, she turned and walked out while the man sputtered. There was no reason to call the man out, but she was frustrated with how things were going this morning, and it was nice to take that out on an unsuspecting bystander. Red deserved it anyway. The man had a reputation for saying truly disgusting things to his underage female employees. And while Carrie Ann wasn't underage, she was at least thirty years younger than Garlock. Good enough.

Feeling better, Lorraine decided to head to Carrie Ann's apartment and see if the girl was in. It was unlikely that she'd already found a new job, so Lorraine was feeling good about finding her at home.

After a few sturdy knocks on the apartment door, Lorraine was rewarded by Carrie Ann opening it. The young woman actually looked quite put together in a gray suit jacket with thick shoulder pads and a tight matching skirt. Her hair was curled to the ceiling, and her pastel makeup was done with a heavy hand. Lorraine had been expecting another neon unitard and leg warmers, so this professional-looking outfit was a surprise.

"Are you going somewhere?"

Carrie Ann nodded. "I got an interview for a new job at the Bottle Stop."

Lorraine shook her head. "Don't go. It's no skin off my nose either way, but the owner is even worse than Red Garlock, so you're better off collecting unemployment."

Carrie Ann looked uncertain, then sighed and opened the door more fully, letting Lorraine inside while slinging her purse on the dining room table and kicking off her black heels. "I don't want to work for another one of those."

"Smart girl." She leaned against the table, recalling how nasty the furniture was and not wanting to subject her clothing to unknown substances yet again. The glass-and-chrome table seemed the safest bet. "Now, the reason I'm here. You were the last one to see Julian . . . before he left town."

Carrie Ann's eyes welled with tears. Shit, had she actually cared about that dipshit? That was surprising. Lorraine also had to be careful—she'd almost said that Carrie Ann was the last one to see him alive.

"Do you need a tissue? He's only missing, you know. Took off."

Carrie Ann wiped her eyes, smearing a gob of mascara across her cheek, and shook her head.

"Okay, my question is, Does Julian have an extra phone?"

Carrie Ann cocked her head. "What do you mean?"

Lorraine needed to be careful here too. "Did he have a phone number that didn't go to his house?"

Carrie Ann's eyes welled with tears, but she managed to answer all the same. "He had a couple a beepers, is that what you mean?"

Lorraine shook her head. "No, a regular number. One that didn't go to his house but went to an answering service."

To her credit, Carrie Ann appeared to think hard. "He said somethin' about a car phone once, but I've never seen one. I wasn't even sure that was a real thing—that's like something out of a sci-fi movie."

A car phone. Of course. Lorraine mentally berated herself for not thinking of that.

This also told her a couple of things. First, Carrie Ann had never seen a car phone in real life, which was very much a real thing, although one was awfully expensive. And while this meant she might not recognize one when she saw it, they were pretty hard to miss, bulky as they were. Second, it was pretty easy to assume that Baker wasn't keeping it in his fancy little midlife crisis or any of the other cars that Carrie Ann had planted her ass inside.

"Did you ever see Julian driving an old Datsun?"

Carrie Ann's plucked eyebrows pulled together. "No, I didn't ever see him in an old car. Like, I can't even imagine him in one."

Well, maybe his wife had. Lorraine needed to speak with Julian's widow again.

Not that Sharity knew that she was a widow. It was unfortunate that she'd need to wait—was it seven years?—in order to have Julian declared dead.

Not her concern, though.

Out of curiosity, she had one final question. "Did Julian ever hit you?"

Carrie Ann looked surprised, but she shook her head. "He raised his hand a few times when he was annoyed, but he never actually swung. It was just sort of a game."

"That is a seriously stupid game. Don't ever put up with that shit again, you hear me?" Lorraine said firmly. Carrie Ann looked surprised but cocked her head and then nodded.

It was a surprising response, but Lorraine still had no regrets about taking Baker out, even if he wasn't a woman beater—or wasn't one yet. As far as she was concerned, he was close enough—he *had* taken a swing, even if he hadn't made contact. They always started with a raised fist and escalated later—at least that had been her experience when she was a kid.

She pushed off from the table and was headed for the apartment door when she was stopped by a question from Carrie Ann. "Mrs. Highsmith, where should I get a job?"

Lorraine turned, incredulous. "How should I know?"

"You're an advice columnist. I thought you would have some advice." Carrie Ann was such a pathetic figure that Lorraine actually stopped and thought about it. She almost asked what the girl was good at, but she already knew the answer to that, which was not much. "Try waitressing or learn how to bartend. With looks like yours, you'll clean up on tips."

Carrie Ann's face brightened. "Thanks, Mrs. Highsmith!"

She shook her head and left. God help anyone served a drink by that girl.

Sharity Baker was Lorraine's next stop. She checked her watch and sighed. She was supposed to meet her trainer at the gym in an hour, so she needed to make this fast. She didn't give a shit about making Cynthia wait, but she did like to get her full hour in since she was paying for it.

She rang the bell at the Baker house, but there was no answer. She paused for only a second—really, she didn't have time for this bullshit—and rang again. Peering through the frosted sidelight, she saw that Sharity was finally coming to the door.

Sharity's mouth was open, and she looked ready to cuss someone out, but deflated when she found Lorraine on the stoop.

"Mrs. Highsmith. I thought it was Detective Mike again."

Lorraine thought it was weird to call Zenoni that, informal, but not quite informal enough? She let it pass. "The detective's been by a lot, has she?"

"Enough that I'd like her to quit," Sharity admitted. "She really has terrible timing."

Lorraine didn't need to know what that meant, but she could guess. She also got straight down to it. "I just spoke with your husband's mistress."

"Oh? How's she doing?" Sharity seemed sincere about this, and Lorraine didn't quite know what to make of that.

"She's upset, but I told her Julian just took off so there was no need to be so worked up."

Sharity shrugged. "She's a sweet kid."

"Does Julian have a car phone?"

Sharity frowned. "I haven't seen it in a long time, but I know he used to." She rolled her eyes. "When he got it, he would call anyone and everyone from it just to brag, you know? Even though it was way expensive. But I haven't seen it around in forever."

"Have you seen an old Datsun?"

"You know, Detective Mike mentioned one of those as well, but I've never seen it." Sharity paused. "Do you want to come in and look for the phone?"

Lorraine looked at her watch. Dammit, she really didn't have time to poke around this woman's house. "Can you look around for the phone, or better yet, a phone bill, and let me know if you come across it?" The brick masquerading as a phone had likely been stolen from

Baker's shitty old Datsun, the car he used for his drug operation. But a bill from that number could prove useful, even if it wouldn't tell her who had made the call.

Sharity nodded. "Is it important?"

Lorraine held her gaze. "It really is."

Chapter 36

MIKE

Saturday

Sweet fancy Moses, Dean's corpse complicated a few things. Although it did seem to support Mike's theory that Baker had killed Rupp—once you killed one person it seemed like a real slippery slope to killing more. Especially in the business Baker was clearly in. And with a full freezer, he would have needed to dump Rupp, although Mrs. H.'s lawn was still a weird place to do it.

Shitty shit. She should have asked Mrs. Highsmith if the paper was doing a piece about Baker. Mrs. H. had been right there, but with the excitement of the body, it had totally slipped her mind. She pulled out her notebook and made a note to follow up on that.

As for Dean Lagerfield, it would be really easy to ask around at the Mucky Duck and hear that Dean was dealing drugs—she would bet money that was why he was in this freezer. Lagerfield probably worked for Baker, and they had a falling out. Mike would of course keep tugging this thread, but she didn't think there'd be any surprises. *A life of crime ends badly*, as her pops used to say.

She rubbed her forehead. Since Dean was frozen solid, it was going to be almost impossible for Dr. Schneider to give a time of death.

Which meant Mike needed to build a timeline of Lagerfield's comings and goings and figure out the last person to see this dude alive. That was her best bet for pinpointing when Dean bit it. Even though Baker was the most obvious suspect here, Baker wasn't around to question or better yet, arrest. She'd have to be clever.

After she got a running start on that, she needed to find out if Baker had any guns. Since he was a drug dealer, chances were real good that he did, but had he gotten them legally? Probably not. But she'd bet good money one of them had been used to kill Dean. If she was lucky, Dr. Schneider would find the bullet, and then the state crime lab could do forensic testing on it. Fingers crossed it was still inside Lagerfield, and then she could get as close as possible to proving that Julian Baker was her killer.

Wherever he was.

It was already past lunch by the time Mike and her team finished bagging and tagging the storage unit. She was a little overwhelmed by how much paperwork this was going to generate and how long it was going to take her to type it up, but she didn't trust anyone else to do it. Could she get out of making the notification to Dean's mom, though? She turned to Hannigan with hopeful eyes.

"No, I will not make the notification for you," Sergeant Hannigan said.

She deflated. "How did you know that's what I was going to ask?"

Hannigan shook his head. "Because they're the worst. Shit like that needs a woman's touch, so you gotta do it. You women folk are better at that kinda thing."

She bit back a choice reply, but Hannigan didn't notice. "This is gonna be a lot of paperwork, though. I can have my guy start on some of it—listing the drugs in evidence and whatnot."

She swallowed both her indignation and her reservations. "Thank you, Sergeant. I owe you one."

Hannigan nodded, but didn't say anything else, instead ambling over to Officer Patoka to let him know how he'd be spending the rest of the day—inventorying everything in the unit. From the look on Patoka's face, he wasn't thrilled, but he nodded—he'd do it. And in the meantime, Mike could get the notification over with and then back to the investigation. This criminal treasure trove was exciting, sure, but it hadn't distracted her from the fact that she had very little time before that drop happened. Although she had a *real* good idea about what was being dropped—this storage unit was like a neon sign. But she still didn't know *where* it would happen.

Instead of heading to the station to look up Dean's next of kin, Mike's car pointed itself to the nursing home facility on the outskirts of town, and she found herself in the parking lot staring at the building before she even realized where she was. It was a squat redbrick building, the entrance flanked by white pillars that should have looked classy but felt forced when you noticed the old folks in wheelchairs parked in front of them, staring into the void while fresh air ruffled their wispy tufts of hair.

She walked past the scattered old people, doing her best not to imagine them as zombies, and signed in at the front desk.

"Been a while, eh, Detective?" The receptionist was kind of a bitch, a prom queen that had graduated a year behind her. Andrea Walters. Mike didn't take offense, though—she figured Andrea had probably pictured a different, fancier life for herself and was just bitter about where she'd ended up. So Mike smiled instead.

"I'll see myself back."

Andrea huffed, and Mike walked down the hallway, her footsteps echoing against the gold-and-white linoleum. She avoided looking into the other rooms, with their doors wide open, the patients staring dully at bulky televisions or simply the wall. It was too depressing. When she came to her dad's room, she knocked on the gray doorframe, poking her head around the corner. He was sitting in a stuffed chair by the window, gazing out.

"Hey, Pops. How are you?"

His head turned and he saw her, but he didn't say anything, the confused film covering his formerly sharp gaze holding tight. She went in and sat on the bed. He regarded her for a few moments, then looked back out the window.

"I caught a big case, Pops. Two murders now." He didn't respond, but she filled him in on the cases anyway. Her heart ached, missing the days when her pops had served as a sounding board, pointing her in logical directions on whatever she was working on. Now he was a husk of a person, a hollow pistachio shell, and she wasn't sure the words were filling him, touching him in any way.

But she kept on pouring until she was empty herself. She sighed. "Thanks for listening, Pops. I'll bring some Mickey D's next time I stop by, okay?" There wasn't so much as a flicker, but she kissed him on the side of his liver-spotted head and made her way to the door. She stopped to adjust the *Maltese Falcon* movie poster on the wall first—it was a little crooked, and it had been one of his favorites. They'd watched it together more times than she could even count. While she fussed with the frame, she blinked hard a couple of times, then took a deep breath to compose herself before stepping out of the room.

At the end of the hallway, she caught sight of Carla pushing a woman in a wheelchair. She hurried forward, just in time to see Carla push the chair out into the garden at the back of the building. Huh. She'd never seen Carla here before. Who did the secretary know here?

Mike paused at the desk before heading out. "Hey, Andrea, who is Carla Robinson here to see?"

"Uh, that's none of your business, Mike."

"C'mon."

Andrea rolled her eyes and turned back to her bodice-ripping romance novel. "Fine. It's her mom, I think."

Kinda strange that Carla never mentioned they both had parents in this place. But then, the chief's secretary *was* super private. And this wasn't a place you put your folks when things were going well.

Feeling both better and worse, Mike stopped by the station, made a few calls, and got the address for Dean Lagerfield's mom, who lived on a farm outside town. Apparently, Dean had been living there until he got his own place on Carriage Drive a couple of months back.

Since making the notification to Dean's mom was the thing Mike dreaded most, she needed to get it out of the way first. Even knowing she was doing the right thing, her car's speed crept slower and slower the farther she got into the country. The city of Sheboygan Bay ended sort of abruptly—there were neighborhoods with houses stacked on top of one another, until suddenly there just weren't any. Once you passed the last clump of new-construction shoebox houses, it was rolling green hills on either side of the highway, interrupted by corn fields and dairy farms or the occasional burst of lush forest, cool and dark. Which was where deer liked to lie in wait before hurling themselves in front of oncoming cars.

In much too short a time, Mike was crunching down the long gravel driveway leading to the Lagerfield farm. The red wooden barn was falling down, the roof sagging in more than one place, although the roof on the house looked new. Half the rambling farmhouse's weathered wood siding had been recently replaced with vinyl, although it looked like the job had been abandoned midstream, a few piles of siding lying in the grass next to the porch. Would the crew come back to finish the job, or had the Lagerfields run out of money?

Mike trudged up the stairs, bracing herself for what she had to do. She paused, but Mrs. Lagerfield was at the screen door before she could even raise her hand to knock. From the look on her face, Mrs. Lagerfield already knew that something was wrong—people often did when a cop showed up at their door.

All things considered, Mrs. Lagerfield took the news pretty well. She only cried a little and asked a lot of questions, which Mike did her best to answer. The detective stayed while she called a friend to come sit with her, and Mike made sure the friend's car was pulling into the driveway before she made her escape.

Once she closed her car door, relief washed over her, her shoulders and spine slowly releasing in a waterfall of unclenching muscles. The worst was over. Now she just had to solve a second murder, get some justice for Mrs. Lagerfield as well as Marjorie Rupp.

No pressure. Super chill.

Mrs. Lagerfield hadn't seen or heard from her son in nearly six days, which she claimed was unusual. She said Dean checked in with her regularly—never going more than two days without a call or a visit. That narrowed the window for when Dean was killed, at least. Mike had a whole page in her notebook dedicated to figuring out Dean's timeline, and this gave her a decent starting point.

On the way back to the station, Mike stopped by her place to let Zeus out real quick. She'd played hooky the night before, so she would make up for that tonight, working as late as she physically could. But poor Zeus shouldn't suffer because of that. She'd let him out now and then see if her neighbor would let him out later. She didn't like to ask Linda to do it—last time, Linda had thumbed through her mail, leaving the pile askew on the counter—but sometimes you had to ask for help. Like during a murder investigation that had suddenly blossomed into two. Passing through the kitchen to the back door, she noticed that the light on her answering machine was blinking red. She hit play while she opened the back door, Zeus rushing past her to relieve himself and sniff around for a few minutes.

There was a whirr, and the first message played.

"Hey, girl, it's Steph. Wondering if you've got time to hit the rink tonight or maybe next weekend? Call me."

Man, she'd love nothing better than to throw her skates on and spend a couple of hours whizzing around the rink, working on her footwork and burning off some stress. But she *really* couldn't afford two nights of hooky in a row. There was too much riding on this case.

The next message started playing. "Hi, Mike! It's Jamie. I had such a rad time last night. I was wondering if you would like to get dinner tomorrow night? It would be pretty sweet if you did. Call me back! Bye!"

Ugh, she hadn't thought Jamie would want a second date. The first had been a really mediocre date, by her standards, anyway.

Was that fair, though? Or was it because she hadn't learned anything from him? Ugh, probably.

Double ugh, should she call and tell him about Dean? No, he'd hear it from someone in town, right? Christ, she didn't want to do another notification. One was bad enough.

Maybe if she ignored the message, he'd take a hint and go away.

Wait. Jamie couldn't be *involved* in some way, could he?

Chapter 37

MIKE

Saturday

On the way to the station, Mike rolled around the possibility that Jamie was involved in the local drug scene. The bakery would make a good front, and his cousin was obviously involved, so maybe he was too. It also made sense why he'd want to date her, in a weird, keep-your-enemies-close kind of way.

But was he smart enough to pull any of it off? That was what she couldn't decide. Could the whole big-dumb-ox thing be a ploy?

She pulled into the station, made some notes about Jamie in her notebook, and then went inside, hoping to find Sergeant Hannigan. She needed an extra set of hands to search Lagerfield's place, and with luck Hannigan would pull one of his guys off patrol to do it. Fifteen minutes later she was back in her car, having both successfully avoided her boss and convinced Hannigan to send Patoka over to help her. She gave herself a high five, which was just slapping her hands together, then checked to see if anyone had seen that.

Nope, she was in the clear.

Mike already had a grisly picture in her head of what had happened to Dean the bartender, but she wanted to keep an open mind and make sure the facts matched her imagination. She could spin all the crazy theories she wanted, but they really needed to match the facts. If they ever did find Baker, she needed to have a solid case so they could prosecute his sorry ass.

Officer Patoka met her in the parking lot, and they walked into the apartment building together. "What do you think we'll find?" Patoka asked.

Mike shrugged. "More drugs. But hopefully the name of his supplier too." They headed down the dank hallway—this building was even more depressing than the one Carrie Ann Williams lived in, and that was saying something.

When they came to Dean's apartment, she paused. Was that a noise in there? She cautiously put her hand to the knob and found that it turned easily. Before opening the door, she shared a meaningful look with Patoka, and they both pulled their weapons. She took a deep breath to try to calm the sudden shake in her hands from the adrenaline dump, then counted down, mouthing the words so Patoka could see, and on three pushed the door open as both cops burst through with their guns pointed. "Freeze!" she shouted at the figure standing in the living room.

The woman's hands went up, and then she slowly turned around.

Mike let out an unsteady puff of air. "Grace Baker. What the *fuck* are you doing here?" This was a rhetorical question—she still had her weapon out and aimed squarely at Grace. "Patoka, I'm going to holster my weapon and search the suspect."

"I've got you," Patoka responded, keeping his gun right where it was.

She holstered her weapon. "Keep your hands where I can see them, Grace."

"I cannot believe you're going to search me," she screeched. "You know who I am."

"I sure do, Grace, and you're a suspect."

Grace continued making outraged noises while Mike patted her down—thoroughly—even ensuring she did the crotch, which was always the most awkward part of a search. But it was also a great place to hide weapons, so you had to overcome the uncomfortable feelings and just get in there.

But Grace was clean. Of weapons anyway. "Sit in that chair, Grace," Mike ordered, pointing at a nearby camp chair.

"This is ridiculous," Grace protested. "I'm in my boyfriend's apartment. I have a key and every right to be here." But she did as she was told.

Mike grabbed Grace's purse from the coffee table and searched it, but there was nothing interesting. She put the purse back down and took a moment since she felt a little lightheaded now. Any time she pulled her weapon, it was supercharged, physically and emotionally, and it could take a while to bring the nervous system back down after a big adrenaline dump.

"She's clean," Mike said, and Patoka holstered his weapon as well.

"I hope you have a warrant, Detective," Grace said, still saucy despite having had two weapons drawn on her.

Mike held up the key Mrs. Lagerfield had given her. "I have a key."

Grace huffed. "Well, so do I."

Mike found Grace's attitude incredibly grating, especially for someone now considered a suspect in this drug ring. At the very *least*. Then she realized that Grace probably hadn't heard the news about Dean. She took a deep breath to calm herself, eyes closing briefly. She found her patience and regarded Grace.

Mike perched awkwardly in the chair opposite Grace, sitting forward at an awkward angle to make room for her holster. Dang, this was uncomfortable. Maybe she should get one of those under-the-arm holster jobbies, instead.

"Why are you sitting down?" Grace asked. She was noticeably less combative.

"You were seeing Dean?"

She nodded. "A couple months now. Why?"

Mike pursed her lips. She really hadn't expected to do another notification, so she put it off for another few seconds. "When's the last time you saw him?"

"Why?" Grace narrowed her eyes.

Mike simply tilted her head, and Grace sighed. "Fine, I think two nights ago?"

Mike squinted. That would be after Baker skipped town. Was that right? She pulled out her notepad and checked. Yeah, no, yeah, it looked like Baker was already gone, but maybe he'd stayed behind to clean up some things before disappearing completely? Like relocating his vehicle. It was weird that he hadn't gone back inside his house for anything, though—at least not according to his wife. But maybe he'd had stuff stashed in the storage locker.

Mike was quiet, thinking through the timeline, and Grace piped up again. "Detective Zenoni, what's going on?"

She couldn't hold back her soft sigh. "I'm so sorry to tell you this, Grace, but Dean was found dead this morning." Her voice was gentle.

Grace's eyes filled with tears. She shook her head, covering her mouth with one hand. "No. It can't be."

"It is. I'm very sorry." Mike's voice was soft. She nearly reached out a hand but kept them in her lap, tensely folded together.

While this was happening, Officer Patoka had quietly excused himself to begin searching Dean's bedroom. He stood in the doorway, just in her peripheral. "Detective, when you get a moment," he said quietly.

Mike nodded but stayed where she was.

"How . . . how did it happen?" Grace asked tearfully.

"I can't say at this time, but I'm very sorry for your loss. Can I call someone for you?"

Grace shook her head again. "I just need a second."

The detective nodded. "Of course. Take your time. I'll be just a moment, but don't touch anything." She thought about telling Grace that she would have to come to the station later to give a statement but decided she could give Grace a minute to collect herself first. "Excuse me." Mike managed to extricate herself from the chair—not easy, since the aluminum arm hooked on her gun when she stood up, taking the whole chair up with her—and went to the bedroom where Patoka was waiting. "Whatcha got?"

Patoka pointed to a few shoeboxes he'd pulled from the closet.

She frowned. "Okay, so Dean liked shoes."

Patoka flipped the top of a Nike box open with a gloved finger. "Ahh, but they're not shoes, Detective."

The blue shoebox was stuffed with baggies of drugs. Marijuana, from the looks of it. Patoka flipped open the other boxes, revealing more baggies with more drugs. This was nothing unexpected, but it was nice to see that the man was organized and hadn't left the stuff just sitting out in plain sight. The bins were even labeled—*MJ*, *Coke*, *Uppers*—she did appreciate a man who labeled.

"Nice find."

"Thank you. But that's not all," Patoka said. He moved closer to the "bed," which was really just a mattress on the floor, not even a box spring. At least it had sheets and a comforter on it—probably courtesy of his mother. Patoka didn't touch anything, but he motioned for her to come closer. "Look what I found here."

It was a gun. Lying neatly on Lagerfield's mattress. It could have had a bow on it.

"Epic find," she said. "But you buried the lede there, Patoka."

"Could it be the one Lagerfield was killed with?"

"It could be, but that doesn't make a ton of sense. Why would the gun that killed Dean be lying on his own bed, not where his body was found?"

Patoka shrugged. "You're the detective." There was only the slightest hint of a snide tone there, so she let it slide. Her mind was busy anyway, working things through.

It didn't look as though Dean had been killed here, although they should do a thorough sweep of the place. So where had Dean been shot?

And why would the killer return the gun here but not take the boxes of drugs with him?

And how was Grace Baker involved?

This case was nothing but unknowns piled on top of more unknowns. A pyramid of mysteries.

Chapter 38

MIKE

Saturday

Mike went back into the front room to let Grace leave, figuring enough time had passed that Grace had pulled herself together. What she found, however, was not a quietly grieving girlfriend, but a woman trying to slip out the front door without being seen.

"Miss Baker, I'll need to look in your purse before you leave."

"How dare you! What are you insinuating?" Grace was sputtering, but a red flush was creeping up her neck. This was all bluster—she was guilty of something. Mike's first instincts were right. Again.

"If you don't have anything, it's not a big deal, is it?"

Grace had her bulky denim purse tucked under her arm, but Mike strolled over and tugged at the strap. Grace resisted for a few beats, still sputtering. When she finally released it, Mike set the bag on the nearest camp chair and peered inside. A large baggie of marijuana peered back at her. A baggie identical to the ones Dean stored his drugs in, one that hadn't been there when Mike searched the purse earlier.

Mike's gloved fingers plucked the bag from the purse and placed it on the chair. She quickly rifled through the rest of the purse but didn't find anything else. "Now, Miss Baker. I'm going to pretend I didn't find you stealing evidence from a crime scene. You get this one pass, since you lost someone today, and I won't arrest you, although I have every right to, and I might go ahead and do it later if I need to." Mike pulled herself up to her full height, towering over Grace, and gave the woman a hard look. "Hand over your spare key."

Incredibly, Grace was still grumbling. "I can't believe this, Dean is dead, and this is how you treat someone who is grieving." The red flush covered her whole face now, and Grace pulled the spare key off her ring, passing it over even while she muttered.

"Come to the station tomorrow to give a statement."

"About what?" Grace whined but shut her mouth when Mike gave her another hard look, and agreed instead.

Mike ushered Grace outside, then shut the door firmly behind her. Was it suspicious that Grace'd come to her boyfriend's apartment to lift some drugs while he was missing? Maybe, but maybe not. It was possible she hadn't even known Dean was missing. And Mike would give her the pass on the pot for now—that was some low-level shit, and giving Grace a pass meant Mike had a marker to call in tomorrow when Grace gave her statement. A little leverage to get her to talk.

Could Grace be involved in the murders? Mike thought her reaction to the news about Dean's death was genuine, so she doubted they would find Grace's fingerprints on the gun Patoka'd found.

She'd still take Grace's prints tomorrow, though. You couldn't be too careful.

She and Patoka called for reinforcements in the shape of the guy from the state crime lab with a great luminol kit. They did a thorough search of the living room and started inventorying the drugs while they waited for the tech to work his magic. It took a couple of hours, both for the tech to show up and for them to fill out all the paperwork—holy man alive, did Dean Lagerfield have a lot of drugs in his place—and it was pretty late by the time it was all said and done.

The most frustrating thing was that no matter where the tech sprayed luminol and hit it with the blacklight, they couldn't find any blood. There was some other really grody stuff—the man's comforter had probably never seen a washing machine and was colonizing all *kinds* of things—but no big puddles of blood pointing an arrow to where Dean had been killed.

So where had Lagerfield been murdered? Before the tech packed up, Mike asked him to come out the next day to Baker's storage unit. Maybe Dean had been shot right there. If he hadn't, he could have been killed anywhere, which would mean the chances of them finding the crime scene were *not good.*

Mike was straight-up exhausted when she got home, tired to the very marrow of her bones, although it was the kind of tired that was accompanied by a circus of thoughts, so the fear that she wouldn't be able to sleep was very real. She let Zeus out and watched him trot around the yard, sniffing everything and watering the fence, before she went back inside and gathered up all her bedding—comforter, sheets, and all. She shuddered again at what they'd seen on Lagerfield's bed under the blacklight—she didn't want anything even *close* to that in her place, even if she had to sleep on the couch tonight before the washing machine was done.

Fine, she had a tendency to forget she was doing laundry and would end up running the washer a couple of times.

Maybe she'd stop at the hardware store tomorrow and buy some bleach too.

What a fucking *day*—so many ups and downs, she coulda spent the day at Great America down in FIB country—Fucking Illinois Bastards, according to her pops and every other Wisconsinite she knew. Seriously, though, that adrenaline rush from pulling her weapon had wrecked her. But they'd pushed through, working that apartment over, and she was confident they'd found everything there was to find.

The gun was a mystery, though. How had *that* gotten there? Patoka had orders to talk to the neighbors tomorrow, after he got some sleep too. Hopefully someone saw—or heard—something that would point to who had killed Dean.

Chapter 39

LORRAINE

Sunday

In the wake of a fresh body—well, not *fresh* exactly, but newly discovered—Lorraine had decided to head down to the Mucky Duck and see if she could find something out about Dean Lagerfield, the Popsicle in Baker's freezer, not to mention who had the absolute sack of brass *balls* to call her from Baker's car phone. The Mucky Duck was a townie bar, and what better place to learn about some local townies?

She'd lain in wait for Youngblood to appear, had even slipped one of the pills into his shitty light beer, but he'd tasted something "off" and had the bartender dump it, then proceeded to slobber all over a girl in denim shorts far too young for him for the remainder of the evening.

Disgusting. And had made the evening a waste of time, but she would simply approach the Craig Youngblood problem from a different angle.

It had only been two cocktails last night, but Lorraine was grateful that she'd taken a couple of Advil and pounded back two glasses of water before bed. A definite drawback to getting older was the inevitable headache from imbibing alcohol these days, even a trivial amount.

She made her morning coffee, and while she waited for it to brew, she replayed the night before.

While she'd been sitting at the bar, she'd overheard some chatter about Dean Lagerfield's demise—news in a town this small spread like poison oak—fast and lethal. Not only was Dean the primary bartender at the Mucky Duck, it looked as though he'd also been the primary supplier to a lot of users in town. All those twitching patrons would have to find a new dealer for their crack needs.

It was a tempting business venture money-wise, but she didn't have the patience for that sort of thing anymore. She also didn't want to find herself on the Outfit's radar again, and she knew better than most that drugs were big business for the mob. Although, most of the guys she'd known back in the day were likely dead, right? It was a tough industry for staying above ground. And maybe she wasn't a worry to them anymore since she no longer knew where they were burying the bodies. She'd headed up that part of the operation for a few years, and she'd been great at it. If only she hadn't miscalculated and killed Epstein's number two, she might still be there, living large in the big city.

Anyway. Best to steer clear of the whole operation.

The coffee finished dripping, and Lorraine poured herself a cup, then took a seat at the small breakfast table. Someone had used Julian Baker's car phone to call her, assuming she would figure out whose number they were calling from. It was more than a little threatening, which she respected, but she needed to crush that person. Especially since this person was likely the same one that had dumped Rupp's body on her lawn, kicking off this whole mess. Both these things led her to believe that they knew at least something about Lorraine's . . . hobbies. Although if they knew the full story, it was odd that they hadn't made any demands. Perhaps they only suspected what she'd been getting up to over the years?

It was hard to say. She needed to figure out who was at the top of this drug circus—the ringmaster if you will—because she was pretty sure *that* was the person threatening her.

There wasn't room in her freezer, but once she figured out who was responsible, she would do what needed to be done. It wouldn't be the first time, and she doubted it would be the last.

Now, what was the best way to get to Youngblood? The man clearly knew more than he was willing to admit about his friend Julian's drug business. And with Julian gone, Youngblood was her best bet for finding out who Julian had worked for. There was always a boss at the top, and it hadn't been Julian; she knew that in her bones.

Lorraine sipped her coffee and gazed out the window, not really taking in the lovely flowers growing there. Those things really grew themselves once you planted them on top of a body. She did notice the sky, however—it was dark, clouds hulking low, ready to unleash their summer fury. The breeze ruffling her curtains felt heavy as well, expectant. Hopefully this was a good sign for things to come that day.

Shit. She'd forgotten to swing by Piggly Wiggly yesterday and grab provisions for breakfast. Should she treat herself to some bakery again? She had gotten a workout in, so it couldn't hurt, although she didn't want to make a habit of it. On the other hand, a bit of kringle might be a good way to hide a ground-up pill for Youngblood. Or was it better to put it in some coffee? She looked at the coffee maker sitting on the flecked countertop, tucked beneath the dark-brown cabinets. The carafe was empty, but she could easily make another couple two three cups and take them along to the ice cream shop. She would doctor the coffee before she left, which was hopefully bitter enough to hide any taste of the drug. She was still amazed that Youngblood had noticed it in that piss-colored beer the night before, so she considered adding some sweetener but ultimately decided against it. She would just grab a couple of packets of sugar and creamer and keep her fingers crossed that he used some of it.

Of course, who knew when Youngblood would drag his sorry ass in to work, so she might end up sitting for a while. The coffee could get cold—was it worth the risk? She opened a series of kitchen cabinets, finally coming across what she'd been looking for: Bob's old thermos from his early-morning fishing trips. Perfect.

Lorraine got another pot of coffee started, then dressed in one of her favorite tracksuits, a lightweight navy blue one that attracted lint, but she thought the color looked good with her silver hair. She wanted to be comfortable in case anything *unexpected* happened to Craig Youngblood. It was good to be prepared to move something heavy under most circumstances—more than you might think.

The threat of rain made her decide to drive downtown instead of riding her bike, which she would have preferred. Easier to park, although the coffee would have been tricky in the wicker basket. The thermos was big enough that it didn't fit in her cupholder, so she strapped it into the passenger seat beside her. The pills she'd dropped in should be good and dissolved, and the jostling of the car ride would only shake it up even more.

Lakeside Bakery was busy, per usual, and she waited patiently in line. No one tried to talk to her today, the novelty of the dead body on her lawn having worn off. Today she was grateful for the locals' reticence about talking to an "outsider"—it gave her time to plan how she would approach Youngblood. When it was her turn at the counter, Jamie greeted her with his usual level of cheer. Lorraine considered asking how the date on Friday had gone, but before she could reach a conclusion about whether or not she wanted to know, Jamie told her.

"Mrs. Highsmith! I'm so glad to see you this morning. Thank you for giving Mike my phone number!"

Lorraine blinked a second. "I'm glad to hear that." For once, she was legitimately glad to hear it—a busy detective was a distracted detective.

"We've only gone on the one date, though, and she didn't call me back? I left a message?"

This was way more than she wanted or needed to hear, although it was annoying that her plan didn't seem to be working out how she'd wanted. "Uh, great. Can I get a bran muffin and a kringle? Actually, make that three muffins—bran, blueberry, and lemon poppy seed—and a couple of slices of cherry kringle." She wanted to cover the bases of what she could tempt Youngblood with. He had to be a fan of one of these sweet things.

Fine, the bran was for her. Fiber was important.

Jamie continued chattering while Lorraine nodded absently, having checked out of the conversation entirely. Jamie passed over her order after what felt like an eternity, and Lorraine asked for her total. "Oh, it's totally on the house today, Mrs. Highsmith. I owe you one, for sure."

That was a pleasant and unexpected surprise. She briefly narrowed her eyes—was he really this wholesome and boring, or did he have some secrets of his own? But she thanked him, took her goodies, and returned to her car. Everyone had secrets, but Jamie was far too simple minded for his to be interesting.

The thermos filled with doctored coffee was still snug in the passenger seat, nice and hot and ready to knock Youngblood on his ass. Now she just had to wait for him to show his face.

Chapter 40

MIKE

Sunday

Mike was groggy, even after her first cup of coffee. Her alarm had jolted her from a pleasant dream, one that had slipped into the ether as soon as her eyes cracked open. All she could remember was that she had *not* wanted to wake up. The weather wasn't helping anything, either—overcast and looking like it would storm. It was doing nothing to launch her into the day.

And she needed to wake up, fast. She had only hours to figure out where Baker was supposed to pick up his drop. If only she could figure out the stupid code on the Post-it. It had been in the back of her mind, always, despite all the other developments, but no matter which way she turned it, she couldn't come up with a plausible location. If she could narrow it down to even just a few places, she could set up surveillance. But it wasn't reasonable to do more than three—they just didn't have the manpower. Even if they called in the county to assist, it was still too wide a net. And honestly, calling in the county was a last resort. Those jackals were less than competent and just as mean.

Who was working on a Sunday? She needed someone to sit with the crime-lab tech while he went over Baker's storage unit, looking for blood. Not Patoka, he had another assignment, so it had to be patrol. She really wanted to know where Dean Lagerfield had been shot, but she sure didn't need to be there while the tech went over the place. Mike went to the wall phone and dialed the number for the station. Since it was a weekend, it was patched through to the county, and she told dispatch to have the day shift officer call her at home.

While she waited for the callback, she stared at the note Rupp had made. *LMP, 6-18-89.* That was today's date, but what the hell was *LMP*? It had to be the drop site. But where?

Her phone rang, and she grabbed it before it had even finished the first bell. "Mike Zenoni," she said.

"Detective, county told me to call you," Officer Patoka said.

She was pleased that Patoka was available today after all. Not only was the man competent, but he was already familiar with the case. Of course, that meant the door-to-door would have to wait. Should she ask for someone else?

"Detective?"

"I know I asked you to canvass Dean's building, but I need someone to go with the crime-lab guy over to Baker's storage unit."

"I can do both. What's he looking for?"

"Blood."

"Got it. Lagerfield's, I'm guessing?"

"Yep. I'll have him meet you at the station if that works for you."

Patoka agreed, and she hit the hang-up button, then released it to dial again. This time she called the lab tech and asked him to meet Patoka at the station.

"On a Sunday? Come on, lady."

"It's important." She held firm and was pleased when the tech sighed and agreed. It was a relief that Patoka was willing to do double duty—he was their best guy. She just hoped the lab tech wouldn't take all day.

After hanging up the phone, the detective cracked her knuckles and looked at the notebook. Who might know what *LMP* meant? Baker spent a lot of time at Mary Ann's Frozen Custard chatting it up with Craig Youngblood, so that had to mean something. And since she hadn't spoken to Youngblood in a minute, it felt like a real good place to start.

Youngblood wouldn't be at the ice cream shop for a while, though, especially if the last time she'd stopped there was any indication. If he showed up at all. Would the man work on a Sunday? Doubtful. All right, she could knock one or two of the other interviews off her list first, then swing by the custard place. If Youngblood still wasn't there, she would track him down at home.

Sharity Baker was first on today's list and was definitely not pleased to see Mike. "On a Sunday morning? Do I need a lawyer?" Sharity asked, arms crossed. "Or a restraining order? You're really not my type."

Mike's cheeks flushed pink even though she willed them not to—why did everyone in town assume she liked women?—then she shook her head. "Neither, I assure you. I just had a couple more questions after I searched your husband's storage unit yesterday. Did you know he had one?"

Sharity sighed. "No, but it doesn't surprise me. He didn't exactly share things with me. He wasn't the type, you know?"

Mike thought that sounded like a sad way to conduct a marriage but kept that to herself. "Did you ever see your husband with Dean Lagerfield?"

At this question, Sharity frowned. "That name sounds familiar."

"He was a bartender at the Mucky Duck."

A light seemed to go on for Sharity. "Oh, I think I know who that is. He's dating Julian's sister Grace?"

"He was." That sparked a different question. "Grace is your sister-in-law; were you close at all?"

Sharity shook her head. "Grace and Julian never got along. Although that didn't stop Grace from asking for money now and then. Julian never told me, mind you, I just heard them arguing about it a few times." She shrugged. "I wouldn't a cared if he gave his sister money, but he like, refused. I never could figure out what the damage was between them."

"Did Julian approve of his sister dating Dean?"

Sharity raised an eyebrow. "It's 1989, *Detective Mike*. A woman doesn't need a man's approval to date whoever she wants."

Mike opted to leave that alone too. But she was quiet while she thought over the connection. Grace was dating Dean, a man that worked for her brother, yet Grace and Julian didn't get along. Did that rule Grace out for being a part of this operation?

She would pick at it some more later. "Did your husband own any guns?"

Sharity frowned. "Not that I know of."

"Would you mind if I searched the house?" She was really hoping Sharity would make this easy, otherwise she would have to get a warrant, which was another trip to see Judge Warner. And that would waste a whole ton of time that she could be using to figure out what *LMP* meant.

But Sharity Baker was fresh out of cooperation. "Nope. Not without a warrant," she said, arms crossed and hip jutting out to one side.

Well, shit. Mike felt her jaw clench with frustration, and she forced it loose. Fine. She'd write out a warrant and take it to the judge.

Right after she talked to Craig Youngblood. She wanted to know how that man was involved in all this and if he knew the location of tonight's drop.

Chapter 41

LORRAINE

Sunday

Lorraine was starting to think that Youngblood wasn't going to come in on a Sunday. Perhaps it was time to look up the man's home address in the phone book. She checked the thermos next to her—still warm. But how much longer would it keep? She'd never used it before, so how the hell would she know?

Just when she'd made up her mind to leave, Craig Youngblood came strolling up the sidewalk, still in his clothes from the night before. Lorraine was delighted. If he'd been up late carousing, he'd be much more likely to drink the coffee she offered. And then he would tell her everything she wanted to know.

She followed him into the building, pushing through the doors, carrying the thermos of coffee, an empty Styrofoam cup, and the bag of pastries. Youngblood had already disappeared into the back, and she followed his path.

"I brought coffee and muffins. Some slices of kringle, too, if you'd rather have that." This was addressed to Youngblood while he openly adjusted himself—he clearly hadn't realized someone else was with him. "I hear boxer briefs are the way to go if you're having trouble keeping things straight down there," she added, taking a look around and finding nowhere to sit. No matter, Lorraine simply planted herself on the edge of his desk, making it even more difficult to ignore her.

Until now, Craig Youngblood had been simply watching her with his mouth slightly agape. Maybe he wasn't quite awake yet. The coffee wouldn't actually help with that, as long as he drank enough of it. She'd put three pills in, trying to account for the quantity of coffee and dilution, but it was a crapshoot how much he'd ingest. A few sips or a whole cupful—who knew how fucked up he would get? Only time would tell.

"I don't have anything to say to you."

"Everyone has something to say, it's just a matter of when they get around to it," she countered.

"Is that what you write in your column? I don't know why you have readers, then." Youngblood's voice had more than a little sarcasm in it, but he did take the coffee cup she offered him and peeked inside at it. "I only take coffee with cream and lots of sugar."

"Well, good thing I brought plenty of both. As well as muffins—which kind do you want? We have blueberry or lemon poppy seed. Or a couple pieces of cherry kringle." She dropped the bag of pastries onto his desk. She'd put the sugar packets and little plastic containers of creamer inside it as well.

She could see that Youngblood was finally tempted. "What's the third kind?"

"How do you know there's a third?" She was annoyed again. She truly wished people would quit annoying her.

"Because that bag is definitely holding three muffins." Youngblood finally remembered his manners, just when she was beginning to wonder if he had any. "I'll take the blueberry. Thank you."

"Good." Lorraine dug in the bag before passing over the blueberry muffin and enough cream and sugar to fill a whole other cup. She hoped the condiments would mask the taste of the drug she'd dropped in there.

"You didn't bring a cup for yourself?" Youngblood asked, sugar packet paused over the top of the Styrofoam.

"I had a cup before I came. And at my age, you can't drink too much. Heart trouble, you know." She watched Youngblood dump packet after packet of sugar into his cup. Ordinarily she would have said something about how both disgusting and unhealthy this was, but today it was necessary to hold her tongue. "Now, you've been friends with Julian Baker for a long time."

Craig huffed. "I told you before, yeah, we were friends, but he was real closed mouthed about his personal life. I didn't even know he and Sharity were having problems." He finally finished mixing up his coffee and took a sip, frowning. "It's kinda lukewarm."

"Well, it wouldn't be if you came to work at a reasonable hour," Lorraine shot back.

He shrugged. "It's a Sunday. I shouldn't be here at all."

"Why are you here, then?"

Youngblood paused mid-sip, shooting a quick glance at his desk drawer. She was certain he didn't know that he'd done it—it had been instinct. Whatever had brought him in on a Sunday was in that drawer.

"Had to pick some things up." He didn't elaborate further, keeping his eyes glued to her. But he'd already fucked up, cluing her in.

She let that go since she would snoop around later, that drawer first. "Have you heard from Julian lately?" She needed to keep up the ruse that everyone—herself included—thought the man had skipped town.

Craig shook his head, his eyebrows pulling together. "No, and that's weird. He usually comes by like every day."

That was a lot of contact for two men who were just friends and weren't sleeping together. But she let that lie too. "You don't happen to have his car phone, do you?"

Now Youngblood just looked confused. "Why would I have his car phone? Wherever he is, I'm sure he has it with him. In his car."

"What about his box of pagers?"

For the second time since this conversation started, Youngblood looked a little shifty, eyes darting around the room. "I don't know what you mean."

"Oh, you don't know about the storage unit full of drugs and beepers that your friend Julian had. Under his own name, too, which was really stupid."

"Well, how else is he supposed to rent one? Stu knows everyone in town."

Lorraine just shook her head. She wasn't going to argue about this, but she *was* watching carefully to see if Youngblood was drinking enough of his coffee to be showing any ill effects. She didn't think so but decided to ask the question she most wanted an answer to anyway. "Who did Julian work for?"

Youngblood took a long drink of his coffee, then took a bite of his muffin, talking around the bakery in his mouth, crumbs spewing onto his shirt. "He worked for himself."

She pursed her lips. Baker clearly didn't work for himself, and whoever he *did* work for had killed a man and left him on her lawn and then made a harassing phone call to her using the dead man's phone. She didn't believe for a second that this idiot didn't know more about Baker's boss than he was letting on. But at least he was ingesting the coffee.

"Did you know he had a body in his storage locker?" Maybe some hard truths would shake some other truths out of this idiot.

Youngblood did not look nearly as shocked as he should have, which was interesting. "What are you talking about? Who was it?" he asked, unconvincingly.

Just then a faint ding and deliberate footsteps could be heard floating down the hall from the ice cream shop. Seconds later Detective Zenoni was standing in the doorway.

Lorraine heaved an audible sigh. Mike Zenoni was getting to be a real nuisance as well.

Chapter 42

MIKE

Sunday

"Mrs. Highsmith." Mike's tone was friendly, deceptively so. "I thought your article was done."

Mrs. H. shrugged. "Doing a follow-up piece, now that there's a second body."

Youngblood's head bounced from one woman to the other, like the ball in *Pong*.

"Mmm. Why do I think that's not the real reason you're here?"

"Because you have trust issues?" Mrs. Highsmith said. "Speaking of, how was your date? Will there be another?"

Mike ignored that and instead cocked a hip casually. "I'm still waiting to hear back from Chicago. That's where you lived before Rockford, right? They're looking for all the records they have on you. I'm keeping my fingers crossed they find some previous addresses."

A gleam lit Mrs. Highsmith's eyes, but Mike couldn't parse out what it meant. Was she impressed? Upset? Worried?

"You're wasting your time, Detective," Mrs. Highsmith said evenly, but she got up from her seat on the edge of Youngblood's desk. Good. She was at least a *little* rattled.

"Well, it's mine to waste. What were you two jawing about?"

"I was just here to ask Mr. Youngblood about his old friend Julian. Wasn't I?" Mrs. Highsmith looked Craig dead in the eye, and he swallowed some coffee and shrugged.

Mike doubted that was all there was to it, not if Mrs. H. brought coffee and pastries. Seemed like Mrs. H. used goodies as bribes when she wanted something that required a little extra incentive. Not just a few innocent questions.

Youngblood started to rub his eyes. Mrs. Highsmith was watching the man with a frown.

"You feeling okay there, Craig?" she asked.

"I don't know. I feel weird," Youngblood said.

"You don't look so good, actually," Mike chimed in. Youngblood really *didn't* look good—he was all pale and sweaty, and looking around like he didn't know where he was. Which was super weird since he was sitting in his own office.

Mrs. Highsmith pursed her lips and shook her head. "All that drinking and then all that garbage you put in your coffee on top of it. I'm not surprised." The woman pointed to a worn leather couch on the other side of the office, tucked under a window covered with crusty blinds. "Maybe you should lie down for a little bit."

Youngblood was now swaying, and Mike came around to help him stand. Craig stumbled a bit, and the detective supported a hefty amount of the man's weight as she lugged him across the room and onto the couch. "Should I call a doctor?" Mike asked.

"No," Youngblood mumbled, then said something else, although she couldn't for the life of her figure out what it was.

"I'll just stay here and keep an eye on him," Mrs. Highsmith said. "He seems unwell."

Was her tone a little flat? It sounded weird, the way she said it, but she *looked* sincere. Mike studied Mrs. H. for a long moment. She didn't trust her, but she also couldn't figure out what her game here would be.

"What are you up to, Mrs. H.?" Know what? It was easier to just come out and ask.

Mrs. Highsmith put a hand to her chest, clearly offended. "I'm not up to anything, Detective. And I resent the implication."

Mike sighed and motioned for Mrs. H. to precede her out of the office. She looked like she was going to refuse, but then Mrs. H. grabbed Youngblood's coffee cup, her thermos, and a small paper bag and stalked out of the room.

Mike motioned to the coffee cup with a nod of her head. "Why'd you take his coffee?"

"Didn't want to leave a mess for him to clean up when he's feeling better."

"That's thoughtful of you, Mrs. H." Mike was now herding her toward the front door. Youngblood needed to sleep off . . . whatever that was, and her gut told her that she should get Mrs. H. out of here. Whatever she was up to, it wasn't in Youngblood's best interest—and he'd be livid if Mrs. Highsmith took a convoluted statement from him and put it in the paper. The man was clearly in no state to be interviewed right now.

Mrs. Highsmith tossed the coffee cup into the garbage can outside as they passed by. It appeared to be half full, and Mike almost commented on what a waste that was, but she kept it to herself. She did, however, want to make sure Mrs. H. didn't go back inside and bother Youngblood while he was getting acquainted with both his couch and his regret. "Can I escort you home?"

Mrs. Highsmith looked amused. "I know the way perfectly well. I'm not *that* old yet."

Mike was preparing a devastating retort when the radio on her belt crackled. "Detective Zenoni, you're wanted at the station." She paused, wondering if she could pretend she hadn't heard it. She didn't want to deal with the boss today—she wanted to get actual police work done. But she clicked on the mic and answered that she would be right there.

Mrs. Highsmith was already walking away without so much as a backward glance. She really did flaunt social niceties every chance she got, but Mike supposed that was a bonus of getting old. As she watched Mrs. H. go, she shuffled from foot to foot. Did she have enough time to go back inside and see if Youngblood knew what *LMP* was?

She'd be fast.

The detective scurried back inside, through the ice cream shop, down the cramped back hall, and into the office. She crossed Youngblood's office in a few steps, then shook the man's shoulder. "Hey, Youngblood. Do you know what *LMP* stands for?"

The man moaned but didn't respond otherwise. She tried again, shaking the man's shoulder, a little harder this time, eliciting a deeper moan. Hmm. That wasn't great, for either of them. "Craig, do you know where Julian's drop is going down tonight?" Youngblood didn't answer, making another guttural sound in the back of his throat, but not moving otherwise.

Well, shit. She looked at her watch, then back at Youngblood. "I hope you're gonna make it, buddy. I'll check back on you later."

Youngblood didn't acknowledge this, and she sent up a little prayer that the man wouldn't die right there on his couch. It was a pretty undignified way to go, especially on a couch that belonged in the dump.

Back at the station Chief Schneider was practically foaming at the mouth. Couldn't be rabies, though; she'd never get that lucky. "Detective Zenoni, I read your report," Schneider said.

"What are you doing here on a Sunday, boss?" Mike clocked his outfit—instead of the white button-down uniform shirt the chief normally wore, he was wearing plaid shorts and a pink polo shirt, his gold chain and chest hair on full display. Weekend duds.

Her boss ignored the question. "There's a big stack of stolen cash involved with this case. Do you have any leads on it?"

"Not so far. I've been following up on forensics for the *murders* and interviewing people about them." Mike really laid on the word *murders*, hoping it would remind her boss what was important here—the victims who'd lost their lives. Real people, with families and loved ones.

But Chief Schneider was not picking up what she was laying down. "Can't you see it, though? It would be such a perfect photo op. All those drugs on a table and a huge stack of recovered cash. You could even be in the photo."

Mike carefully held her face in neutral. What was the best way to distract Schneider right now? He needed something shiny to follow. "I'm trying to work out where Baker was going to pick up a big drop tonight. Probably drugs—lots of them."

Schneider's eyes lit up, clearly calculating what a "big drop" could look like, media-wise. "What do you have so far?"

"I've got the date and time, but not the location."

The chief visibly deflated. "No clues about where? None?"

"Just an acronym. *LMP.* I've been trying to figure out where that might be, but none of the cities around here come even close."

"Could it simply be Lake Michigan Port?"

She *had* considered that, but it was way too easy. On the other hand, a dude had come up with it, so maybe she was overthinking things. It still felt like a long shot, but maybe it was better than nothing, because she was completely stumped otherwise. She nodded slowly. "I'll borrow a couple night shift guys to set up down there."

"I would do the industrial side of the port and the public marina as well," Schneider said, standing. "I'll join you boys." He paused. "And girl."

She tipped her head, acknowledging that yes, she was in fact a girl, although she was lumped into "you guys" and "you boys" so often that she hardly noticed anymore.

She didn't want her boss on the stakeout, but the location had been his idea, so the detective simply agreed and went on her way. What a twist for the *chief* to come up with an idea. Not a great idea, but an idea just the same. Her pops was right—the world was full of miracles.

In the meantime, she had some phone calls to make and a search warrant to type up. Should she send someone over to check on Youngblood? Someone like the paramedics? He hadn't looked good, not at all. Whatever was wrong with him might be serious, and she would hate for something to happen to one of her suspects.

Yikes, that sounded bad. What she meant was, she'd hate for something to happen to *any* citizen.

The detective checked her watch, calculating how much time she had to get things done. She should have enough time to run back over to the ice cream shop and make sure Youngblood was still breathing once she knocked out a few calls and that warrant. It would be smart to make sure Mrs. Highsmith hadn't returned to pester the man some more too. That old bat was relentless.

Chapter 43

LORRAINE

Sunday

Shit that was a close call. She'd nearly been caught slipping Youngblood drugs. But instead of filling Lorraine with dread, her blood fizzed with excitement. She'd played that perfectly, and Zenoni hadn't even suspected. She wished she had access to this drug—and this feeling—all the time. If she could bottle either, she'd be wildly rich.

Lorraine had dumped the coffee cup and then walked off as though she were headed home. The call for Zenoni to come to the station could not have come at a better time—now she could finish interrogating Youngblood. Although she wasn't going to risk going in the front of the shop, that was entirely too suspicious. Instead, she walked around to the back, where an alley ran between the block of commercial buildings and the fenced backyards of shoebox homes, all smooshed together. She ran a critical eye over the houses—most of these looked as though they had small children, toys and play sets littering the yards. But the fences were reasonably tall, and there was some cover from the commercial dumpsters.

All good things to know.

Lorraine located the back entrance of the ice cream shop, a dented metal door that had seen much better days. It was liberally covered with stickers from establishments around town, which made it look like trash, fitting for this part of the alley. Trying the handle, she sighed—it was locked. She dug around in her purse—after scanning to ensure she wasn't being observed, of course—and pulled out a set of master keys. She'd collected them over the years, finding they often came in handy. She tested a few and was nearly at the end of her key chain when she found one that worked. She twisted the lock, and it gave a satisfying *click* before she popped the door open. This led to the back hallway between the shop and Youngblood's office, stacked with cardboard boxes of supplies and plastic milk crates.

Lorraine slipped inside and made her way to the office. Youngblood was still lying on the couch, looking for all the world like he'd passed out. She closed his office door behind her and locked it, just in case. Hopefully any sounds he made wouldn't carry outside the ice cream shop. She rifled through the items on the top of his desk, looking for something sharp. A thumbtack would be great, but Youngblood didn't have one of those. With a sigh, she picked up the stapler. It would have to do, although it was less than ideal. She doubted it would hurt enough.

Lorraine took off Youngblood's boat shoe, finding that he wasn't wearing any socks. "Gross," she said. It was convenient for her, but *fuck*, that shoe smelled something awful. She wasn't going to feel bad about stapling this asshat's foot; she looked forward to it, really. But she gave the bottom of his foot a firm slap with the stapler as a warning before the real fun began.

"Hey, dipshit," she said. "I have questions for you."

Youngblood mumbled something, and she smacked his foot again, harder this time, although she was conscious about making noise that traveled outside. "Craig."

This time he roused a bit more. "What?"

"Where is Baker's money?"

"I don't know," he said, then yelped loudly when she smacked his foot staple first. It didn't penetrate the skin, but it left some marks and obviously pinched. "I don't! I'm sure he took it with him!" Craig was a little more alert, but his eyes weren't open. Lorraine was confident that he wouldn't remember this as anything but a bad dream.

"Is the money here? Why was Baker stopping by all the time?" She was rhythmically slapping the stapler against the soft tissue of his foot. *Whack, whack, whack.*

"He's laundering money through my books." Youngblood's head rocked side to side in a *no more* motion. "I'm gonna have to torch this place if he doesn't come back." This last part was mumbled again as Youngblood slipped back toward unconsciousness.

She wasn't nearly through with her other inquiries, but this did spark an idea for her. "When will you do that?"

"I don't know, next weekend," Youngblood mumbled. The words were sort of smooshed together, but she could make them out. Just.

This was the best news yet. She even had a few more days—plenty of time to get Baker's body into the ice cream shop. She'd have to keep an eye on Youngblood, though, make sure that he didn't speed up that timeline, because dumping Baker here to be incinerated in a fire was the perfect way to get rid of the body.

As long as she could do it without being seen.

She gave her head a little shake and refocused on her current project—torturing information out of Craig Youngblood.

"Who did Julian work for?" Lorraine slapped the bottom of his foot with the flat back of the stapler.

"Ungh, no one."

"That's a lie—he worked for someone." She readied the stapler to send a little metal staple into the arch of his foot, where it would really hurt. After the arch, she would turn her attention to the soft spots between his toes, much as she was loath to touch the nasty things.

"He said he worked for himself, but when he had that money, he was worried. I think he was working for someone else, but I don't know who," Youngblood said. "And then he lost his finger."

Lorraine gave him a good whack with a staple, although it didn't come out, jamming instead. Youngblood gave a little shriek, eyes cracking open, and she paused to see if anyone would come to check on what was happening in here. There was no one in the ice cream shop, but if someone was passing by on the sidewalk, they might have heard that one. After a few beats of silence, which she used to unjam the stapler, she continued.

"You're sure you don't know? You know what will happen if you lie."

Youngblood whined, his body twisting on the couch as though he wanted to crawl away but couldn't. "I don't know. Just don't hurt me anymore."

She sighed in disgust. She'd gotten everything she could from this guy. She wiped her prints off the stapler and returned it to his desk, then held her breath and got his shoe slipped back on—he was already unconscious. Whatever that stuff was, it really worked. She was glad she still had plenty left—you never could tell when you might need a little knockout drug.

Lorraine quietly headed for the back door, wiping prints off anything she'd touched on the way in, mostly doorknobs. It was a good reason to carry a handkerchief in her purse at all times. Mike had seen her in here earlier, but she didn't want her prints found on the rear door once they started investigating the fire.

Back outside, she surveyed the alley once again, looking for the best way to bring a body in. If she could eliminate the streetlights back here, she thought she would be in pretty good shape.

Chapter 44

MIKE

Sunday

Mike made a few phone calls to Baker's credit card companies to see if there had been any charges that would point her to where he'd taken off, but the cards had been quiet. Too quiet, really. Even if the man had a big bag of cash, that couldn't last forever. And a guy like that, he was probably used to whipping out a card and paying for stuff. There had to come a point where he'd forget and slap one down, a gas station or a diner, even a pharmacy somewhere.

Could it be that something had happened to Baker?

That was an interesting theory, one she let swim around in the kiddie pool of her mind while she worked on the warrant for Baker's house. She was still annoyed that Sharity hadn't played ball, but maybe Mike *had* been by too many times.

Speaking of annoyed, she was still pissed that she hadn't been able to come up with a better explanation for *LMP*. They would set up on the lakefront tonight, but she was convinced they were gonna miss the real drop. But there wasn't time to come up with something better, so right now it was their best bet. Their only bet.

She checked her watch. Run over to Mary Ann's and check on Youngblood? She still wanted to see if he knew what *LMP* was. It was a long shot, but she had to ask. She double-checked her list, then remembered she still needed to submit an official request for a ballistics test on the gun they'd found at Dean Lagerfield's apartment. It was an important step, confirming whether it was the same weapon that had killed Lagerfield. And since testing would be done at the crime lab, the tech working the storage unit could take the gun down to Milwaukee with him, and it would stay in the official chain of custody.

Who knew how long the test itself would take, but honestly, it would knock her sideways if it *wasn't* the same gun. In her mind she'd already connected the two, although she was careful to make a big note in her notebook, circling it a couple times, a reminder that they *could* be looking for a different weapon. *Assumptions make an ass of you,* her pops's voice said. He'd never finished the saying, though, which always made her crazy.

She'd already finished the search warrant, so she muddled through the ballistics request as quickly as she could.

Shouldn't Grace Baker be here by now? She'd been instructed to come in and give a statement, and Mike had *questions* for that woman, questions about her involvement with the whole circus. She picked up the phone and dialed Grace's number, but there was no answer. She left a terse message that Grace needed to show her face at the station to give her statement, or Mike would issue a warrant for her arrest.

She probably wouldn't actually take the time to do that, not right now anyway, but if Grace tried to duck her for too long, Mike would—she didn't like to make idle threats if she could help it. Of course, that would mean more paperwork, which seemed to be eating every last second of her days. Fingers crossed it didn't come to it.

"You're still here?" Chief Schneider had actually left his office and sauntered back to hers, a yellow sticky note stuck to his index finger.

"I am." Mike forced a smile. "What's with the sticky note?"

"Oh, it was for you, but it was on my desk." Schneider looked at the note on his finger. "Chicago has no records." He looked at the detective. "Records of what?"

"The Highsmiths. Didn't you say they were from Chicago? Before living in Rockford?" There should have been *something* there, some record of Lorraine or Bob. Her gut told her that this was now *definitely* something to dig into.

Her boss shrugged. "That's what Bob told me. Why are you wasting your time with that, though? I told you not to bother with this."

Distract, distract. Fling a shiny frisbee for the chief. "Oh, it's not a bother. I'm busy writing up this search warrant. We need to get inside Baker's house before his wife can get rid of anything. Like money." As far as Mike was concerned, there was zero chance Baker's money was in the house—it was too obvious, and Baker wouldn't have run the risk of Sharity coming across it. No, the money was stashed somewhere else. But her boss didn't know that.

The chief's eyes gleamed—he'd already forgotten the sticky note on his finger as well as the Highsmiths. "Excellent point. I was smart, promoting you. Are you almost finished writing the warrant up? I'll come with you."

She visibly winced, but just a little. Only minutes ago, she'd been free and clear of her boss's interference. But the allure of a photo op was too much for the chief—Mike shoulda come up with a different excuse if she wanted to do this solo. She forced another smile before telling her boss that that sounded great. Schneider didn't seem to hear, and if he did, he ignored it.

On the way to Baker's place, Mike swung by Mary Ann's. Her boss objected, but she insisted she would only take a second, so she hurried through the custard shop again and found Youngblood almost exactly where she'd left him. Except this time when she shook him, he screamed. She stepped back in surprise.

"No more," Youngblood moaned. At least he was alive and even seemed to be forming words now, although "no more" sounded ominous. Bad dreams?

"Youngblood, where is the drug drop happening tonight?" she asked loudly, bent over to project into the man's ear.

"Lake," Youngblood mumbled. "No more." He moaned again.

She shook her head. It wasn't enough, but it was better than nothing? It made her feel a *little* bit better about staking out the port. "I'll check on you later." Youngblood shook his head side to side and rolled toward the back of his couch.

Back in her car, Mike and her overly cheerful boss drove to Judge Warner's house. This time Warner himself answered the door. She had the unkind thought that it was because his wife was off earning the money that kept Judge Warner in the lifestyle he was accustomed to, but she mentally scolded herself. Mrs. Warner was probably at church—it was Sunday after all.

"Gentlemen! What brings you here on a Sunday morning?" he added, looking at Chief Schneider with a confused frown. Whether he was confused by Schneider working on a Sunday or by his casual outfit to do it in, it was hard to say. Both were a mystery.

"We need you to sign one more warrant, Judge," Mike offered.

"This case just keeps getting bigger, doesn't it?" Judge Warner said gravely. This was also stating the obvious, but she smiled and nodded all the same.

Warner signed the warrant, and the judge and the chief discussed their latest golf scores while she prepared herself for yet another lengthy chat. But Warner handed back the warrant without insisting they come inside, closing the front door behind himself only a few minutes after they'd arrived. She could have moonwalked to the car with relief. At least *this* hadn't been a huge waste of her time.

Sharity Baker was not thrilled to see two cops on her doorstep—she greeted them with folded arms and a scowl. But she took the warrant

Mike handed her, and with a noise of disgust, gestured for them to come inside.

Mike was a little surprised that Sharity was still being difficult about this. Sure, her repeated visits were probably annoying. But there didn't seem to be any love lost between Sharity and her husband, and if they *did* manage to find Julian, he was going away for a long time—and that was just on the drug charges. Given how little Sharity seemed to care about Julian, Mike thought she'd be fine with having her house searched and her husband tossed into prison for longer.

Sharity was still giving them the stink eye. "I'll be in the kitchen with my coffee. Let me know when you're finished." With that, she turned and flounced up the stairs, leaving them standing in the foyer.

The chief blinked after her, left hand reaching for the badge that wasn't there. This was Mike's cue to take over. "I think we should start in the main bedroom."

Schneider nodded, hand drifting back down to his side. "That's precisely what I was thinking."

She led the way up the short staircase, through a corner of the living room to another set of stairs. They climbed up and poked their heads into each room along the hall, finally finding the main bedroom, the last door on their left. Inside they found a king-size bed absolutely *dominating* the space, across from a gorgeous view of the lake.

"This view," the chief muttered. "My wife would love this view." He was looking around with his hands in his pockets, clearly assessing the real estate value instead of considering where they should search. "They call us the Malibu of the Midwest, you know."

It was *such* a stupid name, despite the lake surfing, but Mike made a polite noise of interest. She'd already snapped on gloves and was searching a bedside table. "I don't think the Bakers are likely to sell anytime soon, sir."

"You can't say that for certain, though, Mike."

She always found it jarring when her boss reverted to using her first name, and her nickname at that. Over the years, she'd realized that it was usually when the chief wanted something. Mike kept her focus on the task, but frowned, anticipating whatever Schneider wanted from her.

"I'll start over here," Schneider said, opening the bedside drawer that—by process of elimination—belonged to Sharity Baker. "Whoa."

Mike looked up and found her boss simply staring into the drawer. "What is it?" Another gun? But why was it on Sharity's side of the bed?

"I've never seen so many vibrators outside of a sex shop." The chief's voice was awed, which was hilarious, even though her cheeks heated up; the awkwardness of hearing her boss talk about vibrators made her stomach feel a little squidgy. False bravado and fake laughs were her fallback when the guys at the station made inappropriate jokes or said something gross. She worked hard so they wouldn't see that their shit bothered her. This was different, though; this was her boss.

Oh, *grody toad*, now she was thinking about the chief and his wife in their own bedroom. Could this day get any worse?

"Why don't you start in the closet, sir?" Mike suggested with a strong shake of her head to clear it. "I've got a handle on the bedside tables."

"No, no. I can do this." Schneider looked down into the drawer and back at his hands. "Although maybe I should put on some gloves."

Chapter 45

LORRAINE

Sunday

Lorraine was back in her basement, surveying Julian Baker, who was looking pretty frosty in the freezer. She was a little concerned that the man was too frozen to burn up in a building fire, but she decided that if a Thanksgiving turkey could be defrosted and cooked in one day, so could Julian Baker. Besides, she would soak him in accelerants when she left him there. Soak him and then leave the evidence at Craig Youngblood's house.

Getting a body out of the freezer was just as difficult as getting them in, and she mentally prepared herself for the task. She'd already laid out a black tarp to wrap him in—untraceable, of course, since it was a common brand, mass produced and sold everywhere. She bought hers in cash when she traveled out of state, so there wouldn't be a record of her buying one anywhere near here. And if suspicion ever did come her way, Lorraine would be gone before anyone could blink. On to a new life with a new name.

She had extra identification papers in her safe, just in case.

Lorraine had given things some thought and decided she needed to get Baker's body into the ice cream shop *tonight*. The more the police asked around, the more panicked Youngblood would be, and less likely to wait. And she wasn't going to miss this golden opportunity—so, tonight it was.

She attached the pulley-and-winch system to the ropes still wrapped around Baker's body and, with considerable effort, got his frozen carcass just above the lip of the freezer, then swung it slightly to the right. She released the winch, and Baker fell with an unpleasant *thump* to the tarp below. If Bob was still alive, there was no way he would've missed that one, she mused. Good thing Bob was just as dead as this sucker.

With Baker now on the tarp, she proceeded to wrap him up tightly and bind the edges with duct tape. Then, with a great deal of sweat and swearing, she managed to roll him onto the dolly. Shit, Cynthia would be proud of what she was accomplishing right now.

A trickle of sweat just above her eyebrow was becoming irritating, so she paused to wipe her face on her shirt, leaving a dark streak in its wake. Straightening, she grabbed a strap and tied Baker's corpse to the dolly. He was hunched nearly in two from his time in the freezer, which made him much more difficult to strap down. It would be much easier if he was shaped like a mummy in its coffin—a bungee cord at the head and one at the feet, and you'd be done. But no, here she had to use several vinyl straps, ratcheting them down hard to keep the oddly shaped corpse from sliding around.

Job finally done, she gave the frigid body a quick pat. He'd be fine until nightfall. Sure, it was June, and humid as all get out above ground, but this cellar stayed pleasantly cool. Once night had fallen, she'd work on pulling this dolly up the ramp and then get him into the trunk of her station wagon, probably using a makeshift ramp. There were some old pieces of plywood in the shed that she kept on hand for this very reason.

You know, a truck would be much more useful for this task. A small white box truck would be perfect—it wouldn't look suspicious parked in that alley, and it would be incredibly easy to roll Julian inside, strapped to the dolly. She could just attach the dolly to the wall, drive to Mary Ann's Frozen Custard, and roll the man right in.

But how to do that without making her neighbors suspicious?

It didn't take long for inspiration to hit. Back in the kitchen, Lorraine picked up her phone and made a quick call. It rang so long she thought it would go to the answering machine, but it was picked up at the very last second.

"Hello?" It wasn't the police chief but his wife.

"Dr. Schneider, it's Lorraine Highsmith."

"Hello, Mrs. Highsmith. What can I do for you?"

"I was actually looking for your husband. I'm hoping to borrow his truck."

There was a brief pause. "What do you need it for?" Dr. Schneider asked.

"I have a load of things that I would like to donate to the charity shop, quilts and clothes and such. I need a bigger vehicle to get it all in. I never got around to clearing out after Bob died, and I've finally decided that this stuff should go to a new home. A new lease on life, if you will." And mostly lies.

"Of course. That's kind of you," Dr. Schneider said, voice warm. "Hans isn't home right now—I think he's at the station. Why don't you head over there and tell him that I said you could take it."

"I appreciate it, Dr. Schneider."

"Oh, call me Eva. No one else does."

Lorraine was waiting patiently at the police station when Detective Zenoni and Chief Schneider pulled up. Zenoni looked perfectly pressed in her navy blue slacks, dress pumps, and blouse, but the chief looked a little worse for wear, even in his ugly plaid shorts and rumpled polo. Probably because he wasn't used to doing actual work.

"Lorraine, I didn't expect you to be here," Schneider greeted her.

"Well, I need to borrow your truck. Your wife said it was no trouble."

"Oh?" Schneider said. "Well, if Dr. Schneider said it was okay." He paused. "What do you need it for? I mean, we just executed a search warrant, and I'd like to get home, take a shower. I . . . touched some things. So maybe you could take it in an hour or so?"

Lorraine didn't bother asking what search warrant; she was fairly certain it was one of two places—the Baker house or Lagerfield's place. The cops probably suspected that Youngblood knew something, but they would have no reason to search his shop. Yet.

"Well, I like to get things done, so I'll just take it now. Your wife said she'd come get you." That wasn't true, Eva had said no such thing, and Lorraine thought it was unlikely that she actually would.

The chief cocked his head. "Do you need help? Loading and unloading everything?"

Lorraine thought fast. "Oh, that's kind of you, but no thank you. You have important police business, and the exercise is good for me."

Schneider and Zenoni both looked skeptical. Jesus, how old did they think she was that she couldn't move a couple of bags of clothes and some quilts?

"Well, if you're sure," Schneider said.

"I could always stop by and help," Zenoni chimed in.

"You are so thoughtful. But I insist you stick to your police work." She was amazed she was able to push the treacly words out—they made her feel like gagging. "I've got everything handled."

Zenoni still looked doubtful but went inside while Chief Schneider passed over the keys to his truck. Lorraine smiled and told him she would have it back to him later that night.

She decided not to wait until nightfall to put things into motion. First, she huffed and puffed and managed to get Julian Baker's body up the ramp leading to her backyard. It was fenced, and the people on either side of her kept to themselves, so she felt confident she wasn't being observed. She then grabbed the plywood from the shed and made a ramp into the back of the truck. She tested it with her own weight, then pulled the dolly up that ramp as well.

Damn, she was tired. Her muscles were practically trembling from the effort, and she decided she would cancel her circuit training the next day and do water aerobics instead. It was kinda bullshit, but she'd need to do a lot of stretching after this so her muscles didn't seize up. Her back, especially.

Satisfied that Baker's tarp-wrapped and frozen body was in the back of the truck, she closed up her cellar doors and went around the front to go inside. She drank down a glass of water, then another, before grabbing some trash bags from under the sink. It actually *was* a good time to go through her clothes and see if there was anything she could get rid of—it was smart to make your cover as real as possible. It would also eliminate suspicion as to why she was parked in that alley.

An hour later she had a number of bags, mostly filled with Bob's shit that she hadn't purged yet. She'd done an initial clean out right after his death, junk that was in her way, but then had gotten lazy and left his shit in the other closets scattered around the house. There were a few winter coats, outdated suits from the sixties and seventies that he'd rarely worn, a collection of greasy mechanics overalls he'd worn to work. She also had one bag of her own clothes—items that still had structured waistbands or prints that were simply too wild. Things she would never wear again—they didn't fit her disguise. That and her genuine desire for comfort. Why wear clothes you couldn't wait to get off at the end of the day?

She took the first few bags outside and tossed them on top of the body in the back. She nodded, satisfied that it already looked like nothing more than a bigger, lumpier bag. She dusted her hands together and turned to find Detective Zenoni standing behind her.

Chapter 46

MIKE

Sunday

Mike escaped her boss by dropping him off at his house. It was an awkward ride, but at least she knew where the man was and that his truck had been commandeered—maybe he would have to skip the stakeout tonight. She'd cross her fingers *and* toes for that one.

The search warrant had turned up precisely bupkis, though. It was frustrating that they hadn't found anything, but she also wasn't too surprised—they'd found plenty in the storage locker. Instead of beating herself up for wasting valuable time, she reminded herself that searching Baker's house simply meant that she was dotting her i's and crossing her t's.

She was pretty crushed not to have found anything pointing to what *LMP* was though. Schneider's suggestion and a mumble from Youngblood were still all they had to go on.

Next up, she wanted to speak to Grace Baker again and then Craig Youngblood, if he was feeling any better. But she couldn't stop thinking about how Chicago hadn't turned up anything on Mrs. H. Could she have just flown under the radar? Or, and this was honestly more likely, was Mrs. H. lying about having come from Chicago? Mike's gut told her there was more here, some secret that Mrs. Highsmith was hiding, and that secret had turned into a skeeter bite that needed scratching.

You know what? Right now, Mrs. H. was loading up the chief's truck with bags of junk, and stopping by to help was a great way to get a look inside Mrs. H.'s house without a warrant. If Mike was lucky, she'd see something that would offer a clue about where to call next for records. She hadn't been lucky so far today, but luck had to change, right?

Mike drove to Mrs. Highsmith's house, parked in the driveway, and strolled along the side of the house, finding Mrs. H. and the chief's truck in the backyard. It looked like she'd already loaded quite a bit—how much more could there be?

"Mrs. Highsmith, I've come to help you load up your stuff."

Mrs. H. turned, face glistening, eyebrows slightly raised. "That's kind of you. Should you be taking time in the middle of a murder investigation, though? Two murders, actually."

"A few minutes won't hurt anything. Is there more that needs to go?"

Mrs. Highsmith's expression didn't change, her eyes simply assessing the detective; then she nodded. "Follow me."

Mike followed Mrs. H. into her little bungalow, checking out the decorating style, or lack thereof, actually. There were none of the doilies and knickknacks and glass figurines that she'd expected. Like *none*. Her grandma's place had been full to bursting with that kind of shit, but there was nothing here. In fact, there wasn't personal stuff anywhere—no pictures, no keepsakes. Not even a stray magazine or a stack of books on the glass-topped coffee table. There was a large chocolate leather couch and matching chair that looked both modern and comfortable, and the wallpaper was a wide blue-and-gold stripe down to a mid-wall chair rail with wood paneling below. But there was literally nothing hanging on the walls to break up the stripes. The hallway was painted a simple cream color, nothing hanging there either.

Most people at least had a painting or *something* to look at. A wedding photo or two. The fact that there was *nothing* was more than a little odd. Was this the kind of house that someone in WITSEC lived in? Just who *was* Mrs. Highsmith, and where on earth had she come from?

Mike hurried her steps to catch up to Mrs. H. in the doorway of what might be a guest bedroom. It was honestly hard to tell. "Not a lot of stuff on the walls, Mrs. H. You're not in WITSEC, are you? Hiding out from something?" She added a little laugh at the end, although it came out pretty awkward. Shit, she needed to work on that.

Mrs. Highsmith didn't even so much as chuckle at Mike's joke that was only sort of a joke. She just looked at the detective for a few beats, then pointed to the daybed, where she'd piled a handful of boxes and a couple of black garbage bags stuffed to the hilt. "These are the last of them."

Mike stepped into the room, looking around at the bare walls covered with nothing more than floral-printed wallpaper. She hefted one of the boxes, grunting a little at the weight. "What's in these?"

"I still had some of Bob's things in the closets, and it's time to let go of them," Mrs. Highsmith said. "His clothes, some old hunting gear. Books about World War II," she said with a nod toward the box in Mike's arms. Mrs. H.'s voice was devoid of any emotion, and Mike's eyes narrowed slightly. Something felt *off* here.

"It's hard to let go sometimes," Mike said vaguely, mind spinning.

Mrs. Highsmith nodded and grabbed a bag. The two of them carried their loads out to the truck and tossed them into the back. One particularly large bag on the bottom caught Mike's eye, although it was nearly covered with smaller bags already. "What's that big one?"

"Bob's old golf clubs—I kept them in a garbage bag to keep the mice out." Mrs. Highsmith didn't break her stride back to the house. "I never liked the game," she tossed over her shoulder.

Mike gave the bag another hard look, then made a noise of agreement. She'd never cared for the game either. And it *did* look like it held some golf clubs. What she could see of it, anyway.

It took less than ten minutes for the two of them to finish loading the rest. Mrs. Highsmith thanked the detective for her help.

"Do you want help unloading at Saint Vinny's?"

Mrs. Highsmith shook her head. "Oh, no. They have people to unload." She smiled, and Mike thought there was a reason she didn't do that very often—it looked kind of feral. "I'll be fine. But I do appreciate your help, Detective."

Mike smiled and told Mrs. H. it was no trouble. "Oh, one last thing, Mrs. Highsmith."

Mrs. Highsmith was halfway through her front door already, and she turned, annoyed.

"Was your paper working on an article about Julian Baker by any chance?"

Mrs. H. frowned, and this looked genuine, maybe the first genuine reaction she'd seen from the woman. "Not that I know of, Detective. Why do you ask?"

"Just curious." Mike got in her car, then pointed it in the direction of Grace Baker's house. Grace hadn't called or shown her face at the station, so Mike was heading straight to the teller's apartment to roust her.

But her drive was full of thoughts about Mrs. Highsmith. That house was just *weird*. It was downright creepy that Mrs. H. didn't have anything personal lying around. Mike supposed that she could be a neat freak. But even still. No photos, no nothing. Dusting was an annoying chore, and knickknacks tended to attract a lot of dust, but *nothing*? It was super suspicious. There hadn't been a chance to casually ask, "Oh, did you pick that up in Chicago?" because there was nothing to have picked up *anywhere*.

So this little side trip hadn't been helpful in figuring out where Mrs. H. was from, but it *had* raised a shit ton of other questions.

Mike did her best to push Mrs. Highsmith from her mind as she banged on the door to Grace's apartment, none too gently either. After a second pounding, Grace finally answered, and whoo boy, did she look rough. Bags under red-rimmed eyes were now the focal point of her face, and her nose looked like it had gone ten rounds with a box of sandpaper.

"You didn't return my call or come to the station to make a statement like you were ordered to." Mike pushed her shoulders back, projecting her full height. It was working, too, because Grace actually looked scared.

"I just woke up, I swear, Detective."

"Are you going to let me in?"

"Of course, of course." Grace scurried inside, and Mike followed her into the apartment, the living room chock full of personal stuff. See, this was how normal people did things.

Mike turned her attention back to her quarry, trying to focus on Grace, not Mrs. H. "Now Grace, do you know who Dean was working for?"

"The bar? Yeah, he knew the owner pretty well, and I met him once or twice." Her bloodshot eyes darted around the room while she answered.

Mike gave her a look. "That's not what I meant, and you know it."

A series of emotions flitted over Grace's features, as she clearly struggled with what she was willing to admit. Finally, she sighed. "Yeah, I knew Dean was working for my brother."

Now they were getting somewhere. "And you didn't mind? That your boyfriend was dealing drugs for your drug-dealing brother?" Mike heard herself say *drug dealing* too many times, but she couldn't fix it now that the words were out of her mouth.

"Dean was different," Grace whined. "He was going to get out of the business and go legit."

Mike only had to cock an eyebrow.

"For real," Grace insisted. "He was going to go back to school at night and quit bartending."

"What was he going to go to school for?"

"Auto mechanic."

Even if that was true, Dean was never going to make as much money fixing cars as he did tending bar and slinging drugs. On the one hand, if what Grace was saying was true, Julian Baker might have had motive to kill Dean, especially if Dean knew a lot about Julian's operation. On the other, much more likely hand, Dean had been feeding Grace this story in order to continue sleeping with her. That's where Mike would put her money.

"Were you involved in Julian's operation?"

Grace gasped. "No, I told you. I might . . . do a little weed now and again, but that is strictly personal use. I would *never* get involved in dealing drugs."

"But you were dating someone who was dealing."

Grace shook her head. "I told you, he was gonna get out and go straight."

Mike studied her for a long moment. Her gut told her that Grace really believed this crock of shit. Another good reminder that men lied, maybe *especially* ones you were dating. "Okay. Besides Dean wanting out of dealing, can you think of any other reason why Julian would want to hurt Dean?" She would love to nail down a motive for Baker.

Grace gasped again. "You think Jules did this?"

Mike considered how much to admit, deciding *not* to tell her that the gun from Dean's apartment was being tested and she suspected it was Julian's. "I do." She left it at that.

Grace was quiet. "It's so weird. I thought Julian booked it out of town before the last time I saw Dean." Her eyebrows were pulled together in concentration as she tried to work out the timeline. Her face smoothed, and she looked up at the detective. "I'm almost sure of it."

Grace had hit upon the heart of the problem with the Baker-killed-Lagerfield theory. It really looked like Julian had left town the night he dumped his car in front of his house—no one had seen or heard from him since, not his wife, not his mistress, no one. But Dean was seen on Thursday, which was *after* that. Mike supposed that Baker could still have been in town that day, lying low so he could tie up loose ends before disappearing for good. But it didn't seem likely, did it?

Why clean up loose ends if you know you're in trouble? Why stick around to kill Dean when you're already in so deep that you've got to flee town?

Her gut told her that Grace wasn't dealing drugs, though, especially since she wanted to get out of her apartment and buy a house. She had bad taste in men, obviously, but she wasn't a dealer. Mike would still get Grace's prints, though, just to be on the safe side, and check them against the gun they'd found.

"Come to the station tomorrow. You need to sign a formal statement."

"Okay," Grace said. Her face melted into something close to relief.

"You're actually going to come and get it done, or I'll issue a warrant for your arrest," Mike warned.

Grace nodded quickly.

Mike left and let loose a sigh on her way back to her car. She crossed her fingers Grace would actually show up—she really didn't want to deal with more paperwork.

Chapter 47

LORRAINE

Sunday

Lorraine could not love it more that Detective Zenoni had helped load bags of clothes onto a dead body stashed in the back of the police chief's truck. The irony was delicious, even if it had stopped her heart once or twice. The fear was a drug coursing through her veins, and she felt downright giddy now that the detective was gone.

Zenoni hadn't learned anything from the house, either, which had clearly been the reason for the detective's drop by. Lorraine chuckled. Zenoni wouldn't find anything searching under the names she had for her. Not in Chicago, or where she'd grown up or any of the places in between. She'd been very careful to choose wildly different identities each time she relocated. It was as simple as a trip to a cemetery, finding a name and date of birth, then requesting identification cards where they wouldn't find the death certificate. Easy peasy.

As far as getting rid of Julian's body, it was best to wait until just before Saint Vincent de Paul's closed to drop the bags off. That way it would be after dark, and she could get rid of the body first. She was only willing to push her luck so far, and her luck had been stretched to the breaking point already.

Shit. It was Sunday, wasn't it? That meant it would still be light well past nine o'clock, and Saint Vinny's closed early on Sundays. Waiting until tomorrow wasn't a good idea for a couple of reasons—the first being how ripe the body would get sitting out in the sun until then. It would be like putting him on defrost in the microwave, the black plastic tarp acting as a convection oven. *Shit.* She would just have to risk moving him while it was still light out.

In the meantime, she would swing by Craig Youngblood's house and see how he was doing. It was also worth stopping at a gas station—down in Milwaukee, of course—to fill up a couple of containers of gasoline. Or should she use lighter fuel? She needed an accelerant that would burn fast and hot—that ice cream shop had to go up like a redneck bonfire—one of those huge summer ones teenage kids had out in the fields when there was nothing to do but drink beer stolen from their parents' garage and light things on fire.

Lorraine sat down at her dining table, rifling through the letters she'd left neatly stacked next to her typewriter. One was a letter from Jim Higgins that seemed awfully thick. She frowned and opened it, unfolding the papers inside. Well, look at that. Jim had clipped her column from the *Chicago Tribune* and sent it to her. A little square with her face ran next to it.

And so it began. At least her picture was small and just blurry enough to render her features anonymous—it was unlikely that anyone from her past would recognize her. But she still wanted to get this current body problem cleared up fast, just in case her assumptions about it being a local issue were incorrect.

Another column was due in a few days, but it wasn't worth bothering with just now. She would knock one out at the last minute—it wouldn't be the first time, and it wouldn't be the last. In fact, she did some of her best work under pressure—and that applied to more than writing advice.

Lorraine pulled out her Sheboygan Bay phone book and looked up Craig Youngblood. His address was listed, which was good luck for her.

She copied it down on a pad of paper, pulled the top sheet off, folded it, and stuck it in her pocket. She was getting ready to leave the house when the doorbell rang. She squinted in that direction. Could she get away with pretending she wasn't at home?

With a sigh she went to the front door, where there was now insistent knocking coming from the other side. Obviously not the FedEx man, who didn't give a shit if you got your package or not. She'd seen their usual guy toss packages over a neighbor's fence, which Lorraine found amusing—as long as they weren't hers.

Lorraine opened the door to find Marjorie Rupp. Again.

"What do you want, Marjorie? I'm busy."

"I just want to see what you've found out."

She started to close the door, but Marjorie was surprisingly fast and once again shoved her fat foot in the opening so that Lorraine couldn't shut it all the way.

"I'm not giving you coffee. Or anything else."

"That's fine. I've had plenty for today," Marjorie countered. "I just want information."

Lorraine considered her options. This was the second time Marjorie had made a nuisance of herself, and it was more than an annoyance to Lorraine at this point. She had room in her freezer right now; should she just take care of her? She looked past Marjorie to her driveway—no car, so there would be no trace of Marjorie, no indication that she'd been here.

A dog walker turned the corner and came down the street, staring at Lorraine and Marjorie as he passed. She vaguely recognized him even though her neighbors tended to keep their distance from her. This one lived a block or so down the road.

Well, shit. There went that idea. Lorraine relented and let Marjorie in the house but didn't move away from the foyer, blocking the hall with her body.

"I'll get right down to it."

"Thank God for that," Lorraine said, arms folded over her chest.

"I want the money."

"What fucking money?"

"The money Julian Baker stole. Rumor around town is that he had a huge stash of drug money, and I want it. I'd bet my Elvis collectible plates that's what my brother was after, and that's why he was killed."

Marjorie had a fair point there. Her brother probably *had* been surveilling Julian for the money. Had it looked like there had been a client? She didn't think so, but her memory of Rupp's file was a little fuzzy, and she cursed her slowing brain.

She needed to carry her little camera with her in the future. Or maybe get one of those Polaroids.

"And why are you here telling me this?"

"Because I know you've been sticking your nose in things." This was the same accusation Marjorie had made earlier. "And I'm guessing you have an idea of where the money is. I want a cut."

"What I *think* is that Baker took it with him when he split town. If there ever was any money." Lorraine said this with conviction, hoping that it would convince Marjorie to leave. She had work to do—she couldn't have Marjorie following her all over town.

Marjorie shook her head. "Nah, there's gotta be more. What about the money he stole from his boss—everyone has heard about that. It's why he's short a finger."

"Where did you hear all this?" Lorraine was genuinely curious.

Marjorie ignored the question. "But Baker had another stash. That's the word on the street. I mean, even with that big house and the fancy cars, he was making a shit ton of money dealing drugs. Money he couldn't exactly deposit into the bank. So where is it all?"

Lorraine knew that Baker had been laundering a lot of it through Mary Ann's Frozen Custard, but what if Marjorie was right? What if Baker *did* have more money stashed around town? It hadn't been in his storage unit—she would have seen that right away. So where?

This was an issue to worry about once she'd disposed of Baker's body, which she couldn't do if Marjorie was with her or following her around. Lorraine considered the other woman. "If you tell me where you heard all this shit, I'll let you come with me to check out who might know where the dough is." She could always use new sources of information, and it looked like Marjorie had a good one.

Marjorie stuck out her hand to shake on the deal, but Lorraine ignored it, shooing the woman back outside instead.

Chapter 48

MIKE

Sunday

Mike got the stakeout team for that evening organized before she left the station. The guys had their assignments, although of *course* there'd been grumbling about a woman running the operation—which she ignored, as usual. Now she was home, killing time. She checked her machine as soon as she walked in the door, but for once the red light was dull, unlit. No new messages. She wasn't quite sure if that was a relief or not.

Shit, she should call Steph back. Maybe they could skate next week. Or maybe that was overly optimistic, with the way things were going.

Mike let Zeus out, then wandered into the living room to look at her chalkboard. She was really bothered by the timeline issues, mostly that it looked like Julian Baker did his disappearing act before Dean Lagerfield was killed. Why kill Dean if everything was going to come out anyway? She sat on her couch, staring at her chalkboard, trying to sort it out. Something just didn't work—the motive, for one. But something else didn't seem to fit, and she couldn't put her finger on exactly what.

If only she could talk to her pops, about the case *and* about Mrs. H. But every time she got her hopes up that he might still be in there somewhere, she came away disappointed. More than disappointed, devastated. It was really hard to do that to herself—fill her chest with a balloon of hope only to have it drop to the ground like lead. So maybe not today.

She stared at her own neat handwriting on the board. At least she'd have some answers about Baker's drop after tonight. Either her boss had guessed correctly and the drop was taking place at the port just south of downtown, or he'd been wrong and they would miss it. It was possible the person responsible for the murders was the person dropping the drugs, even likely. Her stomach churned, sending a sour taste to her mouth. Christ, this better go well tonight.

She pulled out the records that the phone company had turned over for Julian Baker's car phone and flipped to the last page.

Well, this was interesting. It looked like Baker stopped using the car phone the same night everyone assumed he bounced out of town. The phone towers could triangulate a person's location, and Baker was probably smart enough to know that. But there was another call *after* Baker split town, to an unknown number. This she found *really* interesting. Had Baker taken the car phone with him? Could they use it to find him?

Mike punched the unknown number into her own phone and waited while it rang on the other end. It was finally picked up, and once Mike identified herself, she immediately recognized the voice.

"Detective," Mrs. Highsmith said. "What can I do for you?"

Her mouth gaped for a beat, and she could hear the sound of another woman's voice asking questions in the background.

"Mrs. Highsmith, this is a surprise," she finally said.

"How is it a surprise?" Mrs. H. asked. "You called me."

"The surprise is that this is the last number called from Julian Baker's car phone. Why was he calling you?"

"I sure don't know, Detective. I never spoke to the man on the phone."

Mrs. H. was lying. "Then why did the call last for almost thirty seconds? That means you picked up the phone."

There was a long silence, which Mike spent frowning. Then Mrs. Highsmith spoke again, voice curious. "Now that you mention it, there *was* a strange message on my machine. It was just silent, went on for a while, though." Mike could almost see Mrs. Highsmith shrug, her face emotionless.

"Do you still have the tape?"

"I rewound the cassette and taped over it, Detective. I didn't think anything of it." She paused. "How odd that it was from Baker's phone. And from a car phone, you said? How funny, I thought only drug dealers used car phones. Do you know who has that right now?"

Mike squinted at a spot on her wall. "Wouldn't Julian Baker have it?"

"Not if he's on the lam, as you young people say," she replied. "However those things work, I think they can be tracked."

She had already thought the same thing and made a mental plan to have the thing triangulated. But she wasn't about to tell Mrs. H. that.

Mike could hear the woman's voice in the background again. "Who is that?"

Lorraine's voice was annoyed. "Marjorie Rupp. Why, you want to talk to her?"

"No, that's fine. I was just wondering. I'll speak with you later, Mrs. Highsmith." She hung up, then made a note about making *another* call to the phone company before staring absently at the chalkboard. Zeus nuzzled her hand, begging for some head scratches, and she moved her fingers, brain whizzing like a Tilt-A-Whirl.

Mrs. Highsmith hadn't mentioned the weird phone call, but then, it was unlikely Mrs. H. had known it was from Julian Baker's phone. But why was Baker calling Mrs. Highsmith?

This felt like one more reason to figure out who Mrs. H. really was.

Chapter 49

LORRAINE

Sunday

"How am I supposed to have a conversation with you squawking in the background?" Lorraine asked once Zenoni had hung up.

"You wouldn't have this problem if you'd let me get on another extension like I asked."

Lorraine didn't bother responding. Instead, she herded Marjorie out of the kitchen—yet again—out the door, off the front stoop, and toward the driveway. "Damn," Lorraine said.

"What?"

"I forgot that I have the chief's truck. It's not exactly inconspicuous." She glanced at Marjorie. "Also, I can only stay out until six." She did some calculations about closing times and unloading things. "Mmm, make that five thirty."

"We can take my car, I guess," Marjorie said doubtfully.

Lorraine frowned. "What car?"

Marjorie pointed down the street about a block away. Both women looked at the banged-up Crown Victoria, clearly a former cop car.

It was a good thing she'd decided to let Marjorie live, since she'd brought a car here after all. "Where'd you get that, a police auction?" Lorraine asked.

Marjorie nodded. "Good engines. A lot of wear, though. But the price is right."

"I'll bet it smells like an ashtray." Lorraine shuddered. "We'll take the chief's truck."

It looked like Julian Baker was getting a final tour around town from the back of Chief Schneider's pickup.

Fifteen minutes later and Lorraine and Marjorie were parked outside Craig Youngblood's place. Lights were on in the living room, and a car was parked in the driveway, all good signs. Lorraine was irritated that she had company, though, especially when Marjorie started rambling to fill the silence.

"Doug was watching Julian. Julian had a bunch of money. It stands to reason that my brother was doing this all for the money. He was such a skeezeball."

Lorraine tried to tune out Marjorie, not even acknowledging her words, hoping the other woman would shut up sooner rather than later.

"I don't get how Doug thought that Julian would lead him to the money, though, ya know? And honestly, my brother couldn't a been that good at his job, so how did he expect to follow Baker around forever without being seen? I can't even believe that he ended up learning something about Baker's wife. I mean, what are the odds?"

This brought Lorraine up short. "What did he learn about Baker's wife?"

Marjorie went quiet, aware that she had let too much information slip.

"Marjorie," Lorraine said in a warning tone.

"I may a looked at the file."

"And?" she prompted, knowing full well that wasn't all.

"I may a taken a page or two out of it before you and the chief saw it."

There it was. Lorraine was kicking herself—she had never once suspected Marjorie capable of it, and that was on her. For a moment she considered diming Marjorie out to Detective Zenoni as being another meddlesome pain in the ass, but it felt too much like tattling. Lorraine had never been a snitch.

"The pages you stole. What exactly did they say?"

Marjorie's face twisted. "It looks like Sharity was having an affair. But my idiot brother hadn't figured out with who. I hope whoever it was didn't get the money."

"You think Sharity and her boyfriend would still be here if they found a pile of cash? You're an idiot for being obsessed with the money—it's long gone."

That finally shut Marjorie up. That and the fact that Craig Youngblood was loading something from his garage into the trunk of his car.

"Are those gas cans?" Marjorie asked.

"Shit." Her mind started calculating fast. She needed to dump Marjorie, like *now*, and then get this body loaded into the ice cream shop. She wasn't going to have time to fill a gas can of her own. There was an old bottle of lighter fluid she could grab from her shed, though.

But how to get rid of Marjorie?

"Marjorie, we're going to have to split up." The other woman started to argue, but Lorraine just spoke louder. "I need you to videotape the front door of the ice cream shop, and I'll take the back. If Youngblood is going to do what I think he is, we should get video evidence. I got two camcorders at home, we'll swing by and grab them."

Marjorie chewed this over, then agreed. "Why do you get the back, though?"

"Because I can sit in the alley in the chief's truck and point the recorder out the window. Your car is a little . . . noticeable. You're likely to get the cops called, parked in the alley with that thing."

There was a long pause, but Marjorie agreed to the deal. Lorraine didn't wait to follow Youngblood to his next destination; she just took off for home. She knew right where the boxy camcorder was—in the hall closet, though truthfully, she only owned one—and grabbed it, praying that the battery was charged.

"I thought you said you had two?" Marjorie asked when she came back to the truck.

"I can't find the other one. I've got a camera in my purse though. I'll take pictures." She put the truck in drive, then sped over to the ice cream shop and pulled over to dump Marjorie across the street.

"Do you know how to use one of these?" Lorraine passed over the bulky black recorder.

"I'm not an idiot," Marjorie snapped.

She let that slide, watching Marjorie dismount from the truck and take up a position in front of the liquor store.

Willing Marjorie to stay where she was, Lorraine zipped around to the alley that ran behind the commercial buildings on Main Street, Mary Ann's included. It was not even close to dark yet, but she didn't have time to waste. She parked close to the fence on the opposite side of the alley, hoping the truck would block most of what she was about to do. Then she crawled into the bed of the truck, pushing boxes and tossing bags of clothes to one side. Fuck, she was going to be sore tomorrow. But she didn't have any other choice right now.

The body mostly uncovered, she scanned the alley for observers—there were none—and then picked the lock on the back of the ice cream shop with her master key. It took her a few minutes to find the right one again, and she cursed herself for not marking it after last time.

Lorraine propped the door open and then set up the ramp from the truck bed. She sucked in a deep breath and then hoisted the dolly up to a rolling position, making sure to use her legs and not her back, just like she and Cynthia practiced at the gym. If only Cyn could see her now, she'd be so impressed.

A small stream of water drained from the lumpy black tarp—the hot and humid weather was doing Baker no favors. She ignored the water and carefully rolled the dolly down the ramp—dolly first, because she wasn't looking to get crushed under the weight of this frozen turkey if this thing slipped free. She congratulated herself for the way she'd placed it in the truck bed—she'd set herself up nicely for this part.

She was panting by the time she got the dolly with its tarp-wrapped load to the alley, but she couldn't exactly take time to catch her breath. She braced her core, then pushed Julian up and over the little doorjamb and inside the ice cream shop. Lorraine let the back door close behind her and let herself huff and puff a little bit, trying to catch her breath now that she was out of public view.

A few minutes passed, and her heart rate started dropping back down to something near normal, although she was sweating inside her tracksuit in a way that was deeply unpleasant. Doing her best to ignore that, she turned her mind to figuring out where to dump this schmuck—he needed to go up in flames and fast.

Chapter 50

MIKE

Sunday

Mike was restless. She couldn't stop her mind from flicking back and forth, back and forth between Mrs. Highsmith and the stakeout, and occasionally to others as well, like Youngblood and Lagerfield. Holy hotcakes, she really needed the stakeout to go well tonight. Not to mention, she really wanted some answers about Mrs. H. But how to go about getting them?

Staring at the chalkboard wasn't helping, so she decided to head out again. Zeus made a show of his disapproval, snorting and slobbering all over her, but she gave him a rawhide to distract him and slipped out the door. She would do a quick run past the port in the daylight, scope out where everyone was supposed to set up. Lordy, if this didn't go down tonight, the department would be paying out overtime for a fat lot of nothing—they'd called in two guys on their day off just to sit in a car and watch the water. Maybe it was time to start praying they'd see more than waves tonight. She wasn't religious, but desperate times, right?

As she cruised down Main Street toward Second, she noticed Marjorie Rupp standing awkwardly outside the liquor store, futzing with a big camcorder. What on earth was she taking video of? The

Bottle Stop? That was weird, but then, Marjorie Rupp was weird, even by Sheboygan Bay standards. On the other hand, she'd just been hanging out with Mrs. Highsmith—that had been Marjorie's voice when she'd called.

Mike should stop and talk with her—see what all this was about. She slowed, but the white Ford pickup behind her honked, clearly annoyed that she'd stopped without her blinker, oblivious to the fact that this was an unmarked cop car. She gave a wave of apology, then hit the accelerator and kept going toward the port. She could talk to Marjorie later, after this stakeout was finished.

The Sheboygan Bay port spanned two city blocks, give or take. To the south were industrial docks, used by small freight ships bringing goods to send north into the tip of Door County or even farther into the Northwoods. There were cranes and equipment parked in fenced-off lots, topped with barbed wire warnings to stay away from the scattered metal containers hulking on the asphalt. It was an ugly area, not the face of the city that you showed to tourists.

But the north end of the port was where locals docked their private boats, a stone breakwater separating the two areas. There were a couple of midsize, expensive boats here. Nothing like the yachts you saw down at McKinley Marina in Milwaukee, but some nice boats, probably paid for with money from Kohler. The rest were fishing boats, speedboats, or pontoons, tied to the wooden piers and bobbing in the water, waiting for their owners to take a spin on the lake.

She'd never been a maritime girl and didn't know any of the terms. What she did know was that the port—both ends, from all reports—was dead quiet tonight except for the crickets, their chirps singing through her open car windows. Mike had been sitting for a few hours already, chewing and spitting sunflower seeds just to keep herself awake, but nothing had moved in or out of the port.

Fuck. Was tonight really going to be a complete bust?

It had been fully dark for hours now, but the glow of lights from downtown bounced off the charcoal clouds that had pooled over the lake while she sat there. A summer storm. Normally she loved them, since a good soaking rain usually dropped the humidity to something tolerable, but tonight was seriously shit timing. If the clouds opened up, they wouldn't be able to see *squat*.

She shifted in her seat again, attempting to wake her ass up, squeezing muscles, then releasing them to try and ease the ache from sitting in one spot for so long. Lightning flashed briefly over the water.

"Detective, it's almost midnight. And the sky is about to open up. I'm calling it," Schneider's voice crackled over the radio. His wife had dropped him off at the station earlier.

She had just grabbed the mic, ready to argue, when her boss spoke again. "We'll leave one car overnight, but I'm sending everyone else home." Drops of rain began a slow but steadily increasing drumbeat on her windshield.

She sighed. "Ten-four." She replaced the mic in its metal holder, and hit the steering wheel with her palm, hard. "Shit!"

Bars usually went quiet when the detective stepped inside, but tonight the few patrons scattered around the place barely noticed her—a pleasant change of pace. And good for them, since she was in no mood for any shit tonight, even curious stares. She shook off her umbrella, stomach roiling from both stress and the number of sunflower seeds she'd eaten over the last few hours. Would a beer help that? No. But she was having one anyway.

"If I Had a Boat" by Lyle Lovett was playing on the radio, and she snorted. Fitting.

She found an empty stool on the far side of the horseshoe bar and slid onto it. Jason filled another drink order before coming over to see what she wanted.

"It's fucked up, what happened to Dean," Jason said.

The case was the last thing she wanted to talk about, but she also wasn't going to miss a chance to gather information from someone who clearly wanted to chat. "Sure is." She agreed. "I'll have a PBR."

"Do you know what happened to him?" Jason asked this over his shoulder while he pulled the beer for her from the cooler.

"I was just about to ask you the same thing."

Jason pressed his lips together while he delivered the sweating beer can, considering. But then he decided in favor of gossiping with the detective. "I told him that was some heinous shit he was getting involved in, and it would lead to no good."

"Did he ever talk about it?"

Jason shrugged. "Not much, but he did let Baker's name slip once or twice. I got the feeling that Dean thought he could do a better job than his boss and wanted to take over the gig."

Her eyebrows went up. Had Dean made a play for Julian's job, and that's why he was knocked off? That was a great motive.

"Dean was like that, though. He always talked about how much better this bar would be if he ran it." Jason rolled his eyes. "For a low-life drug dealer, he had a real high opinion of himself." Then he seemed to realize how that sounded. "I'm sorry he's dead, though. I really am."

"No, I get it," Mike assured him. "After someone dies everyone wants to believe they were a saint and only remember the good things, but that's not helpful, yah know? It's not who they were."

"Exactly," Jason said, relief written on his face. But he still scurried off to fill a drink order on the other side of the bar, leaving her to sip her beer and think.

And eavesdrop. The couple a few barstools down kept glancing at her—she could see it in her periphery—and they were talking about Dean's death, doing their best to keep it to a whisper. She wasn't surprised—it was a hot topic around town right now. Much juicier than Doug Rupp being dumped on Mrs. Highsmith's lawn, since Dean Lagerfield was someone that people bought drinks from. Both men had been locals, but Dean had stayed in town, pulling beer for the townsfolk. And now Dean was dead, dropped in a chest freezer like a frozen ham won at a meat raffle.

Just then Grace Baker came through the door, followed by Jamie Sprout. They shook rain from their hair, laughing, and she tensed, feeling the need to flee out the back door since she was in a foul mood and hadn't returned Jamie's phone call, but Jamie had already spotted her, and while Grace grabbed a high-top table, Jamie rushed over to say hello.

"Dudette! I didn't know you'd be here!" Jamie glanced at where Grace was sitting. "I would invite you over, but like, Grace seems like she needs a friend." He smiled, a little awkwardly. "And like, I don't think she'd like to talk in front of a cop." His eyes got wide. "But there's nothing going on between us. Just so you know. I would never date my cousin's ex. That would be bogus."

"That's really nice of you to hang out with her, Jamie." His reasoning wasn't super sound, but she believed him when he said there was nothing going on between the two. It wasn't really anything that affected her, anyway. The man could date who he liked. In fact, he should, since she didn't have time for dating and wasn't sure Jamie was a good fit for her. "I was just finishing up here anyway."

"Oh, don't bounce on my account!" He smiled. "Even though you're drinking, you're working, right?" One of his dimples winked at her, and then he actually winked at her. "You can tell me all about it at dinner tomorrow night. If you're free, that is. That's why I called the other day—I was hoping we could go on another date."

He said the last part shyly, and her stomach dropped. She couldn't say no to his face, not when it looked like *that*. "That sounds great. Pick me up at six?"

"That's perfect." He smiled broadly before rejoining Grace. She watched the two interact for a bit before turning her attention back to her beer.

Maybe she could call him tomorrow with an excuse. Jamie was nice enough, but she still wasn't convinced that he wasn't involved, even if it had been unknowingly. She could absolutely picture the big oaf running errands for his cousin, not knowing exactly what they entailed or how illegal they were.

But. Jamie might actually be getting some good information from Grace Baker, details that Grace wouldn't give her, a detective. And it wasn't *using* him if he learned something from Grace and then shared it with her, right? She would feel bad about using someone, even a man.

So maybe it wasn't a terrible idea to go to dinner with him, see what he'd learned. Come to think of it, he might have picked up other tidbits, being Dean's cousin. Locals would want to get close to the drama, feel like they knew something about it without grief actually touching *their* lives.

Not to mention it wouldn't hurt to be seen on another date with him. It would honestly be nice if people started to assume she dated men.

Chapter 51

LORRAINE

Sunday

Lorraine was pushing Baker down the hall when she heard banging on the back door. It was making a ruckus, and she let out a growl—she was grateful that she'd locked up behind herself, but *Jesus Christ* the noise had to stop. She had a sneaking suspicion she knew who it was, and she cursed Marjorie up one side and down the other. She was like a summer tick, burrowed in and impossible to get rid of. And for what, some imaginary cash?

Now that her freezer was empty, it might be worth making Marjorie disappear.

Lorraine hustled the dolly down the hallway, the jackass outside still making a racket, and pushed it into Youngblood's office. She pulled the couch a couple of feet away from the wall, then moved the dolly into its place. She released the straps and let the body fall to the floor with a heavy thud, then pushed it as close to the wall as she could before shoving the couch back into place in front of it. It would be obvious in the light of day that something was tucked back there, but hopefully Youngblood would be too concerned with pouring accelerant to notice. If he was smart, he wouldn't turn any lights on to do the deed either.

Sweating with vigor now, she left her dolly in the hallway next to some stacked milk crates and opened the back door. Sure as shit, there was Marjorie, leaning against the truck, playing with the buttons on the camcorder. She looked up when the door opened.

"What the fuck, Lorraine? How'd you get in there?"

"Back door was open, and I realized that I needed to use the bathroom."

"Given the way you're sweating, I'd say you should eat more fiber. Metamucil or something."

"Thanks for the tip." Lorraine's voice was heavy with sarcasm, but she wasn't going to correct her assumption. "Why are you back here? I thought you were supposed to be filming the front of the shop?"

"I got bored. Nothing is happening, and this thing is heavy. I think we should go back to Youngblood's—maybe he hasn't left yet."

Her first instinct was to snarl at the woman, but instead she nodded at the piles of clothes and boxes. "We need to drop this at Saint Vinny's first."

"Uh, *I* don't need to do anything."

Lorraine ignored her and got into the truck, then backed expertly down the alley until they were in line with the rear door of the charity shop. "Get out and let them know we're here. Since you're so good at banging on doors."

Marjorie just chuckled and went to the back of the shop to ring the bell. A young man in a T-shirt and baggy jean shorts opened the door and poked his head outside, surveying the two women and the truck.

"You're gonna need help, son," Marjorie told him. "We're old, and we ain't hauling these bags anywhere."

The kid seemed a little flustered but went inside and came back out with reinforcements, another high school or college-aged kid joining him—it was impossible to tell ages anymore; they all looked like children—and the youngsters made quick work of moving the donations into the shop. Lorraine stood and watched while Marjorie smoked a Slim.

"Those things fucking stink." Lorraine waved her hand in front of her nose. "And they're terrible for you."

Marjorie shrugged. "So are most things."

"Don't come crying to me when you end up with lung cancer."

Marjorie rolled her eyes. "They're done. Head back to the ice cream man's place?"

Lorraine really wanted to get rid of her. "Remind me why you're fucking bothering me with this shit?"

"The money. You think I want to live in that shit box? If I had this bag of cash that Baker hid, I could buy a place on the water, one of those nice places near you. Shit, we could be neighbors."

Lorraine would pay money of her own to make sure that *didn't* happen.

Which meant swinging by Youngblood's house one more time. It wouldn't hurt anything, especially if she was able to prove to Marjorie that she was barking up the wrong tree.

This day hadn't gone *at all* how she'd wanted, but at least she'd managed to get Baker's body unloaded—it felt good to have that little errand done. She needed to retrieve her dolly later, but once she'd done that and Youngblood got his shit together and burned down his shop, she would be in the clear.

Shit, she hadn't had a chance to douse Baker in accelerant.

With everything that had happened—mostly Marjorie interrupting her—she hadn't grabbed that lighter fluid. Well, fuck it. The couch she'd parked Baker behind definitely wasn't real leather, and it would go up fast, taking the body with it. And the dolly wouldn't be noticed as anything out of place if Youngblood did happen to light the joint up before she could retrieve it.

Without a word, she got back into the chief's truck, and Marjorie stubbed out her cigarette before following suit. They didn't talk, but Lorraine did point the truck back in the direction of Youngblood's place. Once there, she parked half a block away, close enough that they could see, but hoping he wouldn't notice them.

Nothing was happening. The garage door was closed, so they couldn't tell whether or not Youngblood was parked inside, and there were no lights on, except for a single lamp in the big bay window at the front.

This was annoying. What if he'd gone to do the deed? She didn't need to be there to witness it, obviously, but she would like to know that he was getting shit done.

"Using accelerant is stupid," Marjorie said out of nowhere. "It will make the place go up, but he'll get fingered right away for insurance fraud."

"That's true, but do you really think the fire chief is smart enough to figure that out? All this guy needs is one spot in the building where it looks like something could have gone wrong—faulty wiring or a space heater left on—"

"Right now? Who's using a space heater this time of year?"

"My point is," Lorraine said, raising her voice, "if he's smart enough—and I really don't know if he is—he'll make it look like an accident, and the fire chief won't even look for accelerant."

Marjorie was quiet. "What about the money?"

"What about the money?"

"I was thinking about it on the drive over here, and I'm wondering if that's what you were searching for inside the place, trying to cut me out," Marjorie said. "Instead of taking a deuce."

Uncouth was the word that came to mind to describe Marjorie. "If I was looking for the money, I obviously didn't find it."

"Did you search everywhere, though?"

She hated to admit that she'd been more preoccupied with the dead body than with finding the cache of stolen money. She *hadn't* searched the place, and Youngblood was about to light it up.

"What if I did and I wasn't able to find anything? Who's to say that Baker didn't take the money with him when he split town? That's what any reasonable person would do. Especially one that needed to start over somewhere. Which is what he'll have to do, what with the shitstorm he started here."

Marjorie nodded slowly. "I suppose that does make sense. I just can't help feeling that he left at least *something* behind. He split in an awful hurry—and depending on where he stashed it . . . well, he wouldn't have had time to collect it all. Rumor has it there was quite a bit."

"You gotta stop listening to rumors. And where are you getting all this from? You said you would tell me—that was the deal."

Youngblood's car pulled past them, and the garage door creaked open. He parked inside, and the door started its slow descent, but before it touched down, they saw him open his trunk and remove a weighty gas can. That was good—it looked as though he'd gone and filled up.

He was limping a little, too, which nearly made Lorraine smile.

But instead, Lorraine turned to the other woman expectantly, one eyebrow raised.

Marjorie sighed. "Fine, I heard most of this from Cindi at the Curl Up 'N Dye."

What the hell? Why was Marjorie getting the good stuff and she wasn't? She spent enough time and money in that joint getting her hair rinsed and cut, she should be getting the good gossip as well.

Because Lorraine was an outsider, that's why. A fucking decade in this place and people still didn't trust her, didn't think she "belonged" here. Even people like Cindi would only give her so much gossip, and that woman *lived* for hot gossip.

Marjorie was watching her with a gleam in her eye. "She's my second cousin on my mother's side."

Of course, she was.

Chapter 52

MIKE

Sunday Night / Monday Morning

Mike couldn't stop glancing over at Jamie, wanting to know what they were talking about and whether it was useful to her case, but she was going to get caught if she didn't quit. It might shut Grace up, and she needed Jamie to learn as much as he could. She motioned for Jason to bring her check. Instead of spying—and getting caught—she would go home to her dog and stare at her chalkboard, go over everything again and see if she'd missed something somewhere. Because she was obviously missing something, and it was getting to her, like a seagull attacking a french fry.

The door opened again, and John Hooper entered. Perhaps shambled was a better word, since the man looked like the walking dead. There weren't a lot of barstools open, and the ones that were free were squeezed in between couples. John spotted her, and the couple of openings on either side of her, and headed her way.

All of a sudden, staying put was looking like a real good idea. When Jason returned with her check, she stopped him. "You know what, I'll have another one after all."

Jason shrugged and went to pull another can of PBR.

Hooper took a seat one down from her, giving the detective a small nod. Mike waited for her beer, sneaking another glance at Jamie and Grace, who looked deep in conversation. She waited until Hooper had a drink of his own before sliding onto the barstool next to him.

"You look tired."

He shook his head. "You don't know the half of it. And my wife wants to have another one! That is the definition of insanity. Adding another sentence of sleepless nights onto the one we are barely surviving."

"You don't think it's worth it?" She was genuinely curious.

Hooper took a long swig of his Miller High Life. "I don't know, Detective. Ask me in three to five years." He rubbed his eye. "Christ, I hope it's not more than that."

She made a noise of acknowledgment but didn't say anything else for a little while, letting Hooper get through most of his beer first. She was hoping it would loosen the man's tongue, so she'd give him a minute before peppering him with questions about his childhood buddies.

But it was Hooper who opened the conversation, much to her surprise. "Heard you found Dean Lagerfield." He signaled Jason for another round.

She nodded, then panicked a little. It looked like Jason had interpreted Hooper's signal as both of them needing another drink, which she did *not*. She had no intention of drinking a third beer—she'd have to get a taxi home if she did, since she would never drive drunk. She tried to get Jason's attention in order to cancel hers, but it was too late—another round appeared in front of them both.

Hooper slammed back the dregs in his glass and set it down with a muffled burp before turning to the fresh one. "I get one night out a week, man. And even if no one else is willing to go with me, I still leave the house."

She nodded. "Who do you usually go with?" He must be real tired if he was this chatty, and with a cop.

He shrugged. "Used to be Youngblood, but that guy has been crazy weird lately. On the nights I'm free, it's like he always has an excuse."

She made a sympathetic noise. "Weird how?"

He appeared to give that some thought. "I can't really put my finger on it. But I did see him talking with Carrie Ann at the gas station a few weeks ago. Like, they were too cozy, if you know what I mean."

"I do. You don't think Julian would have appreciated his buddy chatting up his girlfriend?" She wasn't sure that was especially interesting—Youngblood was obviously interested in chatting up anyone that was young and cute. And she'd bet money that dipstick wasn't above taking his buddy's mistress for his own either.

"Exactly," he said, then shook his head. "Jules and Craig were still pretty tight, so I don't know what that was about." Hooper was lost in thought. "I used to hang with those guys a lot in high school, but our lives really took different paths. I just don't have a ton in common with them anymore—especially not since the baby. Even drinking with Craig once in a while, it's just not the same."

He had said as much the last time they spoke, but she agreed once again. "That happens a lot, I think."

He nodded, and they drank in silence. She was trying to go really slow on this second beer so she wouldn't be tempted to touch the third. "Did you guys still talk to Rupp?" she asked after a long beat.

"Still working on that, eh?" Hooper asked, lighting up a Marlboro. "Nah, I was pretty up front with you before about everything. I hadn't talked to Rupp in years—he turned out to be a real lowlife. And Julian—well, I lost touch with him about a year ago. The only one I still talk to is Craig."

He blew some smoke, then took another long drink. "Gnarly shit about Julian's finger, though, right?"

"Real gnarly." She still hadn't caught wind of how it had actually happened, although of course she had her theories. "What was the story again?"

Hooper gave her a sidelong glance, and Mike knew that he knew that she didn't know what the story was. "Whoever Julian works for cut that finger off because Jules stole money from him," he said.

Harsh. But it made a lot of sense, retribution for the stolen money, right? It also meant that her guess was correct—the big boss had sent a message, and that message was don't steal from me. Baker was lucky he only lost a finger. Knowing that her theory had been right propped her up a little, which she needed after an absolute bust of an evening.

If the big boss had taken a finger, Baker must have made off with a *lot* of money. No one had been able to name a number—not even a guess—as to how much Baker had. Mike was real curious about how much a finger equaled.

She stifled a sigh. Yah know, she might have been able to figure out who the big boss was if they'd caught the drop tonight. But no. No drop, no drugs, no drug kingpin. Baker knew everything she needed to know, but he'd skipped town with his stupid dragon's hoard of cash. Frustration curdled her stomach, souring the beer in her mouth. She had really wanted—no *needed*—tonight to go well. She had a sick feeling in her gut that Schneider would take over the case soon, and that would be a disaster. For both her and the victims.

What would her pops tell her? *Focus on what you can control and let go of the rest.* She was pretty sure he'd learned that in AA, which her stepmom made him join if he wanted to keep her around. Her pops hadn't been a mean drunk, quite the opposite; he'd been quite jolly. But it *had* started to interfere with his job and his waistline. She'd been grateful to her stepmother for that because once her pops quit and switched to drinking nonalcoholic stuff during games, he was more present, had more time for her again. The other bonus was that it made Mike real aware of her own drinking. For instance, she wouldn't be finishing this beer, even though it felt wasteful to not finish what was put in front of you.

She pushed the can away and signaled for the check.

Back in her car, she gave herself a quick Breathalyzer with the little portable reader she kept in the glove box. Only when the numbers came back well below the legal limit did she turn over the ignition and point her car home. On the way, she turned her mind to what she'd learned and what she needed to do tomorrow.

She needed to talk to Craig Youngblood again, sooner rather than later. Julian Baker and Youngblood had still been buddies—Baker had been at the custard shop daily, so she'd wager Youngblood was involved somehow. If she had to guess, Baker was running dirty cash through the place. She might be able to get the judge to sign a warrant for Youngblood's books now, but it would be better if she had some corroboration first.

Maybe Carrie Ann Williams knew something about it. She could talk with her again tomorrow too.

As she pulled into her driveway, she groaned, remembering she had a date with Jamie the next night. *You're too soft, Little Mike. They'll eat you alive if you don't toughen up and learn to say no.* She grumbled at the reminder but knew her pops had been right.

But no matter. She already had a plan to use it to her advantage. She'd see if Jamie was somehow involved in his cousin's drug trade and learn what Grace Baker had to say for herself.

Speaking of. Grace had best show up to the station tomorrow for prints and a statement or Mike would be filling out paperwork on her too. She *wasn't* soft anymore, whether her pops knew it or not.

Mike realized she was still sitting in her car. Her hand went to the key in the ignition, ready to flick it off; then she reached for the gearshift instead and threw the car into reverse.

"You're nuts," she told herself, "just go to bed." But she would sleep better if she cruised past the lakefront one more time.

The squad Schneider had assigned was still parked where they'd left it. Even from a distance she could see that the windows were fogged up—she'd be surprised if the officer could see anything at all. Know what? He was probably asleep.

She heaved a sigh from the depths of her very soul but left it alone. Nothing was happening here anyway, which was no surprise, really. This was too populated, too many boats belonging to locals, too public. With another deep sigh, she pulled away from the marina and cruised south, although she didn't head home, not yet.

Instead, she found herself in Marjorie's neighborhood, which somehow looked even worse at night. She wouldn't walk around this area by herself at this time of night, that was for sure. *But wouldn't that make it ideal?*

"Okay, but where?" she said out loud. But her gut was quiet now, which was frustrating. Why did it only speak to her in riddles?

Turning down the side street that led to the factories, she *did* have a thought. Hadn't the paint factory back here closed two three months back? It was real close to the water, so was there a pier?

Chapter 53

MIKE

Sunday Night / Monday Morning

Mike left her car in front of the abandoned factory, the smell of wet rotting fish assaulting her nose even before she got out of the car. At least it had stopped raining. She shuffled from foot to foot, considering her options. She had her weapon, but was this a bad idea? Checking out the back of an abandoned building by herself? Not to mention the two beers she'd had.

She shook her head. She was well under the legal limit, and the alcohol was probably through her system already. She *would* call for backup, though. This walkabout was probably nothing, just a lark, but it was best to be safe.

Once she'd radioed for dispatch to send the snoring officer her direction, she made her way to the front entrance and pulled at the doors—which were chained shut—just to make sure they really *were* locked tight. Reassured, she cautiously walked around the side of the building, stepping carefully, her Maglite balanced on top of her gun, lighting a path in front of her. She was almost at the back of the building when her bladder decided to make a nuisance of itself.

She really had to pee.

The urge stopped her in her tracks, but she didn't have time to take care of it. She would just Kegel for all she was worth while she scoped out the back of the factory. And since she wasn't likely to find anything, she would be out of here in just a few minutes, probably before the on duty even showed up, and she could hit the nearest gas station for a bathroom on her way home.

Flicking off her Maglite, Mike gave her eyes a few seconds to adjust to the gloom before popping her head around the corner. Holy cannoli, there was a pier. And not only was there a pier, there was a fishing boat tied up at it. One of those jobbies with a little steering cabin and a bedroom down below.

With drugs. Holy shit, there were probably drugs.

Now, the smart thing to do was to wait for her backup. But the pee and two beers united in some bad decision making, and along with the adrenaline pumping through her veins, propelled her toward the boat. Alone. The moon was still trapped behind the clouds, giving her plenty of cover until her shoe actually hit the pier's sketchy wood planking. Stepping cautiously, she tried to mask the loud creaking noises, but despite the noise, no head popped up, not until she was stepping onto the boat itself, gun pointed.

"Aw, shit burgers," the man said when he came up the stairs and found Mike pointing a gun at him.

"Shit burgers, indeed," she replied. "Hands on your head. Interlace your fingers."

The man did as instructed, still grumbling. "I just knew it wasn't gonna be my night when no one showed."

Mike talked him through getting onto the—admittedly slick—deck of the boat, on his stomach. She looked around, hoping the on duty would show his face, but she was still alone. With a shake of her head, she approached the guy from his feet, keeping a close eye on his hands, holstered her gun, then quick handcuffed him while giving him his Miranda rights.

"Who were you supposed to meet?" Her knee was still perched in the middle of his back, just below his cuffed hands.

She felt, rather than saw, him shrug. "I don't know names, man. I just drive."

That wasn't a surprise and only pricked a small hole in her euphoria over finding the drop site. "What's your name?"

"Why would I tell you that?"

"Because I'm going to find out as soon as I find your wallet or take your fingerprints."

His swarthy face was pressed against the less-than-clean fiberglass floor. "Dammit. It's Luke. Luke Prendergass."

Mike would bet cash money his middle name began with an *M*.

It was the wee hours of the morning when Mike finally fell into bed, but she was elated at how the evening—well, early morning—had gone. The on duty patrol had finally showed his face and relieved her of her prisoner, giving her time and space to search the boat—once she'd relieved herself in the lake, which had required some nifty balancing. Luckily, not that much "search" was actually required, since the huge shipment of drugs was right out in the open, in the little cabin below. *Finally* something was easy.

And sure, she might not have learned who the big boss was—yet, she hadn't given up on interrogating this Luke character after she got a couple of hours of sleep—but at least she'd gotten a significant amount of drugs off the streets. Cheese 'n rice, it felt amazing to do some good for her town.

And, *and* she'd cracked the drug drop location. Not her boss. *She* had. It might irk Schneider that he'd been wrong about what *LMP* was, but she was sure that the photo op coming his way would smooth over any hard feelings. All those lovely drugs, confiscated by their department, on the front page of the local paper. Shit, maybe even the *Milwaukee Journal Sentinel* would cover it.

Mike drifted off to sleep with a grin on her face.

Chapter 54

LORRAINE

Sunday Night / Monday Morning

Lorraine finally got rid of Marjorie—a goddamn relief—after they watched Youngblood's house for a little longer and nothing else happened.

After dropping Marjorie off at her car and waiting to be sure that the woman actually drove away, Lorraine was able to go inside. Damn, she was tired. Her muscles ached, and she was going to take a muscle relaxer tonight in addition to some high-octane ibuprofen. It was really too bad that Julian Baker hadn't seen fit to lose fifty or a hundred pounds before she offed him.

Youngblood had filled his gas cans, which felt like a good indicator that he was planning to act, and soon. Tonight would be best, for her anyway. Hopefully he was simply waiting for the predawn hours so he could do the deed with the fewest people around. She should go retrieve her dolly, but at this point she was too tired. She'd just steal a new one.

Lorraine rinsed off in the shower before crawling naked into bed—it was the healthiest and most comfortable way to sleep. And if someone broke into her house in the middle of the night and found her naked, that was their problem.

Especially now that she had room in the freezer again.

As she lay down, she let her thoughts drift. Marjorie was a major pain in her ass, but damn if she hadn't come through with some useful information. Because the more she thought about what Marjorie had let slip—that her brother had discovered Sharity Baker's affair—the more she believed Sharity Baker was someone she should have another chat with. A run-of-the-mill affair wasn't a reason to off a man, but what if there was something more to it?

Something to consider.

Lorraine woke up early the next morning, although it was difficult to drag her eyes open and actually roll out of bed. Her body was protesting from yesterday's exertions, but she forced herself to get up and make coffee—extra strong and extra dark—because she had work to do.

She dressed in a sky blue zip up sweatshirt and a pair of jogging pants—comfort over fashion today and always. Then she grabbed the keys to the police chief's truck. She would swap it out for her wagon as soon as the chief came in this morning.

Lorraine parked the truck in front of the liquor store, which of course wasn't open yet. The hours were flexible—whenever the owner was sober enough to get the door open in the morning seemed to be the rule of thumb. This worked for her since it was one less witness to worry about.

The sun was up, but the downtown streets were still deserted. That said, Youngblood should have torched the place hours ago, and there were no signs of fire anywhere. A little line of irritation appeared between her eyebrows. She got out of the truck and grabbed her thermos of coffee, then stood on the sidewalk, sipping and thinking. She made a noise of disgust and crossed the street, then walked around the block to the now-familiar alley. This was also deserted, although morning noises were coming from a handful of the houses that backed up to the alley, plates and dishes rattling, children crying.

No matter. She would simply walk like she belonged there—people would be much more suspicious if she tried to creep around. But who would remember an old woman out for a morning walk? With that in mind, she marched right down the alley as though she were out for a power walk, only altering her pace when she came to the metal door leading to the ice cream shop. She made quick work of the lock this time, since she now knew which key to reach for, and slipped inside.

Lorraine waited on the other side of the door, hands on hips, listening for the slightest noise. Nothing. Nor was there a telltale smell of gas, which was a fucking letdown. Had Youngblood gone and filled those cans for nothing?

Either way, she needed to find a new hiding spot for the body she'd dumped here. She checked out the front lobby and considered the ugly fiberglass sculpture that Baker had compared her to—shit, that would be a win, wouldn't it? But she'd done research once upon a time, and fiberglass didn't burn; it melted. So that definitely wouldn't work for her purposes.

Where could she stick Julian Baker? She'd had the wherewithal to put that can of lighter fluid in her purse, so wherever she decided to dump him, she would douse him. But she had to find a decent spot first. Good thing she'd left her dolly here.

She glanced at her watch, deciding she had a few minutes to look around for the money, while she was at it. There were still a couple of hours until Youngblood showed up, and she might as well make the best of things. Even though she was still inwardly fuming at the inconvenience he'd caused her.

Karma would come his way, probably in the form of a VD. Twenty to seven said that he never wrapped his dick before he stuck it in something. Wrap it or clap it. Hmm, that was pretty catchy—she'd have to remember that for the column.

She did a quick search for money in the obvious areas, finding nothing but also anticipating exactly that. She moved on to the short hallway, doing a cursory search both there and in the employee bathroom, finding nothing out of the ordinary, except that the bathroom had probably never once been cleaned. She moved on to Youngblood's office.

The filing cabinets were locked, which was interesting. A small ice cream shop like this, who would want his employee records? She searched the man's desk for something to crack them open with, but he didn't have anything in his desk. At all. Not even a pack of Post-it notes. Lorraine got the distinct impression that Youngblood did nothing but play with himself back here, and Baker had handled the rest, business-wise.

Could the money be in these cabinets? Possible, but unlikely. Baker wouldn't have hidden it somewhere where his buddy Youngblood would have access to it. So where would Baker stash it?

And where could she stash *him*? She looked behind the couch and found that there was a growing wet spot on the floor beneath the tarp—it looked like Julian was thawing out quite a bit. Gross, but at least he didn't smell yet. And the shop would be up in flames by the time that happened.

She would make sure of it.

Lorraine considered the body. Could she just tip him on his side so she could move the couch closer to the wall? Ugh, it was still too much of a gap—Youngblood might notice and check behind the couch.

Would that be so bad, though? If Youngblood found the body, what were the odds that he would call the police? Especially since he was involved in other shady shit, like laundering money. She was seriously considering the risk when the perfect hiding spot came to her.

"Of course."

She moved the couch away from the wall again, then grabbed Baker's feet and tugged. Shit, this guy was heavy. She needed to be careful to use her legs and not her back, or she'd be laid up in bed for a week. After pushing the couch back into place—right over that wet spot, nicely done—she paused, considering whether it was worth the effort to get Baker back on the dolly.

It probably was. She grabbed the metal thing and wheeled it into the office, then laid it on the ground and paused before getting onto her knees and rolling Baker onto it. Panting now, she managed to hoist the dolly back up and wheeled the corpse into the bathroom. He would slide real easy here on the tile floor, so Lorraine dumped him off the dolly and rolled that back out into the hall. It was a small space, and she could work better without it. Lorraine opened the miniscule bathroom closet, where a mop bucket dominated the entire space. She rolled it into the hallway and parked it. Hopefully whoever had to clean the shop's floors at night would leave it there as well.

Lorraine managed to get Baker into a semiseated position in the closet, shoving his legs to one side when the door wouldn't quite close. She emptied the bottle of lighter fluid onto him—opening a spot at the top of the tarp to really pour it in.

She hadn't found any money, but at least she'd solved her corpse problem.

Chapter 55

MIKE

Monday

Mike slept great, although it was *way* too short a night, and she had a little headache from drinking the beers and not enough water. Four hours' sleep just wasn't enough, although she was still sporting a grin when she did crack her eyes open and slapped her alarm clock off.

She was going to need a lot of coffee. But it was still a good day.

After two industrial-strength cups of Maxwell House, she dressed in a pair of pleated navy blue pants with a white blouse—minus the shoulder pads, of course—filled her thermos with even more coffee, and headed for the station. Despite the two cups of coffee and her perma-grin, she felt like she could use a pair of toothpicks to prop her eyes open.

"Detective!" Chief Schneider bellowed from his office as soon as her footsteps started down the hall. Normally she'd cringe, but today she practically bounced down the hall. She had good news for once, news the chief would twist to make himself look good. But today even that couldn't dampen her spirits.

"Morning, Carla," she said cheerfully, and Carla gave her a nod. The secretary had a little twinkle in her eye—maybe she knew about last night's bust, that the chief was wrong and Zenoni was the one to figure it out. That was the only thing Mike could figure.

"I've been informed that you made an arrest last night," Schneider said.

"I did," Mike chirped. "On a hunch I checked out the paint factory—they have a pier—and found the supplier with a boat full of drugs, waiting to make his drop."

"He probably saw us at the port and moved locations."

She worked hard to keep her face neutral. Of course Schneider would say that—the port had been his idea. "I'm sure that's what happened, Chief."

Schneider nodded. "Good, that's what I'll tell the papers. Night shift already did the interview—nothing else to report there. He's been sent to county."

She opened her mouth to object to a whole ream of things in that sentence, but snapped it back shut. Would it be nice to actually get the credit for this? It sure would. But she'd known all along that she wouldn't. Not while this man sucked air. And she'd wanted to do the interrogation, but she could double-check the tapes and make sure they'd gotten everything they could.

"We'll set up the drugs in the conference room for the photo," Schneider said. There was a pause while the chief's mind turned. Slowly. "You can be in the photo with me, Detective."

Mike smiled, as graciously as she could manage. "Thank you, Chief. And the conference room is a good idea." Maybe the general public would be able to figure out from the photo that she'd done the actual work. Of course, that wasn't what mattered in the long run, getting publicity, not for a real cop. What mattered was making the city safer, which she'd done by finding the drugs. Yah know, she'd actually found *a lot* of drugs in the last week.

Schneider nodded. "Good work. Now, what do we have so far on the murders?"

She nodded once. Well, at least she'd gotten some praise, right? She shouldn't be surprised that the man was already moving on, since he hadn't gotten the bust himself. "I think it's likely that Baker killed Rupp because Rupp learned something he shouldn't have. Most likely about the money that Baker stole."

"Any ideas about where the money is?"

"I think Baker took it with him when he split town. There's been no movement on any of Baker's cards, so wherever he is, he's paying with cash only." Unless he'd been a casualty as well, but she kept this to herself. She didn't have any good evidence, none at all actually, to back that little theory up.

Schneider nodded. "No, yeah, that makes sense. Although it's too bad about the photo op. All that cash." His voice was wistful.

She ignored him. Wasn't he happy enough with all the drugs? "I'm waiting to hear from the crime lab, but the gun we found in Lagerfield's apartment was probably the one that killed him. Hopefully there were some prints on it. If we're real lucky, those prints will be Baker's."

Carla's rolling chair creaked; then she appeared in the doorway. Mike and Schneider looked at her, surprise on both their faces. "There's a message for you from the crime lab, Detective. You're right about the gun and the prints. Baker's *were* on the gun."

Schneider clapped his hands. "Well, that solves it! We can release a statement to the press today."

"But the timeline still doesn't work, Chief. Dean was still alive after Baker disappeared. And what about the call from Baker's car phone to Mrs. Highsmith after Baker had already left. Why would he call her?"

"To apologize for leaving a dead body on her lawn? This doesn't sound like an issue."

"Are you sure Baker left town?" Carla asked. Mike startled—she hadn't realized Carla was still behind her.

Carla posed a good question, though, one that she's been considering. She didn't want to share it with the chief, however, not without some proof. "I'm pretty sure. There's an old Datsun that was registered to him that we haven't found yet. I have an APB out on it, but no hits yet. I'm hoping the car phone can tell us where he is." She paused. "If the rumors are true, he had huge stacks of cash, so he can probably go a long time without popping up. Especially with shady connections."

She kept her theory about Baker laundering money through the custard shop to herself. She needed some proof before sharing that because she just *knew* her boss would tell the first reporter he saw, and she didn't want to be humiliated in the papers if her theory was wrong.

Schneider nodded. "Well, this sounds solved to me. You write the report, and I'll let the papers know that we've wrapped everything up neatly. They'll be thrilled about the drugs, of course, and maybe even happier to know we've solved the murders too."

She protested, even though she knew it was useless. But she wouldn't be able to live with herself if she didn't at least try. "But, Chief, we still haven't found where Lagerfield was killed, and Craig Youngblood has been acting suspiciously. There are more questions to be asked. I just know it. Not to mention, if we find out who Baker was working for, we could shut down a huge drug ring in the county." It was honestly surprising that the locals weren't more worked up about the thing. Unless there were more users in town than she suspected, but even still.

"But it looks better that we solved two murders."

The chief's obsession with optics was entirely due to the fact that he wanted to run for president of the Wisconsin police chief's association, despite the fact that he was a small-town chief. *Someday,* Mike thought. *Someday I will have this man's job, and I will run the department the way it should be run.*

But today was not that day.

Chief Schneider nodded to himself. "I'll make a statement to the press about how the murders have been solved, suspect on the run, but I do think you should keep chasing whoever the supplier was delivering to. I suppose it would be nice to have a name."

She was quiet. "When's the election, sir?" She knew when it was. What she was really asking was how long the chief's obsession with the press would last, but she was also well aware of who signed her checks, so this was as far as she was willing to push it.

"Oh, in three months, ya know. We still have some time to wrap things up," Schneider said.

Mike closed her eyes briefly before excusing herself.

Chapter 56

LORRAINE

Monday

It had been a couple of physically draining days, and Lorraine was feeling it. Her muscles ached, even more than after a particularly difficult workout with Cynthia. Speaking of which, she'd canceled with her for the rest of the week, claiming that she had a bad cold. Once her body bounced back a little, she'd go back. It was the whole reason she was even able to do what she had done this week. But her muscles needed a chance to recover.

With Baker's body neatly tucked away and her metal dolly back in the basement, Lorraine had a different errand to run this morning—she wanted to talk to Sharity Baker. She had a little theory that had been brewing, and she wanted to see if she was right.

A black Honda was back in the driveway when she pulled up. It was still pretty early, but that was all the better since it would put Sharity and her mystery guest off balance by waking them up. And that was how she liked people—off balance.

Lorraine rang the doorbell once, twice, three times. She was prepared to stand here all morning and ring the goddamn bell, but she finally saw movement behind the frosted-glass panel on the side of the door, so she let her finger off the button.

"Mrs. Highsmith, what are you doing here so early?" Sharity croaked. She was wearing a bathrobe clutched closed at the top, which led Lorraine to believe she had nothing on beneath it. No matter.

She pushed past the woman. "Let's get coffee started so we can have a little chat."

Lorraine ordered Sharity through the paces of making coffee and then herded her into the living room. They were about to take a seat when she caught sight of a woman's head popping out from behind a wall, obviously curious about what was happening but not wanting to be seen. She was doing a terrible job of the last part.

"Aha!" Lorraine crowed. "I was right." She looked at Sharity. "You might as well tell your *girlfriend* to come out."

Sharity closed her eyes, fingers pinching the bridge of her nose. "You might as well grab some coffee and join us, baby."

There was some rustling in the kitchen; then the tall brunette joined them in the sitting room. Both women looked chagrined, but Lorraine was genuinely delighted that her theory had been correct. While she'd lain in bed, she'd gotten to thinking about how the town made assumptions about Detective Zenoni being a lesbian, which led to her wondering just how badly someone would want to hide a secret like that from the judgmental bigots populating the shithole town they all lived in.

Pretty badly, was what she'd guessed. She loved it when a hunch paid off.

"First of all, I never did catch your name," Lorraine said to the girlfriend.

"I'm Louise Williams," the attractive brunette said. "But call me Lou."

Lorraine's eyebrows went up. "Are you related to Carrie Williams?"

Lou and Sharity exchanged a look. "I'm her older sister," Lou said after a beat.

"Small towns," Lorraine said with a shake of her head. Julian Baker had been sleeping with Carrie Williams, and his wife had been sleeping with the older sister. There was a lot of irony floating around these days. "Now down to the reason I'm here."

Sharity was still cranky about the hour. "Yes, why *are* you here?"

"I'm here to find out why you dumped Doug Rupp's body on my lawn after you killed him."

Both women froze, deliberately not looking at one another, and she knew that this hunch was right as well. Something akin to joy fizzled in her veins. She *loved* being right.

"You've already given yourselves away, so you might as well tell me." Lorraine sipped at her coffee—nice and bitter.

Sharity and Lou looked at each other for a long time, before Sharity finally cracked. "It would be a relief to tell someone."

Louise rolled her eyes but motioned for Sharity to go ahead.

"We met in high school, but Louise moved to Milwaukee right after we graduated," Sharity started to say.

"Oh, I don't need that much of the backstory. Start with Rupp."

Sharity paused, then started again. "Uh, for sure. Well, I noticed someone was watching the house. I told Julian, but he told me I was being an airhead."

"He couldn't just look outside and see the car?"

"He refused to look." Sharity rolled her eyes. "I kid you not. And by the time he finally did, the car was gone."

It seemed unlikely, but then, men were pretty stupid, Julian Baker especially. "Then what happened?"

"One night while Julian was at the motel with Carrie, Rupp came to the door. He said that he'd seen me with my girlfriend and that he was going to tell not only Julian, but the whole town."

"Okay, but why do you care about that?"

The women looked at each other. "You know what could happen to us if people found out we're gay?" Both women looked a little scared.

"We couldn't let some scumbag out us," Louise added quietly.

"So you decided to kill him?"

"No, we just wanted to scare him a little. How were we supposed to know the asshole couldn't swim?" Sharity said.

Lorraine let out a hoot of laughter. "How'd you lure him into the lake?"

"We told him we would go skinny-dipping with him in the lake if he wouldn't tell anyone what he'd found out. We met him on the beach over by your house—"

Louise broke in. "I'm renting a house near there."

Ahh. That made sense.

Sharity continued. "It was dark except for the moon, which was pretty bright. Anyway, we all got into the water and walked into the surf. He kept telling us to take our tops off." Sharity closed her eyes in disgust, and Lou took her hand. "And then I jumped on his back. He fell under the water. I just meant to scare him a little, maybe hold him under for a second, but he just started flailing around."

"How deep was the water?"

"There's a pretty steep drop-off. I think we must have gone over that spot. Anyway, pretty soon he stopped flailing. We didn't know what to do."

"We thought about just leaving him in the water, but—" Lou said.

"But I saw this documentary about what happens to bodies in the water and what the fish do. It's so gross."

"So, you decided to dump him on my lawn?"

"It was as far as we could carry him," Sharity said. "And yours was the first lawn we saw that had sprinklers."

"What does that have to do with anything?"

Lou shrugged. "We were pretty panicked. We thought it might explain why he was wet and buy us some time." The women looked at each other. "We weren't thinking clearly."

"Obviously not," Lorraine said. "Why were his hands tied?"

"We thought if we tied his hands and feet together, we could carry him. You know, like a pig on a spit? It didn't work, though," Sharity said.

Well. This was both a delightful turn of events and a relief that the body on her lawn had nothing to do with her personally. Or with her past. Lorraine felt the rest of her tension float away like a red balloon.

Shit. This still didn't explain the phone call from Baker's car phone. Her shoulder blades tightened again.

"Sharity, I asked you to find Julian's car phone. Did you look for it?"

Sharity nodded. "I did, and then the cops searched the place too. I don't think they found it either."

"And you didn't call me from it?"

Sharity frowned. "Why would I do that?"

Louise leaned forward. "Are you going to turn us in?"

"Nah. Rupp's murder is going to be blamed on Julian. I wouldn't worry about being found out." Lorraine was almost done with her coffee. She considered a refill but decided she didn't need more. Time to switch to water.

"But what if Julian comes home?" Sharity asked. "He'll deny everything."

Lorraine looked at the two women. There was nothing in it for her to tell them that Julian was dead—that would only work against her own self-interests. She *did* like seeing women get a happy ending, though, especially when it was at the expense of a dirtbag like Julian.

"Look, I'm not interested in turning you in. Or outing you, for that matter. If men get what they deserve, all the better." The women still looked unsure, although Louise was starting to nod. "You have my solemn oath that I will not tell anyone your secret. Like client-attorney privilege, except I'm a journalist. How about I call you an anonymous source and print nothing about any of this?"

"Okay," Sharity said slowly. The women looked at each other, communicating without words. Lorraine felt confident they would see things her way once they talked it out. Especially when Julian's body was found, which should be any moment now.

Lorraine was still curious about one thing, though. "Why did you marry Julian?"

Sharity looked . . . repulsed, that was the emotion engulfing the young woman. "To hide that I'm gay. My parents are like, fundamentalist Christian and would freak out if they knew. They'd for sure disown me. And Julian had money and a wandering eye. I figured I could basically do what I wanted if I married him."

"Gross." She would have left town first, screw the family. But small-town shit was different, especially up here. "Listen, you don't need to worry about Julian coming back. He wouldn't dare, with what the police have on him."

"You're sure?" Sharity still looked doubtful.

Lorraine nodded firmly. "I'm sure."

Chapter 57

MIKE

Monday

Regardless of what her boss announced to the press, Mike was going to keep working the two murder cases. There were too many loose ends, and they would bug the crap out of her until she could tie them together. Plus she'd had a couple of theories that hadn't panned out, a couple of things she'd clearly missed, and she wanted, no *needed*, to redeem herself, even if she was the only one who'd know. She would just work the drug angle at the same time as tying up the murders, which wasn't too hard since they were so deeply intertwined.

She reminded herself that she'd figured out the drop, though. She'd done some real good for Sheboygan Bay, solved a piece of this case, even if no one would ever hear about it.

Her first order of business was to hit Mary Ann's and see if by some miracle Craig Youngblood was there yet. After the day before, she didn't really expect him to show—he'd likely be at home in bed, but she had to check anyways. The pimply teen behind the counter assured her that her assumptions were right.

Mike's bladder told her that she needed to make a pit stop. All that coffee was making a real pressing appearance—she hoped this wasn't becoming a thing. "Can I use your restroom?"

The kid looked skeptical. "It's for employees only, and I'm not sure you wanna go in there." But he shrugged when she gave him a look. "It's through there," he said, pointing to the hall.

She found the door and opened it. There was a reason it was employees only—it was *nasty*. There was no way it had ever been cleaned and probably violated a couple of health codes. She would not be sitting on that throne—she'd catch something that antibiotics couldn't even cure. Something smelled weird too. She decided that breathing through her mouth and getting the hell out of here were the only real options. She'd run next door to the hardware store to use theirs.

"You guys should clean that," Mike said to the kid on her way out.

The kid shrugged. "It's not on the checklist."

With a shake of her head, she jogged to the building next door. Once she'd finished her business, she would head to Youngblood's house for a little chat.

A few minutes later, she pulled into Youngblood's driveway. The garage door was open, and the man was entering the garage as though he were about to leave. Craig Youngblood wasn't going anywhere, though, not until she was done chatting with him. She'd done a solid job of parking him in.

"That's a lot of gas cans." She nodded to the six red cans lined up against the wall of the garage.

Youngblood looked at the cans. "Gas is cheap right now. I think you gotta stock up when you can. I got a gas-powered generator, and you never know. Lotta storms this summer."

She glanced around the rest of the garage. It didn't look like Youngblood was a survivalist—usually those wackos had stockpiles of cans and bottled water and weapons and other stuff. There was none of that here, but he could also have it all stashed inside somewhere. Maybe he kept his crazy in the basement instead of the garage.

"How you feeling?" She was a little surprised to see him upright.

Youngblood shrugged. "My foot hurts, can't figure out why. But I'm wondering if I had food poisoning or something."

She nodded. That seemed like a reasonable explanation. She wasn't here to check on his health, though. "Have you heard from your friend Julian lately?"

Youngblood was annoyed. "I already told ya, I haven't heard from him in days."

"I gotta ask, 'cause he has to pop up again at some point, right? And when he does, how upset is he going to be about you and Carrie Ann Williams?"

Youngblood looked confused. "Me and Carrie Ann?"

"Rumor has it you two have been getting pretty cozy lately."

"Listen, I get plenty of tail on my own. I don't need sloppy seconds."

Eww. "Why were you chatting her up then?"

Youngblood shrugged. "I honestly don't remember. I 'chat' with lots of people—it's part of being a local business owner."

Clearly not the truth, but she'd get the real story from the other half of the equation—Carrie Ann. If she hadn't spent the morning with her boss, she might have had more patience for the verbal gymnastics, but she'd already exhausted her patience for the day.

"Why was Baker in your shop every day?"

"Look, lady, do I need a lawyer?" Youngblood's arms were crossed over his chest, which was also sort of puffed out. He looked ridiculous, like he might fall over backward.

Mike cocked her head. "I'm just asking questions, Craig. Do you think you need a lawyer for something?" She wanted to follow up that question with something about money laundering, but she didn't want to tip her hand quite yet. She didn't have proof, just her gut and a theory, and so far those hadn't exactly panned out.

Craig opened the door to his car and made like he was going to get in. "I'm not talking to you anymore without my lawyer."

"Cool, cool." Clearly there was a lot here if Youngblood was lawyering up—she was glad she'd followed her instincts to chat with him even if he'd zipped his lips. She did some quick calculations and decided she didn't have enough to ask for a warrant yet, but she would keep tugging at this thread, see if she could pull together enough to search both this place and his shop. Her gut told her that Youngblood was up to his big ears in all this, and if money was being laundered through the custard shop, she'd find evidence of it during a search. She just needed enough proof to take a warrant to the judge.

Chapter 58

LORRAINE

Monday

It had been a fruitful morning. Lorraine had finally figured out how Rupp ended up on her lawn, even if it was an anticlimactic ending. As for turning in the ladies, she wouldn't. There was no net gain for her, and it sounded as though it had been mostly an accident, which was too bad, really.

The only two things she needed to clear up now were ensuring that Baker's body went up in flames with the rest of the ice cream shop and figuring out who had Julian Baker's car phone and why they were calling her from it. Sharity and Lou were no threat to her—they had no idea what she was capable of, that was clear. And they would find out about Julian's demise just as soon as the fire happened.

As she'd left, Sharity and Lou had asked if she wanted to have dinner sometime. Lorraine had waved them off, since they were clearly just trying to keep her close because of what she knew. She'd never admit that it might be nice, not even to herself.

As for Baker's phone and the mysterious calls, her only plan included stopping by the station and seeing if Zenoni had made any progress on triangulating the thing. It was both the beauty and the trouble with car phones—they could be used by anyone from anywhere.

But neither the chief nor the detective were in. "Where are they?" Lorraine asked Carla.

Carla gave a casual shrug. "Hard to say. The detective is haring off after a drug lord, and I think the chief got called home for a nooner."

"Gross," Lorraine said, nose wrinkled.

"Barf town," Carla agreed.

It was unusual to have the secretary's full attention, so she decided to make the most of it.

"Do you know if Mike made any progress figuring out where Julian Baker's missing car phone is?"

Carla shook her head. "I think she put in the request, but nothing came back yet."

Lorraine grunted, frustrated. "I'm trying to figure out who called me."

Carla cocked her head. "Oh, I'm sure you'll figure it out, Mrs. Highsmith."

The secretary's tone gave her pause, but Lorraine thanked her and left.

Lorraine was frustrated that there had been no movement on the whole *burning down the ice cream shop* thing. Youngblood needed to get his shit together. She swung by his house—nothing—then cruised by Mary Ann's Frozen Custard, but that seemed quiet as well. She could see the same kid leaning against the counter reading, but there were no customers. Had anyone noticed a smell in the bathroom yet?

Probably not. Although Julian *was* starting to thaw. She wondered if juice was leaking out from beneath the closet door yet.

Well, it looked like she was going to have to take things into her own hands. First, she would make a trip down to Milwaukee for some gas cans, so she wouldn't be seen in Sheboygan Bay filling them up.

Without stopping anywhere, she headed out of town and pointed the Behemoth south on I-43. If she made any kind of stop first, Marjorie or the detective or someone equally annoying might track her down and stop her or try to hitch a ride—best to just hit the road.

Lorraine's little excursion took a few hours. She bought a variety of gas cans and filled them up at a Sunoco off Appleton Avenue on the north side, paying in cash. Same with the large black garbage bags she picked up at a Menards right off the interstate. Cash was king if you didn't want your whereabouts traced.

It was late afternoon by the time she got back to town. She drove down Main Street even though it was well out of her way, wanting to see if by some miracle the ice cream shop had gone up in flames. No such luck.

That was fine. She made her own luck. She would simply go home and wait for nightfall.

Chapter 59

MIKE

Monday

Cheese 'n rice, what a frustrating day. And it had started out so well, before immediately going downhill after leaving her boss's office, no surprise there. Mike should really blame *Schneider* for setting her off on the wrong foot. With nothing so much as a letter of commendation or even an attaboy for her file after her brilliant work last night. Or was that technically this morning? Either way.

Anyway, first Craig Youngblood lawyered up; then Carrie Ann did the same thing. Mike just *knew* that Youngblood had called her and warned her not to say anything. Twenty bucks said that they would have the same lawyer too. She would love to know who was paying for that lawyer—Julian Baker, maybe? She probably had enough to request Youngblood's phone records, see if he'd been in touch with his old drug-smuggling buddy over the phone recently. So she got right to work filling out the paperwork for that. She'd be able to get the judge to sign off, for sure.

Then she sighed and swished back and forth in her office chair. The rest of this investigation sure wasn't going like she wanted it to. Sometimes police work just felt like talking to the same people over and over again while they changed their lies, and then you had to sift through all the verbal garbage to figure out what was actually true. It was exhausting.

Today, it kind of felt like a blessing that her pops *wasn't* with it enough to ask for an update. It would be crushing to report all this disappointment to him, the whole reason she was even in this business. She cringed, wishing she could physically pull into herself, like a turtle. It was awful to think that anything about her father's situation was a blessing. But you had to look for silver linings where you could, right?

She straightened up and unlocked her desk drawer, pulled out her file on the case, and rifled through the paperwork. What was she missing?

Aha! Here was the page of notes she'd taken from the Rockford Police Department about Mrs. Highsmith. No names listed, though, other than Lorraine and her dead husband, Bob. Wait. Didn't marriage licenses usually have witnesses listed on them?

Mike picked up her phone and called Rockford back, crossing her fingers that the same person was there and would still have their own paperwork. She finally had a bit of luck, and the voice on the other end of the phone was able to not only give her the names of the witnesses from the Highsmiths' marriage license, the officer was also kind enough to look through the local phone book to give her a list of possible phone numbers.

"Sorry I didn't give these to you earlier. Since you were only interested in Mrs. Highsmith, I didn't think you'd need these. And they're hard to read."

She assured the officer that it was fine, despite her frustration. "It only just occurred to me that witnesses sign the paperwork when someone gets married, so I should have thought of it too." She was actually kicking both herself and this guy, but at least he'd come through with some phone numbers.

She tried the ones for Robert Maddox first, since there were five. The first three were duds, and the fourth one was a literal dead end.

Good old Robert had died a few years earlier—heart failure—and the widow hadn't known the Highsmiths. She and Robert had married after the Highsmiths left town, and Robert never mentioned them.

Mike was disappointed, but she still had one good lead left. There were only two possible numbers for Kathryn Blahnik, and the first one was gold.

"Oh, golly, that was years ago, Detective," Kathryn said. "Must be twenty years now."

"Do you remember the Highsmiths, Mrs. Blahnik? You were listed on their marriage license as a witness."

"Yah, yah, I was there. But call me Katie, everyone does." Kathryn paused. "Yah know, it was strange, Bob wanted a bigger wedding because it was his first, but Lori—that's what she went by—insisted on getting married at the town hall. Robert Maddox and I were the only ones there. Well, and my husband, Trevor. His last name was Meyer, but I kept mine."

Mike made an appropriate noise. "Why didn't Mrs. Highsmith want anyone else there, do you know?"

"Can't say. She was a real private woman, and we chalked it up to that. They moved away not long after."

That seemed about right, given what she knew about Mrs. H. "Do you happen to know where she was from originally? Chicago maybe?"

Kathryn—Katie—was quiet for a long moment. "It's funny you ask that. Like I said, Lori never talked about her childhood, or even her years in Chicago. But I do remember one strange thing that happened—it stuck with me."

Mike leaned forward in her chair. Maybe this would be her big break in figuring out the mystery that was Lorraine Highsmith.

"We were at a party in the neighborhood, and we'd all had a few drinks. It was the sixties, you know, times were different." Katie sounded rather defensive, and Mike couldn't help but wonder just what type of "neighborhood party" this was. "Someone brought up Chicago-style pizza, and Lori made an awful face. Said it was 'garbage compared to

New York–style.'" Katie paused. "Well, she used some stronger language than that, but you get the drift, Detective." She chuckled. "I haven't thought about that in years. We did have some good times."

She listened to the elderly woman as she reminisced for a few more minutes, but she didn't have any other information that was useful. Besides, Mike's mind was already working on the nugget she had been given. Could Mrs. Highsmith originally be from New York? It wasn't a lot, but at least it was *something* to go on.

After a polite thank-you—and then another—she was finally able to end the call and hang up.

Well, that at least felt like something. Although it would be quite the digging expedition to find where in New York Lorraine hailed from—New York was a really big state. But at least she had a starting point. And maybe, just maybe, she could get Mrs. Highsmith to spill a city. Or even just a region.

In the meantime, she turned her attention to the issue of Craig Youngblood. She went and grabbed the form, then sat down and filled it out with what she had so far. Was it all circumstantial? You betcha. But she felt confident the judge would sign off on it anyway, and then she would have a legal reason to search both the custard shop and Youngblood's house. And who knew what she might find?

Chapter 60

MIKE

Monday

Well, that had been a total bust. Given Judge Warner's city-wide reputation—well earned—as an idiot, Mike was incredibly frustrated that the man had refused to sign off on either warrant. He said she needed "more solid evidence" for both of them, and when she'd argued with him, he'd closed the door.

Incredible. The one time the man bothered to read anything. She hadn't even been sure he *could* read, but he'd carefully scanned her paperwork and shut it down. Her blood was still thrumming with frustration. Plus, she had this stupid date tonight with Jamie, and she was positive he wouldn't be able to tell her anything useful. Not about Youngblood anyway, which was where she just *knew* she should be concentrating her energy.

Could she be wrong, though? She'd been wrong about other things in the case, had even chased a false lead or two, like searching Baker's house. Was she doing that again? She did a gut check and shook her head. No, she was right about this. Youngblood was her best bet for information.

Okay, should she cancel the date tonight? Jamie had been chatting with Grace Baker last night, so maybe Mike should still go and see if he'd learned anything useful there. She nodded. Maybe he'd learned enough to point her in a new direction. Or give her enough to actually get these warrants signed.

An hour later, she was waiting by the front door in a sunny lemon yellow spaghetti strap dress and her favorite jelly shoes, her eyes frosted blue with matching mascara and just a dash of Malibu Musk. In the mirror it had looked like the makeup was a bit much, but wasn't this how women were doing it these days? She almost wished she'd asked Carla for some more advice, but it was too late now.

Jamie picked her up right on time, and they headed to Randy's Fun Hunters Club—or Randy's as the locals called it—on the outskirts of town. He pulled into the asphalt lot and parked, then tried to get around to the passenger side so he could open her door for her, but she was too fast, on her feet with the door closed before he made it around.

She was a little charmed despite herself. "I see what you're doing. That's sweet, but not necessary."

Jamie smiled but got the door of the restaurant for her.

Stepping inside, they were greeted by a hostess wearing a white dress shirt and black pants standing beside a dark wood podium with a small green-hooded reading light. The thick carpet hushed footsteps, and the clank of silverware and the murmur of conversations could be heard from the dining room to their right.

"Right this way." The hostess smiled and led them to the dining room, where the dark wood paneling and exposed beams were punctuated by taxidermy animals. Mostly deer heads and pheasants in flight, mounted classily, of course. None of that second-rate taxidermy you found in some of the dive bars around town, like the Mucky Duck. Mike knew one place outside town that had a collection of small animals playing sports—the golfing frog was the most upsetting, holding a tiny club, its skin waxy.

Their table was in the main room, overlooking Lake Michigan, and they took some time to appreciate the sun setting over the lake, shades of red, pink, and orange bouncing off cotton clouds and reflecting in the water. The waitress stopped at their table almost immediately, and Jamie ordered a brandy old-fashioned sweet, and Mike ordered the same, except sour and with olives. She didn't like things that were overly sweet.

"How's Grace? It seemed like you two were having a nice chat last night."

Jamie nodded, his face serious. "I'm not dating her. I just want you to know that."

She gave a smile, hoping it looked interested in this update. "Thanks for letting me know."

He looked relieved, then cocked his head like a golden retriever. "She's real bummed. I think she was like, super into Dean."

"It sure seems that way. Did she say anything about what he was up to before he was killed?"

"Gracie was real happy that he finally got his own place." His face took on a hangdog look. "It's too bad he didn't get to enjoy it."

She nodded. "I'm sorry you lost your cousin." She'd sort of lost sight of that fact, that Jamie had lost a family member, and mentally kicked herself for being insensitive. He was probably hurting, too, and not just a source of information.

She was grateful when the waitress dropped off her drink. She took a sip and let the brandy burn down to her stomach, where her frustration was knotting up. She also forced herself to breathe. Even if she didn't get any useful information from this, she was here, and there was nothing she could do about it now.

Except change the subject and ask some questions about Mrs. Highsmith. Jamie did see Mrs. H. quite a bit at the bakery.

"I might have learned something interesting about Mrs. Highsmith, though." Mike paused, considering how much to tell him. "Sounds like she might have been part of some wild parties back in the sixties."

He laughed. "Mrs. Highsmith? What kind of parties? I can't picture that."

She blushed and avoided the answer. She was *not* going to talk about the kinds of parties she suspected Katie Blahnik was talking about, and she never shoulda led with that. "It sounds like maybe she lived in New York. Has Mrs. H. ever mentioned New York to you?"

Jamie cocked his head. "Huh. Not that I can think of. She comes into the bakery now and then, but she doesn't talk really about anything. And she doesn't have a New York accent. On television those are always real thick." He leaned across the table a little. "You know, I think she's a lonely old lady. Grumpy, for sure, but her husband died and she doesn't have kids. I'll bet she doesn't have a lot to keep her busy."

Mike nodded. "I've been thinking the same thing. She's probably lonely." But how was she going to narrow down where the woman was from?

Chapter 61

LORRAINE

Monday

Lorraine allowed herself a midafternoon nap, which she rarely did. But her body craved one, so she crashed for an hour and woke up feeling refreshed. After a quick stretching session to work out the stiffness, she was ready to go. She puttered around her garden to kill the hours until nightfall, deadheading buds here and there, and trimming back branches on those award-winning rosebushes. Once dusk fell, she went inside and sat at her typewriter and knocked out a few responses for the next column.

Stretching her shoulders, she looked at the clock. It was finally late enough to head over to Mary Ann's Frozen Custard. Her wagon was already loaded up with the gas cans and garbage bags, so she dressed in her darkest tracksuit, pulled a black knit cap over her silver bob, and headed out. First, she cruised past the front of Mary Ann's. And it was a good thing she'd bothered too. A light was on in Youngblood's office.

The man's timing was terrible but never mind. She would simply alter her plan just a little. She pulled into the alley and stashed her gas cans behind the dumpster nearest the shop's back door. She put her garbage bags on top of the cans and then drove out, parking two blocks away. Lorraine then removed her cap, smoothed out her hair and headed to the Mucky Duck.

Inside, the place was busy, which was perfect, although it meant that the smoke haze was thicker than usual. Lorraine settled herself at the bar and when the Mustache—her mental name for the bartender—saw her, he hurried over. "What can I get you Mrs. Highsmith?" he asked with deference.

This was great—it would establish a lovely little alibi for her. "I'll take a brandy old-fashioned. No, make that bourbon on the rocks." She scanned the shelves on the wall behind the bar. "Old Forester will do." She almost never allowed herself to drink what she actually wanted to in public, but tonight she was allowing herself a treat, letting her mask slip just a little. Bourbon was her drink of choice. Her late husband had introduced her to it, and she'd really taken to it, collecting pricey bottles to enjoy at home. And normally *only* at home—she kept to the old lady drinks whenever she was out.

Except tonight. Tonight she was celebrating because things were going to work out her way.

The 'Stache poured her a double before returning with it, placing it carefully on a small napkin, and leaving just as quickly. She was a fan of this type of service. She took a few sips, then placed a coaster over the top of her drink, the international sign for "I'm coming back for this," and made a show of heading to the bathroom. She took a little time in there, then slipped out the back door. No one saw her go, as far as she could tell. The dark hallway leading to the bathroom was mostly obscured from the main room, as was the back exit. Lorraine could feel her victories piling up—tonight was her night.

Lorraine walked briskly to the alley behind Mary Ann's and strode down it. She never did take out those streetlights, but they were spaced pretty far apart—the light they cast probably wasn't worth the effort anyway.

When she got to the metal door leading into the ice cream shop, she paused, listening. Nothing. Reassured, she opened the lock with her master key and slipped inside. Now she could hear the sounds of metal drawers being pulled open and then banged shut while Craig Youngblood mumbled to himself. Lorraine crept down the hall and risked peeking into the office. The man was at his desk with his head in his hands, and it looked as though he'd forgotten to relock those file drawers. That was handy—she would love to get a look inside them, just to make sure the money wasn't stashed inside, although that was unlikely since Craig had just rifled through them. Youngblood appeared to come to a decision, because he abruptly stood up, and Lorraine shot back from the doorway, almost knocking into a nearby stack of milk crates. She turned and concealed herself in the bathroom.

Whoo boy, did it smell in here. Julian Baker was getting ripe. Which meant this thing had to happen tonight.

Youngblood slammed around some more before finally taking his leave. Lorraine had the bathroom door cracked—and her nose plugged—and heard him go out the front door and lock it behind him.

Perfect. Time to get to work.

Lorraine went to the alley and briefly propped open the back door while she brought in the gas cans and garbage bags. Then, using only a faint glow from a small pocket flashlight, she used duct tape to secure the garbage bags over the windows of Youngblood's office. It was dark enough that no one would notice the windows were covered, but it should also give the fire some extra time to really get going before the fire department was called. The only thing she couldn't control was the smoke.

Lorraine covered the windows in the front of the shop as well. This took some time, as they were larger, and she had to cover the glass door too. She swiped her hand across her sweaty forehead when she was done.

Now the real fun began.

Lorraine started in the bathroom, dumping a liberal amount of gasoline. Then she ran a trail into Youngblood's office, although she stopped in front of the metal file cabinets before continuing. She opened a few cabinets, seeing nothing but file folders sporting labels of employee names—nothing that looked like a hoard of stolen cash.

She slapped her own forehead. She'd seen Youngblood looking at his top drawer, and in the excitement of torturing him, she'd forgotten to look in there. She tried the drawer now, pleased that this time it slid right open. There were a few files in there, and Lorraine grabbed them all, noting that some were marked *taxes* and *records*. These would come in handy later to point suspicion firmly in Youngblood's direction. Evidence of laundering had to be here somewhere, right? Although Baker probably had the real set of books stashed off premises. Maybe a second storage unit?

Lorraine liberally poured gasoline on the cabinets, metal though they were, and doused the couch as well, taking care of the first gas can.

This really was fun. She should do it more often.

She grabbed another can and did the same in the front of the store, although she was less worried about this area. It was really the back hall and Youngblood's office that needed to go up in flames. She used up her gas in the back and then gathered the files and trotted to the back door. She pulled a matchbook from her pocket—old school was the best school—and lit a single match, flicking it onto the floor behind her as she closed the metal door.

Chapter 62

MIKE

Monday

"What about your parents?" Jamie asked.

Mike shifted in her seat, not wanting to talk about her folks but also not wanting to be rude. He'd just lost someone after all, so maybe talking about family was what he needed right now. "Oh, they were pretty normal." Okay, that was a lie. "Well, my ma left when I was real little. I don't really remember her." She had to look away from the sympathy on his face—it was too much, too *sweet*. She forced herself to sit up a little, forget about her mother leaving her behind. "My pops was a good dad, though. Most of the time." Cripes, why had she said that? Making out like her father had been a monster—he'd just been a single dad. And sure, the drinking got to be a problem when she was a teenager, but then he'd turned it around. She hurried on. "Things were real good once my stepmom came on the scene."

"That sounds hard," Jamie said.

"Oh, it was fine. She died a few years back." This was *not* going well, and she needed to direct the conversation somewhere else. "Did you grow up with Dean?"

Jamie nodded. "Yeah, we did almost everything together 'cause our moms were sisters."

"That sounds nice." And it did, especially since she hadn't had anyone like that, which was why she'd spent so much time reading as a kid. "You two were close?"

"Yeah, we were pretty close. But we kinda stopped talking once he started dealing drugs." Jamie looked real serious. "I don't touch the stuff."

"Good to know." It was the best she could come up with. "So you don't remember when Dean and Grace started dating?"

"Not really. I hadn't talked to him in a couple months." His face fell. "I feel really bad for Gracie."

"Bad for her? Why is that?" She was pleased they'd come back around to this.

"Dean was an okay guy," he said, then looked sheepish. "I know, he was my cousin. But he had problems. And I don't think he was good for Grace."

"Did *you* ever date Grace?" Maybe he had some insight into the woman. Mike was still on the fence about whether or not Grace was involved in her brother's "business." And it didn't work in her favor that she'd been dating an active drug dealer.

Not to mention the weed Grace had tried to steal.

"We went out a couple times." He hurried to explain himself. "But that was years ago now."

"Who broke it off?" She cocked her head.

"I did. I wasn't ever really interested, to be honest." Jamie ducked his head, embarrassed. "I was bored."

Mike filed this away. It was the first thing she'd learned about him that she really didn't like. And while she wasn't necessarily interested in actually dating this guy, she realized that she hadn't completely ruled it out either. He was easy on the eyes, and maybe it would be nice to date someone who didn't fight with her about her job. Her job would always come first, and maybe he wouldn't care about that. This revelation was a tick in the minus column, though.

But instead of address it, she ignored the growing feeling that this wasn't a great side to Jamie Sprout and changed the conversation back to Grace Baker. Which also wasn't great, morally, but she told herself there was something here that could help the investigation. There had to be.

"Grace was pretty upset," she prompted.

Jamie nodded, then looked thoughtful as the waitress arrived with another round of drinks. "I couldn't really tell if she was actually upset about Dean dying, though."

Her brow furrowed. "What else would she be upset about?"

"It seemed like she was more upset about who might have done it than she was about him actually being gone."

She leaned forward because this was really interesting. "Who does she think did it?"

"She wouldn't say, but I totally got the feeling she thought Craig was involved."

That wasn't a surprise. A lot of things seemed to come back to the custard-shop owner, which was exactly why she'd been trying to get warrants to search his places. Her mind flicked back to their last chat and the row of red gas cans, neatly lined up, and her stomach nearly dropped out of her body. Sweet fancy Moses, Youngblood wasn't a survivalist; he was a man about to take drastic measures.

"Oh, shit," she said, blood racing. She shot up and grabbed her purse, nearly upending the table, rifling for her wallet. She'd leave some money on the table for the cocktails, but she had to go, like now.

Jamie stood up too. "What is it?" His eyes were wide.

"Youngblood is going to set fire to his shop," she said over her shoulder as she hoofed it toward the exit, Jamie right on her heels.

Goddamn it, she couldn't believe she'd missed making that connection. *Fuck.* She hoped she wasn't too late.

Chapter 63

LORRAINE

Monday

Feeling certain the fire had taken hold, Lorraine strolled away from the back of Mary Ann's Frozen Custard. She reached the sidewalk at the end of the alley and ambled in the direction of the Mucky Duck, then slipped inside the back door and reclaimed her drink and her barstool. Within a few minutes the first faint whiffs of smoke were noticeable through the cigarette haze. She nodded to herself—the fire had taken hold—and waited.

Ten minutes or so passed while she sipped her bourbon. The ice had melted the perfect amount while she'd been gone, and it was easy sipping now. Lorraine watched while other patrons in the bar started to notice the smell of a fire instead of the smoke of their own making. A few of the more curious went outside. She grabbed her glass of bourbon and joined the stream of people headed out to the sidewalk, excited shouts preceding her.

At the end of the block was the edge of a park that led down to the lake. A series of benches sat on the border of the green space, and Lorraine sat herself down, glass in hand. The smoke was a downright plume now, and she was a little concerned that the fire department would arrive before the fire could really take hold—one of these fools from the bar would inevitably call this in, although she hadn't seen anyone run to the pay phone. Not yet.

Flames could be seen in the front window of the ice cream shop now, having melted the garbage bags away, and the plume was becoming a dark tower above the building. Excellent. Lorraine found the acrid smoke somehow pleasant, although she knew she shouldn't breathe it in for too long. Jamie came running from the west—Detective Mike only moments behind him—and she smiled. Wasn't that nice? They must have been on a date. Too bad it was interrupted by the fire.

After a few minutes the wind shifted, and tiny pieces of paper began littering the street. The roof must have caved in, or at least part of it, if detritus was already drifting on the wind. Lorraine frowned. What *was* all this paper? Leaving her drink on the bench, she took a few steps into the park and found a large hunk of paper that had floated to the ground. Bending down to retrieve it, she let out a string of curses that would have done a sailor proud.

It was money. Burning money.

Some of the pieces had melted plastic on them, and it didn't take long for her to put things together. "That son of a bitch hid the money inside that ugly fucking statue," she muttered to herself.

"I should have thought to look there as well," said a voice to Lorraine's left. "But I didn't realize it was hollow."

Lorraine turned to find Carla Robinson standing beside her bench. Lorraine looked at the woman, eyes narrowed, trying to figure out what the secretary might know and why she was here. Carla gestured for her to move her drink, and Lorraine picked up her bourbon, both women then taking a seat. Neither spoke for a minute, watching the flames in the ice cream shop. The roof was long gone, and the fire trucks that had arrived were concentrating on preventing the fire from spreading to nearby buildings.

Carla reached into her purse and took out a Ziploc bag that looked a little frosty and passed it over to her. Lorraine turned it over in her hands for only a few seconds before realizing it was a human finger. And she knew exactly who it had belonged to.

Julian Baker.

Chapter 64

MIKE

Monday

Mike and Jamie jumped into Jamie's car as fast as was humanly possible and raced to the center of town, where a smoke plume was already visible. Mike was practically sitting on the dashboard, fuming that she wasn't driving, although he *was* doing an excellent job. She directed him to park a few blocks away, out of range of floating debris, and they both took off on foot. It wasn't long before Jamie was well ahead of her—he really was in magnificent shape, and these jelly shoes were tearing up her feet.

She slowed to a stop a block away from the custard shop, gasping in air that was thick with smoke, burning her esophagus and lungs as she pulled it in. It was only going to get worse the closer they got to Mary Ann's, so she let herself pause for a second to catch her breath.

She needed to start running more. She was really sucking wind.

Jamie had slowed to a walk some distance ahead of her, probably realizing that he didn't know what he should do once he got there. They were still a block away, and she didn't bother continuing the rush because it was obvious from the flames leaping from what used to be the roof that she wasn't getting inside the building. She was a cop, not a firefighter. If it had been mostly smoke, she would have tried to see if anyone was still inside, but those flames were no joke. It was a little shocking how fast the place had gone up, really.

She caught up to Jamie. "I decided there wasn't a reason for me to run," he said. "And I remembered that I hate running."

She did, too, but she was going to have to take it up again. This little display had been nothing short of embarrassing—it had only been a couple, three blocks and she'd nearly died, not to mention her cheeks were red as a tomato, and blisters were already forming on her toes and heels.

"Should we call someone?" he asked, looking around for a phone booth.

She shook her head, pointing to the crowd on the sidewalk in front of the Mucky Duck. "I'm pretty sure one of them will have."

And just like that, the sound of sirens—multiple ones—could be heard. The town had a mostly volunteer fire department—a few full-time guys were always at the station, but for a fire this size, they would call in every available resource and then some from neighboring cities. At least the local trucks were on their way already.

It sounded like the on duty patrol officers were en route as well—she could tell that at least one of the sirens was a cop car. This was good 'cause she needed help controlling the crowd—the bars were emptying, and the growing number of idiots were jostling each other to watch the blaze. All these folks needed to move farther back—it was just *stupid* they were getting so close to a raging fire. The air was already thick, and the last thing emergency services needed was to care for a bunch of rubberneckers who'd inhaled too much smoke. People really were dumb.

She plowed her way to the front of the crowd. "Everyone move back. You need to get out of this area and go home—all of you." There was some mumbling and shifting of feet, but no one followed her instructions.

A familiar voice joined hers at the other end of the crowd. "You heard the woman! Let's move it!" Jamie stood at the front, facing the onlookers, waving his arms in the air. His voice was shockingly loud. He turned his head and shot a wink at her, and she found herself grinning in return, even though it was annoying that people were more willing to listen to Jamie than to her. She shrugged it off—at least they were making progress herding them back. She figured they needed to push the crowd at least a block away to be safe—two or more would be better.

As the group shuffled away from the burning building, she spotted Mrs. Highsmith and the chief's secretary sitting on a park bench together watching the excitement. She'd leave them there for now, but they needed to move down the street, too, even though they were technically the farthest from the smoke.

Chapter 65

LORRAINE

Monday

A lot of pieces suddenly fell into place, and Lorraine realized that for the first time in a long time, she was actually impressed, *really* impressed. Carla reminded her a bit of herself in her youth—heartless, calculating, and motivated. She felt an unfamiliar feeling in her chest . . . was that . . . pride? In someone else's accomplishments? How unusual.

Well, there was a first time for everything.

"Right under everyone's noses, eh?" Lorraine handed the finger back.

"Something you know quite a bit about, it seems," Carla said.

"You're running an entire drug enterprise from the police station." Lorraine nodded. "Clever."

"I like to think so." Carla shot Lorraine a sidelong glance. "And you used the police chief's truck to move Julian's body, didn't you?" Carla chuckled. "Damn, I had a good laugh about that."

Lorraine smiled. That *had* been a great deal of fun. She cocked her head. "Why stay here? You could be operating out of somewhere larger, like Sheboygan or Green Bay."

"There's very little oversight of the port here." Carla shrugged. "But also, I have . . . personal reasons. A mother who needs care."

Lorraine respected that that was all she was going to say on the matter. But then she frowned. "Are you the one who called me?"

Carla sighed. "I was. I do apologize for that, but I was hoping you'd find the money Julian stashed. And I needed to egg you on to do it."

"Looks like we found it." Both women watched the scraps of bills falling from the sky. Lorraine wished the secretary—no, *kingpin*—had just come forward and talked to her, but no matter. She was tempted to ask Carla whether she knew about the graves in Lorraine's yard but decided not to invite more trouble by giving Carla information she might not already have. For now, it seemed they were equally matched, information-wise. Mutual destruction if either of them talked. Lorraine didn't want to tip those scales, but she did have a few incidental questions.

"Why out yourself to me?"

Carla's smile was small, mysterious, a living Mona Lisa. "Oh, you'll find out in time."

This was a deeply annoying answer, but Carla was likely thinking that Lorraine might be useful down the road, willing to help her out in some way. It was unlikely that Lorraine would, but you never knew what kind of opportunities might arise. It was best to let it go for the time being and move on to more relevant questions.

"Julian's car?" Lorraine asked. "The Datsun that everyone thinks he skipped town in?"

"Already taken care of at the scrapyard. I figured it was best to help make it look as though he really did leave town." Carla nodded at the fire. "Clever way to get rid of the body, though."

It seemed the other woman had been helping her along the way.

"Some of my suppliers to the south have heard of you," Carla said casually, but Lorraine knew what she was getting at. She was asking about Lorraine's time working for the Chicago Outfit.

"Mmm, yes. Your 'suppliers' and I had a bit of a falling out after working for them for a number of years. Running numbers is easy enough, but body disposal is a tricky business." Lorraine wasn't willing to tip her hand any further—arrogance and more than a little bit of pride in her work had loosened her tongue, but only so much.

"I would love to hear those stories someday," Carla said.

Lorraine chuckled. "To see if you can use any of it for blackmail?"

Carla gave a too-casual shrug, then laughed lightly at being called out. The women were quiet again before Lorraine asked something else that she'd been wondering. "Who killed Dean Lagerfield?"

"Craig Youngblood, if you can believe it." Carla shook her head. "It's too bad because Dean really moved a lot of product for me. I was thinking about promoting him once I got rid of Baker."

"So, I did you a favor."

"I think we both did each other some favors here," Carla said. "And there's no need to discuss this ever again, correct?"

Lorraine nodded and held out a hand. Carla shook it, a nice firm handshake, displaying neatly manicured nails painted pale pink, before she gathered her modest brown purse and left without another word.

Chapter 66

MIKE

Monday

Officer Patoka soon arrived and took over the job of moving rubberneckers back from the smoke, so Mike marched over to the bench where she'd seen the two women sitting; Carla seemed to have disappeared, but Mrs. Highsmith was still perched there.

"I need you to move back. It isn't safe here." The wind was no longer blowing in this direction, but all the same. The air was far from clean.

Mrs. Highsmith simply looked at her, then glanced back at the Mucky Duck. "I suppose I should go close out my tab. A lot of excitement, don't you think, Detective?"

Mike filed it away that the woman had been out drinking, which she thought was kind of weird for someone of her age. She saw the empty glass in Mrs. H.'s hand. "It's illegal to have open beverages on the street, Mrs. Highsmith."

Mrs. H. tipped the glass over, eyes still locked on the fire. "Nothing in here, Detective."

With a sigh, Mike turned to face the fire once more. She noticed that the ground here was littered with scraps of paper, blowing over from the blaze. Picking up a larger piece, she gasped—it was money.

Holding up the charred corner, she turned to Mrs. H. in amazement. "This is money."

"Looks like there was money in the ice cream shop," Mrs. Highsmith said, then stood and stretched. She coughed once, her fist covering her mouth. "Maybe you're right, Detective. I should get out of this air."

Mike nodded absently, focused on the scraps of cash littering the ground.

Hours later, Mike was still on the scene. Jamie had gone home long before, just before the police chief had finally shown up, fluttering around the scene and squawking like a chicken before going home himself once the news crew had packed it in.

The fire department managed to keep the fire from spreading to other buildings on the block, although Mary Ann's was a total loss. It was now nothing more than a blackened, wet shell. A husk of its former self. Craig Youngblood had also shown up toward the end, staring for a while before swiping a hand over his face and leaving. She'd considered arresting him on the spot for starting the blaze, but she didn't have enough. Yet. Although she did radio Sergeant Johnson and had him assign one of the night shift guys to follow Youngblood. She didn't want him skipping town like Baker had.

Once the building was cool enough, sometime tomorrow morning, she and the fire chief would do a walk-through and see what they could see. The fire department didn't think anyone was inside, and she could only hope that was true. Because there was zero chance they'd escaped if someone had been in there.

Mike was angry, even as she drove home, both at herself for missing the obvious signs, and at Youngblood for going through with it before she could search the place. There wasn't going to be anything left in there to find, not unless Youngblood had taken all his money-laundering records home with him, and why would he do that? They were probably the reason he was lighting the place up.

It was crazy how much money had burned up in the fire, though. Was this Baker's stash of cash, hidden in the custard stand? Why hadn't Youngblood known that the money was there? If he had, he wouldn't have torched the place with it inside; that would have been beyond stupid. Which meant Baker must have left the money behind and not told his buddy where it was hidden.

Mike had a lot of questions for Youngblood, but she was going to try to catch a few hours of sleep first, then get some of this gunk out of her lungs.

Chapter 67

LORRAINE

Tuesday

Lorraine awoke the next morning feeling fantastic. She sipped her coffee, looking out over her rosebushes, lovely in the golden morning light. Even the sky was agreeable this morning—a crisp bright blue, not a cloud in sight. She felt lighter than she had in weeks—dark weeks she'd spent trying to figure out who'd learned something about her. Now she knew for a fact who it was, and she trusted that Carla Robinson would keep her end of the bargain. And Lorraine would do the same, of course—it benefited both women.

If only she was a little younger, and didn't need to avoid Carla's suppliers, she might have wanted a piece of the action that Carla was running. But it was a younger woman's game, and she was satisfied to know that it was a woman running things. Right beneath the cops' noses, out of their police station. In this day and age.

Truly masterful.

Lorraine had two tasks for the day—first was making sure that Marjorie knew the money was gone so that she wouldn't come knocking on Lorraine's door anymore. After that, she would check in at the station to see how the assumptions were shaking out about who killed whom. She would hand over Youngblood's files and hopefully learn whether they'd found Baker's body. Fingers crossed it had been burned beyond recognition.

Speaking of, what would Carla do with Baker's finger? Leave it in her freezer?

Lorraine rode her bike across town to Marjorie's, enjoying the sensation of moving her legs despite the exertion of the previous day. It was a several-mile bike ride from the north side, through downtown, and to the south side of Sheboygan Bay. She proceeded to knock on Marjorie's front door with as much vigor as Marjorie had used on hers. It was certain to be annoying, and that made her heart sing.

Marjorie's mouth was twisted up when she came to the door, and she smelled like she'd been chain-smoking all morning. "Yeah, I heard," Marjorie said.

"About the money?"

"Yeah, about the money." Marjorie was clearly unhappy. "Cindi called first thing this morning."

"I'm sorry you won't be striking it rich."

"There's always tomorrow," Marjorie snarled and then shut the door.

Which was just as well because she missed Lorraine's satisfied smirk.

Were her feet floating? They may as well have been. Lorraine strutted into the bakery next, expecting to see Jamie Sprout, but a beige man in a beige outfit was behind the counter instead. "Where's Jamie?"

"Called out sick. Something about inhaling too much smoke." The man rolled his eyes. "What'll you have?"

Jamie Sprout had been at the scene last night, shooing back rubberneckers. Lorraine briefly wondered if he'd gone home or gone to the detective's place instead—she hoped for the latter, just so the detective would be in a pleasant mood this morning. Then she set aside her musings and ordered an assortment of muffins and pastries. She loaded her goodies into her bike basket and rode to the police station, where she found the front door locked. This was definitely a new development.

Lorraine set her bag of goodies and thermos of coffee on the sidewalk while she eyed up the city block. There was a phone booth outside the grocery store, so she strolled over, popped in her coin, and dialed Hans directly. He picked up after one short ring, which told her he was staring at his phone.

"It's not a good time, Mrs. Highsmith," Chief Schneider started to say, but she stopped him short.

"Hans, I'm out front, and I have pastries."

"Oh. Well, we could all probably use something to eat. Carla," the chief yelled, and Lorraine held the phone away from her ear before hanging up and shaking her head. She crossed the street again, picking up the pastries just as Carla opened the door. The two women locked eyes, then nodded at one another. After a beat, Lorraine moved past her, through the lobby and the swinging door that Carla had left unlatched. On her way past, she pulled out a muffin and left it on Carla's desk. "For you."

"Thank you, Mrs. Highsmith," Carla said, breaking a piece off the muffin and popping it in her mouth before taking a seat in her chair. "I'm doing Weight Watchers, but I suppose I deserve a treat." She gave her a quick wink.

Lorraine smiled, then wiped her expression clean before sliding into the chief's office, where she deposited the bag of pastries on his desk. Detective Zenoni was sitting in the chair closest to the wall, so she sat in the other, sipping at her thermos of coffee. She glanced at Zenoni.

"You look like shit. Not a lot of sleep, eh, Detective?"

"I stayed late at the fire," Zenoni rasped.

Too bad. The detective hadn't gotten laid then. "Pretty exciting night," Lorraine said. "Why was the front door locked?"

Chief Schneider shook his head. "We've been swamped by the media. I had to lock them out until we decide how much information to release."

There had been no one sitting outside. Not a single news van or reporter to be seen, but she let Hans have his imagined moment of glory. "Maybe you should run it by me, so I can see if it will play well in the papers," Lorraine suggested.

Zenoni made a noise around the big bite of muffin in her mouth, but Schneider thought it over and agreed. "The detective and I did a walk-through of the ice cream shop—what's left of it—this morning and found a body. We're guessing it belongs to Julian Baker, although we'll know more when Dr. Schneider gets through with it."

"Your wife."

"Erm, yes." He cleared his throat. "We have Craig Youngblood in custody. He's claiming he didn't kill Baker and has lawyered up, but we have quite a bit of evidence against him—his prints and Baker's were on the gun that killed Lagerfield. And we just heard back from the crime lab. It's likely he murdered Baker too."

Lorraine nodded. That was all to plan, then. "Oh, I almost forgot. I have these—you might find them useful. They belong to Mr. Youngblood." She pulled the folders from her cavernous purse.

Both cops looked startled. "Why do you have these?" Zenoni's voice sounded like she'd sucked down four packs of Marlboros.

Lorraine shook her head. "I went to see Mr. Youngblood, and I got a real bad feeling about what he was up to. I may have borrowed these from his office."

Zenoni opened her mouth—without a doubt to admonish her for stealing—but Schneider cut her off. "These will come in very handy. You might have to testify, of course."

"Whatever you need, Hans. I was going to have an accountant look at them because I suspect he was laundering money."

"What makes you think that?" Zenoni asked, eyes narrowed.

"I heard him on the phone while I was outside his office. Or maybe he was talking to himself. Either way, he mentioned it."

The chief clapped his hands together with glee. "We've done it! We've cleared two murder investigations." Neither Zenoni nor Lorraine pointed out that Hans had actually done nothing while the other two had taken care of business. "Mike, finish writing up the reports. We have our man. And I'll start working on a statement for the press." The chief brushed streusel from his tie, and Lorraine stood to excuse herself.

"I'll see you out, Mrs. Highsmith," Zenoni rasped.

Lorraine shrugged casually as the detective followed her onto the sidewalk outside.

"Kathryn Meyer, Katie to her friends," Detective Zenoni said. "Does that name mean anything to you?"

An uncomfortable zing of recognition sailed through her, but she did her best to keep her face neutral even as her body stiffened. How the *fuck* had Zenoni gotten that name? "I don't have the slightest idea who that is, Detective. A new case?"

Zenoni chuckled and shook her head. "How soon we forget old friends." She tapped her lip, feigning thought. "You know, I wouldn't have pegged you for a New York–style pizza lover, Mrs. H." Despite the smoke inhalation, her voice was playful, which meant she hadn't gotten any further than New York—which was a huge state—but it was too close for comfort. Way too close. Fucking Kathryn Blahnik. She hadn't thought about that loudmouth in years. Should she pay the old woman a visit?

Lorraine had the uncomfortable feeling that she was being toyed with. She did not care for it one bit.

"I'll be in touch," Zenoni said.

"Looking forward to it, Detective." Lorraine was seething inside. She'd been looking forward to puttering in her garden with an empty freezer and a clear conscience, the case neatly wrapped up as far as she was concerned.

Now she had some more digging to do.

Zenoni had opened the door to the station and stepped through but turned to look at her over her shoulder. "I'm sorry you couldn't get your hands on that money."

Lorraine considered her but said nothing.

Zenoni winked, then stepped inside, the door thumping shut behind her. Lorraine stood on the sidewalk for a moment longer, fists clenched, before taking a deep breath and striding to her bike.

The detective was far too clever for her own good. But Lorraine was still better.

Acknowledgments

First, I want to thank Jessica Tribble Wells and Angela James who are real-life wizards. Thank you for sharing my vision and tirelessly helping me get this story where it needed to be. And further thanks to the absolutely stellar T&M team.

Huge thanks to my amazing agent, Courtney Paganelli. From the bottom of my heart, thank you.

Big love and thanks to the friends who have cheered and championed this book. Some of you (looking at you, Megan) have read it numerous times, and either way, I cannot thank you all enough for believing in both me and Lorraine. Thank you, especially to Shannon Baker, Tim Hennessy, Carrie Hennessy, Megan Kantara, Jessie Lourey, Beth McIntyre, and Nick Petrie.

Thank you to the readers, the booksellers, and the librarians. You make this job possible.

I grew up watching *Murder, She Wrote* (among many, *many* other shows) with my dad, who was a small-town police chief. I never understood why he watched detective shows since he was one, but I do think he would have been deeply amused by my take on the nosy old woman tripping over bodies. Thanks for the hours and hours of detective shows and movies, Dad. I miss you every day.

My dad was a *much* better police chief than Schneider, though. As for the rest? Yes, some of the characters are based on people I grew up around; no, I won't tell you their real names.

To the real Mike Zenoni, I'm sorry I made you a woman. It was better for the book, though. Also, Carrie Ann Williams is a lovely person, not at all flighty like this character.

Big love and thanks to my friends and family who support me and my crazy schemes. Especially Jessie, Shannon, and Susie; Sandy, Sue, and Sara; Gunther; Katie and Trevor; Erin and Beth; Tasha and Andrew; Chris and Katrina; Dan and Marie; Tim and Carrie; and Bryan and Kyle Jo.

And thank you, always, to Mike B., a.k.a. Mikey Biscuits, who never fails to roll with things, no matter how wild. I love you. To the bones, babe.

About the Author

Photo © 2019 Rachel Neubauer

Erica Ruth Neubauer is the Agatha Award–winning author of the Jane Wunderly Mystery series. She spent eleven years in the military, nearly two as a Maryland police officer, and one as a high school English teacher before finding her way as a writer. For several years, she was a reviewer of mysteries and crime fiction for publications such as *Publishers Weekly* and *Mystery Scene* magazine. She's currently a member of the Sisters in Crime and Mystery Writers of America organizations. Erica Ruth lives outside Madison, Wisconsin, although her heart will always be in Milwaukee.